Walks for the Unemployed

Andrew Brown

Contents

One: Resistance – "Mrs Dowd"

This is the joyless story of Jimmy Suzuki.

Jimmy is forty years old. He is unmarried and childless. He is alone. He is independent of desires, or, seemingly so. Jimmy Suzuki has never attained a day's remunerated employment in his entire life. He has been succoured by the welfare state. Jimmy has never admitted this as failure; he knows it is because of his art. The state has labelled him as a "Deviant Artist". When he was young he wanted to be an artist. He had had a feverish imagination always sketching absurd depictions of hairy demons and hobgoblins. Convinced by his own idiocy he had presented some of these sketches of hirsute weirdoes in his application to the Imperial Society of Gifted Arts (ISGA). Jimmy had had pretensions of training as an art student at the prestigious ISGA in Colling Town. He was soon disabused of that when less than a week later a Poll Inspector was knocking on his door with his staff of office. More than twenty years later Jimmy could still remember him to this day – the venerable Alderman Lennon.

Alderman Lennon was all bombast and pomp. He was shrill in explanation, declaiming and clarifying, citing to Jimmy's parents, Harold and Doris, the righteous path. Harold and Doris were plain, honest, but ultimately, gullible folk. Harold was a lock-keeper on Plints Wharf, Doris a breadwoman. They were bamboozled by the Alderman and took a shine to his effusive argument that their only child Jimmy (their special child) should take an allocated apprenticeship at the School of the Suspect Norm (SSN) in Snoods Droop - out there in the invigorating countryside, far away from the urban grand metropolis of

Banana Delta. There Jimmy would learn his contribution to Great Society; accomplished artist or otherwise. Jimmy would leave his home in Trenchtown and receive further education in Snoods Droop.

Jimmy had been given a vocation. He had been allocated his counter-profession: Deviant Artist. Counter-professionals are the burden of the state. They do not work. Instead they become the charge of the state. Great Society is burdened with the conditioning of such sad fellows to be blended back to normality. It is a long project.

It was indeed a long project. Nineteen year old Jimmy spent six years in the backwoods getting the demon out of his eyes. No artistic freedom in SSN Snoods Droop. No intelligentsia as found in the Colling Town district of Banana Delta. Instead there was basket weaving. Lots of it. Counselling support groups in which intermingled cocca addicts, sex miscreants, gambleheads, all there shooting the devoid breeze with Jimmy.

A very successful education was given too. SSN made sure of it. By the time they passed him out at the age of twenty-five poor Jimmy Suzuki was a deluded soul. Since that time he has had the confidence of a failed opium addict, has been tongue-tied in front of women and pig ignorant about enterprise and how to make a living. The SSN men made a disserving man out of him. He had passed the course, had been cashiered out with the classification "Unemployable Category B+" and with the official value status of "Social Welfare: Factor 5". Before leaving the school in a moment of high social euphoria he elected to take the "Life Enhancing Vasectomy Plus" package which the SSN men confirmed to be a wise course so as to alleviate future burdens (a nod and a wink too that this would add increased durability to the Factor 5 rating).

At the age of twenty-five Jimmy S. came back to Trenchtown. He came back to an empty abode. Mum

Doris had died suddenly of a heart attack the year before; she had become very large. More diminutive Dad was in a care home suffering dementia already at the age of 62. Harold Suzuki had had a hard life and it appeared that he could hardly wait to escape it. Jimmy had returned to his parents' empty dwelling abode. His benefit payments covered the lease, but not much else on top. For fifteen more years there Jimmy remained alone with few pleasures; the occasional beer, a modicum of tobacco, a very occasional hand-job at the state collective with Miss Pussy (he could afford no more). Simple survival in what is called a life whilst maintaining his Factor 5 status. Jimmy was deep under cover, well embedded and suffocating in the system, but with a flame of anger smouldering through this long darkness. He existed and persisted and kept quiet his remaining ambition about turning out great painting. Such ambition subsisted barely on some occasional practice through his use of cheap chalk on low grade sketching paper. James Donald Suzuki, burgher of Trenchtown in the precinct of Banana Delta, wanted release from a long dying. His want was agonising and numbing. There seemed never to be any satiation.

Jimmy was simply "pale scum". A sobriquet accorded by the Malaccans to the underclass that originated from the far east Oriens. The pale ones were the race of privilege, but the ones they had discarded were the pale scum who lived in the tenements of Trenchtown, Frasertoon, Tusker & Mansion and other less salubrious parts of Banana Delta. Jimmy's class held little upward mobility. Those who progressed were often those who became members of a privileged underworld and there were few from Jimmy's area who found elevation in the generous bosom of Great Society. In Jimmy's class of pale scum most were of poor professional status and many counter-professionals sacrificing their right to work to uphold the stanchions of Great Society.

When Jimmy thought hard about it he could convince himself that this is what he really deserved. He had been arrogant back in the day and could understand that he needed to be taken down a peg or two. He had looked down on his parents, had sneered at their simple ways and had been enraged by their pointless patter. "It's very hot again today, Harold. We could really do with some rain". Or: "I've got us some lovely pork pie and tomato for us tea, Doris". The bloody man did not even have the palate for some chutney or other relish; so small-minded and unadventurous. His mother was always complaining when Jimmy played his lap-harpsichord looking to improvise some experimental spiker pod music. "Don't you like it, Mum? Don't you appreciate its fineness, its subtlety?" "I don't like that experimental honky-tonk. Just plain old fashioned island music for me!"

He had felt stifled. Constricted by their small minded attitude. Thought and attitude for his parents had been stringing green runner beans and winding up the decrepit looking grandfather clock as if it were their philosophy and purpose of the world. That old clock's chime had resonated like a call of oppression to Jimmy's ear at that time. His parents had revered that clock as a family heirloom. Jimmy had regarded it as a risible signal of lack of ambition. He had seen it as the symbol of negative soul.

The young Jimmy wished to break out. He wished to question. Somehow he could not tolerate his lot. After the poor school education everyone in his demographic was given he was apprenticed to an undertaker by the name of Willy Werner. Jimmy did not relish this apprenticeship, but Mum and Dad had convinced him that he would not find a better more regular trade, so he stuck with it. Jimmy found it uncomfortable handling dead people and often during this time had unsettling dreams about talking cadavers. Nonetheless Werner had an older apprentice by the name of Joffrey Jonkels who had a bit of a rebellious spirit. Jimmy looked up to Joffrey and Joffrey took him under his wing. Joffrey took the young Jimmy to a lot of street art exhibitions up in the Decayed Barrier and Jimmy became fascinated by the freedom of putting road detriment together in curious provocative poses and saying that it was to look at, and then giving it an enigmatic name like "No License". It was so liberating, it was so broad minded. Jonkels would talk to Jimmy about these displays and share some of his fantasies about putting together sculptures formed from corpses and coffin pieces. Joffrey Jonkels revealed his plans to Jimmy to hold a clandestine art exhibition on this concept and discussed with the impressionable Jimmy how this might be done covertly without the proprietor Willy Werner cottoning on. Jonkels wanted to call it *Definitive Deathly*. Alas, Jimmy was unable to see Joffrey's plans come to fruition.

Jimmy before his incarceration and conditioning was into art. Art fed his rebellion and disquiet. It had at times the ability to quiet temporarily that overall sense of disquiet. Nevertheless along with this wish to be artistic Jimmy held a sense of shame about this plan to be an artist. He wanted to wear the wish like a Sunday morning frockcoat, but he could not. He essentially kept small and closeted about the desire and the only person he shared any part of it was with his older apprentice peer at the charnel house. For that reason he still viewed his sudden application to the Imperial Society of Gifted Arts as something of a quirk. Still a quirky action that led to a lot of misery, but he might have had a lifetime of misery in the embalming rooms.

Jimmy thought on and remembered his adolescence. There had been no discussion of art and music, only futile banter on what Pa would have said if he were still alive now, or, what Mister Jones had said to Mum Doris about new immigrants coming to take jobs and turn us all into counter-professionals. He had regarded their simple ways with the utmost disdain, and now his mind was prisoner in the physical manifestations of simple ways. It was this hubris, Jimmy acknowledged, which had brought him down. It was that hubris and contempt for his parents which had led to that ill-starred application to the ISGA. It was well known, and he recognised it, that the fates revenge hauteur.

Enough of this heartstrings pulling background. Jimmy Suzuki lived and expected no more. Then in this condition one day something was thrown up on to his life. By chance another sequence of events could finally begin. Although Jimmy's life is dour and monotonous there are things set to begin. Even though Jimmy's life has been wall to wall monotony some things are yet to begin like those things that had begun before and were still hidden blended into the wall to wall monotony. Jimmy despite the fact that he could see no future for his life, yet still had some dark drawers in the back of his life. He had a past and it was chequered, so that it had some light and shade to the overwhelming drab bland majority of his existence. Yes, there are drawers which from time to time he has to acknowledge are there, but within which he does not easily care to look; to take any peep at again.

So to set the scene on this latest set of happenings; it is right at the beginning of January with the ubiquitous palm trees swaying in the balmy breeze and the sun is shining on the disused carcass of the New Year's revelry and Jimmy has popped out to smoke a fag (Great Society having deemed smoking indoors illegal on the grounds of passive smoking – neighbourhood sneaks were everywhere). He had bought some rolling tobacco the day before to celebrate his birth date. Again there had been plenty of celebration this time. Trenchtown is an impoverished district, but they still liked to whip up a storm to see in the New Year. This is some old pagan tradition but Great Society in its wise benevolence humours a holiday on it. It allows the masses to let off steam and it gives all Value Providers the chance to be honoured. Jimmy has taken the habit of late of locking himself indoors on the 16th. floor of his tenement building (the Massive Tivoli) during the celebration, the Hootenanny. As is the norm it is very hot and steamy, yet a strong sultry breeze registers. Empty champers bottles and dead fireworks adorn the urban concrete palisades; no sign of wounded merrymakers, the rozzers have already done their cleaning up. From afar Jimmy can hear the sound of the Assembly from the Poorhouse clearing away the trash about a block away. The team are singing "The Poor Go Gathering", and there is the sound of the scraping of spades sweeping up the old revelry rubbish into barrows and carts. A pigeon is startled by Jimmy and almost flies in his face. Jimmy is startled too for a moment and further startled when the wind whips up a piece of yellowy foolscap paper into his face. Jimmy is about to scrunch it up and throw it back into the debris from whence it came when suddenly his attention is brought to its title:

Walks for the Unemployed: A Self-Help Guide
By Mrs Rosemary Dowd

The print appears faint but the letters glimmer in the radiant morning sunlight. Jimmy reads on:

There are more and more of us losing our jobs in this post-industrial age. Being temporarily unemployed can be disconcerting, particularly when economic insecurity is coupled with feelings of loss of worth and value to society. Nevertheless, such time can be used valuably to reset oneself and take stock on life; to think on God's purpose and divine real meaning from life. No matter which political or religious persuasion you hold, Mrs Dowd offers practical walking exercises as frameworks for building back your self-worth so that you are able to re-enter the job market reinvigorated. She offers us profound and original insights into how we can find spiritual worth and reinvention in the catharsis of this post-industrial world.

Although the walks themselves are based mainly around Salisbury and the Avon Valley, she paints a delightful mind's eye picture of this charming solace and useful artefacts to create your own walks of solitude and meaning within your own locality which mirror her own original inspiring thoughts.

"Walks for the Unemployed" is a little gem. Whether you are unemployed, suffering some loss or generally feeling a little under the weather, or, just wish to reinvigorate the soul, then I thoroughly recommend this little masterpiece of walks and contemplations.

This is a little book which yet aspires to be your closest companion.

Walk well, read well, and think on all well.

The Very Reverend Tony Walters

See of Salisbury

'What is this? Is this some sort of subversive pamphlet?', worries Jimmy. He had heard of subversive elements present in Trenchtown, particularly out near Hard Shoulder and Decayed Barrier – areas where illegal aliens were coming into Banana Delta. 'Maybe a bit risky to hold on to this. Don't want to get caught up with those Chamberlains', he mused. Then some of the old fire cuts in. 'No. I'll take it back up to me digs and have a proper gander at it'. Jimmy folds up the foolscap page of paper and stuffs it into his trouser pocket.

Jimmy feels a faint tremor. The Brown Dwarf system would appear to be active again heaving away at the surface of the earth. Suddenly there is a crack in the paving and he is alerted to another sheet of foolscap similar to the first appearing through the crack. He moves quickly to collect this as if he had to harvest quickly a gift from fate.

It seems to be from the same source. He quickly notes the headline:

WALK 1: FROM THE JOB CENTRE AMESBURY TO SOUTH WOODFORD SUB-POST OFFICE (4.5 Miles)

He scrambles up the second piece of paper, folds it and puts it in his pocket alongside the first. Finishing his smoke Jimmy returns upstairs. Taking the stairs is a slow laborious process as again the two winch lifts are out of order, but at least it has forced Jimmy into some economies and the physical effort is efficacious for the health.

A good ten minutes later Jimmy is back in the small two bedroom abode where he has lived his whole life (apart from his attendance at Snoods Droop). He is out of condition. Jimmy Suzuki at six foot two inches tall and approaching 110 kilos, with sweat oozing out of his cheap shoddy waistcoat, sitting on a dilapidated divan infiltrated by crumbs, reads properly the second piece of paper. Again the print is faint but quite legible.

WALK 1: FROM THE JOB CENTRE AMESBURY TO SOUTH WOODFORD SUB-POST OFFICE (4.5 Miles)

I talked to Mr Dowd in the vicarage last week whilst he was repairing our dishwasher (our motto is "Waste not, want not" – Mr Dowd has trained himself to applying himself with great diligence to solving all irregularities with our household appliances).

"Stephen", I said "Why do these unemployed people complain so emphatically and so earnestly? They have a jolly lot of free time. Couldn't they go for lots of nice walks?"

"You're absolutely right", replied Mr Dowd. "Still you have to remember that a lot of these chappies don't have lovely country

areas they can ramble through. A lot of them are living near slurry pits, disused tenement buildings, industrial wastelands and the like. Some of them might live in dodgy areas where it might not be so safe to go for a brisk walk. But in essence you're certainly right, they could do more with their time than simply whinging and malingering".

"That's settled it", I said.

"What?" I had roused Mr Dowd's curiosity.

"I'm going to research and write a nice book of walks for unemployed people. I'll start with one from here down the Woodford Valley."

"Your book might have a limited circulation if these walks are all in south Wiltshire. Remember unemployed people can't exactly travel far afield to do a walk."

"Stephen, I realise all this", I interjected. "I will take that into account. These walks will be emblematic, representative of walks they can do in their own neighbourhoods. I will set out some of my local walks and add internal thoughts, contemplations on which these people can think on their respective value to society. If you like it will be a set of Christian reflections as they ramble. They can look for similar types of walks in their own vicinities and apply similar reflections on their own local paths. Indeed, I can go further afield to more industrial and urban environments. You know I could take a walk from Wigan Pier to somewhere else in Wigan".

"Oh, it would be like a sort of self-help contemplative guide?" clarified Mr Dowd.

"Yes, that's it. Walking as a vehicle to inner contemplation and a means to reflection on how valuable these souls are to the world. Indeed, how lucky they are that we have adequate social security and benign Christian values here".

This is the last paragraph on the second page that Jimmy had collected. Jimmy goes back to the first page and reads it again voraciously, and then the second page again, and then both again and again. It is like a great relentless thirst in him has been triggered by these manuscripts. Jimmy has never read anything quite so radical and thought provoking. His thoughts are tumbling with questions.

Although the text is written in English and is plain enough, things are still not exactly clear to him. What was this reference to God and political and religious persuasion? Were the unemployed chosen or freely appointed? What is the See of Salisbury? Could this be a misspelling for some foreign body of water? What is a job centre? Who was this Mrs Rosemary Dowd? The name Dowd had a familiar ring to it, but Jimmy could not exactly recollect.

None of it really made sense, but Jimmy finds it bold and original and wants to learn more. The text seems to touch a gap in Jimmy's being. The gap being there, however, Jimmy cannot connect to it, cannot identify any surface near or around the gap. What is this feeling of something unsaid, something missing? Perhaps there were more sheets down there in that debris of the revelry. Might they be lost in the clean-up by the Assembly? Jimmy feels that there is something of the subversive about Mrs Dowd and is willing to take a chance. She has burnt something up in his soul that none of the library books from the Institute of the Scholars had ever done before.

Jimmy Suzuki pulls his portly frame out of his dilapidated divan, brushes back with his hand his greasy lank hair and makes to go outside once more consoling himself that at least he would be able to get in another smoke. Perhaps that is his real reason for this additional foray. Stepping outside his front door he sets off on the long stairwell down to the bottom floor. He is unlucky and with his cumbersome large frame not quick enough to avoid the skateboarding joyrider on his career down from the 31st. floor. He is hit. He is bowled over spectacularly and clonks his great sentient head on the steps; the joyrider apparently unscathed and escaped. Jimmy S. unconscious and concussed lies waiting for assistance. There is no joy of further knowledge from Mrs Dowd; at least it is unlikely.

"Consciousness leads to reflection and improvement. 'I am awake' said the Buddha", says Mrs Dowd.

The venerable Alderman Godfrey Lennon sat his portly frame down on our dilapidated divan. He solicitously wiped away some crumbs in the process of doing so. He wore a bright red frockcoat with golden buttons, white breeches, long white socks and shiny black shoes with silver buckles. He was a massive man, bald and sweating profusely —around forty I would say, but the jowls around his chin made him look older. His obesity was pronounced by the tight cream waistcoat under the frockcoat which gave the overall effect of a whale constrained in a corset. Again the waistcoat was held together by bright golden buttons. I was sure he was going to explode at any moment and launch an onslaught of gold buttons at us. The groaning of the belly was quite mesmerising, but also made me feel on edge. He took off his tricorne hat and laid down his staff of office by his feet prior to speaking to us. We had an actual Poll Inspector in our house.

"Would you like a cup of tea, Honourable Alderman", asked Mum.

"Indeed Mistress Suzuki, that would be most kind of you". Mum went away to the kitchen.

Is this my imagination running away with me?

Our visitor said: "Now then young Sir, you wish to become an artist do you?"

All my attention, all my focus was honed on to his shiny garish uniform of office. I had seen Poorhouse inspectors dressed quite similarly to him. I was still inexperienced when it came to officialdom.

"Speak up son", said dear Dad.

"I suppose".

"I've seen your application to the venerable ISGA. I have to say I found it quite disturbing", boomed the Alderman. "All these pictures of hairy demons, grotesqueries and other degenerates. Deviant art has no place in the Imperial Society! The curators were quite appalled, I can tell you. This is to be cured. What is to be done with your boy, Mister Suzuki?"

Mum brought in the tea while Dad sat ashen and quiet. Mum poured out the tea. She had brought out her best china. From the corner of my eye I could see Dad's face twitching; a tear in his eye.

"What say you, Marm?". The Alderman was probing for a response.

"I say fuck you". Was that really me?

It was.

"Well", smiled the Alderman. "I was afraid that might be your reaction. I will have to file my report and state that you are *counter-profession*, counter-profession Deviant Artist. That means you have no profession in Great Society. No weaver, candlestick maker or bookbinder, but counter-profession! No place for you in Great Society as a counter-professional. My, my. When things are done wrong it is so difficult to right them back again".

I remember that I then left our dwelling. I wasn't going to take any more insult from this charlatan. I went out in the ubiquitous steamy heat to try and clear my head. To try and walk off the emotion and anger, sure in the knowledge that Mum and Dad would clear this up. I got home about an hour later and Alderman Lennon had departed. The problem though was that his great malevolent presence was still with us. My parents had signed the forms. The very forms that the Alderman had wished them to sign. My own parents had sold me down the river. So it was that the next Monday I was to be pressganged to the School of the Suspect Norm at Snoods Droop on pain of incarceration. Mum and Dad had acknowledged me to be a Deviant Artist, a serious category of counter-professional. They had given up hope on me.

"I'm so sorry", dear old Dad sobbed, "but it's for your own good Jimmy".

On such a cliché my life of banality and pain had begun.

Jimmy Suzuki where are you? Are you in your present, past or future? Are you a memory thrown back by time? What part are you displaying? What side of your personality is going to come shining through?

Hidden eyes are seeing into your subconsciousness. There is a little toad of a man who is holding a tattoo needle who wants to give you exquisite pain. He is ready to tattoo *agony* on your tongue so finely so that every time you lick your lips you will remember him and the process that you have undergone. Consciousness, consciousness; it is indelible.

And the bats. The bats. They are flying through you as if they exist within you. Evil blood suckers sucking at the pernicious blood who gave their mother form.

Stormy dark night. The earth shifts and the bats give way to all the leery characters you have ever met, and you have ever been with, and you have ever been.

Two: Resistance – "Nurse Kendra"

Jimmy wakes up. It appears that some time has passed. He is lying in a hospital bed. Nurse Kendra is smiling at him in the process of administering to him. The usual drips and bottles and things. She is wearing a long white pinafore dress with a stern starched cap of matronly office, but Jimmy immediately notices that she is quite beautiful with bright white teeth and malacca skin. She is an exotic beauty in her early twenties.

"Where am I?" he whispers.

"White Cross Hospital", she sings back whilst clanging around bedpans.

"What happened?"

"We're not quite sure. It appears that you fell on the stairwell of your tenement building. We're clueless as to the circumstances, but a kindly burgher found you there unconscious. She alerted the Day Watch and Bob's your brother – you're here!"

"I see".

"There's more", she continues. "It now appears that you have a blood clot in your head".

"Is it serious?"

"We have to take it seriously. You'll have to stay here for a few days while we use blood thinners to try and remove the clot. The clot was likely caused by your fall. However, we're hoping you'll be alright. Surgeon-Captain Sir Frederick Roper will be making his rounds later this morning and he'll be able to advise you more".

"Thanks. And who might you be?"

"I'm Nurse Kendra", she sang. For Jimmy her voice just sang; her very persona a melody in a tone deaf world.

"Then I'm pleased to meet you Nurse Kendra", he croaks.

"Pleased to meet you too finally, Mister James Donald Suzuki!"

"How long have I been here?"

"Three days. Look I've got to see to the other patients. I'll be back later and will tell you more".

It is at this point that Jimmy notices that he is lying in a bed in a huge room seemingly a hundred yards long, ten yards wide with beds on both sides. The place is choc-a-bloc with beds, tubes, nurses, groans, splutters and coughs. It is an immense hospital ward as big as a ship's dry harbour.

"Oh, I almost forgot". Nurse Kendra reappears. "I was asked to give you this once you woke up".

Jimmy takes a sheet of foolscap from her hand. *And that's how I entered into this first walk and this entire project*, Jimmy immediately notes at the top of the page.

"Who gave you this?" he asks.

"It was given to me by a nice old gentleman out in the Visitors Corridor. Somehow he must have known that I was administering to you. Actually, I should have asked how he knew. Said his name was Arnold Copperfield Esq. and that you'd be interested in the message."

"I don't know anyone called Copperfield. What did he look like?"

"In his seventies I would say. He was very courteous, a real gent. He doffed his top hat when he addressed me. Long grey hair, about five foot nine. Posh accent and well groomed, but was wearing a wool cape with a top hat, which was rather incongruous, I might venture!" She laughs like rain dew cascading over the back of a rainbow at the humour of her observation. Jimmy is smitten.

"I'm none the wiser", states Jimmy concentrating on the wider circumstance. Then there is a wave of panic. What about the other two sheets? The two sheets that were in his trouser pocket. Things are starting to come back to him now. Mrs Dowd and all that.

"Nurse Kendra, what happened to all my things? My possessions?"

"Everything that you were wearing and that was on your person is in that locker next to your bed. Anyway Mister Suzuki, I really must get along". With that she turns and goes. Jimmy feels love. He feels for love in the way that he aches for love. He has never had a proper lasting relationship with a woman. Even in his hospital bed he can pang for this woman. And even if she might be more than fifteen years younger, he still has skin in his game. Jimmy closes his eyes and moans inwardly in the snug crispness of his hospital bed.

"By the way," Nurse Kendra is mysteriously back. "Who is Fumi?".

"I don't know. Why?", he blurts.

"You called her name a lot when you were unconscious".

"Really. She must be a fantasy girl", smiles Jimmy nervously.

"And Nicole, you romancer?". Nurse Kendra has a smile like raspberry jam.

Jimmy just smiles ever so coyly.

Nurse Kendra charmingly nods her head ever so slightly and simply leaves again. Jimmy waits a full minute for some privacy. He is about to read the new sheet of paper when ......

"Bed Stations! Bed Stations! Surgeon-Captain Sir Frederick Roper is on his rounds. Look lively!" A hand-bell is rung and again the same statement is shouted out by a large lady in a Sister's blue dress-uniform. She looks like she brooks no argument. Jimmy puts the sheet of paper under his pillow.

Nurse Kendra glides past purposely.

"Nurse Kendra! Can you help me get my belongings out of the bedside locker?" Jimmy calls.

"Mister Suzuki", she admonishes. "Pray remember that White Cross is a Poorhouse hospital. That means you have to sit to attention until the Surgeon-Captain has done his rounds. You heard the Sister! We give charity here, but in return expect discipline!"

"Sit to attention? I can just about lie comfortably!"

"Then lie nicely then!" she exclaims.

"I'll be good, Nurse". He feels comfortable now just dealing with the uncomplicated authority of a hospital.

Jimmy observes the Surgeon-Captain's progress. At first from afar he sees a blur of people as the length of the large open ward is really quite long. He makes out only a very abstraction like an impressionist painting. 'Deviant art, the bastards'. Then the picture starts to slowly take shape as the entourage perambulates up through the long hospital ward. He can hear one voice above all others. This is the voice that is doing all the talking; occasionally another timbre is allowed to cut in. The principal voice must be the Surgeon-Captain Sir Frederick Roper. 'All the fuss over this guy would indicate he should be a bloody admiral of the fleet, not just a captain', he thinks.

Jimmy starts to realise as the party approaches nearer that the voice has been heard so far away because the big cheese is absolutely bellowing and words are starting to become discernible now.

"No, no, no, Miss Parfiter, this patient's recovery will not be aided by a homolgonous saline solution. No, no, no, not at all; this is a disgrace! This will not do at all!" the voice booms on and on. "When things are done wrong it is so difficult to right them back again".

"Next!"

"John J. Perriwinkle, your Worship", announces the large Sister heaving in her blue uniform.

"Sir John J. Perriwinkle, 15th. Baronet of Sandown. I would appreciate Madam if you would accord me with my proper name and title", asserts the geezer in the bed to the left of Jimmy.

'He's got pluck', thinks Jimmy. The geezer is sitting up stiffly in his bed. He has a shock of grey hair and a grey goatee beard. He does not look particularly ill. Piercing blue eyes glistened with unusual intelligence for this type of Poorhouse Hospital ward. 'He stands out a mile among all these old codgers', observes Jimmy. 'A fish out of water. He looks professional class', he muses.

"I demand to see the Visitor!" declares Sir John J. "I have no place here. In fact, I consider this to be a case of habeas corpus. I demand to see the Visitor and I shall appeal to Equity too!" he adds.

'Spunky guy. No low-life. I wonder what this Equity thing is?', thought Jimmy.

Jimmy notices that Sir Frederick is adorned in a fantastic navy blue uniform garnished with braids and medals. He is of average height, about five foot eight, but his face hair is flamboyant and aggressive. Jimmy puts him in his early forties. He has a wonderful twirled up moustache and bushy beard going down so far to cover the top of his club cravat. A splendid sight and plumage, with an aggressive edge to it. In fact he looks actually more flamboyant than the old singer entertainer Franzi Joe. All in all a fiercesome specimen

"Indeed? Baronet of Sandown? Which club?" booms the Surgeon-Captain in response to this riposte.

"Milliwhigs!" is the immediate rejoinder.

"If your Milliwhigs then I'm a Dutch duck's confessor!", retorts Sir Frederick.

Artificial laughter is articulated amongst the Surgeon-Captain's entourage.

"Perriwinkles have been Milliwhigs for five generations", replies the spunky one.

"And you wish to meet with the Hospital Visitor, Lady Elizabeth Swann?"

"Yes".

"And pray why would Her Ladyship condescend to receive you?"

"As I am being held here against my free will".

"But you are being treated man! You are a dissolute and a drunk. My staff had to perform an emergency stomach pumping on you last night. Your whole system was toxic and drowning in Old Ship's Bells! You, fellow, are in your appointed place and we provide for you out of the beneficence of our charity. Great Society demands that we care for our counter-professionals and degenerates as every single one of you here is in this dormitory."

"I object most seriously Sir! I am no idle counter-professional. Immediately discharge me or call for the Countess of Tischent. I am a close personal friend of hers". Perriwinkle has not yet lost his spunk.

"Keep this fellow on an extreme saline drip. He is bound to have the collywobbles. To guard against self-injury restrain him to his bed. Gag him please until I finish my rounds. If he is still giving you trouble then we'll saw off his legs as it would obviously be blood distemper that is so playing with his mind". With that two burly orderlies do what the good surgeon has ordered. Sir John J. is taken aback, he is restrained and muted with brutal ease, but Jimmy still notices the light of defiance in his eyes.

"Next!" It is Jimmy now.

"Jimmy Suzuki, your Worship".

"Right, right, let's see his notes. A blood clot in the head I see. Suzuki this will not do, old fellow! Put him on the major disseminator straight away".

Nurses emerge from the back of the entourage and pull tubes, twiddle knobs and Jimmy goes out like a light.

"Nobody is invincible, Jimmy", said Alms-Master David Lincoln.

I was sitting in the Great Counselling Hall at Snoods Droop. My mind's eye remembers The Banners of Import strewn around the walls of the hall. The bloody banners of import were all over the institution; in the dining hall, in the solitary cells, in the ablutions – everywhere. One could not escape their menace and their puerile all effecting statements indelibly itched etched on to the brain and the very core of memory. The one my memory is being drawn to is: *Only Some of Us can have an Outcome*. Another was: *To Serve and to Disserve Preserves Our Balance*. There had to be a mythos for the scrapheap. At the age of nineteen my whole life had been concluded upon and finalised. I just needed to go through the formal indoctrination process. You see they needed me to be aware of my situation and accept it. Great Society compelled that I be cognisant of my limitations and that I resolve to accept them. It was the desired outcome that a cripple learns to love and embrace the Poorhouse. To disserve was as equally important as to serve. To disserve was to fulfil the grace of Great Society. I had been categorised and now I had to understand why; indeed I had to assume and live the why. More than that I should embrace the why so that I could hold and revere the universal balance. Such was my importance to all by virtue of my total banality, and thereby the others can thrive.

David Lincoln had been assigned to counsel me on the why and wherefores. He was to work on me, get me to accept my lot – that I was counter-professional and would be for the remainder of my life. Not all could work. Not all work out, some fail. It is a simple law of physik. Great Society only had limited endeavours. Individual utility is a scarce resource, and only some of us can have an outcome.

"You see son, you can continue to rebel against your station, or, you can learn to accept and embrace your Disgrace. No-one is invincible. You will feel less vanquished by taking your part in the natural order rather than trying to rebel". His voice would go on and on in this vein for hours. He expressed all of this with his kindly face, his stubbly bearded nice face of mixed ancestry and accent of urban post-industrial correctness. I hated the fact that it was so difficult to be unkind and rail against his kindly tone.

"But I wanted to be an artist, Alms-Master!"

"Jimmy".

"Or even a gamekeeper or plongeur! What about dolphin expert?"

"That is beyond your ken. You cannot dispose to that. It is all beyond your means. You are not capable".

David Lincoln looked toward me benign in all his urban chic. Handsome in his cross-over mixed ancestry, radical stubble and with the whiff of "Grey Highwayman" water of Köln, he was the stylised epitome of the caring society's caring profession.

"It's beyond your ken; beyond your wherewithal", he reiterated, but there was a tear in his eye.

There was a tear in my eye too. Social place conditioning – it was all they could ask, and it was my grace to comply. I was to become noble in my sacrifice.

Then my waking voice declares.

'Piss off! Piss off, Lincoln! I don't want to hear any more of your claptrap in that quiet reasonable voice of yours. I don't want to see that pained expression in your face any more. You come across as a bleeding-heart liberal, but scratch the surface and you'll find an evil calculating ambitious state official. You turned me like a number on a state quota. I was part of your bonus. I don't want you fucking with my mind any more. Enough said? I'm so sorry, Fumi'.

Jimmy sleeps on in his induced subconsciousness fighting in his fugue for clarity. Arnold Copperfield Esq. is in the outer corridor of the hospital wishing to aid Jimmy in that quest. He is wearing a bright yellow blazer and Lamonti tartan trews and orange galoshes. For an older man of seventy-two it was remarkable that he still liked to strike a fashion chord. In a hard life, in which many painful compromises were given, his non-compromising on fashion details had been a strict constant. A style warrior he was and would be and the manifestation of his clothing would continue to signify his consternation and bewilderment about life, and its many illogical vagaries. One might think it poor or outlandish dress sense, but Copperfield knew it reflected emotion and sadness and an attempt to see a ray of optimism in an otherwise drab world.

So there stands Copperfield like a faded dandy in the Poorhouse hospital corridor amongst the great unwashed. Standing there erect and poised he has three pocket watches dangling from his green gingham check waistcoat today. He impatiently checks them all in a finicky manner. He waits for Nurse Kendra. He expects her off shift at any moment. He has ten sheets of manuscript with him this time. 'A very great walk; maybe her greatest', he considers. The southern aspect of the Pembrokeshire Coastal Path with divine reflections at both St. David's Cathedral and the St. Merthyr shrine. The description of the sunset over Whitesands Bay would move Jimmy. Mrs Dowd had managed to describe the aspect of that savage beauty in the wild sea framed in cold weather. 'Had Jimmy ever experienced the cold?' Arnold Copperfield remembers the cold. He has not experienced it for some time; the frosty breath, the shrivelled skin and the aching upon going to the toilet. 'Maybe better these humidified garbs .....'

"Mister Copperfield?" He is brought out of remembering.

"My dear Nurse Kendra. I have been waiting here to invite you to a glass of chocolate. There is a very nice place down a hundred yards on *Pretty Penny* which does a very passable glass."

"Why Mister Copperfield, you know how to capture a young girl's heart. I hope that this is no assignation! A tryst d'amour?", she says coquettishly.

Arnold smiles knowingly.

"Well why not, dear Sah? I'm off shift, partial to a glass of chocolate and not due at the Princess Beatrice Guides until seven-thirty".

"Mam, let the radiance of you and this evening cast its spell on this pale pallor of a feller!"

"Well said, Sah! Lead on."

Mister Copperfield courteously gives Kendra his arm and they stroll decorously down the corridor out of the hospital into the early evening outside. Copperfield adopts an exaggerated walking pattern where he shifts his feet left and right and left again in the process of moving forward whilst erratically digging his heels into the pavement and then moving his free arm airwards at a dalliance as if greeting acquaintances or shooing off maverick pigeons. At once it is exaggerated and stylish and Nurse Kendra moves innately to its convulsions.

"My Mister Copperfield, you adopt the Skittish Walk! You are so stylish, Sir!"

"I do the Skittish Walk not for the style, my lady. I do it to ward off the effects of anti-matter. Have you not read the words of O'Tone? The walk he has expounded is very efficacious against the dark matter contusions that are untoward us at the moment. Arnie O'Tone is extremely sagacious. Who would have thought that the Skittish Walk would be an antidote to the perils of dark coincidence. That a style of walk developed for foppish stylery be stand-guard against this great approaching cosmic irregularity. That surely is the most manifest of white coincidence, is it not?"

Kendra nods her head sagely. She could not get that pretty head of hers around all the vast implications of the Brown Dwarf thing and did not wish to expose her lack of understanding thereof. Instead she elects for a glistening smile of her pristine white teeth and she continues her up-tempo flow into the stylised manner of the Skittish Walk as she embarks on her outrageous stylised arm movements in concert with Copperfield. If there is one thing a Malaccan beauty can do is to hold rhythm.

They arrive at the beverage house in full style and procession with all the appearance of intimates; perhaps like father and daughter. Perhaps like patron and protégé, or something else. Who knows? Copperfield decorously orders the chocolates emphasising to the waiter that the rumba punch be kept on the sideliner.

Kendra sips on the exquisite Chocolate Marango. Copperfield notices for the first time how exquisitely beautiful she is and is captivated by her Malaccan beauty. He wonders how at his age that he can still stand an appreciation on such matters. He thinks of an image of an old stag rutting right up to its death; young male vanquishers goring at him and yet the strain for immortality carries on beyond. Beyond where there is any hope at all. 'Yes, the painting by Jonnie Turner at the National Treasures'. He pictures it. The old stag dying in and for the lust for life. Arnold Copperfield empathises with that old stag. Jonnie Turner was in his eighties himself when he painted that masterpiece. It was that bright flame at the end of the candle.

'What is happening to me? Where go these thoughts? I'm practically old enough to be her grandfather', his long abiding conscience shrilly remarks. He has an overwhelming wish to clutch her delicate hand. He concentrates fully against the desire so that he does not hear what she says. He only hears the speaking voices in his head talking over the desire of a dark temptation.

"So what is the interest in patient Suzuki then? How do you know him, Mister C? He says he does not know you."

"Pardon me?"

"He says he does not know you, Mister Copperfield. James Donald Suzuki. My patient."

"Oh, yes. He's probably still a little confused from the head injury. Indeed he knows me very well".

"How's that then?"

"Mister Suzuki and I go well back. Jimmy – you might not think – has had his gallivanting days, and if you wish, I've been a little like his older conscience so to speak. But enough of that for the time being. Please tell me about you circumstances. How did you become an 'angel of mercy'?"

"Oh Mister C, I haven't heard that moniker for a while."

'She speaks like a singing nightingale', thinks Copperfield. Her words glide effortlessly like a melodic song. Nurse Kendra has the high lilting accent of the full islands. An enchanting accent from one so animated and she speaks music now so that her form becomes abstract in his mind as well as in his gaze. Pure notes. The words are lost in harmony. Copperfield is lost in another age and starts to recognise it. He thinks Jimmy would be lost too in this. Jimmy is probably lost in his own world. He must get more words to him. The words of Rosemary. The stormy Pembrokeshire Coast, the contemplations – the natural things which will dispel all this magik.

".... So my mother did not think I would make it on the Big Island, but here I am. What do you say?"

"I say that often parents believe in their own limitations for their children. It must be in the passing of the blood lines. I have read many alchemies on this matter, and I think they are generally agreed that children are starved by their own parents' childhoods."

"Sah, that is deep. Poetic". She finishes her beverage. "I really must be going now Mister Copperfield. I have to prepare for the Guides. Perhaps we can liaise again soon?"

"Yes, indeed my dear. But before you go, I'd like you to give him these on the morrow. Ask him to read these and he will start to remember me again. Tell him I shall visit as soon as appropriate."

"Will be sure to do, Mister Copperfield."

Nurse Kendra collects the manuscripts into her satchel and turns away intent on her next stage in life. She walks off and after a few paces unexpectedly turns around.

"What is it with these pieces of paper that you are wanting me to pass on to him?"

"Ask Jimmy. He'll be able to tell you. Just let him come to his senses again."

"Ship-shape, me old mate." And this time she does saunter all the way out of the beverage house.

Arnold Copperfield Esq. remains a while and contemplates. She is more than that just what is shown on the surface. So is Jimmy too. He is prisoner and warden and revolutionary all wrapped in one.

N urse Kendra lives a good distance from her workplace at White Cross Hospital. She takes the stage back to her habitude in Gaolers Knoll, a cosmopolitan student area of the city. An area where she felt particularly at home as many others from the Islands inhabited the area giving her a feel of home. It had been a hard four years since her arrival in Banana Delta and a lot of difficult water had flowed under the bridge. She had fled her home on a tiny planget plantation; the small homestead of her parents. The family had no sons, just the two daughters. Her elder sister, Sophia, had already escaped the plantation by marrying a Royal Marine and was currently ensconced in familial bliss on New Minger. There were no strapping young boys to farm plangets; just Kendra as the family future. Nurse Kendra had no desire to farm plangets for the rest of her life, breaking her back and submitting to the capricious will of a drunken bully husband. She had no wish to emulate her mother in this regard. Even so for some time she had hung on in the miserable household because she could not bear to leave her mother. However, there was more; much more, that somehow is stored away in a crevice of the mind, brooding and skulking – threatening to come out some fine sunny day when everything is alright just to say that it is still there.

Beyond that, there had eventually come a breaking point when Pa had brutally beaten Ma in a rum soaked fury. Nurse Kendra had been at a dance at the local village and had come back to find Ma black and blue and in a desolate state. Pa had wandered off to collapse somewhere in the surrounding fields. Nurse K told her mother that she had to leave Pa or he would surely soon enough kill her. Ma resolutely refused. She struck a martyr's pose. Nurse Kendra issued an ultimatum. If Ma would not leave this misery then she surely would. This had had no effect on Ma. She simply became more obdurate in her sobbing and self-pitying. It was evident that she would be soon ready enough for another day of punishment. Kendra at the age of nineteen had been having chilling recollections about little fingers. Little fingers that liked to go a wandering down jolly passages. Something in her determined that she would not take further punishment to protect Ma, when Ma seemed freely to accept hers. There had to be an end to this aberration of events.

It was really time for her to be out of it. She could protect Ma's ruined conscience no more. That very night she cadged with a bounty of smiles a passage on a banana boat leaving Abergavenny for the Delta and two days later was in the great metropolis armed with her Value Provider

(VP) certificate which her father unbelievably had won for her on a municipal lottery. She entered the Tomdog training hospital to train as a nurse and procured cheap digs on credit earned from her VP certificate. She had done well, but she was lonely. She had over the past four years a number of beaus, but she wanted to do no more than flirt. Every man could be an intrusion like her father. With older men strangely she felt more comfortable; maybe because they were more like the father that she had hoped to have. She was lonely for sure and that accentuated her concern for poor old johnnies like Mister Suzuki and Sir John J. Perriwinkle. No time for young men when there were so many concerns to be aired.

The stage is quite crowded, but she is able to get herself seated on part of a bench. The occupant next to her is lank and greasy and smells of garlic and is intent on having a rather threatening sounding conversation with his small pinkie, but nonetheless she puts up with it to rest her weary legs. She decides to read the missive for Copperfield that she was bound to pass to Suzuki. She folds open the manuscript and reads the greying print.

WALK 17: PEMBROKESHIRE COASTAL PATH FROM ST. DAVID'S TO WHITESANDS BAY: WITH DIVINE REFLECTIONS AT TWO HOLY SITES (2.5 Miles)

My dearest reader this is my final walk: No doubt you will agree that we have walked together quite far. When we first started out on that lovely walk down the Woodford Valley we did not have the most confident gait. Mr Dowd said to me that I was just to start the mission even though I might be stumbling along. I trust that we have not been stumbling along for too long, rather that we are now striding out together with strength and purpose armed with an inner confidence that we can rely on our very selves in any walks of life and in whatever elements the weather and the road throws up at us.

Well here we are at the final walk and in the final event we know, that should we stumble out of our confident gait, that we have a friend and guide who will clearly steer us back on to the path again. In that knowledge I have included two holy sites for divine reflections for solitude of thinking and profound inspiration. The first is the immaculate St. David's Cathedral, a world famous heritage site and place of worship for eons. The second is far lesser known. It is the St. Merthyr shrine. A shrine to the remains of a young woman ceremonially sacrificed some 1,500 years ago. Recently discovered this is quickly becoming a place of growing importance for pilgrims to a site which archaeologists have established as a burial site of a woman who had been buried in accordance with what we know now as Christian tradition. There is strong historical evidence that "St. Merthyr" had been sacrificed cruelly and ritualistically by Druid priests for the very fact that she was an early Welsh Christian.

Like the previous walk from Wigan Pier to Standish Cross, this final walk signifies an adventure for me in that I have had to leave my own locale to step out on the high road in a complete other part of the ....

"Cloppety-Clop! Red Nought Street. All change!", intones the conductor. "End terminus for this stage".

'How bothersome', thinks Nurse Kendra, although this was a regular change on her journey back to her home in Gaolers Knoll. Every day she did this change procedure twice. Nevertheless she is frustrated by the interruption as the language was difficult for her to read and she was just getting into it, albeit very abstract prose. 'Obviously the type of stuff those intellectuals like to read.' She resolves to continue on the next stage even while recognising that the next stage is always particularly busy and crowded. She might only have a slight chance of getting a seat where she would be comfortable enough to read the remaining sheets.

She turns out right, the next stage taking her to Gaolers Knoll is indeed crowded out. No chance for further reading. After fifteen minutes of being thrown around with her neighbours while hanging on to the straphanger she arrives at her stop in Newmarket Plaza. There she walks a further five minutes avoiding January downpours and amassing puddles. When she arrives at her humble abode she realises she is running a little late for the Princess Guides meeting. At the age of twenty-three Kendra is considered to be a senior guide and mentor to the younger girls. This "teaching" role or capacity accords her with vital additional VP points which ease her progress in the hospital meritocracy, In that way her *Badges of Honour* that she has been earning give her kudos in her hospital career, so it is important to keep the activity up. Soon she may be considered for elevation to PBG mistress which might put her in contention for ward sister at White Cross.

In her hurry she downs her satchel, changes out of her wet clothes into her starched and toggled Guide uniform and is out of the house in five minutes flat. Mrs Dowd's mysteries remain secreted away in her satchel.

Although it is a beverage house it still stocks brannet and Arnold Copperfield Esq. asks for a large one. 'What in the hell am I doing here?', he thinks. 'I'm flirting with a Malaccan beauty whilst trying to get portions of hallowed text to an ingrate who is not even a Value Provider! Why are the forces driving me this way so that half of time I'm not fully aware of my actions?' Arnold Copperfield Esq. is a seasoned campaigner and a man of the world but he had never known in his wisdom such a self-appointed path of foolishness and folly.

He does not want to go home. It is well appointed in Prison Oval, but his dwelling manor is lonely and populated by sad paintings. Portraits of ones long dead, deeply loved and grieved, and even some so by Arnold. It is a sitting room of sombre ghosts. Besides which, amongst those portraits, amongst all those stern unsmiling faces, Arnold is more likely to become possessed by the action – possessed by the action to help Jimmy, and that meant facing Rosemary Dowd. He does not want always to be facing her. He is drawn to her poker face, even among all those other faces in his grand sitting room, and she has the ability to give the greatest reproach. She has the ability to disarm him with quiet argument so that he can reason only with emotion and the strength of it is like a giant blood clot in his brain; it is like rusty water overpowering him and he can taste its choleric. When she makes him deal with all this internal emotion he is thrown to exhaustion, wanting to weep and mortified by the miseries of past failure and neglect. 'Life is complicated enough without the duty of communing with doleful portraits with their bitter ghost memories. I shall stay here anon, methinks', thinks he.

He indicates to the waiter who is able to notice him in the increasingly lively beverage house.

"Another brannet, Sir?", enquires the waiter.

"Gladly, my man!"

"And perhaps an extra cushion too for your tired body?"

"Aye, I think that would be grand", grants Copperfield cautiously. 'I'm driven to death to be alive', muses he.

The new brannet comes with fresh glamour. "My name is Annabelle", says she.

"What's your tipple, Annabelle?"

"Karmesan, but shall we have it up in me room?", she winks knowingly.

"Well it's getting rather crowded down here", ventures Copperfield and noting that life should always be played with adventure.

Nurse Kendra gets home exhausted from her Guides meeting. It has been a long day and she forgets altogether the remaining Dowd manuscript in her satchel. It is not until the morning in her rush and upon opening the satchel to put her gear in is she aware again about her wish to read the manuscript in whole. It is the same procedure as the last night. The stages are packed tight; no chance for leisurely reading hanging on the straphangers like monkeys in the high jungle canopy. Even the sedate chairs more frequented by the more posh folk appeared to be spoken for on this work day in the thriving metropolis.

Brisk, brisk is the nurse's day. Upon arrival Nurse Kendra is briskly into the changing room and in brisk time she is briskly into her nurse's starched and bonneted uniform; the curls of her long luxuriant dark hair abstinent from appreciation during the course of this yet another working day.

"What news me girl?", she calls out to Nurse Trevor Chargehand who has covered her station during the night duty.

"Watch it cheeky!", he rejoins. Nurse Kendra always makes him smile even though he does not think on her. " Astrologer Royal is reporting that the Brown Dwarf is on the move again. Oh and Mister Suzuki is conscious again. I wonder if the two are related. In fact he's even calling for you. Something about his possessions, and also Roper

wants to see you, so you better get to it and be a busy bee.
I'm off to Bed Town!" And with that Chargehand is off.

'I wonder what the Surgeon-Captain wants. Very
unusual that he wants to speak to me personally. Very rum
indeed. First, I better call round to Mister Suzuki and see
what he wants quickly.'

Jimmy lies in his bed looking groggy but determined.
He seems to perk up when he notices Nurse Kendra
gliding towards him.

"Ah, there you are Nurse".

"Yes, Mister Suzuki. Here I am. What seems to be the
trouble?"

"Well it's my belongings. They're not here, you see."
Jimmy points at the locker next to his bed.

She peers at the locker. "It says John J. Perriwinkle on
the tab. There must have been a mix-up when you were
taken for your procedure and more or less at the same time
Perriwinkle was transferred to isolation. He was roaring
up a storm, you see. Doesn't he have anything good to
read in there?", pointing at Perriwinkle's locker.

"No, not really. Only Diskey's account of the Second
Seturk War. It looks very dry indeed!", moans Jimmy. "I
wanted to read my stuff. Personal and family papers and
the like, you know", he whinges on.

"Well I'll see to it in a jiffiness. I've just been
summoned by our big cheese. Read these for the time
being", giving him the most recent papers from
Copperfield.

"But Nurse Kendra......."

But she is off. Priorities take their precedence. A minute
later she is standing in the anteroom of the great man
Surgeon-Captain Sir Frederick Roper. A stern junior
matron acts as gatekeeper like a mastiff at a gate. She is
piggy faced fierce looking and looks like she eats starch-
yamamas during every minute of her entire spare time.

"Nurse Kendra reporting for the Surgeon-Captain", she announces. "I've been told that His Honour wishes to see me".

"Oh, yes. He wants to see you", responds the matron peevishly. "Wait!" Matron knocks on the door of the main office and goes in.

Kendra thinks nothing of this as she knows matrons have had the training in peevishness. Nevertheless, she is still on tenterhooks wondering what is up and why she is summoned for an audience.

The gatekeeper is back. "You may enter".

Nurse K enters into the palatial office of the chief for her very first time. She notices straight away that its ostentatious grandness made its single occupant look rather small and insignificant. Even so Surgeon-Captain Professor Dr Dr Sir Fredrick Roper is bristling with buttons, braids and brass; like a small size peacock in naval attire. The chief does not move from his chair. He remains seated behind his large mahogany desk, and neither does he offer his guest a seat, only an immediate question without ceremony.

"Do you know someone called Arnold Copperfield?", he enquires neutrally.

"Yes, I do your Honour. Why?".

"Well, I am sorry to say that the gentleman died in the early hours of this morning. Furthermore he actually died in only what can be called a knocking shop! While conducting his business there he suffered a major heart attack. It proved fatal in the end. Orderlies were able to get to him whilst he was still alive and were able to revive him for a short period, but ultimately unfortunately unable to stop him passing on. Before he died though he asked for you by name and identified you as a member of staff here. He gave one of our men this small envelope to be passed to you. It is written in his hand and personally addressed to you. One can tell from its weight that it contains something therein. Here it is yours." Roper passes her a small envelope.

Kendra looks sheepishly at it clutching at it too tightly.

"Aren't you going to open it, girl?", he enquires.

"Well, it is private".

"That granted, but at least do me that honour considering the effort we have placed to get this to you!", bristled the Surgeon-Captain.

"Yes, indeed Sah", and Kendra opens the envelope without further ado.

"It's a key", she said.

"It is that".

"What is it for?", Kendra plaintively asks the S-C as if he were omniscient.

The Surgeon-Captain does not pause to think on that. "Apparently Copperfield did not have the breath left to explain before he popped his clogs, but to me Nurse Kendra it looks like a normal door key or possibly for a strongbox, wouldn't you think?"

"I see."

"Yes, but what I do not see is your connection to the elderly gentleman, and, more so I am particularly curious to know the connection as he came to our attention with his trousers down in a house of ill repute!" The S-C's sideburns bristle with disgust.

Nurse Kendra has no answer for Copperfield's final location.

"In truth I hardly knew him, Sir. He was simply a visitor to the hospital. I met him a couple of times as he was enquiring about the health of one of my patients. Yesterday evening he invited me down the road to take a chocolate with him that's all".

"Which patient, Nurse Kendra?"

"James Donald Suzuki."

"And this Copperfield, was he some sort of relative of Suzuki's? Or a close friend perhaps?"

"I'm not entirely sure, your Honour. Only that he knew Suzuki, but that Suzuki seemed to be having problems remembering him, probably due to the head injury."

Sir Frederick clears his throat. "I am not sure why you have been concerting with a visitor to the hospital and cavorting over chocolate in a honky-tonk bar. I'm not entirely of the opinion that this is the professional behaviour becoming of a professional". He stresses particularly the last word.

"I'm sorry, Sir. I took it for a respectable beverage house".

"Did you now? That may well be, but nevertheless you will be put under formal investigation for this matter. An investigation, after which a report will be drawn up by Matron Stoneywell. In any event we shall be respecting the dying man's wishes", concluded Roper. "Take the key freely if you wish it. I will though inform Copperfield's executors and you shall have to deal with them about it. What say you?"

"I will take it".

She is then dismissed. She leaves the great office and exits through the anteroom.

"Goodbye Matron … ah…"

"Matron Stoneywell. Please remember well my name", is the reply.

Jimmy leafs through the leaves of paper like an obsessive collector. He is beside himself with excitement. He devours page one of Walk 17 wondering about Pembrokeshire and the so-called Druids who were cited in the text. He is fairly irritated by the absence of continuity in that he has barely read the first walk and now it has jumped to Walk 17, the final walk indeed. For a member of a recognised underclass he could at times be as fussy as a high academic. Nevertheless, he recognises that the profundity of the text is masterly; the joy invincible. The pyjama topped intellectual devours on blissfully unaware of catheters and bed pans below the surface of the picture:

Like the previous walk from Wigan Pier to Standish Cross, this final walk signifies an adventure for me in that I have had to leave my own locale to step out on the high road in a complete other part of the country

('By Domingo, this Copperfield is the collector', he thinks. 'Where could he have got his hands on such an artefact and why does he want me to see it?', he muses further).

*and thereby I have left my own particular zone of comfort to reach out to you readers who are in different parts of this our great nation so that I can experience a different nature to my walks of solitude. More so in doing this, this walking away (*pun for association football lovers*) is intended to provide affinity to you dear reader, so that I can reach out and feel the type of places where you might walk in solitude and achieve resolution. It was important that I could imagine in my mind's eye something other than the verdancy and valley of South Wiltshire as it is vital that I could write up a set of universal reflections which would fit with all landscape, weather and regional character. I hope that I will have succeeded. You will see the result after the account of this Walk at the Appendix thereafter entitled:* "Set of Universal Reflections". *Now that I have set out my rationale for this, and the Wigan walk, let's take our starting point of St. David's Cathedral, or Lincoln Cathedral, or Giant's Causeway, or White Cross Hospital, or Times Square, and so on.*

First I enter the Cathedral itself knowing that this is a landmark, a place which has provided meaning to visitors and supplicants for nigh on a thousand years. I could also be walking to the head of the Grand Canyon a natural wonder that has inspired visitors for hundreds of years. Upon entering the Cathedral itself

('But how did the first two sheets come about? I got them outside on New Year's Day. In fact the second quite literally came out of the ground', thinks on Jimmy. "Did Copperfield arrange this by magik? Giant's Causeway, Times Square – something feels so familiar.')

one immediately perceives the cold early March light rushing in through the stained glass windows, for I am here on St. David's Day, 1ˢᵗ. March. Dear reader, you know how I like my ceremony! Also, as it is my final walk of this series, the Reverend Mr Dowd is walking with me, for I know that if you have been following the walks and practices of this book you will most likely not be walking alone either. When you are joy, then the whole world is joyful with you.

The first things that strike me is the silence and the space. The whole impression of the space therein is of quiet waters. A non-showy self-confidence; it just is. One's eye is soon drawn to the Norman style nave which is actually the oldest part of the cathedral. Work was commenced by the then bishop, Peter de Leia, who was an appointee of Henry II to the position. The story goes that the original construction of the cathedral was owed to the fact that the original cathedral existing there was deemed by Henry himself to be too small. The King had visited St. David's in 1171 and seeing the ...

"The man who has been giving these papers to me to give to you .... Well he's only died, hasn't he!"

"What?" She has caught Jimmy in deep concentration somewhere in the nave of St. David's.

"Copperfield! He's brown bread! Dead", amplifies Nurse Kendra.

Jimmy's first thought is actually who is going to supply him with further instalments of this story.

"Why that's horrible! What happened?"

"I've just been with the Surgeon-Captain and he says Mister Copperfield died of a heart attack last night, how do you say it? In flagrante delicto with a woman of the night! Almost directly after I took a glass of chocolate with him".

"What this old Copperfield fellow? Unbelievable!"

"You knew that he was old?"

"Yes, you told me."

"Then you have a good memory, Mister Suzuki. How is it that you knew Arnold Copperfield?"

"I didn't".

"Well, he said you did. Why was he at pains to get you all these sheets of paper? What's all this stuff about Whitesands Bay and the like?", Kendra rasps.

Jimmy feels under a peculiar pressure from this short onslaught. He has never stood up well to pressure; a hint of criticism he took morbidly personally. He becomes aware that beauty under anger transforms into something terrible giving him terror. The primeval force of angry beauty. Some old survival instinct from the past appears to be cutting in and overriding his considerate self. An instinct which knows nothing else other than self-survival and knows no other consequence than this. If he does not respond to that instinct he will be overwhelmed by forces of self-repulsion.

"Sister! Sister!", he calls. "This nurse is giving me wicked palpitations". It was nasty to do this to the much put upon Nurse Kendra.

"How could you?" Nurse Kendra is shocked. This action, is something she did not see coming from Jimmy, like a man fighting for his life where she thought there would be no life at all.

"By Gad! You are a fraud Sir! I'm going to have the contents of that locker with Perriwinkle and I will expose this mystery", she promises like she means it.

"You cannot touch my property!"

"There is no property in the Poorhouse. I have also a key passed to me by old Copperfield before he died, and I wonder what that shall expose too".

Jimmy looks like he could propel himself out of his hospital bed and blaze her out with his fury. Nurse Kendra is now starting to look worried here.

"Now what is happening here?" It is Ward Sister Solice.

"Sister, this nurse is throwing me into consternations!", Jimmy gets in first like a nasty sneak child. "Trying to insinuate that I'm in cahoots with immoral philanderers".

"Really Mister Suzuki. What is all this funny-buggers stuff?", rejoins the Sister.

An authoritative sounding voice in the background asseverates, "Maybe it is Nurse Kendra that is funny-buggers? Could it be that she is procuring for such immoral philandering? Is it mere coincidence that she took the elderly gentleman to this house of ill repute for a **chocolate**?" It is the stony voice of Matron Stoneywell, the Inquisitor-General.

At this awareness Nurse Kendra faints gracefully to the floor.

'Beautiful in all aspects', notes Jimmy. 'I wonder if it was deliberate?' Jimmy uncomfortably recognises and pushes away this base side of his character. Even Alderman Lennon might have been more gracious.

Kendra was a dancer. Daddo liked dancing. When all was misery and the silence suffocating he liked to have a jig. The family was poor, but Daddo insisted that little Kendra should still have her reel dancing lessons from Miss Marigold. Kendra was invited to show Daddo her new tricks. The new steps, the flicks of the head; poise and grace. Dado would whip out his concertina and get the young Kendra out on the kitchen floor to perform a jig.

"Daddo's little girl is gaying to perform", he would say in his rough full islands accent. "Come my little princess. Come and dance for your Daddo."

Daddo would insist that Ma and Sophia should be there to witness the performance. Ma would sit there masked in misery and Sophia with a face like thunder and they would have to sit there listening to Daddo's idiotic exhortations while Kendra pranced and preened around the hard stony kitchen floor.

"My, my what a little ballerina. What a little angel. Encore! Encore! Give us a little pirouette. There that's the treat. Lavaly, lavaly". And so on.

"Kendra, come and sit on Daddo's lap. There's me good gal. Ooh you looks pratty in that there dress. Should Daddo get you a little pet? A wea hamster perhaps? He would climb over you and snuffle in an out of thee. In an out."

"It's so tickly, Daddo!"

"That them snuffly hamsters. That's what they're like. Snuffling, snuffling". And then that smile out of cracked teeth and the whiff of stinky rum breath. Mood changes like a tropical squall.

"Where's me supper you dozy bitch?"

"But you said you wanted to go to the public house for a drink with Jim first", Ma entreats. Sophia shifts and looks concerned in a surly sort of way.

"That was yesterday, pig-head! Get your wits about you!", snarls the family's dance connoisseur.

Little Kendra sits in a dark corner of the kitchen and bides her time.

In the splendour of the isolation ward Sir John J. Perriwinkle has been mistakenly raking through the contents of Jimmy's bedside locker looking in vain for Valentine Diskey's account of the Second Seturk War. Instead he unearths some grubby foolscap pages which he reads. He does not like what he reads and he knows why.

Sir John had been for most of his fifty-two years living the life of an aristocratic fop and dandy. He had old money. The sort of serious money and lands that Great Society dare not abominate for Great Society, despite its meritorious principles, depends still intrinsically on the bounty of Capital. Great Society knows that Capital tolerates regimes, philosophies and orders when it is left to regulate its own. Nevertheless, although Sir John was a member, he had not been an active dogma giver. He had left dogmas of Capital to others. He was too filthy rich to care. Instead he had embraced experiment; some might call a dissolute lifestyle. He wore the wears of the bawdry and the tawdry, keeping company with actresses and Tula wolfhounds. Whether on the plantation, or in the city, his world had been one of sensation; gambling, gamesmanship, trying addictions, life swap wagers and so on. He had never considered marrying some aristocratic bossy-boots. He remained extremely well connected throughout the Old Class and would make a fine catch for some down at heel Old Class family. Despite his flagrant hedonism he had over the years supported a number of philanthropic projects – the Chair in Erotic Poetry at Issacheim, the Old Sailor Women Home at Port Authority and the Royal Society of Science's deep space telescopes at JaJa Point.

Six years ago the last of these had brought astounding news about a Brown Dwarf system. Professor James Riddell, the Astrologer Royal himself, had called upon Sir John at his city residence in Rumpole Street. A tiny star, so old and fantastic in density had been unearthed by one of the JaJa telescopes. Sir John although sponsoring the JaJa project really did not understand much astronomy preferring to read the astrology charts in the *Daily Bugle*. He liked to sponsor scientific projects for the common good and promotion of knowledge, not because he wanted to know anything about the scientific findings. One Friday morning, whilst nursing a hangover, the AR had unexpectedly turned up in his drawing room and he was at a complete loss to understand quite why the AR himself was here with the news about a brown dwarf.

"Well Professor, what does this Brown Dwarf do for the price of bread?" Sir John believed in cutting to the heart of the issue. He did not wish to hear about quarks, Betelgeuse and disruptions in interstellar mediums and the like.

Professor Riddell, who was in his early forties, was a sharp dresser with the appearance of a politician in waiting. He was in full decorum in grey morning coat, Earl Grey spats and topper hat. Sir John was aware that the Prof had earned an inestimable number of value points and could be in line to be the next Culture Minister.

The Professor knew that Sir John could be known for his irascibility, but nevertheless moved the topic on with confidence.

"A Brown Dwarf, your Eminence, is very difficult to perceive in the glasses. It is a very small star. In fact smaller than the largest two planets in our own star system. Nonetheless, it is still a star and because of that it has a fantastic mass and density. In other words, it exercises a mighty considerable pull in gravity. For the fact that it is so small, maybe not so much larger than our own planet, we have just spotted it some days ago. Not just a star too, but a small star system. We had already detected two small planets orbiting it. We would like to call it after you our benefactor – the Perriwinkle System".

"I am mightily honoured and that is why you rushed here during my morning toilet to inform me of the bestowal of this honour?"

"Well, it is two o'clock, almost time for luncheon, but no, it is rather to inform you on the extraordinary details of this discovery."

"Being?", Sir John rasped impatiently.

"It looks like we have discovered a runaway star. I've had one of my top people Doctor Egregious Daedalus checking on it to confirm. The doctor has confirmed that the Perriwinkle System – if I may, Sir- has broken free from the gravitational pull of the outer orbit of our Milky Way galaxy and is spinning away at unfathomable speed!"

"Ye gads, Sir! What is this, the story of a runaway star slave? I can tell this story at Lady Mary Pavingstone's soiree tonight. It will be an amusing insert during our game of Golddigger", chuckled Sir John.

"May I go on?", ventured the Professor.

"Pray do, but I'm having a snifter. You want one too?" Sir John poured a brandy into a glass.

"No, thank you. Sir John, I wish to inform you that the Brown Dwarf is heading in our general direction at fantastic speed. In breaking free of its gravity hold fantastic fabulous velocity has been garnered. At the same time its own extreme dense gravity is pulling our star system towards it. A fantastic gravitational pressure is brewing due to it putting pressure on innumerable star systems during its passage. The mathematik on all this is immense. We will need to research the calculus and I would wish to employ many additional inquisitors to engage in the calculations. To do so, Sir, the Society would ask humbly for more financial support from you."

"I see I'm sure Great Society will wish to contribute."

"The effects of this astronomical aberration are presently incalculable Sir John, but through your research stipend auspices Doctor Daedalus has set forth many theoretical calculations on the effect of anti-matter which we call the *G Gauge Effect*."

"I am sure Professor this theoretical research is very absorbing, but I am not made of money".

"I understand Sir John, but this is no mere intellectual pursuit. We already know from Doctor Daedalus' asseverations that the anti-gravity effects of this heavenly occurrence are likely to be very anti-physik".

"Anti-physik?"

"Yes, ultimately Perriwinkle – if I may again, Sir –, or the Brown Dwarf if you prefer, will pull us into its gravity and chew us up. A sort of doomsday scenario, if you like. We have to calculate how long until that happens, but daresay more than a year of Mondays, I would hazard. Nevertheless, the anti-G will start to effect much much sooner, even in the next fortnight I'm led to believe. You see, the G Gauge Effect has the ability to distort reality. We simply do not know how this will affect time and space without much more research being applied".

"If not our own government then, why doesn't Oriens do it? They have far more resources to throw at it".

"To be absolutely candid Sir, we absolutely need to have a head start on all this. The good Doctor needs more inquisitors to analyse the figures so that he and I can do the advanced calculus, but the preliminary findings are suggesting that we can harness the absolutes of anti-gravity to procure the Philosophers Stone".

"The Philosopher's Stone!"

"Yes, Sir John. I am absolutely deadly serious. Daedalus and I are of the firm belief that we can harness the anti-G to produce the circumstances for eternal life. Not an elixir, if you will, more how to employ the gravitational shifts of Perriwinkle to warp the space time continuum in the very continued favour of our mutual existences. This is a secret we would not even wish to share with a few select and loyal friends, let alone with the Orientals. Of course, we shall have to publish the physical possibilities; increased volcanic activity, tidal effects and so on, but the metaphysical aspects I would wish to keep Marm on. Strictly between us."

"Am I to understand that you are offering eternal life?"

"In a nutshell, yes".

"Stakes are large", thoughtfully murmured Sir John J. Perriwinkle, 15th. Baronet of Sandown visualising an infinity of dissolution day and night.

Why had he been wondering on this particular episode in his life? Why had this recollection surfaced to his consciousness? Sir John J. Perriwinkle reads on curiously through the mysterious Suzuki tract certain he can make sense of it all. He is confident that he could make all the loose ends tie up. There was no such thing as coincidence. He is confident of that, but extremely unsettled about all else.

"Yes, that's it. Walking as a vehicle to inner contemplation and a means to reflection on how valuable these souls are to the world. Indeed, how lucky they are that we have adequate social security and benign Christian values here".

"Well, I think it is entirely commendable. A good Christian work in the Church's finest traditions. But do you think that anyone is going to want to buy it; particularly your target group: the unemployed*", enquired my spouse quite rightly.*

This gave me the chance to build my philosophy on the book, and yes dear reader, we have not as yet set one foot ahead of the other!

"Well Stephen", I interjected. "The working title I had in mind is Walks for the Unemployed. *Of course, I have been thinking ultimately of publishing. It would only be Christian to put out the good word to the wider world. Nevertheless,* Walks for the Unemployed *is only a snappy title that works for a book cover. My real intention is to have a wider audience which in its extent could not be included in a short book title cover".*

"What do you mean?", he asked.

"Well, I would intend this contemplative guide to include all those who have recently suffered some sort of major loss, not just loss of employment itself. For example, bereavement, loss of physical or mental faculties, loss of optimism, loss of faith, loss of soul, loss of joy, and generally those who feel they have been or are being passed over. It is for all those who feel at a loss for life. Through walking contemplations I would wish to aid the lost mind back to the compassion and optimism that is within the fold of our Lord Jesus Christ. It is as simple as that".

"Brilliant!" was the one word uttered by my redoubtable husband.

"Well, I better get started then", I said and my heart sang with this commitment.

So here goes.

I set foot from the Job Centre at Amesbury. I have deliberately chosen this site as there are many unemployed people within. Poor farm labourers, squaddies who cannot transition on from the army, disadvantaged souls who cannot handle the challenges of NVQs, and their like. It is indeed a place where people appear somewhat despondent, and the staff employed there to help them equally so. In a charming little town like Amesbury it is a place resident with despondent souls, and it has the feel of a betting shop or a travellers pub.

So what better way to dispel this despondency by setting out from there and strolling down the road!

Amesbury is a vibrant little market town which ....

Sir John breaks off from reading and examines again the Mrs Dowd manuscript. He has just again reread the third sheet which frustratingly ends on a point of great excitement. 'This Amesbury, this Amesbury .... Could the system and Daedalus have led me to this strange Amesbury?' It leads him to ponder on again that first awareness of the renegade Brown Dwarf system conveyed to him by Professor Riddell. Perriwinkle the reaper of planets, named after him. The bane of mortality. A lot of troubled water had flowed under the bridge since then, such that Perriwinkle feared for his sanity, but his quest would go on and he knew deep in his bones that the temporal shifts in time, space and reality had delivered the Mrs Dowd papers to the Poorhouse Hospital of White Cross. Negative effects - negative effects - the Brown Dwarf remorselessly spins on.

He tosses and turns after lights out.

'How could the great Sir John come like some destitute to this paupers hospital. It is barely more than a prison', he wonders.

Sleep though takes him.

Mrs Dowd stands before him among the stones. It is night. There is moonlight and the snow falls.

"Mrs Dowd, I presume? So good to meet you at last! I am one of your most dedicated followers."

"Indeed" rasps Mrs Dowd with eyes like terror. "Who are you to address your Queen so? I am Eleanor! How dare you a poor vagrant address my majesty!"

The moonlight shows fittingly the majesty of the stones. Within their circle there are white fluffy sheep whiter than the cascading snow. The sheep turn into armoured soldiers holding blood axes. These quickly manifest into nurses holding brutal looking sharp syringes.

"Low born Sir John is insane!" laugh the sisters hysterically licking the tips of their syringes.

Mrs Dowd laughs herself into Surgeon-Captain Sir Frederick Roper and exclaims: "Poor little John. Out of the poorhouse into the madhouse now".

Sir John wakes in a sweat and thinks the world unkind.

'Why would I wish to prolong my time in it?'

"You fainted". It is the voice of the mean-hearted Stoneywell. She is holding a bottle of smelling salts. "Often a bad conscience can manifest itself in physical reactions", she continues tartly.

Nurse Kendra registers but is still too confused to react.

"But you appear fine now, girl. Nevertheless the Surgeon—Captain does not want anyone who is not at their best cavorting through his wards. You are to take the rest of the week on sick leave without pay. After that you and I shall come to terms with your transgression with Mister Copperfield. I will hear you out about that, and it better be plausible. However for now you are dismissed until next week", concludes Matron Stoneywell.

Kendra is too aggrieved to even argue. She retires into slow sobs sitting on a hard chair in the nurses' office. After some five minutes of feeling betrayed, and thinking that the whole world is against her, she determines to get out of the hospital and find some normality. She takes the stage to Gaolers Knoll homeward bound. As it is the middle of the day the stage is not too crowded so she is able to be seated and muses about all the events of the day. She turns around and around Copperfield's key in her hand wondering what it opens. A glint of noonday light comes in to the carriage so that she can suddenly discern small discreet markings on the head of the key.

PCB 591

'PCB', she thinks. 'That seems familiar'.

The coach enters the banking district of Beet Market. She likes to look out at the great banking edifices and spot the bank workers in their fine bureau apparel. She has always felt a little envious of their chic style and self-importance.

Then it suddenly comes to her.

'PCB is the People's Credit Bank. Roper was right it could be for a strongbox or safe deposit box.'

Kendra is too exalted to think of inaction. She gets up from her seat intent on alighting at the next stop, Newcastle Pool. Getting off the stage she knows that the People's Credit Bank is a short five minutes' walk away. She sets off there and is not thinking. Her sole concentration is on getting into that bank.

When she arrives there she notices its grandeur. She has never been in a bank before let alone held money in one. She is unsure as to what to do. A red liveried doorman opens the big wooden door for her.

"G,day Marm".

"Good day, Sir", immediately realising that she had taken on the role of servant in this interchange. She feels embarrassed. The marble hall is large and intimidating. She starts to feel that she should backtrack out of there. She edges slowly and automatically towards the exit looking to exit.

"May I help, you Marm?". It is a middle-aged man in full bank livery regalia looking very clerk like and professional.

Kendra is taken aback, so taken aback that she does not have allowance to think but merely to blurt out: "I have a safe deposit key", holding it out as if it were some powerful talisman.

She was about to add that she thinks that it is a safe deposit key presumably for the PCB and that would it be alright to check and enquire if it is; if it is not too much trouble, that is.

Yet she has no chance to say what she was going to say for the official without asking any leave or permission immediately snatches the key from her dainty hand.

"Just a moment", says the official and puts an eyeglass next to his nose. "Yes, number 591. Please come this way, Madam", and she follows him obediently to a side bureau.

"My name, Marm, is George Cadger, assistant under-manager", says he opening a larger ledger. "Yes, here we are number 591. Arnold Copperfield, Esquire; Justice of the Peace."

George Cadger smiles at Kendra as if to say what on earth are you doing here with this key and Kendra is about to utter a paltry explanation.

"And let's see, of course, there is a co-trustee on this safety deposit box whom Mister Copperfield has conferred access and full power of attorney rights; that being?"

"Nurse Kendra Okvicha", she suddenly answered confidently.

"Yes, indeed, Mistress Okvicha", he says. "Proof of identity and statement of professionalism?"

Kendra Okvicha, who is now feeling something like a human being with some status, searches in her clutch bag for her documents and hands them to Cadger for inspection.

"Good all is in order, Mistress Okvicha. Would you like a glass of portillo for fortification before I take you down to the vault?"

" I don't mind if I do, Mister Cadger", she answers thinking a bit of fortification would steady her extremely fraught nerves.

"Certainly Marm", and he pours the libation into a tiny crystal glass quickly without undue ceremony.

Kendra downs it in the one gulp.

"Capital! To the vault then Marm", Cadger instructs.

Cadger leads her down to the vault where he unlocks box 591 with the bank key and she does the same on a lock the other side of the box with Copperfield's key. Cadger eases out the box and takes her to a small anteroom so that she can privately interact with box 591.

"I shall be waiting outside, Marm. Pray take your time."

"Thank you Mister Cadger", and George Cadger removes himself from the room.

She opens the box 591 tentatively as if something nasty might spring out. However, the contents are quite mundane. There are a number of stock papers for the South Ocean Trading Company, a pay the bearer bond from the Legal Cooperative Fund for two hundred sovereigns, a small bag containing three minute but flawless sapphires and a letter manuscript which has been sealed with the stamp of the Copperfield family. Above all this is a short declaration manuscript with no enclosure and which reads open and face up:

My dear Nurse Kendra,

The contents of this box are all for you and for no other. Rest assured that the contents therein are not to be declared through my estate and be aware that my executors know nothing of these. They represent a tidy sum which may help you launch a new life. Please take particular care of the personal letter stamped with my household seal which is also herein. Take it away with you and read it carefully at your leisure. It has much import on our recent dealings together.

Yours sincerely,

Arnold Monteloupe Copperfield, Esquire, Justice of the Peace

Kendra is astonished, but not too astonished to stand up, remove the letter from the strongbox and put it into her clutch bag. She definitely feels too awkward to read the content of the special letter down in the bank vaults. The remainder of the valuables she elects to leave in the security of the bank.

"Mister Cadger", she calls.

He is there in an instant as if he had not been away at all.

"Do you wish the box to be returned, Madam?"

"Yes, indeed kind Sir!". Kendra is sounding more confident and cultivated as if Copperfield's legacy has uplifted her.

"Just a moment then. I will return the box to its position in the vault and then I will escort you back upstairs".

Kendra gives him one of her haughty looks with arched eyebrows, that she learnt with the more dramatic moments of her reel dancing lessons as a child, and Cadger scampers away.

On their way back to the foyer Kendra comes across more and more haughty and in turn Cadger turns more and more ingratiating; so with the goodbyes.

"It was a great privilege to have your visit here today, esteemed lady. If there is anything more that I can do to be of service ....."

"Farewell, Cadger". She could do rich and arrogant.

As luck would have it, directly upon leaving the bank, she is immediately embarked onto a stage and in no time at all is at her private residence in Gaolers Knoll where she boils herself a strawberry tea and sits down to read the letter. She opens it and begins.

My very dear Kendra,

I have always expected my demise at any moment and these recent times have been no exception. I have thought about it constantly and I have had very many premonitions about my departure. So many premonitions. These premonitions have been strong of late, though, I do confess, I have felt them strongly before in the past and have survived them. Nevertheless and correspondingly I have always set out my affairs for the unfortunate moment, and I am doing so again in the context of the recent contact that I have had with you. Such obsessive behaviour you might think, but if this letter comes to you, then I should have been commended for taking these particular precautions. Thus I have been again taking these usual precautions over the last few days in my dealings with you and the Poorhouse patient in your care, one James Donald Suzuki.

I still have a deep shudder even now recollecting as to how I almost lay dying not so very long ago. I have on one occasion seen death flow parallel to me in the river of my life. He drifted dark along with me even though the day was bright and glorious.

[Kendra is baffled by the obscure metaphor and her irritation points her to note that there is a date at the top of the letter, and, indeed the date is only from yesterday.]

Nevertheless that aside, the first thing I would ask is if you would once again pass another missive over to Mister Suzuki. You will see it appended in thin paper to the back of my manuscript. Tell Suzuki that I hope it gives him comfort.

[Kendra looks to the back of the letter and finds another memo to do with these strange walks. She determines to read it later after finishing Copperfield's letter, and before handing it over to Suzuki.]

Why have I wished him comfort you might ask? What is the relation between us two? Why do I want him to seek redemption through the profound musings of Rosemary Dowd? Well, I shall fill you in on the second part of the story that irrevocably connects us. It is the second part which is clearer for me. You will have to ask him himself to describe you the first part of the strange story. In doing so he might be redeemed and you shall know that he is a man of stranger character than you might have estimated. He might wish to deny any connection to me as he may feel embarrassed about some ignoble enterprise he conducted. We shall see. Or rather you shall see. I forget myself. I forget my imminent demise − for once. I have been passing the Rosemary Dowd reflections to Suzuki as I wish to forgive him. I had wanted to speak with him upon these reflections to open up a road to forgive him for his past iniquity.

For James Donald Suzuki and Arnold Monteloupe Copperfield Esq. did indeed know each other and were partners in a desperate escapade. The circumstances were these, and in drawing them I am not proud about those circumstances which led me into the path of Jimmy Suzuki. It was some six years ago and I was suffering from great moroseness. I was feeling very low, paralysed with fear about departing this life so that to counter this melancholia I took to trying to embrace life in its very full. One of the initiatives in this respect was to increase the spend of my sexual libido. I do wish to spare you this child, but I do simply want to justify how Suzuki came across me in the arms of a common hussy. He caught me at a most embarrassing moment for a gentleman of my standing and although he had caught me in such an embarrassment I had also caught him out similarly in the unedifying position of actually carrying out a villainous kidnap. You will need to ask him how he had been embroiled in this imbroglio, but to cut a long story short, in that as I had witnessed the capture, I became a captive too. Jimmy Suzuki and his motley crew of criminals made me their prisoner.

The escapade concerned a young woman, not much older than you – and a lot like you in looks and temperament, I might add - and of high professional standing. Suzuki had kidnapped her along with two others. They were mere henchmen for some underworld baron. Well, at a crucial phase in the development of this increasingly disturbing crime Jimmy Suzuki did something which appeared quite heroic which led us to make our escape; that is the damsel, Suzuki and I. However, we did not in the end make well our escape. Suzuki did not continue his heroic streak. Instead he did something quite nefarious which might have actually saved my life, but was most injurious on the poor maiden that we tried to help evade captivity. The thought of that maiden I hold precious to me now.

Her name was Fumi. Ask Suzuki about Fumi. Tell him you know about the kidnapping; that Copperfield told you. Force the issue with him. He has to speak about it to gain redemption under anyone's faith or philosophy.

I cannot tell you any more in this medium. Time is passing and I have to stay set in the action. Learn more from Suzuki. You are very like Fumi and you will be able to get him to reveal all.

So if you are reading this Kendra, then I wish you a true goodbye and a good life. I would that I had gotten to know you better. It is down to you now to get Suzuki to confess for redemption.

Yours aye,
Arnold Monteloupe Copperfield, Esquire

'Fumi. That is the very name I have heard him call in his sleep', she reflects.

"I will have this out of him over the course of next week when I'm back at hospital", she murmurs to herself and sheds a lone tear for Arnold Copperfield Esq.

"So Mister Suzuki, what is the complaint that you have against Nurse Kendra?", asks Matron Stoneywell.

"I have no real complaint, Matron, and I would give her no trouble."

"Well, what was the earlier commotion about? It couldn't have been about nothing. You cried out asking that Nurse Kendra be removed from your presence", she retorts. "She is due back next week and before then I want to know if there is any issue between you that means that it would not be professional for her to continue to administer you".

There is a great imposing silence while Jimmy waits for a brainwave to propel along a plausible explanation but none is forthcoming and the great silence starts to assume epic proportions.

"It's just that she she sh…", Jimmy stammers.

"Are you two sharing some guilty secret?", enquires Stoneywell.

"Sorry?"

"You haven't proposed some how's your father, for example, and she rejected your advances?"

"How could you conceive of such a notion?"

"Well it has been put about here that Nurse Kendra is known to have a bit of a libertine attitude. With this reputation in mind, maybe you thought you could push it a bit and make some amorous advances towards her".

"Matron, what an extraordinary assertion!" Jimmy is on stronger ground now. "What gives you grounds for imputing such a charge?"

"Do not forget Mister Suzuki that you are in a Poorhouse hospital. You are counter-professional and you are being administered here through the grace and benefaction of Great Society. This is no hospital of the Sisters of Mazuma. You are here entirely on charity. Therefore you will live by our rules and procedures, or else you will be summarily discharged. It is my duty to investigate any imputations against my staff, and if my staff have done anything untoward it may be that the patient is not entirely blameless and I will have this out too in fairness to my staff."

Jimmy shifts uneasily in his bed covers. The matron's use of stern sounding words is making him feel guilty and gutless. A feeling that he has too often known and would rather again avoid.

"Now having put the record straight on that", she continues. "I have had my eye on Nurse Kendra. She has had a record of being importune with persons' feelings, especially with the more mature gentlemen. She may well have been provoking your feelings in view of the exchange of some pecuniary award or otherwise."

"Well…", a slight hesitation, "she has been asking about my Sacrificer cheque ". Jimmy is starting to think on his rump now.

"In what connection?", she enquires further.

'Oh, Jimmy. You are truly despicable!', he thinks, but nevertheless his mouth continues with the baseless charge.

"Wanting to know how much I get for my Social Welfare: Factor 5 status. Whether I had a girl; that sort of thing. It was getting to be a real harassment, Matron. Money and girls questions are not a palatable mix for a poor unfortunate like myself who just wants to recover and recuperate. That is why I laid my objections earlier."

Jimmy listens to himself talking. It does not seem like him, but like some actor in a pub-stage drama. Jimmy does not recognise himself, but recognises what an accomplished liar he has become. He sounds so believable, although he does not believe himself. The trouble is that he does believe himself to a fair degree, especially when the issue of self-survival cuts in. 'Do I represent a spineless survival?', he wonders. 'A sort of animal that sinks in the sand so it need never fight at all'.

"I see", says the Matron solemnly. "I am going to have to investigate this further."

"Yes", says Jimmy equally solemnly, but wishing to have this hell-brand away from him and to float his wanting eyes on the soft bosom of Nurse Kendra.

"When she returns from her leave of absence next week I will examine her. You Mister Suzuki may be required to formalise your complaint against her. Think very hard then upon her actions; her words, particularly with regard to your money and her affections. Such licentious behaviour is not new to us in regard to the nurse. The paragraph and line that you shall be providing will go significantly towards building up a very credible case. You, sah, have given substance to some of my suspicions!"

And with that Matron Stoneywell blustered out; no doubt to torment some other poor soul.

"My God, my poor Fumi what have I done. My poor Kendra forgive me", sobs he quietly in the large expanse of the enormous ward in White Cross Hospital.

Kendra is restless. She cannot get to sleep. There are counter emotions going on inside her. Box 591 has given her a small but effective maintenance. With the bonds and the sapphires she calculates that she may be able to give up her professional post as a nurse at White Cross. If she were careful she might not need to work again. She wishes she could get advice. She would have liked to speak to Copperfield for such advice. Maybe she could also confer with Sir John J. Perriwinkle on money matters. Despite the incredulity of the Surgeon-Captain, Sir John's provenance still seemed credible to her. He might very well be able to advise on stock, securities and the like.

However for Kendra there was also the matter of justice. She wants to resume her post at the hospital simply to be vindicated; for them to withdraw their terrible and base suspicions of her. She will not let it go with Roper and Stoneywell simply because she now has some money and does not need to clear the defamation. What is right is right, and she wishes for things to be righted. She does not take lightly or gladly any false aspersions against her.

Furthermore there is the wish of her benefactor. Arnold Copperfield has spoken to her beyond the grave asking that she absolve James Donald Suzuki of his transgressions. His story has to be made known to her. Added to that, she feels extremely betrayed by her patient. A patient on whom she has solicited so much care. Even more betrayed by the fact that it was so unexpected. She had indeed not expected such pernicious behaviour by one James Donald Suzuki who prior to that had been all sweetness and light towards her.

She would have to go back to the hospital and face the orchestra and have it out. Have it out with all of them. There were now quite a number of issues to be resolved there. The sapphires and the other stuff would resolve her confidence. They were her insurance. She has nothing to lose, but her reputation to regain. She tosses and turns not believing in sleep and then sleep is talking with her.

"How could you have led him on so", sleep is saying.

Kendra is sobbing inconsolably and not replying to admonishing sleep.

"Your Papa is a good man, but you led him to temptation!", upbraids the dream character.

"You are a dirty slut who perverted a good man into such unnatural actions", further admonishes the dream crone.

For that which was Kendra, in this fecund dream, it is too much.

"What have I done? I'm a child. You are a mother who has not protected me! I am fourteen and have been suffering his attentions for the past two years and more. He has taken my innocence and you have connived and I am the one who is accused as the temptress; the slut. This is double injustice on me!"

Kendra in her dialogue with sleep is not sure who is talking now. The Kendra that then was or the Kendra that now is.

"She led me along Ma. I was drunk and she asked me to come to her bed. What's a man to do?"

In her sleeping, or her waking, Kendra is now sure that it is the Kendra of the now that is speaking. It is just that little Kendra just sticks around and keeps reminding her of everything.

Kendra wakes in the middle of the night now firmly resolved to go out on a limb for her reputation. She would cower no more.

Jimmy spends the rest of the week toadying to the powers to be in White Cross Hospital. He has reverted to form, an ever so humble counter-professional who is ever so grateful to sponge charity from the benefactors of Great Society. He has wheedled his way into the confidence of Matron Stoneywell. She from time to time administers to him in person granting him her special favour of measuring his pulse, cooling his heated brow and so on. She brings him healthy cooled pulla juyces from time to time. In her ministrations she leans over him to attend to tubes and bed fittings her spacious ample bosom caressing his nose like a motherly canopy. Matron Stoneywell is ugly, but Jimmy has been starved for a long time of the affection of the female sex. He never had a mother who was motherly. Matron Stoneywell even in her pure ugliness is pure security which he accepts without reservation. He begins to wish for her administrations and the smell of her starched uniform has a primeval carnality for him. Matron Stoneywell in her starched malevolence is the capricious earth mother that sustains faith for him.

Of course, Jimmy broods upon Nurse Kendra. There is a sense of shame in him upon how he treated her. He has shopped her just to save his own skin. When he is not gazing upon the ample bosom of Matron Stoneywell his attention becomes diverted to what remains of his conscience. He has done wrong on Nurse Kendra. He does not know how he will handle it if Nurse Kendra confronts him.

The week of remission is almost up. Kendra could be soon back to admonish him for his disloyalty.

"Matron Stoneywell, will Nurse Kendra be coming back to this ward. I am afraid that if she were to bear me any malice then this would do much to deter my recovery."

"Never you mind, Mister Suzuki. Rest assured, that even if the hospital authority were to reinstate her here on this ward, that she will not be administering her attentions to you. Ward Sister Solice or myself will be tending you. You are our own special patient", she adds oleaginously.

The short and ugly Matron Stoneywell in her starched white uniform then approaches Jimmy closer by coming over to the bed and very carefully and very slowly checking all the tubes and callipers around Jimmy's person. She extends her squat body to the furthest attachments, her heavy bosom resting languorously up and over Jimmy's prostate face as if she were taking some religious communion with him. He hears himself give out a little sigh.

"Now, now Mister Suzuki don't be worrying", the mass of flesh is whispering. "We will be protecting you against her and her poison".

"Poison?"

"Don't be vexed. No-one is going to poison you with your guardian angels around".

"You talk figuratively, Matron?"

"Do I? The autopsy on Arnold Copperfield Esq. suggests that there were elements of strychnine in his blood. Very recent too."

"What does that mean?", gasped Jimmy.

"Well, let's just say that it is strange to behold that Nurse Kendra goes for a chocolate with the man and hours later he is found dead with traces of poison in him."

"Somebody else could have given him the poison", lightly defends Jimmy.

"That's for the authorities to find out, but it appears that we have more than just a professional standards matter with Nurse Kendra. It could be a criminal matter. She hasn't given you a nice pulla juyce where you've felt a little queasy after the drinking, has she?", tartly enquires the Matron.

"Surely that is nonsensical", quips Jimmy.

"Is it? Hasn't she been asking about the amount from your Sacrificer cheques and at the same time your recovery is taking longer than expected. Be prepared. You may be speaking to the rozzers as well as the Surgeon-Captain when she returns".

Jimmy has a lot to think on about. This is escalating to a position far more serious than he wished to be involved in. He is not certain if he wishes to help put a rope around Kendra's neck. He considers that he has been too indifferent towards Kendra; too selfish in his own self-preservation. He resolves to help her out of a selfish hope that she could be his. A beauty that he has no right to be close to. Nevertheless, he may be redeemed. Fortune may smile kindly upon him.

Five days later Jimmy notices that Kendra is back in the hospital and working. He could see her at a distance down the long ward. In fact he could almost feel her presence in the vicinity before he actually sighted her. It was as if he were elementally attached to her, but it is plain as day that they are trying to keep her away from him. Stoneywell and Solice marshal around him like protective mothers. He is a long way from Kendra and he has to figure out a way to contact her.

Suddenly the next morning the opportunity comes.

"You are very fortunate, Mister Suzuki", announces Matron S suddenly. "You have been allocated a steaming as part of your rehabilitation programme. This very afternoon too. It is a great privilege to be granted a steaming, you know."

"Pray what is it, good Matron?"

"A bloody good steaming? It is when you are put in a hot room to soak in your own fleshy juices for an hour. Normally it is only the upper orders that get the chance to do this, but the Surgeon-Captain has ordered it for you. It is extremely efficacious for promoting the health. Lucky you!", she warmly exhorts.

Jimmy is not filled with the same excitement about this treatment, but will go along with whatever ministrations they prescribe for his well-being. It is easy to be administered to. Best just to be administered to and cause no trouble.

That afternoon White Cross Poorhouse patient Jimmy is laid out into a bath chair and is being wheeled along the main ward by Nurse Girtles (a simple, very plain girl from Trenchtown). It is a long way down the main ward and most of the staff are scurrying around as some top brass are planned to visit the very next day. All the senior staff are absorbed in making sure that junior staff clean scrupulously in every nook and cranny.

"Watcha cock!"

It is Kendra smiling at him and Jimmy thinks her to be rather nonchalant given the pressure that she is under.

"Sorry, I mean how are you feeling Mister Suzuki?", she adds rather mockingly.

"Very well Nurse and doubtless feeling even better to see you."

"Oh, good", she replies. "Where are you off to with the patient, Girtles?"

"He is going to a steaming", says the soft girl.

"Right you are, Mister Suzuki". Kendra winks at him and skedaddles off.

"Nurse!", Jimmy plaintively cries, but she has faded into the commotion of the ward. Nurse Girtles continues the procession with her patient down the main ward and eventually they are out into the west corridor and into the bathhouse area.

Upon arriving at the steaming room 8, Girtles instructs Jimmy that he should be in his birthday suit to be comfortable for the experience. She offers to help him undress from his hospital pyjamas but she is so plain that Jimmy feels that it is better to handle this operation himself. He undresses himself while the little stove is fired up. Girtles advises him to take in with him some of the rough hospital towels to avoid skin burns and discomfort. Eventually he is left in the small steamy room to sweat out all the jaundice and sweat in new vigour. Soon he is perspiring and feeling very uncomfortable. Beads of sweat have manifested themselves in every single one of his' fleshy folds and he can hardly see through all the steam and the sweat trickling off his forehead. It is horror and he is feeling palpitations and some slivers of panic on account of his rapid heart rate. The door to the steam room opens quickly and abruptly. Someone comes in, but in all the steam Jimmy cannot make out who it can be.

'Perhaps another patient', he surmises.

"G'Day" is his rather involuntary utterance not knowing what else is done in such a circumstance.

"Jimmy, it's me, Kendra!"

Sure enough it is and Jimmy can make out her form in the steam filled light of the room. Her body is a sight for Jimmy's sore eyes as she is clad only in hospital issue towels too; although her towels are a smaller version to Jimmy's. Jimmy's towel looks like it has had a tent pole put inside it.

"Well I had to look the part", she explains. "That way I avoid suspicion".

"I so wanted to see you, Kendra. I am verily glad you are here".

"I can see that", she smirks.

"Oh, Kendra", he sighs.

"They have so got the rumble on me…"

"Yes, I know. That's why I have been desperate to see you, but it is clear that for whatever reason Stoneywell is keeping you apart from me."

"It's this Copperfield thing! They are making so many malicious allegations about me in respect of him".

"Kendra .."

"I don't have much time, Jimmy. I could be discovered here at any moment ...", she swallows. "It has gone beyond just the fact that I was with Copperfield just prior to his heart attack. They are now saying that there is reasonable suspicion to suggest I poisoned the fellow. I have been put on caution for the time being whilst they conduct further enquiries, but it is not looking very straightforward for me. Jimmy, you have to tell me about your connection to Arnold Copperfield. I need to know for it all to make sense. Indeed it may be essential to clearing my name, for indeed I did not poison the man or wish him any form of malice whatsoever."

"I told you Nurse Kendra! I don't know the man."

"That will not do at all".

"Why so?"

"For he has left me a message telling me that he did know you and that you should give me a further account on that."

"Utter nonsense".

"Is it?", she questions. "Then how do I know about a certain Fumi?"

"What!" Jimmy is very steamed up now.

"Yes, that he Copperfield and you were connected in some misdeed to this Fumi. A damsel that you put in distress. Have you something to confess to me, Mister Suzuki?".

Kendra body swathed in towels is heaving now through her agitation. Jimmy does not know whether to go closer to it or run away from her altogether. Jimmy reverts to form. He charges out of the door like a hippopotamus escaping the sun.

"Nurse Girtles", he screams. "I cannot stand the heat in there no longer. It is making me most poorly. I have to return to the ward most immediately!"

"Oh, poor Mister Suzuki", Kendra hears along with further commotion. "I will get you right back to the ward, but first we must get your jim-jams back on", Nurse Girtles is saying.

"Get on with it!", she hears Jimmy testily say.

Kendra hangs in the background of the steam unnoticed by Nurse Girtles vowing that she will be revenged on the scoundrel Suzuki. Revenged on his lack of character and moral baseness. Her reputation restored with Roper and Stonewell, and all this poisonous talk of poisons be dispelled.

Kendra keeps her head down and does her work. She realises that with Copperfield's legacy to her, stashed safely away in the bank, she need not continue with her tribulations at the hospital. However, it is important to her to be vindicated. Nevertheless, the aspersions concerning poison put a new complexion on it. Thus far it has been solely Stoneywell who has mentioned to her this allegation. If this were to result in some serious charge then she would have to be prepared to fight to clear her name; money or no money.

Kendra has been given lowly work to perform. As she is mopping the floor Stoneywell and Solice come close.

'They have come to sneer', thinks Kendra. 'I shall ignore them. They are beneath me and beneath my contempt'.

"Would you credit it?", Kendra hears Solice say. "That is most dastardly!"

"Absolutely perverse malice", is the reply of Stoneywell. "To do such an unspeakable act against a nice old gentleman. He was a septuagenarian and with strychnine too! It is a terrible cruel death."

"Strychnine, you say?"

"Yes", answers Stoneywell. "The Surgeon-Captain explained to me that this poison when inhaled, swallowed or absorbed through eyes or mouth, causes a poisoning which results in muscular convulsions and eventually death through asphyxia. Traces of strychnine were found in the old gentleman's stomach. This was established at the autopsy. What a horrible way to go".

"And who do they think was responsible?", queries Solice.

"The last person he was consorting with. Nurse Kendra Okvicha."

"How dare you?" Kendra cannot believe that she has risen to the bait, but risen to the bait she has. "How dare you make such a spurious accusation. Was I indeed the last person with him? The Surgeon-Captain himself informed me that his last encounter was with a dubious woman of the night. Why is she and her cohorts no greater a suspect than me? If Mister Copperfield was in some house of ill repute, then they may have poisoned him to steal his belongings."

"There was actually no evidence that any of his possessions had been taken", is the withering reply. "And", continues Stoneywell, "tell me why they would risk a fatal poisoning at their own establishment and then report it in to the authorities?"

"You find a lot of mitigation for the so-called knocking shop, but none for me. I find that strange. Don't you too, Sister Solice?", questions Kendra.

Solice looks embarrassed but says nothing. Stoneywell does not respond to Kendra's last comment. The two senior nurses look at each other as if conspirators. Nothing is said between the two.

"As soon as you finish washing and polishing the ward floor Okvicha, you can go and slop out the lavatories", simply says Solice.

Kendra realises that it will be a hard job to garner any sympathy here.

So in the course of the next day ritual punishment and humiliation are meted out to Kendra. Doing the job of a cleaner, not a nurse. Washing and polishing, slopping out the heads, bed baths for the most disgusting patients and being made to run pillar to post on the most menial errands as if she were some young apprentice intern. Meanwhile it was apparent that the rumour mill was being exercised ruthlessly by Stoneywell and her cohorts. Wherever in the hospital Kendra went she heard whispers of 'nice old gentleman' and 'strychnine'. Sometimes she was not sure whether she actually heard the cruel words or imagined that the people were saying them. Under the pressure Kendra recognised that she was undergoing a paranoia, but she felt powerless to prevent it. Her mental stability was being challenged. She dallied with the idea of seeking help from one of the resident phrenologists at White Cross, but thankfully in a more lucid moment decided against it. It was tough to keep going and she felt that she might crumble; just not show up for shift one day. Kendra cries herself to sleep at night and seriously considers throwing in the towel, but somehow what keeps her going through this ordeal is the sense of indignation. An outrage that this is being done to her, transferring into an extreme hatred of Matron Stoneywell.

Outrage. Hurt. Humiliation. Demonization. Cruelty. Kendra's daily lot.

"Okvicha!", growls Stoneywell. "Go clean up the mess that madman has made. I swear if you were not here I would send him to the Demeans and put him with the other funny farmers."

"The Captain thinks that he might be highly connected so that is why we have to put up with him up here", laughs Ward Sister Solice.

"That may well be. Sometimes Sir Frederick can lose his nerve", acknowledges Stoneywell. "Just the threat of higher-ups puts him in a cold sweat. Why are you dallying?", she suddenly shouts at Kendra. "Look lively!" and pointing towards the bed of a rather dishevelled gentleman who had seen better days.

The person in question is the noble Sir John J. Perriwinkle, 15th. Baronet of Sandown amongst other things, although nobody on this hospital floor appeared to believe that is who he actually is. Sir John is sitting up in his bed in a pool of his own vomit. Kendra smiles faintly at him not relishing cleaning him up and his bed with its plethora of puke.

"Now Sir John, what has become of you?". Kendra realises that she has accorded him the title that all of the others had been scoffing at in their disbelief.

"Good of you to ask, noble lady", smiles the baronet.

'He can be quite beguiling in his strange sort of way', thinks Kendra.

"I have had nausea again, and again it is because of the unspeakably bad quality of the hospital food. It is as if the hospital chefs have been instructed by the board of administration to poison all the hospital inmates!"

At this Kendra blanches and Sir John reacts.

"I am sorry to have used that term. Even I have heard of the scandalous stories against you. I recognise that they are baseless and unfounded, and fabricated by the monster matron to ruin your reputation. She sees you as some sort of threat. Who knows why. The why will kill you. The only thing to do to survive is to fight the injustice. Kill it and ask about the why later."

"These are wise words which do much to support me, Sir John", states Kendra as she starts to strip the vomit laced sheets from his bed. "Please get on to the bath chair so that I can take you to the ablutions for washing."

Kendra wheels her important patient down to the bathhouse.

"Nurse Kendra, you have to let me help you through you helping me first."

"I am listening."

"Get word to the Visitor about my plight. Get a message to Lady Elizabeth Swann."

"She would not receive me."

"Yes, she will. Go to her house. It is No. 15 Thunneycliff Grove in Ripside. Say to the butler – should be a fellow by the name of Kampmann – 'ducks and drakes'. It is a code word known to him that recognises the visitor into the company of Lady Elizabeth. She will grant you an audience if you use that code word. Our close ensemble of friends have used it confidentially for a number of years now. It will secure you the access to tell her of my poor circumstances here. She will come to me immediately to attend to me. When I see her I will ask her to call off the hounds from you."

"You can do that?"

"I have that influence", he replies confidently.

Kendra holds the water hose.

"It might be a little cold, so please brace yourself Sir John."

The water jet reaches the body of Sir John and he braces himself manfully.

"Yes. I will do it", she adds and smiles through relief.

That very evening finds Kendra in the elegant drawing room of Lady Elizabeth Swann, the Countess of Tischent. Kendra stands while the countess sits in a grand chair next to a sterile and ornate marble fireplace.

"Do you know how to skim stones across placid areas of water, Nurse Okvicha?" The voice is cool and considered. The lady is elegant and confident. She can be direct in her own drawing room.

"No, my lady. My family was poor and we lived next to the ocean. As a child I never got close to an inland lake where the water was calm enough to try it." Nurse Kendra finds the finery rather overawing and yet is surprised that she starts her conversation so lucidly in such overawing surroundings.

"You are right, my dear. The calm comes from privilege. As children we used to enjoy this pastime at Lake Tacka or Estuary Mine. That is part of the reason why we have 'duck and drakes' as the clandestine code word for our select group. We children of privilege used to have fun playing skimming stones. Moreover it is an allegory for our noble class surviving through the upheavals of Great Society. We of the great families have to skim through life elegantly, briskly and without causing much rupture on the pool of placidity. We have to be fit and nimble in the areas we have placed placidity. We never go to troubled waters as we cannot skim over them. Sort of like the swans who bear closely to my family name. That is why ultimately we are doomed to go finally. The fact that the most noble Sir John has surfaced in an alms hospital is an indication that we are going under in the waves of Great Society. Yet whilst I still have influence I will see that Sir John is raised up again; albeit I have heard that he lost his entire great fortune through a Chuzzle-Dorritt scam. You shall be rewarded for coming to me in haste." Lady Elizabeth appears mysterious. Her features are hidden in the gas light shadows of the grand drawing room.

Although Sir John has promised his personal intervention with the great lady, Kendra decides to be forward.

"As for reward, your ladyship, I would beg your help".

"Name it", coolly from the gaslight shadows.

"As Sir John neatly put it, you can call the hounds off."

"And who is hounding you, child?"

"Principally Surgeon-Captain Sir Frederick Roper and one Matron Stoneywell. They wish to do me down and destroy my character."

"And these same two are largely responsible for Sir John's discomfort, I bet", she laughs.

"Yes, largely," and Kendra goes on to give a quick account of her predicament. By the end of her woeful tale she feels quite teary but better for opening up even though it was to the marble countess.

"Rest assured, Nurse. I will right you. Now leave me be. I need my rest for the fortitudes of tomorrow."

So it is that Kendra has quickly set some things into action.

Sir John J. Perriwinkle, 15th. Baronet of Sandown has not just been issuing noblesse oblige to Nurse Kendra. There is also the small big matter of James Donald Suzuki. Around about the time of Kendra entreaties to Sir John, Jimmy Suzuki comes shambling in to the hospital quarters of the great man carrying an unexpurgated tome.

"Your Honour, I am returning your Diskey. His discourses on the Second Seturk War."

"Are you a student of the Seturk wars, Sir?"

"I can't say I am your Honour, but I can understand how conflict and rancour can generate from the poor and oppressed when they pick up religio-myth to solve their poverty and inequality."

"Yes, that is about the most salient point one can take from it all. We should not allow our weak and oppressed to be shepherded into the hands of fanatics, especially fanatics as organised and cunning as the Seturks."

"Yes and in the second war Enel was a great strategist. The way he routed Maximus Ba was outstanding."

"Quite so, quite so", nodded Sir John knowledgeably. "You appear to be very well read, Sir".

"I am a mere counter-professional. No man of characters."

"Maybe so, doubtless nevertheless you have an enquiring mind. How did you come by my Diskey?" Sir John is warming to his fellow scholar.

"There appears to have been a mix-up with our lockers. When you were transferred noble lord my locker was transferred with you and your locker went to me."

"I see, and you are?"

"James Donald Suzuki, counter-professional of Trenchtown. Mainly I go by the name of Jimmy".

"Well, if I may … Jimmy. I believe I have something of yours. Some very abstract writings. I first thought that they were some experimental works from Posey or Dyker, but now I think I am well off the mark. What do you make of these so called *Walks for the Unemployed?* Maybe you are more than just the owner of these manuscripts, but the author too?"

Jimmy is abashed.

"Alas no Sir. I have scrawled a bit in my time, but I could not come near to assembling such rich prose. A prose that comes from a sort of never-never land."

"I see, but how did you come across these rare writings?"

"It has been most passably strange, your Honour. I have received some from the very cracks in the earth, some from unknown acquaintances and some appear as if magik pressed them into my very hands."

"I suspect it is the doings of the Brown Dwarf. The Perriwinkle system", chuckles Sir John.

Jimmy looks enquiringly awaiting more clarification.

"I have consulted with scientists of high order who have alerted me to the fact that the anti-gravity of the approaching Brown Dwarf system more than just puts physical stress on our planet but also distorts and palpitates our whole reality belief systems so that we are aware of things that we never used to be and unaware of things that had been normal to us before."

"I don't understand, your eminent peerage".

"It plays tricks on our minds, Jimmy! Why do you think that I, a peer of the Islands hierarchy, am here at this poorhouse hospital? It is the disruptions and distortions to reality that the Brown Dwarf is engineering."

"This is stupendously bad news", replies Jimmy.

"Yes, and for you to understand this, I should give you brief familiarisation on how I was ruined by a scam where the actual law of physik is a principal architect. Let me tell you and I hope the account does not warp your mind in the way it has made me crazy and forlorn."

Jimmy listens while Sir John tells him a lot rapidly and with precision to the point. After precisely fourteen minutes of listening absolutely attentively Jimmy understands how Sir John is now down on his luck. His luckless circumstance bonds Jimmy with affinity to the great man. After the quick account, which Jimmy assimilated immaculately as if it were some Great Society parable, he no longer felt quite so alone in his suffering. Sir John's was a like mind that he could and would aspire to.

"These walks, Jimmy. They are messages that come from the singing spheres. They are riddles as old as history. You and I shall have to decipher them".

"But how, Sir John?"

"For next time. Here come more doctors and nurses. Next time, friend."

Jimmy rushes off before the wave of officialdom.

'Friend! He called me friend", reflects the status bereft Jimmy Suzuki.

Three: Destruction – "An Independent Voice "

So there verily had been some extraordinary goings on in Jimmy's crumpled obese ramshackle life. Every life no matter how mundane can have an edge to it. Some things which were completely out of place, different – a turn up for the books. Incidents and persons who run into lives like accidents; near misses, misses but which are hushed up, not talked about, compartmentalised in silence in remote places of the mind. Every humdrum person has that distinction, a dark secret, a brooding lingering of a dark secret of guilt and shame. These goings on are like revolutions of maverick spheres through our solar system. They come hurtling at you at speeds beyond your understanding and come ram-jam at you, with you not realising until it is simply too late, and you think what was that, was that really me? Has this been happening to me? They come at you at high speed, at speed beyond your belief, and at impact all is at a slowed down speed. There you see it happening to you, like an out of body experience.

It was some years ago, maybe about six years ago, when Jimmy was feeling reckless with his emotions, when things just could not remain easily bottled up and he would lose his rag over nothing at all; he was really taking things far too personally. When I say six years ago, then perhaps that period had started even some four years before that. In a difficult life this was a particularly difficult time, and particularly difficult times can run for a long time. Then the difficult becomes the norm and the normal harks back to a golden time which can just about be remembered although not quite believed.

During this tumultuous period Jimmy really particularly hated it when his guys lost. He could be inconsolable for days. He would be in a foul mood and terrorise the cat, even though she was about his only friend and companion. His cat was called Nicole and was quite big and very black of fur. She would bugger off through the cat-flap and make herself scarce until the bad vibes evaporated. Of course, he had never seen an actual real life footie match. He had only listened to commentary on the squawk-box. It was difficult to comprehend what was happening through the commentary on the squawk-box, but it was all Jimmy had as he had no recourse to visual arts on his balance of state credits. Nevertheless he was madly passionate about his club; *Yor Mama's So Fat* and their star dribbler, Christian Dale. He was also partial to their imperious crack sweeper and skipper Lord Alisdair Ferg. He was a wag, always saying the drollest things like, 'We're going to try and equalise before they score'. Jimmy remembered the time when he could kick a footie; when he was part of a team. All before the ISGA and Lennon stuff. He loved *Yor Mama's So Fat* with their strip of navy blue and white, the way the fans called themselves the Trenchtown Tigers, and the jaunty way the players wore their club blazers and straw boaters. The coaches were always footie masterminds with cred names like Big Ed and Uncle Tony. By the sound of it the team played with real swagger, but always lost the important championships to teams who didn't play fair and resorted to unfair play and shenanigans to win matches, like prime arch-rivals Blue Lagoon. Jimmy sort of liked that in a way; that they were noble and pure, but would ultimately lose. He felt that that was a mirror image of life. Jimmy loved his *Yor Mama's So Fat*, his precious Tigers, but there was hell to play if they lost. It was as if it were an aggravation of his real lost life. All that he had lost, his years of disservice and not belonging, not being part of a team. If his beloveds lost, it was like the pain of all that he had lost in his life. It was personal.

Jimmy loved the game of wicket-taking too, but he was not so upset when his favourites the Vale of Glamorgan lost. With the footie, with the Tigers, with the swagger, was a sense of tribalism; being part of a movement – a fierce feeling of somewhere where he could belong and where no-one would deny his love. Yeah he would get seriously pissed off when Mama lost or just drew against some indifferent side and he would plummet the depths when they lost to the Blue Lagoon. It was such torture to lose to them. They were slimy, status kept, not like the barrow-boys of Mama. They were synonymous with everything he had not had, could not have.

"My name is Belsingham by the way. And so I say."

Bobotie Bruce was a poet. During the day he made bobotie for a living, selling a good homemade classic to keep together body and soul. However, it was a competitive market down in the rickshaw market of Frasertoon and prime lamb was at a premium. Sometimes you just had to make do with a bit of nag from down the knacker's yard. The important things were the sauce, the preparation of the topping and the fusion in the hot oven of the spices and the ingredients. You had to make do as it was such a competitive business.

Bruce had been told by many in his family, and among his other familiars, that Bruce was a noble name. It was a name going back to an aristocratic clan being free-form leaders who challenged absolute monarchy and their land enclosures. This had been before Great Society, of course, and the family had been disowned by all they had sought to protect. That's why the Bruces were in decline and Bobotie was on his uppers selling bobotie to the hoi-polloi.

He had noble blood which was evinced by his noble thought – his poetry. Bobotie making was so consuming that he had only composed 46 poems (five of which were fully finished), and then after all the bobotie making Bobotie had to have some time for leisure. At the age of sixty-seven Bobotie enjoyed the pleasure houses of Government Yard and he was still thranging strong. He was a professional with a lust to work and thrive – he had been officially designated a candlestick maker so he had free licence to conduct business widely across Frasertoon and nearby Trenchtown; pray forgive the irregularities – a liberal mind would understand the need for flexibility.

Bruce, although a dilettante, supported the Blue Lagoon, and he was in a particular good mood and willing for experimentation - the Blues had just thrashed those Trenchtown Tiger losers in the Islands Challenge, a great put-down for those noisy Trenchtown neighbours – when a big fluffy black cat came waltzing down his alley.

"Here kitty, kitty!"

You just had to go with the flow; a quick bit of butchering, a bit of je ne sais quoi with the sauces while you're firing up the kiln and then you can do a bit of quick bleak business on a Saturday night before celebrating a famous victory at the *Ruskie Perry* with all your mates. 'God wills, me's a poet', I would imagine him declaring before a quick route to fine thinkings. You had to free-coast to free up more time for your literacy.

"Here kitty, kitty".

T he terrible time finished for Jimmy Suzuki. His massive sulk finished, it always did. He had been through it before. The lost Cup Final eleven years ago, the 9-1 humiliation against Rovers and the time the great D'artagnan despicably deserted for Richmond Park

United. He had gotten over all of those and would more. This was emblematic of his tarnished life. Besides which he had to come down from the 16th. floor of his tenement (the Massive Tivoli) to procure some rolling tobacco. 'Where was she? Little Nicole'. He needed to smoke. He would look for her. He was hungry. His depression like a hangover. He would treat himself to some bobotie on the cash proceeds of his weekly "Sacrificer" cheque.

Jimmy Suzuki stepped out into a steamy February night in search of food, diversion and the hope of coming across his big black fluffy moggy whom he was now starting to miss so much. The normal bobotie seller, Ogdens, was shut. There was a sign saying closed due to a family bereavement. He would press on to Frasertoon, there would be more there. Jimmy S. trundled along until eventually he fished up at Bobotie B's stall. Bruce looked like he was about to close up, but was glad to do a last minute trade before winding up for the evening. He liked the look of Jimmy's spondules and persuaded Jimmy to take a double portion of the bobotie for the price of one and a half.

"That's half a bob for your cash, mate", said Bobotie B, "and it gives me the chance to clean out me kiln for the night".

"Glad to be of service to you too!", exclaimed our Jimmy. "I'm indebted to you Sah. I'm so hungry I could eat a horse".

"Not today, Messoo!", Bobotie winked.

Jimmy dug in with a gusto. It was a makeshift moving restaurant and dallying was not normally done in the course of eating.

"Special recipe?" enquired Jimmy. "Tastes bit different from normal".

"Thursdays are exotic dish day. This is a variant recipe from Cape Sarawak. Kuching cooking".

Jimmy had no idea what he was talking about so he nodded his head sagely and said "Methinks you've added lime to the caterpillar chilli sauce".

"Hah!" extorted Bobotie and winked conspiratorially.

Jimmy finished his meal with an extravagant burp and then was in mind of some ale to wash it down.

"Know a good alehouse in the vicinity, squire?" he enquired of the vendor.

"You might try 'The Dog and Hound' round the corner. Good brew and good company, especially if you're alone if you know what I mean?" Again another conspiratorial wink.

"Thank you, good trader". Jimmy shambled on and found the alehouse and then found it to his liking and then liked the ale and then really liked it until the landlord liked him to move on. We have all had times like that. It's the stress you know, with the booze it makes one behave strangely. In a semi-drunken fugue Jimmy arrived at the next port of call. An inn called "Ruskie Perry" where the ambience was flowing and the girls were easily smiling, even at a portly chummy such as Jimmy. Jimmy got ensconced with a bunch of lovelies. He knew that his weekly dole money was running away like the beer, but he could not stop himself anyway. Inebriation and insolvency, so many bad things starting with "in". He just wanted to be part of the "in-crowd"; a bit of love and respect from strangers was alright, wasn't it?

"How's the fucking bobotie business going then Bobotie?" roared an immense man from the corner of the bar near to where Jimmy sat. Jimmy's attention sat up even though he was preoccupied with other things.

"Inestimable, dear Trevor. Inestimable. I make enough to meet ends meet, you know. Enough so that I can pursue the devising of my poetry and to get up to the Ridge to see the Blues play from time to time".

"I don't know how you can afford the price of there then lamb, dear chap. Those moors are making daylight robbery out of the little fluffies!", retorted Trevor.

"By Gad Sir! I'm an entrepreneur. One needs to be resourceful!" In a conspiratorial whisper as per a drama on a big stage. "I've passed my money around the *Nag's Head* in my time, if you take my meaning. Sometimes that fails and this very week not to be **cat** out, I've had to raid the **kitty**".

"Meow", said Trevor.

Bobotie Bruce nodded his head and smiled. "Another pint, dear Trevor? Ah look here comes Jonas and Nigel. Over here, dear fellows!"

"Look there's your daughter too. She coming over also", added Trevor. "Is that Starfish Cill and Fleesa that she's with?"

Jimmy lost track of the conversation in the added commotion. A girl called Sheila was working hard for his attention. She was a superb worker and he soon lost interest in Bobotie, Trevor and their chums. When he regained focus Bobotie Bruce and Co had disappeared.

The next morning Jimmy S. woke up with a mega hangover in his abode in the Massive Tivoli. As usual with these type of things he had no idea how he had got home, but did recognise straight away that he was cleaned out and Dad's old vintage JWB pocket watch was missing. Jimmy felt shame and horror. Surely he had not pawned that for God knows what? He was disgusted with himself and he had no-one for solace. Where was the cat? Where was Nicole? Stupid moggy. It was Friday. The big cup match had been on Sunday. Why did he kick her in his rage? Poor cat, it had been almost a week since she had scarpered. Then he remembered something. He had seen that street vendor Bobotie Bruce in a pub last night. He had overheard something about lamb prices being high and an insinuation about other types of meat having to be used. *Meow.* It couldn't be, could it? Jimmy really wondered.

He spent the rest of that doubt purged day spread-eagled on his run-down divan sobbing, starving and screaming at himself as if someone else were responsible for him until it was time to quell his hunger and fill his bulk.

You couldn't say that Jimmy was an accomplished cook by any means, but what he was actually was a dab hand at pancake making. He had quite the predilection for them and probably, given his great bulk, was too liberal in the eating of them. In order to minimise laundry activity it was his want to cook only in his worn out threadbare mariner shorts; his giant girth like a colossus in the kitchen. He liked to get the tub of *Old Rusty* margarine on his cooking surface, set out the other ingredients, such as the deverera flour, sugar and goat's milk and talk to Nicole while he went through his ritualised cooking routine. He loved to toss the flapjacks up in the air and catch them in the pan while Nicole stroked herself against his hairy white legs. The cat too was partial to a bit of pancake. She was well capable of consuming half a jack while Jimmy scoffed the other twelve and a half.

Today was different though. Jimmy was splashing batter haphazardly and burning pancakes. It got so bad he had to open a window. He was ruminating. He was not in love with his purpose. He was missing the dear little moggy. Something was really amiss. He had his suspicions, by Janna. He was just too hung-over to act. He had to eat. On the morrow he would put himself in the know.

And so I can come now and say that Bobotie Bruce had a daughter. A twenty-six year old mixed race beauty who went by the name of Fumi Lartal. Ma Lartal was one of the Kloondock Malaccans out of the Banana Sea. Mister Bruce had taken advantage of her for a few krugerbands and then, for once (really for once), had not been proud of his actions when he discovered that he had put her up the duff. Bobotie had not exactly moved in with the lady Lartal; he had to think of his poetry, and an independent soul was the only type of soul that was going to reach the heights of sublime poetry. Nevertheless, he felt responsible for his little family and kept in more or less daily contact. The bobotie business was popular and the cuisine long-established in Frasertoon. He could afford to throw them some crumbs and Ma Lartal often obliged with a little rumpy-pumpy. As time went by Bobotie Bruce became very connected to his daughter, less so with Ma Lartal (he had never thought to ask her first name – Orange Myrtle actually). There you go, that's the ways of these gigantic intellects, these poets and troubadours.

Although he never really liked to admit it freely, he paid in to his daughter's educational trust. He got her into a good Grammarsarium (*Dorothy's Girls* in West Argyll) and from that platform she won the Alderman Lennon Bursary admitting her to Sharp's Law Faculty at the Emporium University, Banana Delta. Fumi had taken a treble first and had been incorporated in Fustigans Chambers in Millbrook. At twenty-six she was already the Right Decent Fumi Lartal, JJKC at the Equity Bar. JJKC being Junior Junior King's Counsel – not that there was a monarch anymore, but we adore tradition in the legal fraternity.

Fumi Lartal was gorgeous and brilliant and knew a number of good jokes. Moreover she was Bobotie's little girl and he cherished her completely. In his life she had no equal, apart from his poetic masterpiece "The Nation's Distress" perhaps, which he had been working on the last fourteen years. She walked on his water as far as he was concerned and he would not have her sink on his water.

So it was on the very next morrow saw Jimmy a man of action. A person of grim determination; a man on a mission. He was going to find his beloved cat, his Nicole. He was garbed in his best street garb; Mouchino moleskins, Prof. Hinkelstein wader-boots, his beloved old grey waistcoat and AC leather frock coat. For street enquiries he found you had to look the business. No-one would pay you much attention if you didn't look sharp. He greased back his long lank hair with some *Old Rusty* margarine, took a quick douse of his father's old eau de cologne (*Sophisto Gent*) and put on his urban AC apparel sun-goggles. Down into the mean streets he went. He did not particularly feel comfortable in those streets, but for a time he could be an actor playing a part. In his bulk and ugliness he could portray a certain malign brutality and ghetto sophistication.

It was another muggy day in Banana Delta. Jimmy although he had lived there his whole life could never quite get used to the intensity of the humidity. It was a dank overcast day, but every action of his caused sweat to roll down and across his accumulation of skin; he had too much street clothing on. The sweat enhanced the lankness of his hair and the unkempt wildness of his demeanour. For the participating public it seemed quite reasonable to field questions on a missing kitty from this uncomfortable looking lumbering giant – answer politely or there might be trouble. The relative humidity accentuated the intensity of the questioning, kind of made reasonable the import of questioning concerning a missing feline. Alas, although all those questioned were polite, none could offer head nor tail of Nicole.

His feet were taking him towards nearby Frasertoon. Maybe it was an unconscious connection to the bobotie maestro. The conversation overheard in the *Ruskie Perry* was still there in his consciousness. The memory of it appeared irrational to him but he hadn't discounted it. Somehow there was a pull to Paul Street and the rickshaw market where Bobotie Bruce was likely serving his celebrated fare.

"Have you seen a cat?"

"Yeah, lots mate! Not unusual is it? It's not like seeing a fucking blue whale here in the Toon, is it? Lots of the pesky moggies here, that's those that escape being thrown in the pot by that's lot over there".

It was the first uncivil response that Jimmy had received to his line of questioning and it came from one of the rickshaw market vendors – in this case perri-perri juyce. The residents of this part of town were known to be hardnosed and mean spirited. The man looked gnarled and weather-beaten, as if he had spent his life at sea, thought Jimmy. Above his stall hung the sign *Kurt Tempels: Purveyor of Fine Natural Juyces*.

Tempels continued on this line. "Cats! You ought to ask them food sellers over there what happens to cats. It's a public scandal. It's not right. It's downright lawlessness! Ask them kebabie sellers, those hino purveyors, the bobotie blokes and the like. I've mentioned this to the Honourable Wholesalers, but graft is rife here, me old china. They's all keep stumm. Your dear pet may have long been eaten!"

You might imagine that this discourse has put a train of thought into action in Jimmy's great sentient mind. The overhead conversation and Tempels' intervention have drawn the connection for Jimmy. Meow, he had it. He was going to confront Bobotie Bruce. He was going to have it out with him, and with that thought Jimmy lumbered over to the stall of Bobotie Bruce with all the defiance of one strung out on grief.

"Ah, my dear Sir!" cried Bruce. "Come to sample my wares again? I can very much recommend the chilli bobotie today. Come Sir! Are you game".

"Have you seen my cat, Mister?", was the strange response to Bobotie's entreaty.

"Pardon me?"

"Have you seen my cat? My Nicole?" Jimmy seemed to be staring insanely at Bobotie.

"She's a black west-tailed mouser and has very fluffy black fur with green eyes. Her movement is very elegant. She has a very loving nature".

"Sir, I see a gamut of cats every day here. They're drawn to the rickshaw market by the rickshaw market rats. Because of the rats we're swimming in cats. Mongooses too."

"But have you seen my Nicole?", persisted Jimmy.

Bruce was becoming irritated by this line of questioning. "How would I know if I've seen your bloody cat. A black cat or white cat is all the same to me. For some people ratatouille for others catatouille. It's all the frigging same to me!"

At that Bobotie Bruce felt the full weight of Jimmy Suzuki's large fist. Bang in the nose. Blood spurting from one very sore hooter.

"You bastard", shouted Bobotie. "You'll pay for this. Just like you paid to eat your own fucking cat. You big dipshit!"

At this Jimmy was not impetuous. Like a man who is resigned to fate his response was considered and neutral.

"Thank you. That's what I suspected. You'll be hearing from me. Just you wait. Watch your back, chummy".

Jimmy was cool and indestructible. He turned his back and walked away whilst a small crowd looked at him and ogled over the scene of disharmony.

Jimmy walked all the way back direct to his tenement building perspiring and giving over to a small amount of sobbing.

The next day Jimmy received a missive through his letterbox.

Dear Sir,

I witnessed your anger at the bobotie seller yesterday. You were right to punch out. I heard what he said about serving up your own cat to you. That's disgusting and should be punished. I think I know how you can get back at him. Can you meet me this evening at "The Seven Bottoms", the inn half a mile south to you?. I'll be there by seven and will have a dram waiting for you. You will know me. We talked at the market yesterday when you were looking for yer cat. I'm the juyce seller, by the way. It was me who pointed you in the direction of Bruce and those other ne'er-do-wells.

Yours honourably,
Kurt Tempels (Master Juycer)

Jimmy thought it odd that Mister Tempels had to add his professional qualification at the end. It irritated him somewhat, as being someone counter-professional and not allowed to earn money for a living, that he had to be pointed out precisely what Tempels' profession exactly was. Nevertheless the main thing at hand was to put right the situation regarding his beloved Nicole. He had to put personal considerations aside for this. He would see Tempels that night even though he seemed a rather seedy fellow. He had heard the expression "Don't get mad, just kill them later" and he wanted to put it into operation.

So Jimmy went and was spotted by Kurt Tempels as soon as he entered the public house.

"Mister Suzuki! Mister Suzuki! Over here!", he hissed across the crowded tavern.

Jimmy felt more comfortable that the inn was so full of people. It made him feel less self-conscious about meeting Tempels. True to his word Tempels had a wee dram waiting for him.

"Mister Suzuki, Sir! Thank you for coming". He thrust the dram at Jimmy. "Nothing like a spot of sheep-shlog to settle the nerves! Come Sir, come Sir, make yourself at comfort. I've chosen this table as there is a nice cool draught of air coming in here".

"Thank you kind Sirrah!" Jimmy could remember some manners. Jimmy smiled amiably and broadly and then asked, "How do you know my name? How did you get my address?"

"Why Sir, I am a Carnival King. My status as an officer of the Carnival allows that I can question any member of the Day Watch for information I need. After all the needs of the Carnival are paramount and no-one will stand in her way. Actually I had you followed home by a Subterfuge of the Day Watch after you slugged it out with Bobotie Bruce. Alas that the influence of Carnival does not supersede that of graft when it comes to the Honourable Wholesalers and the Chamberlains, otherwise Bobotie's pheasant really would be cooked."

"Why did you send me the note?", Jimmy asked.

"I sent you the note because I think folk like Bobotie Bruce should be stopped. As a juycer I am still by no means a vega-vegetarian, it is just that I honestly wish that their cavalier disregard for public health should be put to a stop. They should no longer serve up what is unwholesome and unfit for public consumption. By Gad Sir, they should be stopped!" At this Jimmy's spotted a tear in Tempels's eye.

"You seem to be very outraged, Mister Tempels", he hesitantly ventured.

"Horsemeat, cat meat, then it will be rat meat".

"You can't honestly believe......"

"Not believe. Know, Sir!"

"How so?"

"Twenty-two year ago my little daughter died of food poisoning. She got ill after she bought and consumed a mince corpilla from a street vendor. I blame myself Sir! Her mother had died of black ache two year before and I had been negligent concerning the child by too constantly pursuing my craft. I would toss her coppers for her to procure her dinner. I had been meaning to find a day mother, but you know what it's like with the pressures of industry".

"I don't ..", Jimmy was about to say.

"Too easy I know to make excuses", interjected Tempels. "Mister Suzuki, I've had to live with the results of my ineptitude. Suffice to say when little Sandra became ill I first chose to try and ignore it thinking it just the tropical sweats. By the time I did start to take it seriously it was too late. She was taken from me very swiftly in a little over two day. I'm not a man of the established Creator persuasion, I have other beliefs. Nonetheless I commissioned a full funeral in the old faith in mitigation for her soul at any rate. The sky shepherd presiding, a Mister Dowd, offered autopsy as part of the full heaven package service. He did that autopsy, Mister Suzuki, and what he said after confounded me. He said that he found traces of rat meat in my little Sandra's stomach, and, what's more that rat meat had been tainted by poison! My Sandra had suffered a cruel and unnatural death for the trick of the turn of a cheap profit! She was only six."

"This Dowd. Was he a member of the College of Surgeons? Did he really know how to conduct autopsy?"

"No, but I have no reason to doubt his findings. There were no reasons on his part to fabricate such a monstrous story. He told me he had studied medicine before taking his shepherding." Tempels paused in his story to bellow, "Barman. Bring me the whole bottle of the Fictish Water!".

"Right, what does this all have to do with me?" enquired Jimmy of his distraught host.

"I grant you that Bruce himself was not my daughter's killer, but the cynical and immoral behaviour of him and his kind will lead to the deaths of other innocent children. Great Society will not move because its officers are corrupt and made bereft of their duties through the leveraging of their own greed. We must act therefore. The cynical death of your dear pet, whom you loved as an only child, is just another example of the continuing deaths of innocents and the consequent heartbreak it brings to their families. This outrageous behaviour has to be nipped in the bud, and we should do this through our morally compelling enforcement of executive citizen action!"

"How?"

"We make an example of this Bobotie Bruce. We hit him where it hurts in order to send out a message to all of his kind. We are going to kidnap his daughter. We are going to make him suffer as we have suffered through the losses of our dear Nicole and Sandra. We are going to have to take the law in our own hands!"

'You're crazy', thought Jimmy. Nevertheless, Jimmy had always had a fondness for a dose of hard liquor which most of the time was unaffordable for him. If the fellow kept on pouring, he would keep on agreeing.

"I entirely support your endeavour", said Jimmy Suzuki. "Pour me another dram and tell me precisely your plan. I'm a believer."

"May Sand have Salt!", murmured Kurt T.

'What a rum saying', thought Jimmy, but decided against querying Tempels as to its meaning as there was a wild unsettled look in his eyes.

"Down the hatch!" countered Jimmy.

So it was that Fumi Lartal had spent a demanding day at the Bar at circuit assizes in Further Plokington. She had harangued, threatened and bullied eye witnesses and expert witnesses to win a successful prosecution for Great Society. She had damned the tradeswoman with the charge of fraud. The defendant she had successfully argued had defrauded the public through manipulation of weights and measures and thereby overcharging for her eichnuts. Fumi had appealed to the jury's sense of outrage and moral indignation so that the jury came back with an unanimous guilty verdict and with the recommendation to the Lord Justice presiding for a sentence of eight years transportation to the very inclement Northern Islands. In that transportation programme the fraudster would join the punishing forest clearing project. Fumi Lartal had been tough, the public opinion tough and the punishment tough (the judge too had been tough and revised upward the recommendation of punishment to a minimum of ten years transportation before parole), but Fumi Lartal, State's Prosecutor, could live with herself. She was giving value to Great Society through the process of extending the common good in the prosecution of miscreants opposing the civilising mores of Great Society. She was moving on to the next case, back in the capital; a case of a celebrity entertainer who had knifed his girlfriend to death "in his sleep".

She arrived at the Greater Plokington staging just in time. The boardwalk was all a steam and the carriage ready to go. Fumi Lartal made a magnificent sight. She deliberately kept all her court gowns on for the travel. She liked everyone to see the intimidating sight of an officer of the law in full garb. A JJKC, one of the elite, in her ceremonial wig and staff of state, ready to prosecute the nefarious and unworthy. Even the Chamberlains deferred to her when she was in her full majestic apparel. It must be the majesty of the office symbolised through the robes. She was brilliantly punctual just on time on the very time of the departure and effortlessly moved without breaking stride into the first class compartment quietly relieved to see no other passengers therein. She seated herself inside and started to sprawl out as the trahere started to pull away when suddenly the door opened as they were just about underway and in stepped a large unkempt man with ugly long lank hair. 'Definitely not first class" was her immediate thought.

"By Gad, Sirrah! Out with you! Third class is down back", the lawyer shrilly commanded.

The intruder did not react. He merely took a bottle out of his shabby trouser pocket and a rather used pocket handkerchief. The bottle was medicinal brown.

"Chloroform", he explained, and before she was able to react the combination of chloroform and handkerchief was enveloping her nose and she went out like a light.

"You see all this lot my girl. These are the counter-professionals. The scum of the earth. Alas that we don't have a good war for them to be cannon fodder", explained her father. He went on with a passion, as he looked at the queues of populace holding brown envelopes waiting to get into the central-amt building. "You are a Bruce. I will never allow you to be a member of such an under-class. Don't listen to the small-mindedness of your mother. She may be an immigrant and she may consider you then just as the daughter of an immigrant worker, but never you forget that my blood courses through you – that you are a Bruce, a member of an old and noble family."

"Yes, father". She kept to the observance and humoured him in the right way. The noble family Bruce which was disenfranchised from its fortune by fighting for the care of the poor and weak and so on and so on. At the age of twelve Fumi was getting more savvy at this. She felt herself on the crest of becoming a woman and of being able to assert herself by using an easy growing surfacing charm.

The day was warm with the February sun beating down on the swathes of the great unwashed on the far side of the piazza. She and her father sat in the chic eatery

Crocodillo in the heart of the Altstadt of Banana Delta drinking Long Dreamies and observing the Saturday morning signing-on ceremony. In the mass of confusion, on the far side of the piazzas past the crowning fountains, it was a wonder if anyone could collect their benefit credits at all.

A loud horn blew. Twelve o'clock and the end of civil servantry hours.

"That will teach that remaining scum to get off their dole beds a bit earlier. Teach them to be so bone idle", her father commented and he sucked up the remainder of the cream from his ice escapade. A platoon of redcoats moved in around the government building yonder. Fumi could not see what they were up to due to the sun glinting off their raised bayonets on their weaponry.

"Education, education, education is key. Education I cannot stress it more", went on Mister Bruce. Her ramshackle daddy with his haughty mores. Then he laughed, "You've been a good girl. You've done fantastically well with your grades and all your good work has brought you results. I've got you a place at Dorothy's Girls."

"Oh, Daddy! Really?"

"Yes, really. Only yesterday I was with Mistress Marchant and got it sewn up. You start in August at the start of the Larchus Term. You will be with the elite."

Fumi gave her father a coy little kiss. "Now Father you'll surely wish to change my name to Bruce, won't you?"

"Well chickadee it might be a little tricky at present. Part of the funding – that's the money we have to pay for a private school – is coming from charity benefactors on account that you come from an immigrant background and need a leg up for assistance so to speak."

Fumi looked perturbed.

"No reason to worry chickadee. Great Society likes people making their way up through hard work and dedication. It's all part of the service doctrine. You can become of service even though your background is of immigrant standing disservice. It's all part of the Great Society dream. That you can make something of yourself to be actually of service and become a Value Provider. So that means you'll really be fitting the mould at Dorothy's as Miss Lartal. Besides which your mother will keep her stranger benefits if you stick with the family name of Lartal".

"Oh", exclaimed Fumi and tried to think it through.

Her father had spotted an acquaintance who was perambulating by. "By Gad, Jonny Loudsticks!", he shouted. "Just a moment, me girl. I'll be back in a mo".

The young prepubescent Fumi Lartal looked around her from her café seat on the grand piazza of the noble Altstadt. This seemed to be worlds apart from Frasertoon where she had been raised, but yet it in fact was a mere league away. Her father was deep in conversation with a red faced man in ceremonial attire. All around elegant ladies in long dresses and parasols promenaded with dashing moustachioed gentlemen. She would be part of this world she determined and thought more about the circumstances.

She had read much through her schooling and had been many a time to the Institute of Scholars. Many people believed that information was not freely accessible and that one should only gather information from the official information sources, but in her limited experience this was simply not true. You could find out far more than what was contained in the official broadsheets; there was more than just the "official" information given in the broadsheets. The library at the Institute was such a place. Another she had heard was the Hedge of Mature Arts, though she was still too young to gain access there. Fumi had done some research. She was bright, coming from "immigrant stock" (discarding all that noble family Bruce stuff), and she had always wished to learn context and background on all things. Great Society pooh-poohed notions of a Creator, a divine omniscient and omnipotent deity, although chapels were open and tolerated everywhere (less so the dogmatic cruel Sand religion believers) and there were daily missives in the regular broadsheets, such as *Truth* and *The Despatcher*, about the origins of the universe. The Astrologer Royal knew so much and wanted all to know that too. Fumi wanted to know how you could get something out of nothing and if the universe was expanding what was it expanding into. The problem was that most people were too intelligent to ask that question or preferred to talk about the Creator or rant about the Great Sand and so on, but Fumi wanted to know. So she got to read a lot and learn a lot. The information was there. You had to get there and simply take it.

Great Society, she learned, had come about through opposition to the Orientals. The Orientals had been growing and growing so that their populace was so large that its vast tracts of land, Oriens, had not been able to sustain it. The Oriental nations were great seafarers and were very good with ships and ocean travelling. Three hundred and sixteen years ago they reached the Islands. Their technology and weaponry were greater than ours, and so they had conquered and colonised us. They were red haired and pale skinned and looked down on us because our skins were more swarthy and our hair dark. They were freckled racists who had kings, and the warm climate was amenable to them growing foodstuffs here which they transported back to their hungry Oriens. In the end they used the Islands for profit while at the same time creating an aristocracy here which just exploited and taxed our earth and our people. The Bruces of her family clan was one such. There had been one Sir Henry Bruce who had been governor of Luckyland. However, if her family clan had hit hard times by supporting the poor, then she was not able find any evidence to support her father's claim.

The Orientals spent the next century sending their sail boats to us. Pressing the Islands with more and more exploitation, establishing a grandee class to lord it over us and even bringing to our lands Malaccan slaves to work farms and plantations for the overweening demands of Oriens. Oriens, however, was in trouble; civil wars and discontent had become rife on the continent. It became so that income generation became the purpose of the islands. Income generation was not contrary to the interests of the grandee class here. What did run contrary, however, was income generation where the lion's share had to go back to the rulers of Oriens. As a consequence one hundred and thirty-four years ago the Islands (the so called "colonies") rebelled against their ruling Oriens states and declared a republican government in the islands. Circumstances were in their favour; Oriens was still in the grip of its own set of civil wars and at the same time the Nicadeans had started to plunder their eastern seaboard. King Alfons I of the dominant Eastern Oriens was simply inundated with problems and two years later he brokered an agreement leading to the independence of the Islands as long as certain favourable trade agreements were maintained. The sweet potato would still be sent back east to relieve the famished masses.

A rebellion became a revolution. The landed classes had to become more democratic and allow everyone the vote. There was a backlash against the Oriental monotheistic religion. Creator and privilege were replaced by Man and equality. Notwithstanding that a lot of intellectuals behind the revolutionary movement came from the grandee stock, from the stock of the original colonisers and inevitably there had been some fusion of the old institutions and artefacts with the radical new movement. Over time it had appeared that the radical movement had been watered down by the still resilient status quo. Trade relations with the old country, Oriens, had been maintained and many people had prospered by them and the influence of Oriens over the Islands was starting to grow strong again. Oriens had suffered some major devastation and population loss through war and consequent pestilence, but its star was on the rise again. Oriens had developed more sophisticated means of mass agriculture and had started to be a little more choosy about its imports. There was less demand for the sweet potato and the lava-cane; rather more emphasis on horse-plant and cuckoo clam. These were luxury products and the giant farms and plantations providing the former products started to decline. Jobs were lost in a wholesale manner and it was time for a popular leader. It was time for the revolutionary Porto Dominigo to step in, and he did so seventy-two years ago.

Porto Dominigo was poor and of ethnic family from the Islands. He was a product of a rough upbringing in Decayed Barrier. He formed the social welfare based party named *Movement* to unite the islands in proletarian solidarity and got the populace to celebrate and have confidence in their history and ethnic roots, but at the same time embracing the modernity that had come with the influence of Oriens. He leaned towards progressive and preached equality and fairness for all without reference to class, standing, race or sex. At the same he was deeply influenced by the economist Randall Snoggs. Snoggs was of the view that modern society could not offer full employment to all its citizens. In the demographics of the Islands some 20% of those of working age would not be able to fulfil proper remunerated employment, whether it be as employee or freelancer. Snoggs held the Chair in Wealth at the Emporium University and he was great chums with Sally Dambey who held the Chair in Self-Help Studies. Together they formulated their principle of *social place conditioning*. Snoggs held the view that large scale unemployment was inevitable and that the state could not pay significant sums on universal educations for all, job seeking emoluments and re-training projects. Better to grasp the nettle now and dispense with a fluctuating unemployed and have instead a class of permanent non-employables (the counter-professionals). Dambey added that it would be better to condition persons into being non-employable, that this would be kinder on them and ease social unrest and friction. However, for such people if they could be inculcated with the notion that they were of disservice it would be easier for them to accept their classification. No hope would engender constancy and resignation to their condition. They would learn that it is a sacrificial privilege to have no rights and with it no real obligations. Better that they had no hope at all, but that hopelessness would, through the administration of proper caring and precise instruction, be accepted and embraced as a worthy quality of altruism.

Dominigo, the great populist, ran with this and enveloped it within the concept of Great Society, i.e. that all individuals gain if there is no individual gain. He had a great propagandist to help him, one Franzi Joe. Franzi was an old vaudeville theatre comedian and coined the slogans "Only some of us can have an outcome" and "To serve and disserve preserves our balance". Franzi was appointed Minister for Culture and he went out to install these new virtues, or strictures, into popular culture. Many plays and vaudeville musicals had these themes central to their heart. Carnival marches had *Movement* members singing out these virtues sloganized into popular marching songs. The new government made a start by unilaterally annexing the district of Hard Shoulder with its large immigrant community (largely from Port Doe) and declaring wholesale the neighbourhood as an area of National Disserve. Thus it began and a wave of government officialdom and bureaucracy, official elites, disenfranchised, one party democracy and statements - many statements about how great the new state was - and so it was now some seventy years later.

Sometimes Fumi's thoughts ran too quickly ahead of her. Her father thought her a genius. Perhaps she was.

"Now where was I young lady?" Dad had returned.

"Something about education and not being part of any underclass".

"Oh yes".

"Oh yes. My name is Belsingham", he said.

The next staging post was at Lamb's Slaughter. Jimmy was out of the compartment like greased lightning with Fumi Lartal over his back. A gent was trying to get into the compartment but Jimmy Suzuki pushed him aside shouting "Plague victim!", and this was enough for him to build up a momentum and make headway through the steam of the staging post area. Waiting nearby on the lane was the wizened Kurt Tempels with a horse and cart.

"Did you nab the tart?", snarled Tempels. The tart was starting to feel semi-conscious already.

"No, I just bought a sack of tatties", she heard the outlaw Jimmy reply.

Fumi was really starting to become conscious again. 'The tart?' she thought. 'Me a tart? I suppose I am a bit', a strange foreign voice in the back of her mind mused. In her blurry consciousness there was felt a frisson of sexual excitement.

"Are you molesters? What's in your wicked minds for me?", a very detached voice emanating from Fumi Lartal asked.

"Moron!" Tempels shouted. "I told you to apply a liberal portion of chloroform!"

"What's a fucking liberal anyway?" retorted Jimmy S.

"Now you're going to have to bind and gag her, you nincompoop. There's some rags in the back of the cart and some blankets too. You'll have to do it on the move. Come on Big Bess, away with you!"

At this the horse started into a trot and was trundling down the country lane at night with the sound of jimmy-crickets all around.

Jimmy got started with the binding and gagging with all the expertise of a drunk wrestler. It was difficult work all this roping and groping for knots, especially as the cart rolled over the unsteady ground. Jimmy had never really quite felt a feminine form like this before. She was lithe, muscular but bouncy-curvy, not floppy-curvy like Miss Pussy was. The feel was nice, but very distracting and with all her moaning Jimmy found it hard to concentrate on the job at hand.

Equally Fumi Lartal seemed to experiencing something new. She could not really rationalise it, but there was something liberating and exciting about being under someone's control; strange for someone who was always striving to be in absolute control and in mastery of all those around. She really felt a sense of being turned on when Jimmy put his overpowering bulk of flesh up against her heaving bosom and drew in the drawstrings of her bonds. When he gagged her with a disgusting oily rag she positively gurgled with muffled excitement. Even Jimmy's musky sweat was not reviling to her. What Jimmy took to be moans of pain were actually, she was realising, moans of pleasure. Eerily she did not feel frightened, she actually felt enlightened.

Jimmy grunted and wiped off the sweat from his brow declaring, "She's done".

"It took you long enough", exclaimed his counterpart. "We're already halfway to Potter's Vale. God, I hate the frigging country".

"I don't know", said Jimmy. "It's a nice smell that cow shit, and I like the singing of those jimmys".

"Bah!" spat Kurt Tempels.

Jimmy didn't say anything, but noted to himself that right from the point he had secured Miss Lartal, Tempels attitude and behaviour toward him had remarkably changed. There was no semblance of the ingratiating fellow who felt so much for Jimmy and his heartfelt loss of his feline. Tempels now appeared as a rasping bully who had no respect for Jimmy at all. After all, hadn't Jimmy done the dangerous job of the abduction on the trahere. Not even a "thank you" or a "well done". It was not polite or respectful.

Fumi Lartal all wrapped up in her cocoon state picked up on this antipathy between her abductors, but this strangely added to her heightened state of frisson like a drug. She moaned the more ostentatiously.

"Get her to shut the fuck up!" demanded Tempels.

Jimmy's huge fist hovered over her. "How would you like a bunch of fives? Shut your gob!"

Fumi moaned once more, but very imperceptibly and discreetly. She decided to enjoy the ride and avoid those fives for the time being.

Oh, indeed, yes. I have to take the strain in relaying this experience; in recounting this story. After all much of it has been of my making. Sometimes I have to speak the parts as the players have not been aware of my machinations. I have to give them context as it has been my plan. I have brought it about through malice to myself. My character is very controlling, but it is complicated, so wearisome, and I feel when I do others wrong then I wrong myself. I do not understand, I do not conceive of the injustices that I have done to others, and how they have blemished my own character.

Thus our narrator has narrated.

I could have been such a jolly chap.

I could have not set up all to fail.

I could have conceived it that life is about embracing, winning and succeeding. It is just that I have never believed it. You did not smile at me, sah; I was the one smirking at you.

I have really started to gravitate towards you. Perhaps you can hear my spheres singing. If you truly listen you can hear an almost imperceptible sound. I have drawn dully and inexorably closer. You have not gleaned my presence, my creeping up on you. You look in the hand mirror and see yourself as always, but my gravity is upon you, and you look again and see the distortions I have been causing. You cannot believe what you have glimpsed and you shut it out as the effect of the dark sultry candle light, but I am forming, I am coming and I will come to pass.

I am the change. I am the only thing now that it is believable and with credibility. You will pass out imaginings to deny my awful existence, but whichever way you dance, whichever way you are deluded, I am coming to crack away at you for there is no room in my universe for your terrible consciousness.

I perceive that the temporal shifts in physik and reality have become more alarming.

It was the first time that Sir John J. Perriwinkle, 15th. Baronet of Sandown and Protector of the Wold, was to meet the great intellect behind the baffling calculations that Professor Riddell had been feeding him – that being the inimitable Doctor Meritorious Egregious Daedalus. Riddell and Perriwinkle had agreed that the basic discovery of the Brown Dwarf system should be made public. The analysis of the more obvious effects of the maverick star system were included in that public sharing. What was not to be shared were the more radical calculations of Doctor Daedalus and their perceived outcomes. This was kept on the strict QT between Perriwinkle, Riddell and Daedalus. It was another oppressively hot February day and two punkah wallahs were cooling Sir John using large ostrich feather fans. The overbearing butler announced Professor Riddell and Doctor Daedalus.

"Riddell! My dear Doctor Daedalus. How good to meet you at last!"

"And you kind Sir". Daedalus was a small gnome like man and quite perfectly ugly. In a grey frockcoat, uncared for boots and battered looking spectacles he appeared quintessentially like a man down in the archives continuously poring over calculations.

"I do hope you calculations are on the money, Doctor Daedalus."

Sir John noted the Doctor's poor pock-marked skin. His face was a ferocious angry red rash as if some internal fire was blazing out from within. His hands partially covered by half-mittens also looked uncared for. Sir John as a gentleman who prided in his appearance gave a slight arched look of disapproval.

"Some room for error Sir John, but I am six sigma and I am continually removing my errors", replied Doctor Daedalus quickly and steadily before there was any further breakout of Sir John's displeasure.

"Errors?"

"Yes, Sir John. I have by precise metrics calculated that we will all commit 27,000 errors before we meet our graves".

"Then I'd better be very careful", replied JJ drolly. "Tell me more!"

Riddell nuanced his head towards the punkah wallahs.

"Leave us!" commanded Sir John. The servants shuffled out.

Doctor Egregious Daedalus sauntered forward confidently to lay claim to a Gellvidere salon chair. He took off his battered top hat to reveal a tatty grey skullcap. Sir John noted that the hair not covered by the skullcap also was lank and greasy and looked like it was rapidly thinning. Nonetheless, Daeadalus looked the inch the eminent alchemist and researcher. He was more than just stuff and calculus. He had a strange academic swagger and Sir John was impressed by his confident manner. No school mouse here.

Professor Riddell a little more apprehensively also took a chair and Sir John did not demur.

"Of course", started the good doctor, "the tally can always be reduced". Daedalus appeared to be itching severely in the leg and began to give his lower thigh a sound scratching.

"Sorry?" Perriwinkle is perplexed. He is still able to conduct the conversation although captivated by the Doctor's contortions.

"What the Doctor means is that the mistakes will gradually accumulate towards the 27,000 threshold whilst we continue on a straight line time continuum. One mistake becomes two, becomes three and so on as we have always experienced", explained the Professor. "However, advanced Physik tells us that time is not a straight line. It is in fact warped. Actually time is not an absolute in the way gravity is".

"Or anti-gravity!", exclaimed the Doctor. "Gravity or anti-gravity can manipulate the less than absolute material force which we know as time. Therefore, through the warps and disruptions of a gravitational or antigravitational pull one can cause 26,999 to shift to 291 to 18,880 and so on. The possibilities are endless. We can shift the count of our errors so as to be in control of our destiny. The universe would be our dance floor and we would be cosmic dancers".

"Are you suggesting time travel?", ventured Sir John.

"Not really. In a common parlance you might call it time resting. We can go and rest at various points of time, if that is what you want to call them for ease of reference. The mathematik is more complex than that. Pray Sir John let me try and explain and do interrupt if I resort to mumbo-jumbo".

Doctor Daedalus fidgeted a bit in his chair and hesitated to take a breath before embarking on giving his big explanation. An explanation he knew which were successful would have the potential to shift the known paradigms of the universe and complicate even further all the other big questions.

"Well Sir, how do I start? First, I'm sure that Professor Riddell will attest to my credentials in this field."

The Professor nodded solemnly and pouted his lips waiting for Daedalus to go on.

"For a number of years I have been researching advanced notions in mathematik and physik. In that regard, I'm sure you are aware that what is natural law on this planet is also natural law in the vastness of space. Of course, with space you get the big picture. Everything with spades so speak. The natural laws that we learn on earth are acted out on a minute scale as within a confined petri dish; controlled and reasonably restrained. When one applies these natural laws to the vastness of space different permutations arise as they are not constrained in the stability of our preserved environment. The sheer space of space allows the natural laws to fulfil themselves to a limitless unrestrained conclusion. These are often surprising and violent. Suffice to say the gravity that holds us on this planet and puts us in thrall to our sun, we hold to be gentle and sustaining. It adds consistency and security like a direct line going forward. We might call that reassuring line "time" or "timeline". Timeline means that we all go forward to the future, decay, replenish and ultimately as a species or a plant or a star die out to be replaced by another energy or mass. The driving mass that moves us forward ultimately shall have a reduction in momentum. When this constitutes we physicists say we have anti-gravity and very different effects do occur, especially in the absolute range of our cosmos. I have been expostulating for many years now the likely effects of anti-gravity when events of the magnitude of the cosmic scale come about. One of the great perceived effects is the warping of straight line time so that time runs in a very different fashion. I have calculated that in such environs it is possible to run slow time and to distort the effects that normal timeline produces." Daedalus paused for breath.

"Professor? I'm sure that you can confirm that the scientific community is in agreement with my conclusions".

"Yes, indeed my dear Doctor".

"Now what happens when anti-gravity comes up against positive gravity?" Daedalus continued.

"Dash, if I know", said Sir John pouring himself a glass of port wine. "Anyone for a snifter?"

Both boffins declined and Doctor Daedalus immediately went on.

"Well usually according to my well respected measurements, the anti-G will prevail and suck up all the gravity. It comes out through the other side and forms another parallel universe. That universe will be a little out of synchronisation, so that indeed at this very instance with our good company here then I would be wearing brown shoes with the picture of a golden hamster on the soles, or, you Sir would be a Malaccan maiden."

Sir John chortled into his port wine.

"That anyway is a little beside point, fascinating though it may be – I digress. The point that is interesting is when the anti-G is appreciably smaller than the normal force of G, the anti-G cannot do its usual sucking up, but at the same time the anti-G persists and remains. Then some unusual things can come to pass."

"Like what?", Sir John was becoming interested.

"Shall Daedalus cut to the chase, your Honour?"

"It might be as well as I have to attend a soiree with Lady Elizabeth Swann".

"The Countess cannot be kept waiting. Please Doctor Daedalus cut to the good bit".

"Gladly Professor. Where was I?"

"The ruptures between gravity and ant-gravity", prompted the Professor.

"Indeed. Theoretically there would be very pronounced ruptures in our reality when these two forces would happen to coincide. Hypothetically yes, indeed very most extremely bloody likely. In fact I'd stake my reputation and my livelihood on it", the Doctor was in the verve. "If the two coincide then the friction between these two opposing forces can be manipulated to produce temporal shifts, provided the anti-G is at a proportion smaller than the normal gravitational field. Given the right calculus and the right machine, one could move back and forward in time by synthesising enhanced temporal shifts caused by the anti-G source. We could piggy-back time, time after time and time again"

"Pardon me?"

"He means, Sir John, that you can use these gravitational effects to go back in time so that you would remain younger so to speak, but then shift your younger self swiftly forward again to the present. This done at regular intervals – yearly I believe – would allow your body and mind to be continually reinvigorated against the approaching future. Not an elixir of eternal life, but a flux of eternal life. My the ancients would be dismayed that they had been looking in the wrong place! This is time gravity warping. Not really time travel as such; more time gravity shift optimisation that ensures the ageing process is infinitesimally slow. Not time travel, rather than time gravity warp dissimilation. Not the Philosopher's Stone, rather the Astrologer's Nugget!"

"Yes!", Daedalus was getting quite excited now and was slightly slavering in his haste to get words out. "And with the discovery of the Brown Dwarf system the Professor informed you about last week, these actual astronomical and gravitational influences are coming about! We are ahead of the game, Sir John! No-one yet is aware of the approaching Brown Dwarf, yet alone the efficacy of its life extending qualities. When we report it all persons will have to be made aware of the physical reactions such as earthquakes, severe tides, volcanic activity increases, plagues of frogs and the like, but nothing so ill, as I calculate it, that would have really disastrous effects that would definitely downright obliterate us for at least 181,900 years or thereabouts. It's existence is known between only the three of us —our secret -, and I can provide us with close on two hundred thousand years more added life before that disaster befalls us. Furthermore, I have great confidence to provide many more years on top of that given the much more additional research time I would be gaining and thereby find a solution to avoid obliteration by the Brown Dwarf!"

"Additional research time for what, pray?", enquired Sir John.

"High speed space travel", winked the doctor.

"I see."

"For our get-away", clarified the doctor.

"Just the three of us in on this scheme?", enquired Perriwinkle tentatively.

"Yes. The Prof is unmarried, as are you I understand, and Mistress Daedalus couldn't get her head around these figures. It would be a lost cause. Not worth booking a passage really".

"So what you are promising is a somewhat virtual eternal life, not truly immortality, but quite acceptable in this day and age. I have been feeling my age lately. The pall of mortality falling on me. At what age would I be during these manoeuvres?"

"Why you remain as you are as at the age we first implement the process", quickly answered Daedalus.

"Then what can I do to support it, dear fellow?", sighed Sir John.

"Release us the necessary funding", entreated Doctor Daedalus, "the funding for a Big Warp Tenderer. Only someone like yourself has the private means so that we can benefit without it going public. We must have a private enterprise. Going to Great Society would entail the kidnapping of our true goal".

"What is this thing?"

"The divine-head machine…..

"A Big Warp Tenderer, did you say?"

"Yes, indeed. It is the machine that will provide for our salvation; for our virtual immortality. It is a large and complex machine, extremely expensive to procure and likely to be seven years in the making. Even though it is large and expensive it will only have the facility for temporal gravitational shift for up to three persons. The shift would have to be performed on an annual basis to restore our immortal efficacy, dear Sir! Therefore the need for secrecy. We don't want any Tina, Denise or Hilary getting wind of this. The great plus is that the BWT …

"What?"

"Big Warp Tenderer".

"Righto".

"Yes, the great thing is that I can configure everything on the surface for it to look like it is a machine to register and calculate the physical effects of Perriwinkle – sorry, the Brown Dwarf system. People would be none the wiser as to what we are really up to, but some of the sager mathematicians will recognise that with the BWT we will be able to observe and calculate some of the more metaphysical shifts and imbalances, although they will not be able to fathom exactly that we are after our particular Philosopher's Stone".

"Explain these metaphysical shifts to Sir John", requested Professor Riddell.

"I have already hypothetically calculated that the gravitational disorders will lead to psychic effects affecting human consciousness and appearing like reality shifts. A fusion between wakefulness and dreaming, between past and present and between identity and non-entity. Very strange disorders for us all could be likely I calculate."

"You will be telling me next that counter-professionals will be running the country", chuckled Sir John.

"Possibly" said Daedalus quite earnestly, "but the result is we need to get a lot of things done in the next seven years or so. The gravitational circumstances through the approaching Brown Dwarf will be mature enough in seven years for us to get our certain things done – to be able to engineer the shift that my calculations irrefutably demonstrate. At the same time by the passage of the next seven years, or even earlier, we may be already experiencing these physical and psychic effects that I have been alluding to. At the same time we are looking at a seven years project to get the BWT up to snuff for it to propagate its miraculous powers".

"A universe of perfect sevens", commented Sir John. " I would be 53. Not too old and decrepit by then".

"The universe is a programme of profound coincidences", retorted Daedalus. "And yes, by the look of the very stuff of you Sir you should still be in good vigour seven years hence".

"You mentioned capital", said Sir John. "I like the notion but you have to lay my curiosity to rest regarding the money. What is the cost to procure this miracle machine?"

Daedalus looked sheepish apparently at a loss of words.

"You do realise Sir John that we are putting a price on something that is invaluable", interjected the Professor. "The BWT is a device that cannot be procured on a shoestring".

"How much?" Sir John adopted a more menacing tone.

This time it was Riddell who appeared sheepish.

"A princely sum worthy of unfailing life!", came back the good Doctor finally realising that to shilly-shally about would be to no good avail. "By my latest estimates we shall require 183,500 sovereigns to put BWT into full running order".

"By Gad, you may as well say two hundred thousand!" Sir John was clearly staggered. "Where do I find that sort of money? I'm rich indubitably, but I'm not made of money". Sir John went and poured himself another stiff one.

"Well? Well? What say you?". Sir John was obviously frustrated; something he could have desired and seemed so close to its potential perfection had been snatched away again from him. "Hah! How farcical! You come to me with the deepest notions borne out of the astronomical, only to throw an astronomical figure at me! What irony."

"You could raise the sum from the Catcaldis Venture Financiers. I'm sure they would accept your mortgage on the great house at Chatham Cheap", ventured the Professor.

"Would they now? What makes you think that? Besides which the plantation and the house has been in my family for generations. I am a mere custodian for future generations of Perriwinkles and custodian of this thing of beauty for Great Society and the Nation."

"But Sir John under our current realisations you would be custodian for endless generations to speak of. Family heirlooms would belong to a different paradigm – another universe - and Doctor Daedalus is …."

"I am also an expert at actuarial calculations", picked up the good Doctor. "A property such as Chatham Cheap is eminently mortgageable. I have reckoned the debt that can be serviced under such a rent bearing estate and the required sum for the BWT is easily within its burden bearing capacity. Additionally, I hold by absolutely immaculate and irrefutable calculus that the loan of such a sum would never exceed the marketable value of the estate. You would soon be paying off that mortgage easily and providing a more than modest estimable profit margin for the Catcaldis. *You play they pay, you pay they play*, as we are wont to say in Lower Itooland".

Sir John J. Perriwinkle shifted uncomfortably in his Arbunkle chair, then he stood up abruptly and paced around the ornamental bay windows of his exquisite drawing room. He ruffled and rummaged through the luxurious locks of hair at his most pronounced and cultivated widows peak. He looked as if he was in a rush to get somewhere, but something was preventing him bolting to it.

"My dear Sir John …." It was the suave voice of Great Society's Astrologer Royal. "We have prepared for you a most confidential dossier for you to consider giving out all the facts and permutations of this very singular case. May I leave it with you and we shall bid you good day".

"Yes. Yes. That may be wise", whispered Sir John.

The two eminent scientists made their leave and departed.

Entering out on the busy thoroughfare of Rumpole Street, Professor James Riddell softly remarked to his colleague: "Methinks he is in".

"Just as Belsingham predicted", enjoined his learned associate.

Daedalus looked at his calculus anew. The blackboards in his study were ram jammed with chalked calculations. Usually his calculus was unassailable against mysteries. Everything could be eventually explained through recourse to logic and algebra. There was a formula to explain everything. Every problem could be reasoned out. It was a matter of defining the parameters; elucidating the value of everything.

The good doctor Daedalus could practically explain everything. He could model the most imponderable and understood the gravity of stars beyond infinity. He could reason a wrap-round universal tenet that could encapsulate eternity. He could theorise on matter that ceased to exist as the door of time began to open. He could compare the synapses of the human brain to the unlikeliness of creating good tunes. He could put into place an equation which would also balance out mass to gravity. He could convert the highly complex into the natural. He was breaking down the greatest intricacies of the universe into immutable clear law of physik so that their effects could be seen to be applied in Long Longbridge or the Window Nebula.

His reason and his quantum mechanik were infallible. Not many knew, but some few did know, that his was the greatest mind that had ever lived, but notwithstanding this, on his principal hobbyhorse he was failing. He was failing absolutely. To crack the problem would glean true understanding. He simply could not explain in his calculus the property of consciousness. He could not find the physik to put into his natural laws, the ability to think, to feel sensations, to divine one as a self that in all this conjoined matter was a thing that recognised its own profound loneliness.

He was willing to conclude that consciousness was outside the natural law of physik. But physik contained all things, so this had to be nonsensical. The ability to feel yourself, to acknowledge your own being, was outside all physik relativity.

He was struggling. He was losing hope in divining the natural elements that could be fused in consciousness. The human brain, a thing so compact that it transcended the complexity of the infinite universe. Something so superior to the natural making forces of the universe. However, the great natural universe did not have the wherewithal to recognise the superiority of consciousness and merely destroyed it like everything else not stopping to reflect on anything in a grinding business. If the universe were only to recognise our mindfulness, to appreciate our beauty, then it might halt to ponder the incorporation of our sentience into the eternal scheme of things. We rail against its indifference to us so that we spend so much time of the little we have trying to make our mark of posterity on this earth; an insubstantial sliver of the whole everything.

He just needed more time. More time to be able to commune with the runaway star.

Cloppety-clop went the slow horse's hooves on the cobbled country lane. Fumi Lartal could hear, and then feel, the cloppety-clop like a metronome of sexual arousal.

At the same time she was aware of the horse's breathing. It was very wheezy and discouraging, bringing her back to the fear of it all – this mortal coil all coiled and sacked up. All sacked up and bound up by Jimmy Suzuki she felt the strange perversity of fear colliding with erotic awareness in a base elemental contest as to who should have the upper hand. She was confused. She was not often confused, but she was now and felt a curious relief in her surrender. What was happening to her? 'What will become of me?', she wondered but in a rather removed way as if she were the protagonist in her own theatre play.

"I'm pleased you put the slag into some composure". It was the voice of the other one. Not the fat grunting sweaty giant who had transported her from the trahere against her will. She felt that this other one was the decidedly nastier one of the two hoodlums.

"Now Mister T. Hold your tongue. This personage is a lady, a scholar and officer of the court. She's no slag."

"What did I say about names! She could be conscious again."

"Oh, did I say Mister T or Master Z or Grand Master Zillock? Or something like that? Silly me. I must remember not to break our cover through an accidental misspeak", replied the more avuncular one.

'Methinks he is a mite cunning and he is playing a scaring game. Making our Mister T feel that his identity could be exposed at any moment', pondered Fumi. 'Is he passing some sort of reassurance message to me?' Her mind was still exercising whilst her passion was continuing to be aroused.

"Alright let's keep quiet. We've got to pass through the village of Bolsover-Belsingham. Make sure she's all wrapped up and not going to give off any alarm. We don't want any argy-bargy from any concerned onlookers, do we? ", instructed the tetchy one.

"No, we don't squire", and the horse and cart continued to amble along its way down the quiet county road at evening tide where there was no other traffic and no-one around to pass Fumi Lartal any concern. The procession of the abductors and abductee passed quietly through the village of Bolsover-Belsingham and if there were habitudes there Fumi was not able to glean any intelligence of civilisation or human kind. Big Bess just kept ambling on in an inexorable way like a life going nowhere apart from in one certain pre-ordained direction. Fumi consequently surrendered to her destination like we all do with a certain resignation when one sees the odds very clearly. Fumi was embracing this resignation to fate, but in that resignation she was finding pleasure too. In that pleasure she found herself spontaneously moaning. It was primal and it did not emerge as a moaning of pain or suffering. More the moaning of a realisation that there need be no more fighting, no more imposing of the will and denying another. It was the moan of come and take me if you will and I will experience it. It was odd and unsettling, but also for Fumi liberating and perversely empowering.

"For pity's sake get her to shut the fuck up!" snarled Tempels. "We'll have the Night Watch upon us if we're not careful".

"I'm not going to give her any more chloroform. It can't be good for her", argued Jimmy.

"Then kick her into quietude. Gag her with your fat dick, but do something you fat baggage!", ordered Tempels.

"Stop the cart. I need a piddle", exclaimed Jimmy. He then peered down at Fumi in the approaching half-light. "And you girl better give over your moaning or else Grandmaster Zillock or Pillock will do something to you which a scholar and gentleman would never entertain to do unto you. You do understand me, girl?"

Jimmy could just about make out Fumi eyes alert to his message. The eyes implored and at the same time accepted.

"Right I'm just off to those bushes over there to shake a leg. So behave as I cannot vouch what this bogeyman will do to you if you do misbehave. Perhaps he would feed you to his wild horse here". As if in acknowledgment of such a desire Big Bess went into a round of particularly shallow but loud asthmatic breathing.

At that Jimmy shambled off into the night grove to do his bodily business. At the verge of the shrubbery he began to pee with great equanimity.

"My dear Sir! Please desist in directing your whizz in this direction. We are in grave danger of being deluged by its frothy properties!"

Jimmy was startled by this male voice in the darkness and then even more disoriented by a woman's laughter. He drew his artillery barrage to the direction of the road.

"Did we startle you dear Sir? No more than you startled us, I daresay." More feminine laughter, cackling and not very ladylike.

"What?"

"We are here for the discretion, Sir. I trust that you are not from these parts."

"True. We're from the city."

"Well I shall ask of you for your word as a gentleman to keep this encounter strictly confidential. I am a gentleman of means in these parts and I would wish to keep my assignations with young Rosali here on the strict QT. I cannot be allowed to be spotted in the *Sparrow's Elbow*, the tavern in Bolsover-Belsingham, or, indeed anywhere near my own residence, with such charming ladies such as Rosali who are easy with their favours. I am a man of property and a Justice of the Peace. I trust very much on your honour Sir, that you will not divulge any of these delicate personal details. Alas, I did not wish to open up to a very stranger, but still consider it less of a hardship than a grand soaking of my fine silk waistcoat or young Rosali's bounteous corsets".

Jimmy noticed with his expanding night eyes that there were two persons lying on the ground on a picnic blanket. They looked like they were in a state of casual undress.

"Oh I get it. I get it!", exclaimed Jimmy conscious of his somewhat delicate position himself with the kidnapped Fumi Lartal only ten yards or so hence. "Please let me clear my way out of your business, dear Sir. There will be no further need for explanation and no more of any asking." Jimmy moved to shamble off.

In the dark night there was a sharp shriek of pain. Jimmy recognised it coming from their prisoner. Also he heard Tempels's rasping voice carry across the night. "I warned you, you strumpet. Next time I'll turn you into dog meat".

"By Janna, what have you done!", shouted Jimmy and he ran instantly in his shambling sort of way back to the cart whilst at the same time trying to sheathe his weapon. It was a bit of an ungainly run, but urgent no less.

"She was fucking me around!", declared Tempels anxiously.

"What did you do?", asked Jimmy anxiously.

"I just cut her a bit as a sort of a warning to behave and stop with all her moaning nonsense."

"You cut her!"

"Yes, a little bit with me baccy razor. Sorry, but it's a bit blunt really; not like when it was new."

"You cut her you imbecile! How are we to negotiate with tarnished goods? You cut her where?"

"Across the cheek. Actually on the back cheek. A bit of a blunt cut across the arse. Not life threatening and no doubt will not spoil her future prospects."

"Miss Lartal, are you alright?". Jimmy felt very concerned. Just a muffled whimpering from the dark cart in reply.

"What do you mean negotiating? Who said anything about negotiating? May Sand have Salt! We're simply going to sell her sweet cut arse to the highest bidder, me lad", blustered Tempels.

"You never said anything about that", uttered Jimmy.

"What's to do here. And me a JP", said the voice of the stranger in the night darkness. "What is this pretty commotion?"

"This pretty commotion is a Slavanger blunderbuss trained at your temple", menaced Tempels.

"Now, now Sir. No need for consternation. Your esteemed colleague will confirm that like you that I have been caught with my trousers down; although mine are particularly fine Jonson lungwort green Worsteds." Jimmy glanced around, but there was no sign of the courtesan. She had evidently hopped it.

"After the confidences I have shared with this fine fellow", the dark figure in the night turned towards Jimmy, "I am sure that I am in no position to tittle-tattle about your sensitive predicament."

"Who are you then?", growled the testy Tempels.

"I am Sir, Arnold Copperfield Esq., at your service."

"What's to stop me blowing off your bollocks with this blunderbuss and leaving you to lie at the wayside to die while the crows pick at your entrails?"

"Sir, you have a lovely turn of phrase, but let's be pragmatic here. Young Rosali, my erstwhile cohort here, is fleet of foot. She is clean out of here and she is sure to raise the alarm if I'm not back at Cribbers Hall by the morning. Nevertheless, I swear to keep complete Marm on this for I am too equally compromised by the events of this evening."

"She'll raise the alarm anyway. You sent her away, didn't you. I'll spare the noise from the blunderbuss and cut your throat instead. Grab him!", he shouted to Jimmy.

Which Jimmy did at surprising speed, but unsurprisingly Jimmy was not necessarily in for all of Tempels's plan.

"I don't think we should have any killing, dear colleague. That would end up making us really parties outside the law. At the moment we still have the force of moral retribution as a recognisable mitigation. If we kill an innocent bystander, and Justice of the Peace to whit, we would lose all chance of clemency. Let's take the old fellow hostage for safe passage insurance", for the fellow was old; Jimmy could feel his saggy body and folds in the skin.

"May Sand have Salt! You really are a walking lexicon of big words. Mitigation and clemency, you say?", then Tempels spat dramatically on to the ground. "Still, you may have a point there, and besides which, he just may buy us safe passage should the going get hairy. Truss him up with her then", he commanded.

"Don't bind me too tight, otherwise I'll have an apoplexy", moderately advised Arnold Copperfield Esq.

"Right you are kind Sir. The ropes will do their job, but they shall not be unkind". Jimmy was becoming a man of adventure. He was feeling in his element and so like a seasoned adventurer he made fast Mister Copperfield with the minimum fuss. Copperfield seemed moderately resigned to it and loosened his body out as if he were that special present waiting to be gift wrapped. Copperfield and Miss Lartal made strange bedfellows on the floor of the cart. Two dark figures immobile in the villainous fastness of the night.

With the two parcels secured and Jimmy back at the head of the trap, Tempels signalled Big Bess to move on ahead again into the night. "I expect you're wondering where we are heading to", he whispered to Jimmy. "Best to leave that in my mind alone. Need to know basis so that the mission is not compromised should you be captured".

"Ah", sighed Jimmy. "Mission protocol, I fully understand. I know the importance of it amongst naval men".

"Exactly", resounded Kurt Tempels.

All seemed quiet and inexorable as the light patter of rain was felt. Big Bess ploughed through the dark sea of night as if her continued passage would be the only thing that would stop complete and utter darkness holding on to the world.

A footman came into the drawing room to announce: "A package from the Royal Society of Science has arrived, Sir. It is marked as *extremely confidential and personal only to the eyes of Sir John J. Perriwinkle, 15th. Baronet of Sandown*", stressed the pompous footman.

"Bring it in without further ado", ordered Sir John J. Perriwinkle.

It had been eight days since the visit of Riddell and Daedalus and Sir John had to admit to himself that he had become a little anxious at the lack of palpable news since the very extraordinary conversation he had had with the two eminent scientists.

The head butler himself, the Eminent Egon Swinson brought the delivery into the drawing room. Swinson knew how to bring proper ceremony to Sir John's household activities. He unfurled a tube of architectural documents with great solicitousness wearing the type of pristine white gloves used for cleaning the best silver. Sir John could immediately see that they were drawings of machinery. There appeared to be arcane looking calculations on the sides.

"Thank you Swinson, that will be all".

"Would your Worship like fresh coffee to be brought, or, perhaps a fortifier?"

Sir John knew that Swinson was curious about the parchments. If he did not watch out there would be rumours abound in Milliwhigs Gentlemen's Club.

"No verily, that is all **for the time being**", with added emphasis.

Swinson recognised the imperative and beat a retreat to leave Sir John in his own solicitude.

Sir John opened out fully the parchment documents and immediately noticed the heading *Big Warp Tenderer*. There were a number of detailed engineering documents with strange calculations. It all appeared Ob-Ugrian to him. How was he meant to interpret all these? They did appear serious and authentic though. There was a brief inside.

Most honourable Sir John,

I apologise for the length of time in getting these plans to you. It was not due to any reluctance to engage with you as a benefactor of this remarkable project; simply that I wished Dr Daedalus to be absolutely certain on the engineering plans for the Big Warp Tenderer. These plans are now well conceived and executed to my utmost satisfaction. Naturally, they now have my personal warrant on them. I do, however, entreat you not to share these with anyone. The execution of our plan is absolutely hinged on exclusivity. The efficacy of the Brown Dwarf system as to our aim is predicated upon an operation of no more than three persons. That means should anyone get to this goal before our venture, then the game is up.

Furthermore, we have re-costed the project and can finally affirm a sum of one hundred and ninety-three thousand sovereigns of the realm shall be required for the faultless execution of the project. We have revised our original figure admittedly, but assure you that this cost is now an absolutely comprehensive one. As you said before, you may wish to call it a round two hundred thousand sovereigns to allow reserve for caprice.

I realise that this is a vast sum and few could afford it. Dear Sir, recognise though the prize at stake for which you will not forfeit a princely sum but receive instead a supernatural bounty. The reward is beyond calculation; simply priceless. For this we should be thankful that I have the enterprise, Dr Daedalus the genius, and you Sir, the nobility of purpose and resources for the greatest undertaking humankind has entered into.

Concerning the raising of capital, I have been giving thought to how this might be done. I advised you already as to the likely willingness of Catcaldis Venture Financiers to hold good your mortgage on Chatham Cheap. To that regard I have a close associate in government circles very sound in the regard of Great Society who also has impeccable connections into Catcaldis. I am sure that he would be very willing to broker a deal in strictest confidence and to that effect I have put out some discreet feelers on the matter.

Our utmost secrecy has, of course, to be maintained, so please be assured kind Sir, that I have put out a cover story to disguise our deep import. The story to be fabricated is that you wish to make a benefaction to the war effort, that being the grant of eight Fighting Temeraire class war frigates. You wish that this be an anonymous gift from you to Great Society; your small part in upholding liberty in the face of Oriental dominion. Both Catcaldis and my associate will understand your wish to do this selfless behest to the nation under the cloak of secret benefaction. My associate will make clear that this would be a simple mortgage against your family seat; no instalments payments are to be aligned to progress payments set against shipbuilding!

Should you wish to progress our plan (and I do urge alacrity to ensure its success), then please convey back to me your satisfaction. I would like to arrange a meeting for next Monday between us, dear Dr Daedalus and my associate whom I mentioned above, one Horatio Beeswax Belsingham. I would suggest we assemble at Daedalus' bureau at JaJa Point.

I remain your humble servant,

Professor James Riddell, Astrologer Royal

'This Riddell takes liberties', thought Sir John, 'but he also knows how to conceive and execute a plan. The prize is too big to be concerned with my sensibilities', he further mused.

He determined to go a little deeper with these soundings. He wanted to hear the sound of deep space and the time to enjoy it. He wrote back that day to Riddell at the Society and affirmed the proposed meeting for that coming Monday. He put the brief letter in the normal delivery pouch as it was commonplace, as a benefactor, for him to write to the Royal Society of Science. Swinson nor none of the footmen would give it a second thought.

'Let Monday come!', he thought.

Four: Destruction – "Among the Professionals"

Far removed from the divining of immortality, on another slice of the strata, in the suburban district of Prison Oval, with its leafy boroughs, state's lawyer Belsingham sat on the rocking chair on the porch of his mid-size mansion and listened to his two small daughters, Missy and Jessica, singing *Sur le pont d'Andlau* in the comfort of the balmy night. They were seven and five respectively and quite delightful and filled with grace like their mother. State's lawyer Horatio Beeswax Belsingham (HBB to his closest intimates, and there were many who were close) sighed with pride as his lovely spouse Nicole appeared on the porch dispensing iced punch and lemonade. Nicole, nee Naismith, was a child of the plantation and had instilled in her grace and old worldly charms and the well-bred etiquette of the plantation class. HBB was well satisfied with his delightful, beautiful, and of course, gifted family. Nicole herself had achieved a double first in Botany and Classics at Emporium. Belsingham's career was on the up. He had just been appointed State's Prosecutor First Class and a judgehood and knighthood would soon be in the bag. Everything was going swimmingly; all was just so and perfect really.

However, there was one thing that had to be amiss. There always is really. HBB had a big guilty secret; he was a slaver. Slavery had been outlawed by Porto Dominigo much to the horror of the plantation class. Domingo had come down hard and swift to liberate the slaves and discontinue this perverted sense of ownership. However the business had not been entirely eradicated and it was generally known that the Sand religion people did not hold any scruples about doing a trade, especially if it concerned trading in non-believers. It was not as if Horatio Beeswax Belsingham needed the money. What he did need was the sense of danger; a sport, a sense of being able to ride lucky all this perfect life against the crest of something that could smash it thoroughly to smithereens. He just wanted the simple joy of doing something so thoroughly invidious and then not being caught. It was his grubby pastime and at the same time his simple thrill of being alive. The misery of others should not of course compromise his thrill of being alive and the pursuit of his grubby pastime, and such uncompromising commitment and dedication consequently meant that he always had to move up to a next level of this esoteric sport, thereby meeting a challenge that became more and more difficult; making it more thrilling. His next target would not be an easy one at all. It would not be just some poor underclass moll, it would indeed be one of his very own august legal profession. He had set his eye on the delectable Fumi Lartal, JJKC. She was going to be exactly the type of target to test his skill. She had become far too uppity in their shared profession. She was simply too good a rival and had to be taken out. He would take her out and he would take her out in the style of a great hunter. He would do so with the debased morals of a white slaver. This challenge searched his waking awareness and sub-awareness looking constantly for an elegant solution. That, he had no doubt, he would find eventually.

"My dear, more punch?", his charming wife enquired.

Belsingham smiled indulgently and held out his glass for the offered re-fill.

"If you have finished with *The Thunderer*, might I read the broadsheet?", further enquired Nicole.

"Yes, of course, my dear". HBB retired back into his thoughts.

"Oh these too disgusting people!", exclaimed Nicole.

"What do you mean?"

"I'm just reading that the Chamberlains have discovered another slave prostitution ring centred around some market traders down in Frasertoon".

"Really, that's too despicable", replied HBB. 'Now there's a thought', he thought.

Big Bess ploughed on through the night doughtily and somewhat wheezily, but unerringly. Dawn was on the horizon as they approached a remote farmhouse. Jimmy noted a sign pointing to it – "Marmalade Fields" and as he observed the sign Tempels guided the horse off the general path down that fork to the house. Jimmy was confident that they were coming to their final destination although he did not venture to ask Tempels. Need to know basis, best not to know everything. It felt good for a little while to be controlled again; to save his adventurous spirit a mite.

"Whoa Bess".

'So we are finally here', thought Jimmy.

"You can get them off now. Put them in that barn there yonder", instructed Tempels to Jimmy. "You should find in there restraining chains and the like to make them both snug and comfy. But be aware there is only one set of wall manacles in there. Reserve them for the bitch. We weren't expecting further company during this trip. There are separate cells though, so that will stop them conniving."

Jimmy with the dexterity of a drayman started the unloading process when suddenly a fellow walked abruptly out of the barn quite startling him. Tall and grey in the cool dawn light, the fellow announced:

"Hello there! My name is Jan Gloop. Mister Belsingham sent me to make sure that you get all you need and that you're being looked after and all."

"Ah, Mister Gloop, I've been expecting you", responded Kurt Tempels.

'Who in the hell is Belsingham?', wondered Jimmy. 'Name seems familiar'.

Jimmy scrutinised Jan Gloop. Gloop had all the demeanour of a plantation overseer. He looked like he was in the prime of life. He had a big nose and tussled hair, but was not ugly. Gloop wore white breeches, green hunting frockcoat and brown riding boots. He had the look and feel of the veritable country about him.

"Mister Tempels, I presume?", and when Gloop gave a large grin Jimmy could see that the state of his teeth was country bad though. 'Must be the chewing on all that beef biltong', mused Jimmy.

"I was expecting the delivery of only one package", commented Gloop.

"Yes, I know. We got a sort of two for one insurance package. We picked the fellow up on the road after he discovered what we were up to and I was persuaded to take him hostage against our safe passage."

"No doubt Mister Suzuki persuaded you?", Gloop cheerfully added showing another smile full of decrepit teeth. He turned to Jimmy: "And you must be he, James Donald Suzuki. Mister Belsingham sends his sincere regards to you, my dear Sir."

"I would reciprocate if I knew the gentleman".

"Oh you do. You do."

Before Jimmy could enquire further Fumi Lartal entered into a round of pitiful moaning pressing Kurt Tempels into immediate business.

"Come along Suzuki. Let's get them out of sight. Pray Mister Gloop, will you help us?".

"Come Mister Suzuki. Let's take in our lively guest. We have excellent accommodation awaiting her." Gloop moved solicitously to help Jimmy with the now rather animated Fumi Lartal. Both Jimmy and Gloop manhandled the rather writhing package, otherwise known as State's Prosecutor Fumi Lartal, into the barn. Already set out and prepared inside was a small makeshift cell made out of steel bars and with grubby straw on the floor. A solitary blanket lay therein.

"We're not leaving her in here, are we?"

"My dear Sir, you have entered into an abduction. Freely according to Mister Tempels. What did you expect? Milliwhigs Gentlemen's Club?".

Jimmy felt the disdain and hauteur in Gloop's voice. He very decidedly did not feel at home with these circumstances.

"Let's get her into the cell, shall we?", added Gloop.

They moved her into the cell. Gloop took out a sharp knife and released Fumi of her bonds. Fumi did not say a thing. She looked shocked and abashed.

"Take off that fine court uniform, gracious Sir! She's now a prisoner. Like all those she has sent to stiff sentencing!", bellowed Gloop. He suddenly looked to Jimmy like a veritable ogre. The very epitome of a person who would kill someone for simply looking the wrong way at him.

"What leave her in her under-things?". Jimmy was uneasy. Fumi looked extremely frightened.

"Yes indeed, we can be kind I suppose and leave her in her underclothes. I could grant you that. Personally, I would leave her in her birthday suit. She needs to learn that she is nothing now. A creature she has become like the creatures she has herself made out of honest folk with her cruel unjust criminal sentencing!", shouted Gloop.

"Yes, under-things, of course", complied Jimmy always knowing how to strike a good compromise.

"If we hear anymore of her blethering, my dear fellow, we shall have to punish her. I know ways of disciplining with a hot poker which will not leave a mark on her body. We would not wish to reduce her value on the market."

Jimmy was aghast and wanted to enquire further on what was meant, but Tempels had entered.

"Hurry! Hurry, my fine fellows. Daylight is in its ascendancy and we still have not lodged the venerable Copperfield. We must get everything out of sight, Gloop!"

"Get those clothes off!", boomed Gloop. "Here use this! It'll speed the process. You don't look like the type who could quickly undress a wench", smirked Gloop. He showed Jimmy a sharp evil looking hunting knife. "This is how you do it", and Fumi Lartal's fine embroidered bodice was glimpsing in a flicker of an eye. "Right me fine fellow Suzuki, get her chained with those wall manacles. Come Tempels, let's leave these two lovebirds to it and attend to Copperfield".

'I wish. I wish', Jimmy felt himself unconsciously thinking.

Meanwhile outside in the farmyard Arnold Copperfield Esq. was determined to be resolute as he lay waiting in the cart with Big Bess voluminously farting. Every time he was about to formulate in his mind an appropriate entreaty to be used on his captors Big Bess passed wind with a thunder. Apart from the unsettling noise, it was extremely malodorous. This process really put him off his own thought process.

"Yikes, Big Bess. I've got to keep you off the frigging turnips", growled Tempels. "Mister Copperfield let's be having you". With that Tempels whipped off the gag from his mouth.

"My dear Sirs", gargled Copperfield, "I entreat you!"

"Let's cut out the pig shit. It smells bad enough here already", said Gloop and bonked Copperfield deftly on the head with his shillelagh. Copperfield was transferred to the land of Nod. "This way we can get him in safely without all the whining and entreating", added Gloop.

Arnold Copperfield Esq. had a most profound fear of death. It was always there somewhere in his consciousness and then in times of his subconsciousness it really gave vent to its feelings. In sleep, half-sleep, cat naps and those drooling times in the rickety-rick of the moving carriages of the trahere - it would really let rip. Then it became a fear without abandon. Consequently Copperfield never felt fully rested. He desperately feared the entire messy conclusion and would have liked to have signed up for some creator myth to ease the fear of passing. Nevertheless, he was a man of science and through his fear he had to accept the persisting doubt of a random natured universe based on impeccable natural laws of physik. At the end of the day one had to accept that he was just another piece of detritus in the cosmic accident.

For this reason he did from time to time rebel against the fear and act with a bit of gumption. In that regard as a sexagenarian he was prone to try and do some things that verily smacked of life; womanising, pit-bull fighting and gambling, opium snorting, dandy clothes and the like – at least he had the money. He was hell-bent on outliving death, even though most of the time he felt so tired and morbidly discontented with the whole process of struggle throughout life. The sort of behaviour that has led to this pretty pass – a voice of doubt dark deep in his being cries out. A sort of behaviour of a foolish old man that is going now to draw him ultimately to his death.

'At least you have the money, but you have no-one to pass it to', the demon voice swirls in the depths of his decrepit dis-consciousness. No money to pass, no loved ones, no-one to give it to; money or love. Just shiny gold sovereigns on the whirl of cosmic circumstance. No-one will know any more.

'Where are you my son? Why have you abandoned me? Sixteen years and no contact from you. No brief, no token and no sign. Why have you forsaken me? Why have you turned your back on me? My dear Donald ......'

Demons, dark doubts, good feelings all lost, an aching in the groins, a wanting to be loved, a realisation of the cold isolation unfeeling infinity, and a weird voice crackling "This is Belsingham" – Arnold Copperfield Esq. had started to stir in the hay loft of a barn in the vicinity of Ford Bolsover. Though it could have been at the furthest tract of the old universe.

So his delectable consort had sprung for him the idea, but HBB was just the genius to spring the plan and put it into operation. HBB as state's lawyer knew some shady persons. Narks, loan sharks, reprobates, persons who sailed close to the wind and the like. He would ask one Angus Oiler to put the feelers out. Oiler was an ex-rozzer from Zentralpolizei who had been in the heinous crimes unit. On that basis he knew some heavy duty villains, and Oiler was on the verge of being heinous himself. It takes one to know one, and HBB could rely on the dubious Angus to find one. It was all a question of price and payment terms. Oiler came back to him quicker than expected.

"So Mister Oiler. What do you have for us? I must say that you are back to report earlier than expected. It has only been a couple of days. I trust that this is not because you have drawn a blank on this enquiry?"

They were in the grand sitting room of HBB's fashionable home. HBB was not particularly gratified to receive house guests like Oiler; unsavoury types. Nevertheless, it was a better place for this type of sensitive rendezvous than his bureau, the staging station or some other similar public place where they could be exposed. HBB looked his guest over and although having met him numerous times before still concluded once more that Oiler was an apt name for such an oily and odious weasel like person. Angus Oiler looked his years, a very lived in fifty-seven years old. Long lank hair, a bit too much bristle showing and clothing much too long utilised and shabby. The shiny brass buttons on his shoes could not give out any more shininess – they had simply been shined out of allure. 'Maybe his thriftiness is borne out of the fact that he has so many mistresses and bastard children to endure', considered HBB.

"Oh not at all good Mister Belsingham. Quite the contrary!", expelled his guest. "There is a very wave of antipathy towards Miss Lartal. Many in Frasertoon would like to see that dear lady out of the picture. She has been rather over-zealous in her prosecution of the law and has been rather unsusceptible to the usual arrangements of bung-a-lung which cause the wheels of trading and merchandising to turn. She has been just too a fussy paragon of virtue that lady, especially since her own father is a Frasertoon street trader."

"Her father?"

"Yes one Bobotie Bruce".

"Bobotie?"

"Yes, it's what he serves. It's a Frasertoon cum Trenchtown local delicacy. A type of rumbustious curried meat concoction. No-one seems to know his real first name! They are a rum bunch in Frasertoon."

"I see."

"So what I'm trying to say Sir, is that there would be no-one down in that hearty community that would be sad to see her disappear. Many in that most sincere community would wish to sponsor such an endeavour, and many in the august hierarchy would be prepared to give most generously to your fighting fund for that desire. You might have heard of a certain Lord Roy Gibbons?".

"I have". 'So not only would I get rid of the bitch and satisfy my sates, I would actually be paid for it too', thought HBB. "Tell me more, Oiler."

"I would like to put you in touch with one Kurt Tempels a purveyor of fine natural juyces and high up in the Great Sand movement. He should be able to help us with your scheme, your Honour. I've already sounded him out and I think he is ready to put a concrete proposal in front of you."

"Fine, Oiler. Set up a meeting for Tuesday evening, but not here. You and I should meet with him at the Mariner warehouse down at the Southern Docks. Can we rely on his discretion?"

"We can, Sir. Trust me. I'll set up the meet. Good day, your Honour."

B obotie Bruce had been feeling some heat. First some crazed cat lover and anti-trade protectionist had planted his knuckles in Bobotie's face. If that were not bad enough he now had Slim Tennyson making him a visit to deliver some "intimations" from Lord Roy Gibbons. Of course, Lord Roy Gibbons was no lord at all. This was his given street name as a boss in the Frasertoon underworld, but he did carry similar influence to a titled aristocrat. Some said that he was considerably more regal, and that simply said his word was law. Yes, in that regard he was a formidable character, and his diplomat and representative, Slim Tennyson, had a tart way of making simple words appear very menacing.

"My, my Mister Bruce", started Tennyson. "I hope that you didn't get all cut up simply in anticipation of my visit to you." Jimmy's fist visitation was still clearly available to see on Bobotie Bruce's ruddy complexion. "My, my, quite a shiner. Try Pompander powder, it certainly works a treat with my laughter creases." It felt like mock concern from Slim Tennyson as a preface to the real matter. "Anyway, that being said, the real sympathy I wished to express is my very palpable concern that your daughter hasn't had a holiday in some time. Fumi has been positively overworking, don't you think?. It is not right, Sir. She needs a visit to the spa and replenishment. Yes indeed, she is very much in need of a very long holiday. A spa cure perhaps. And far far away from here, away from all this debilitating hubbub and hurly-burly with all its work concerns. You too Mister Bruce are probably in need of some time away as well. Maybe you should join the state's prosecutor in a nice long trip away. I'm sure that the venerable Lord Gibbons would support fully such a notion. I could book you both a handsome passage"

On and on in this kind avuncular vein continued Tennyson in a soft reasonable tone whilst waving delicately and ostentatiously a scented lace handkerchief. Bobotie sweated in the heat of the February afternoon whilst acknowledging demonstrably that there was much good counsel in this advice. Bobotie Bruce knew that they were really putting the heat on. This was the shot across the bows he had been expecting. Sort your daughter out or else we will. Slim Tennyson stood next to his stall incongruously in the heat of the afternoon sun with his light purple tinted wig and dressed in an outfit of high court foppery. Tennyson looked like a rich young dandy from George Square Quarter slumming it up in the poor area. Nevertheless not one bobotie customer or local bystander came close to this scene as Tennyson waved his handkerchief and doffed his ornate walking stick to his forelock every time he exhorted upon some wise reasonable words of wisdom which might have occurred to the venerable Lord Roy Gibbons also.

Eventually after what seemed a lifetime of chastening and derisive berating Slim Tennyson departed. Even his departure was long drawn out, and this merely added to Bobotie's tension, as Tennyson continued to employ the cumbersome and extremely outlandish *Skittish Walk* which was the very mode of perambulating for extreme high fashion. Eventually after much extremely contrived perambulations Tennyson was removed from sight. It was so humiliating for Bruce to be hassled by such a transparent queer. Bobotie was all hard knuckle, hairy chest and Captain Seward crew, and it was demeaning for him to be terrorised by such a flagrant poofter. Lord Roy Gibbons was not noted for his sense of humour. He was as funny as a pewter beer tankard breaking your nose. Bobotie wondered if Tennyson was kept around for simply more than his acid tongue and his high turn of fashion.

In any event for Bobotie Bruce it was becoming increasingly aware that he would have to act soon to keep his natural daughter safe and save his own bacon too. He knew his own daughter though. He knew her as quite an obstinate and intractable individual. She had not lessened her zealous prosecutions around the market community of Frasertoon despite his many pleadings to her to slacken off. A more subtle and devious approach might be required he deemed.

'If only I hadn't got her into that pretentious school. If only I had not raised her up to be so high and mighty', he rued.

Horatio Beeswax Belsingham never had trouble sleeping. His was an easy conscience. He somehow knew that his conscience was unburdened in his nightly dreams. He was a dreamer, a doer, and then again a dreamer. It was just that he was able to think through his waking dreams, put them to stratagem and then carry them out efficiently and without compunction, but he could not recall his nightly dreams. He was somehow able to dispel them without any scarring of his consciousness. He had faith that there was some sort of strange process, but he had no real ken of its inner workings. Sometimes Nicole would comment on the dampness of his sheets or his crying out in the night, but whatever it was it was locked away in the mental equivalent of a night safe. The unsavoury details were not seen in the day. He could never recall at all and he was not haunted by it.

That night after hearing about the ruffian Kurt Tempels, he slept soundly as per usual hugging on to the backside of the delectable Nicole. Snug up against her soft backside and dreaming.

"But what a strange profession to get into David. Why?"

"I don't know Beeswax! Why not?"

"Don't call me that. You know that I don't like it."

"It is a divine name. Why wouldn't you just love it petal?"

"You would play with my mind?"

"I would play with everyone's minds for that is where true power lies. Porto Dominigo knew that, Franzi Joe knew that. Real power lies not in your quest for wealth Horatio, but in the ability to control people's mind. That's the future. The power of guilt, shame and blame, and the giving of worth, value and absolution – that's where it's at. It is the provenance of the past and the absolute certainty of our future."

"But to qualify as an Alms-Master, David? Surely that is a little too modest for someone with your faculties?", I enquire.

"Modesty is the guise of real power, Horatio", he says. "The power of them thinking you give sacrifice, but in reality that modesty is promoting them to make the actual sacrifices. I will do my training as an Alms-Master and work with the counter-professionals. It is said that we will

all commit 27,000 errors before we meet our graves, so
there is no room for doubt for doubt causes us to make
mistakes; for doubt perceives for us that we have made a
mistake. Doubtless I will have a long and good life and I
am firm in my calling and hold it to be true that as it is
said *"only some of us have an outcome"*. My outcome, dear
chap, is conceived upon the valuelessness of the great
unwashed. Their giving will be my provision. I am firm in
my destiny to contribute to the science of social place
conditioning. I will take my humble position at Snoods
Droop and give comfort to all the maligned. It is my
calling and stairway to greatness."

"Well said then Alms-Master David Lincoln!", I cried.

We were both so young and idealistic then.

Old school chums.

"Hush now, my darling", murmured Nicole as if it were
unclear that she was still sleeping.

Bobotie Bruce was nursing the shiner given to him
randomly by an enraged fat feller. Bobotie Bruce was
ruminating on all his cares and increasingly becoming
more and more anxious. He was adamant that his mortal
coil should have some considerably more time to run yet.
It was Fumi, Fumi who had placed him in this precarious
position. There was no point reasoning with her. She was
just too inflexible, too married to her state of office from
Great Society. She would contend, he knew, that she owed
utmost loyalty to Great Society – there could be no
compromising, he imagined her shrilly declaring. No, no,
the direct approach on her would not work. This called for
a more devious solution, but what?

He remembered something that Sheila Jack mentioned
down at the *Ruskie Perry*. Something about the Sand
religion crazies becoming a little too cock-sure of

themselves. That their Grand Demonizer Rasta Habs had issued a believer's bull rationalising legitimacy of slave trading where non-believers were concerned. The immaculate rationale to this was plain casuistry; that their enforced servitude to believers brought them into close proximity to the belief and the high likelihood of salvation. Not surprisingly that this high moral authority from the GD had promoted a spike in slave trading, and, unsurprisingly too, young females constituted the largest part of the spike. Believers were apparently known to sigh and say that was because females were furthest away from understanding the belief and needed to be brought back closer; it was the way the world was -"May Sand have Salt". Also Rasta Habs had suddenly gone into deep purdah after releasing his moral authority. Rumours were abound that Frasertoon market was a hotbed for the new religious activity. It had also been reported on the jungle drums that one Kurt Tempels – the guy who did the juyces- had become a born again believer and for that was keen to see the GD's bull enforced.

"After all, who wants frigging cranberry juyce in Frasertoon?", Sheila put her finger to her nose knowingly and cackled a smile of those deplorably bad teeth.

Bobotie Bruce could still get a whiff of those malodorous teeth even now, but she had given him an idea to work out on. Bobotie resolved to see the fellow the very next day.

The very next day he did. He tried to make it natural. It was a very hot early February morning. Just the sort of weather for a cool natural fruit juyce. As per the norm there was nobody at the stall of Tempels. In fact there seemed to be no-one around at all. Bruce decided to illicit an appearance.

"Shop!"

"At your service, kind Sah!" Tempels had seemed to materialise out of nowhere. "It is a thirsty day, is it not?"

"It is indeed and that is the purpose of my enquiry."

"My old grand-marm used to say for February there is fallucca. It just so happens that I have freshly picked fallucca fruits from the great ocean road down at Perak. I would humbly recommend a fine juyce concoction from these delectable falluccas. The fallucca is also most efficacious for any sort of injury and by the shiner on you, you look like you could do with a pick-me-up."

Bobotie Bruce was conscious of his ugly present appearance but was determined to move discussion along without reference to it. "Mister Tempels, I shall try your recommendation. Squeeze me a concoction".

"Gladly, Sah" and Tempels started to cut and squeeze the faluccas in the large wrought iron squeezer.

"How's business, Mister Tempels?"

"You know how it is. All these recent wars have made folk more conservative in their spending. I sometimes wonder if in this modern world anyone appreciates a fine juyce. It is hard to make a living."

"I know, Mister Tempels".

"Aren't you Mister Bruce?", enquired Tempels.

"I indeed am, Sah".

"Then you must understand my experience".

"I do indeed. I do indeed. But Mister Tempels I cannot but notice on your arms your seafaring tattoos. It looks like you sailed on *the Implacable*" .

"You are very knowledgeable, Mister Bruce. The Implacable a ship of the line. I saw some bloody action I can tell you. I was with Commodore Stabler at Herty Hole and we were part of the flotilla that pursued old Crookie down the Galss river. I was witness to seeing that scum blown out of the river", at which Tempels ceremoniously spat on the ground.

"Old Crookie. Lord Archibald Crook, 6th. Marquis of Beef Common and scourge of our precious islands. Now he was a formidable opponent plundering and pillaging in the name of the combined Oriental Navy. I seem to recall that he raided villages up the coast to secure slaves and pressganged our young to service his warships. Servicing in all sorts of manners I heard. Very salacious."

"That's right, Mister Bruce. Great Society as is its policy has always been reticent about giving all the historical facts. I understand that it is so as to not induce panic and despair about our fragile constellation in world politik in these here vulnerable islands. Nevertheless, it is a great pity that there is no official record about what we seafarers had to see and endure and the valour we had to summon up to cast away these demons. Crook was a first rate bastard and what our poor youngsters that were kidnapped had to endure defies credible belief."

"So one might say Mister Tempels that you're a man of the world?"

"I've crossed the six seas and done things I'm not proud of. Still, let's talk of happier things. Mister Bruce you must be very proud of your daughter. I cannot compete with you there in having such exalted family members."

"Yes, I'm very proud of her Mister Tempels, but I have to admit I'm losing some connection with her. She's moving in different circles to me now. She has become hoity-toity. I'm afraid that my Fumi needs reining in. She's forgotten her roots. She needs to remember where she has come from. I'm a market man Mister Tempels. My duty is to my market profession and to my fellow traders; in that I am Professional. Now I understand the need for the rule of law, otherwise there would be anarchy and that I would not wish. Great Society had caused us all to prosper under proper conventions and observances and brave persons like yourself have gone to sea to protect our valued principles. Nonetheless there has to be proper balance in the scheme of things, and I'm afraid that my Fumi is upsetting that balance and she no longer listens to my fatherly counsel. Her dogged unrelenting pursuit against some of our ancient market trading customs is now just going too far. It is well known about here that she is about to prosecute a tradeswoman in Further Plokington for weights and measures abuses on eichnuts! Talk about taking Krog's hammer to crack a nut! It makes people here very uneasy. Quite frankly it makes me uneasy too, but she is immune to my entreaties. What is to be done with her? The daughter that I love so."

"Indeed, what is to be done?"

"It might just take one enterprising tradesperson to put some of the fear of the mortal in her. Make her realise that there are base elemental mortal forces at work in this world that have to be respected in balance with her high browed principles and her sincere respect for the strictures of Great Society. Make her realise there are other forces prevalent in this Great Society."

"You mean like Lord Roy?", interjected Tempels.

"Just if the frighteners were put on her for a few days then she might become a little more meek and humble. A bogus threat to her that might apprehend a real threat to her. And to me I daresay."

"Umph", Tempels was musing demonstrably.

"If there were some enterprising individuals who could arrange her apprehension, give her a bit of a fright and then I could valiantly negotiate her release back in to my arms. She might then think differently upon my situation and temper her prosecutorial resolve."

"Umph".

"Can you think of a project initiator for this type of thing? You being an old seafarer and having diverse contacts and all."

"Umph".

Tempels was clearly not biting. It clearly was not such a delectable worm for such an old fish.

"Well, Sah! Your juyce was most invigorating. Our conversation most stimulating. I bid you good day!". Bruce was trooping off.

"Wait!", snarled the worldly-wise Tempels. "I may know someone, but we'll have to procure a fall guy. What was all that kerfuffle that I saw you having with that large fat fellow yesterday?"

"Oh, that was some silly misunderstanding about a stray moggy. A mere bagatelle, Mister Tempels."

"Matters feline are extremely important for some folk. Quite a shiner he gave you. Please amplify on the circumstances, Mister Bruce. These feline matters may be more important than you might imagine". Kurt Tempels extended a crooked grin as a man of the world is wont to do.

'Coincidence is a remarkable thing', thought Kurt Tempels as he watched Bobotie Bruce shamble away from his stall into the stark noon sunlight. It was getting hotter and hotter every year. Tempels was sweating heavily and contemplating on all this coinciding of late. The prophets had prophesied the coming of this period of coincidences prior to the *First Cataclysmic Event* and the Grand Demonizer Rasta Habs had in his hallowed writings interpreted this period as the precursor to the *First Cataclysmic Event* as the sacred prophets had bestowed. Matters of faith were reinforced in the strangest of circumstances. Only the day before yesterday Tempels had been to the Orators Stone to listen to the rant of Arnie O'Tone. O'Tone had been establishing an esoteric and cult reputation for declaiming against the forthcoming extremely negative effects of something called *the Brown Dwarf System*. O'Tone had been ranting on about contusions between temporal time and space and increasing constant reality shifts. O'Tone's most infamous declamation was that the extremity of these contusions could cause life to be a dream, or, the other way around. The ranter had been gaining a quite notorious reputation and was starting to put quite a fear into the people of Whitecircle and Bogenhausen in the vicinity of the Orator's Stone. Now that stir was going around the people of Frasertoon and Trenchtown and inciting dissension in the immigrant quarters of Decayed Barrier and Hard Shoulder. The Brown Dwarf System, O'Tone and the vapid heat cast a negative pall over the underclasses of Banana Delta. Great Society had now reacted to O'Tone's preaching with the Astrologer Royal himself, Professor James Riddell, who had now gone on record officially confirming that the Brown Dwarf had been indeed discovered by Great Society's advanced optical lookers and that the discovery had been held back from the public until the scientists and other eminent persons could study the likely effects of the system. Riddell had officially denounced all supposition of contusions of time space reality axes, although had admitted that there could be more incidence of gravitational impacts in terms of earthquakes and increased volcanic activity.

'Absolutely extraordinary times. May Sand have Salt!', thought Kurt Tempels. 'Absolutely amazing to have a visit this morning from Bobotie Bruce himself just after last night's visit to the Southern Docks to meet a certain Horatio Beeswax Belsingham and his agent Angus Oiler', he mused.

"May Sand have Salt!", he roared to a whisper. The prophets were in order. His faith was in order. There was no such thing as coincidence.

There was no such thing as coincidence as Kurt Tempels, purveyor of fine natural juyces knocked on the door of the dilapidated Mariner warehouse in the Southern Docks. It was dark and the night was musty with the smell of tropical heat and old hemp. The door opened discretely and without ceremony. Tempels looked at the man carrying an oil lamp and concluded that it might be appropriate to assure him of his credentials.

"Kurt Tempels, Sah. I was asked by a mutual acquaintance Arthur J. Henpeck to join you here tonight".

"Indeed, Mister Tempels. Angus Oiler, once of the Metropolitan and Zentralpolizei. Though I am not the principal here tonight. Please come this way".

Tempels followed Oiler through the deserted dark warehouse building wondering if the reference to Zentralpolizei was some sort of veiled threat .

"I trust you are a gentleman of the greatest discretion", enquired Oiler as they proceeded together. "We are about to meet an extremely important personage and extreme confidentiality is absolutely required. For that, Sah, you can expect great profit. You will be rewarded handsomely."

"Have no fear, Mister Oiler, discretion is my middle-name!"

"Good because the trust we have in you has to be impeccable, otherwise calamity is inevitable. We reward most handsomely on the basis that we simply, simply cannot be let down! Do you savvy?"

"I understand you, Sah. Most assuredly."

"Good. We shall soon be in the presence of the great man himself."

They were coming to an office at the end of the warehouse. It was dimly lit. They entered to find a fine dressed man sat on a leather chair behind a large teak desk. There was a quiet opulence here at odds with the dingy warehouse. The man behind the desk looked handsome, lean and with a fine head of curly dark hair. There was not a blemish on his clean shaven face and he appeared to be in his early forties. He looked slick and sharp, conservatively dressed in morning coat but with a hint of opulence with a silver grey silk cravat and a jaunty purple sash on his top hat. Tempels felt correspondingly shabby and tugged with his fingers on his whiskers in unconscious acknowledgment of the fact. Nevertheless he was determined not to be overawed by the gentleman's finery.

"Mister Tempels! I am sorry for all this subterfuge", was how the dialogue began. A sympathetic and courteous acknowledgement towards him which made Kurt feel immediately more at ease. The man was tall, about six foot two, and lean and muscular with it, as he rose to greet Tempels. "But sometimes confidentiality is key to immaculate operation in the most discrete of commercial transactions. I'm sure you understand. Allow me to introduce myself. I am Horatio Beeswax Belsingham, but do call me HBB!".

And with that he extended his hand to Tempels most politely.

"Please dear Mister Tempels, do take a seat and allow me to pour you a libation. I have some fine Malacca rum of forty years provenance – a Westly no less!".

Tempels was quite taken aback by all this courtesy and hospitality, he had been expecting only skulduggery.

"Please savour it, Mister Tempels. It is very fine indeed. You probably wonder how I acquired it as Westly went out of business a decade ago. Let's just say that I am a man of means and I know how to get what I want and I know too how to get the best out of people. I like fine things and I love fine company, Mister Tempels"

Tempels started savouring. It was truly fine rum. Angus Oiler had somehow merged into the background of the office and was not apparent. The man known as HBB was sitting across him staring at him most earnestly. There was more of a fierce impression about him now. Intense. Yes, HBB was examining him intently and Tempels was feeling a little self-conscious once more.

"Mister Tempels let me tell you, I hold an office of serious state in Great Society. I have responsibility to ensure that we do not become a criminal state. I am a State Prosecutor of senior order and this means that I must prosecute so that the rule of law is sacrosanct and seriously observed. Laws ensure that order prevails and that commerce is sound. Laws are guidelines enshrined, but law again is principled behaviour. It is ethical behaviour, Mister Tempels, that we all accept and observe. Yet, apart from law, there is economics. Trade and barter makes the world go around. It cannot be confounded! And yet again Great Society in its wisdom has recognised that there cannot be valued employment for all and sundry. There simply cannot be that much legitimate value creation. We hold it to be true that *to serve and disserve preserves our balance.* However, there comes the lacuna …"

"Sorry, Sah".

"The hole in the patchwork – the seamstress's one in a million oversight; the dilemma if you like."

"I see, Sah".

"Science tells us that the universe is served by the fusion of the positive with the negative. We have black and white, we have pro and contra and we have form and abstract. The balance is a sensitive one. We have to have entrepreneurship for value creation and simply said we have to have a black entrepreneurship for the non-value creators too. There's the symmetry of the inverse and converse. In the balance we need a wealth creation scheme for the underclasses. We cannot house every villain in a prison or fund every miscreant from our dole. In short we cannot be too overzealous with our prosecutions. The fundaments of the natural system would dissipate and die, Sir!"

"I am of one with you, Sah!

"Good, kind Mister Tempels. Every enterprise should have a code that we all buy into, and that now brings me to the enterprise in question. Do you know of State's Prosecutor Lartal?".

"Aye, Sah, I know of her, but have not had the pleasure of meeting her as yet. She has the reputation of being a veritable avenging harridan amongst my fraternity. I must say in the world of my living market she is much feared and despised."

"Exactly! And that is why something must be done with her. Mister Tempels, I am a man of impeccable connections going to the highest echelons of Great Society. Massi Burgess herself is godmother to my younger daughter and the finest of the elites dine at my table. Just so you should know; I have taken soundings at the highest levels of state about this enterprise which should be considered an "opaque" operation. My superiors have concluded that Miss Lartal is a loose cannon who needs to be removed from the deck that she is so seriously damaging. Her prosecution of the thieving class is such now that it will upset the balance of our black economy and will only lead to insurrection amongst our counter-professionals and immigrant communities. Such potential insurrection is too great a risk. It has to be snuffed out. Miss Lartal has to depart the scene of her crime for the greater good of Great Society, and this is where you step in Mister Tempels as we in office cannot do something officially about the problem. You are not in office. Unofficial so to speak!", HBB guffawed.

It all sounded quite convincing and reasonable to Kurt Tempels. 'Let's go with this flow of his and see where it leads us', he thought.

"The symmetry of the universe. That's why you are here Tempels! Mister Oiler please explain the particulars of the devising", called Belsingham.

Oiler approached from the low light to take a chair next to Tempels.

"Mister Tempels, I believe that you have knowledge of persons skilled in the arts of abduction. You yourself may be adept at these particularly when it comes to matters of faith", began Angus Oiler.

"I don't know where such mischief comes from!", retorted Tempels.

"And if it weren't mischief? If it were a kilo sack of sovereigns like this one just here?" Oiler moved to open the sack and clasped a handful of sovereigns. "Nothing as textural as the feel of gold in hand, wouldn't you say?"

"I'm listening, Mister Oiler".

"Well, Great Society can make certain deals which are not declared to the revenue collectors. One of them is this transaction in question. The abduction of Fumi Lartal does not need to be passed over the books Mister Tempels. It's a sack full of gold and no questions asked for her abduction and delivery to a remote farm known as Marmalade Fields in Ladrokeshire. We don't mind you being a little rough with the package to be delivered; just that the package is delivered, shall we say, in substantially working order. A little shaken up that package may be, but essentially there should be no record of its despatch. Once you get the package to the farm we'll have someone on the ground to take it from there. We'll pay you a third now and the remaining two-thirds on delivery. What is paramount is that absolutely no-one is aware of this transaction. If not, Sah, you run the jeopardy of being such a transaction yourself or worse. Do you understand?"

"I understand", replied Tempels a little caustically. "And if hypothetically one were to do such a thing, then one might require an accomplice to help with the shipping".

"I don't want a veritable army involved!", snapped Belsingham.

"Well, I was thinking that such an accomplice would be innocent as to what was actually going on. One could work diligently to ensuring that the accomplice is doing the co-work on entirely different terms and should anything go wrong in the execution of the delivery one could fit this accomplice up as the perpetrator of some hare-brained scheme of revenge against the honourable Miss Lartal. Every shipment package should have way insurance, wouldn't you agree as men of commerce?"

"I grant you latitude on that basis as a seafaring man Mister Tempels", responded Belsingham, "but you absolutely must ensure there is no foul-up leading back to this present creation, otherwise you will be turning in the waters also like the seafaring ships!"

"Maybe under the bows of the seafaring ships", added Angus Oiler.

"I understand you good, kind patron", said Kurt Tempels. "Allow me to conceive a little more in further planning to get us this package to ah ..... Mustard Flats?"

"The farm is called Marmalade Fields", snapped Oiler.

"Yes, Marmalade Fields", rejoined Tempels. "I saw something that happened this very afternoon involving the very father of Fumi Lartal. Quite an altercation concerning a bobotie, a cat and a fat feller which by the purest coincidence may give rise to an immaculate plan."

"You talk cryptically, Sir", said Belsingham.

"That's because the code is in the devising in my mind, Sah. I may have our "accomplice" and "fall guy", but I only need now to fashion it into a battle formation. I accept the assignment, or consignment, but allow me a couple of days to ponder through its execution".

"Very well, Mister Tempels. Oiler will be in contact with you the third day after this. Oiler show him out, would you?"

Kurt Tempels made to leave the office in the company of Angus Oiler.

"Oh, Tempels! Make sure the plan is good", ordered Belsingham.

" I will, Sah.".

The very next morning Kurt Tempels, Purveyor of Fine Plans was at the back of his stall cogitating upon big plans when per chance Bobotie Bruce fortuitously called.

'Sand have Salt!', thought Tempels, 'my faith hath a way of stitching things together. Fuck State Prosecutor Belsingham and his lacunae. Thy People come!'

Arnold Copperfield imagined he had a son, but that did not stop him waking. Even he had to give up dark thoughts to the banality of nature, so he found himself waking to the sound of the cockerel, the distant mooing of cows and the ripeness of the smell of the country. The light appeared dim as if the day were dawning or the opposite. He noticed that he lay on old straw and was situated in a cell in what appeared to be some sort of big barn house. With his fear of dying in the night with no hope of reviving, he was always extremely relieved to wake again, so that in the abandoning of his dark ruminations he could that next day glean some further glimmer of hope in that he had a further fresh day to live. Nevertheless, he registered perturbation to see that his cell had all the appearance of a prison cell with its iron bars and dungeon trappings. It looked serious; it looked like this was no small time hoaxer in charge of the escapade. This was no garden party. The seriousness of the situation momentarily made him feel helplessly hopeless and he let out a little cry.

"Hello, Sir!"

Copperfield was mightily disoriented and allowed his little cry to translate into utter abject sobbing.

"Ho Sir! Be upstanding!"

Copperfield pitched his perception to reality and began to take in the wider picture. There was a cell adjoining his. In it was a young woman. An attractive one too, although she looked as if she had been knocked around a bit. Unlike him she was chained by her arms to the wall of her prison. 'Even more of a serious predicament', mused Copperfield. 'At least I am free to scratch around the empire of my cell'.

" I am Fumi Lartal, Sir,", she introduced, "and I have been abducted unlawfully by these villains whoever they are."

"I see. I see". Copperfield felt that it would be good form to sound sympathetic bearing in mind that she was chained and all. She looked really like a maiden in need of a gutsy hero. "Why have you been kidnapped, lady? I realise that my situation here is because I inadvertently got caught up in your kidnap operation."

"I have no idea. The only thing that I might hazard is that it's because I am state's prosecutor and senior chamberlain, and as I prosecute my job well I have likely made a number of enemies in the criminal fraternity who indubitably would be glad to see me out of the way. And you Sir? How did you come to be in this pretty pass with me in this den of iniquity?"

"Well ..", Copperfield stumbled, "a long story though perhaps not as long as yours, but nevertheless first let me introduce myself too for I am Arnold Copperfield, Justice of the Peace and Squire of Cribbers Hall; an upstanding gentlemen in the all!", he added. "I fear that I am your fellow prisoner, Marm, by the mere fact that I accidentally came across the ruffians who apprehended you in the middle of the night on the road near to my estate. As a JP out for my evening stroll it is incumbent of me to take up the responsibilities of the night watch. Your ruffians looked suspicious so I challenged them as to their business after nightfall and was met by the way of answer with a loaded blunderbuss to my temple." Copperfield skirted away from the less salubrious details of his night-time elopement with young Rosali. "So it appears that you Marm are very much here by design, while I'm merely collateral to that very design."

"I see", considered Fumi.

"That's probably why you are restrained by chains fair lady and I lie on the hay at my own reconnaissance. You are the far more valuable hostage while I just cost inconvenience. I fear that I might be dispensable while something wretched lies ahead for you."

"They might be taking us both out", further considered Fumi.

"Out where exactly?" Copperfield was unclear.

"Out of the calculus. It is criminal fraternity slang speech for murder. Alas my profession brings me into contact with such dark despicable expressions. These folk are so gutless that they cannot speak of plain murder as murder."

"That's what I was thinking, dear lady, but I dare wished not to say it. How now? What's to do?"

"We must conspire to escape Mister Copperfield, and we must do so with the utmost innovation and commitment, otherwise we are regularly done in …….. Yes, I mean brown bread ….. dead. I am afraid in my distress I become as spineless as them in avoiding putting things plain."

Copperfield got up and tried the barred door of the cell. It did not give.

"It appears that my cell has been locked and we are thoroughly restrained here with no rescuer in sight".

"I am too well aware Mister Copperfield. I fancy not that there is an elite guard of rozzers hounding down their very tracks. We can only use our own resources. I see that you are fully attired Sir in cloth of handsome cut."

"Indeed, I pride in it. As my years advance the more solicitous I have become about fine fashion and grooming."

"And amongst that handsome attire I see you wear a jaunty apricot coloured cravat. A man of your fashion no doubt holds that fine Bodander cravat together with a cravat pin, pray?"

"I can see your forensic skills as a state's lawyer. You are absolutely right."

"Then pin and persuasion are going to be the arms of our weapon of attack, and accordingly we should plan our attack on where they are weakest."

"What do you mean, lady?"

"Well what do you make of the big fat one?"

"The fat one? Is one of our assailants fat?"

"I refer to the more portly of our assailants. He comes across as a little less brutal than the other two, don't you think?"

"Got it! Yes, you are right. He seems less a scoundrel than the other two; more a reluctant accomplice, I would say. I have the feeling that he has been a little pressganged into the whole affair, and he is definitely more moderate of tone and action than the other two."

"I feel that too, even though he was the one who originally abducted me in the carriage of the trahere. I discerned the feeling too that he was being leveraged into this escapade. Also ... and how can I put this? .... I think he is a little sweet on me. Bearing in mind that he is less enthusiastic than the other two in the full prosecution of this misadventure, and that he could be influenced by my let's say – "engaging smile", then on that basis the only desperate plan I can come up with is to get my release from these chains on the basis of me offering my body to him and in the process of the very carnal act disarm him with your sharp cravat pin. What say you? Can we operate such a plan of action?"

"You mean to seduce and then submit to him? Marm, on your honour, I entreat you not!", implored Copperfield.

"I'm afraid its life before honour, Mister Copperfield. For all the ethics we learn, it is always the case that life is more sacred than honour; it's just that we should never put ourselves into a position in which we have to trade off one against the other. I console myself that it was not through my actions that I was put into this predicament."

"I understand, Miss Lartal. Then it is the greatest plan we have available at the moment. You will seek to seduce the chubby one and in his rapture disarm him with my cravat pin."

"Yes, a great plan", she agreed. "And me a virgin too", she added.

"When needs must Marm", comforted Copperfield; now suddenly the more pragmatic. "Now how precisely do I get this Fabergian pin over to you? Then should you disarm that big fellow and get the keys off him, how then how do you unlock yourself with your arms in those chains? It will require extreme dexterity. Such accomplishments are made in the romantic novellas, but how you would pull it off I would not wager!"

"That is a problem that is vexing me", she confessed. "Maybe in the act of seduction I must seduce him into unmanacling me".

"Oh, Miss Lartal, I have been thinking of my death for a long number of years now, so long that I wonder if I ever had any life, but I never thought that my nemesis would come about in such a dramatic manner. I just thought simply that one day I would wake up dead. I'm extremely perturbed by our predicament. Extremely perturbed."

"Steel yourself fine Sir! At least you'll go down fighting. Not for us the slow descent to permanent decrepitude."

"I don't doubt it, Miss Lartal."

Jan Gloop was ruminating with a purpose on the further plan. It had been made clear by Belsingham that the design was to hurt and humiliate the captive before selling her on to slavery. Mister Belsingham expected artistry. Gloop was in the farmhouse at Marmalade Fields with his fellow conspirers Kurt Tempels and Jimmy Suzuki.

"We have to take her down a peg or two, gents", mused Gloop. "What say you? How do we do that?"

"Well she's all trussed up and ready to shag, is she not Mister Gloop? Methinks in such a position she is desirous of a bit of rough. Her cultivation is in want of such an education", volunteered Kurt Tempels.

In Jimmy's mind though there was undergoing a quite different situation. In his mind there was a fragile beautiful human being; a being you could love. To have her smile at you every day would be to be living in a dream, and these two ruffians are plotting abuse and horror to her. It could not be countenanced.

"A capital proposal, Mister Tempels", considered Gloop. "And who should have the honour?"

"Why Mister Suzuki, of course. She should receive all that negative psyche from her very abductor. Miss Lartal associates all her present travail with her abductor from her trahere compartment", smirked Tempels.

"Are your love juices just ready to explode, Mister Suzuki?", enquired Gloop.

Jimmy made a calculation. He was starting to have strong feelings for their feisty yet vulnerable captive and did not want things to go badly for her. This whole thing had started with revenge for a cat and was escalating into unspeakable acts. Better he took the lead role in what was being proposed rather than the odious Gloop or Tempels he considered. It would be hard to talk them out of the plan so it would be better to go along with it, but on his own terms.

"Or an old fashioned gang bang", countered Tempels.

"No, I think I'm peppy enough". Jimmy sounded convincing. "I'm ready to ram some sense into her", he grinned. "But I don't want any leering audience like you two when I do!"

"Then we better take that old Copperfield out of the barn also", proposed Tempels.

"No, he's alright there. His venerable presence will simply add to her humiliation. It will shame her that one of her cultured class was here to witness her being taken down by my trusty peg!"

At that his two accomplices guffawed with laughter.

"You are a spotted hound, Mister Suzuki!", belted Gloop.

"I'll be about my business then", said Jimmy.

"Give good report", smiled Jan Gloop.

Arnold Copperfield stared at the gold cravat pin he was holding in his fingers.

"I'll have to throw it very exactly to you so that you are able to obtain it bearing in mind that you are lying manacled to the wall. In such circumstances a very expert lob of precise placement will be needed. Please take into account though Miss Lartal that I did not make the school team for wicket-taking. Regrettably I have always been cack-handed, and, for that matter, it is probably consistent to report that I have never learned to play music, or indeed, play music very fluently from the female form for that matter."

"This is very interesting Mister Copperfield, - and I look forward to many interesting conversations on such with you once we have retrieved our liberty -, but I really think you should now make an attempt to get the pin over to me. I am sure that you have enough accuracy to toss the thing in the region of my person. From the bars of your cell we cannot be more than eight feet apart. Remember Sir that I still have within my will plenty of ambidextrous capability in my legs and feet should your lob fall short. I am sure that the brave wicket-taker will now surface in this great hour of need!"

"Just so, just so, fair lady. I shall now come out to my maximum extension and toss it to you!"

"What could sound more inviting, Mister Copperfield!"

Copperfield moved and was preparing the final trajectory for the tossing of the cravat pin when Jimmy Suzuki burst in quite startling Copperfield and causing him to drop the cravat pin just inside the confines of Fumi's cell.

"You wanting to get close to the young lady, Mister Copperfield?"

"No, not all. My throat is quite dry and dusty and the dear lady had trouble hearing me with this croaky voice I have at present. Hence the need to move closer."

"Conspiring then, were you?"

Copperfield look abashed and was quiet.

"Well your jailer's back to look after you. My first responsibility is to ensure proper maintenance of the merchandise. Now I don't think that any experienced slave trader is going to think that you are a virgin, Miss, but there will be the expectation that your womanly parts are homely and give off fair affection. So on that I have been asked to give my warranty!"

"I am a virgin", said Fumi quietly.

"Miss Lartal …", croaked Copperfield.

"What?", resounded Jimmy.

"You can give any slave trader you like a warranty on my virginity", replied Fumi.

"That puts a different shine on things", said Jimmy.

"For pity sake. Why?" Arnold Copperfield wanted to know.

"Because the stranger and more barbaric clients of the slave traders, that we are soon to negotiate with, apparently would always prize most handsomely a virgin. Particularly one of your age, beauty and intellect Miss Lartal. These more unusual clients put out hefty bounties for virgins and are wont to desire cruel and unusual punishments put on to the flesh of maidenhood. Virginity and barbarity are one of the universal pairs. You've heard of the stranger customs of these islands. Sex and religious practice ally themselves commonly. No doubt you have heard of the even stranger customs of folk across in the Orient. There are persons who will pay absolute top premium for the combination of virginity and intelligence such as yours. Even more for a virgin who has achieved a certain ripeness such as yours. Virgins are particularly sought after for debasing and dehumanising punishment. There are cruel persons who would relish taking your tongue out just to stop the flow of your intelligence, before then taking your maidenhood by using bizarre instruments. They would delight in torturing your mind simultaneous with your body. If you were deflowered already then probably you would just go as some house or boudoir slave to some tin-pot Oriental or sandraker".

Jimmy had been unaware of what the effect of his statement would be. There was ashen silence. Both his captives seemed totally taken aback by what he had said.

Then after what seemed a monumental pause in the dialogue.

"Are you offering to take my virginity?"

Jimmy was flabbergasted.

"Well, I actually had come to rape you which I had been ordered to do by my two seniors in this enterprise."

"O, happy circumstance then", she said and smiled.

Jimmy admired how she kept her humour under such grave circumstances.

"But, seriously now. It could put you in a more secure circumstance", Jimmy countered. "Particularly if we translate into an act of lovemaking from sexual assault. The one thing you do not wish to be is a virgin at the time you are passed on to the traders."

"I think you just want to get your end away, but don't want to force it", she taunted. "On the other hand, you could just simply let me go. That way I wouldn't have to learn carnal knowledge or slavery, and there goes your moral dilemma".

"Be Gad. The lady has a point!", seconded Copperfield.

"So many choices", mused Jimmy unlocking the cell door and withdrawing a sharp looking knife from a halter on his trousers. He walked straight over to Fumi and punched her true in the left eye. Fumi screamed with a venom and Copperfield voiced strongly his protestations. Jimmy forthwith took the knife and started to shred away at Fumi's petticoats and bodice.

"Don't struggle so much, otherwise you will get cut by this knife!"

Fumi screamed stronger. "So you are to rape me you, villain!"

"It's better for that way it to seem and it will seem that way if I destroy all the fine work of your seamstress! Relax."

"What?"

"What I'm telling you Miss Lartal, and your chivalrous champion opposite, is that I will let you go, but it has to be later when my two charming compadres are asleep. Meanwhile we must maintain authenticity. Now that I have bashed you about a bit, kindly allow me to masturbate over your thigh, Miss Lartal."

"What?"

"What?", repeated Arnold Copperfield.

"My charming companions", started Jimmy "are probably assuming that you are not a virgin, so they are not expecting a pool of blood in these proceedings exactly. However, they are expecting some unseemly evidence from an act of sexual violence and debasement of the sort they have wanted to engineer. They will no doubt wish to give you some sort of cursory inspection to add to the humiliation. Best that they see some sort of discharge of gooiness consistent with the fact that you did not volunteer me free access. It has to be messy, right? With the two free of suspicious thought and less inclined to vigilance, I'll attempt to spring you both deep in the night".

"You, Sir, are deranged!", spat Copperfield.

"Wait, kind Sir! He may a have a point", Fumi said. "Mister Copperfield, the other two of our captors will be looking for some evidence of sexual congress. Mister … here, sorry I don't know your name …."

"Suzuki is my name, and I give you my name freely so that you can put trust in me."

"Mister Suzuki", Fumi continued, "is obviously mindful to help us. In our dealings in this encounter so far he has evinced more human decency by far than the other two miscreants. As a lawyer I recognise that there is always a need to manage expectations, and, I can surmise that Mister Suzuki's description of the expectations of the other two parties to be a realistic one. Their expectations will require that degree of authenticity that Mister Suzuki has offered. Are you afraid of the other two, Mister Suzuki?"

"Indeed I am, Marm. I don't know what pernicious evil and craziness those two came possessed with. It is really best that we conform to the picture they will now be painting in their heads."

"Then Mister Suzuki, I give you leave to disperse your fluids over me. Pray turn away Mister Copperfield".

"Dear lady", whined Copperfield and turned his face in to the straw.

"I'm sorry Miss, but I'm quite stored. It has been some time since I've opportunity", explained Jimmy. "Nevertheless, it should give us ample to make the best artistic impression".

"I understand that you mean no harm. Please do your stuff and don't hold back on my sensibilities."

Jimmy unhitched his breeches and withdrew his member. It was not stiff, but rather perturbed at the peculiarity of the place and position it was starring in. Jimmy tried some rubbing. He thought about Mona La Car. He visioned up Miss Pussy and the tarts on the waterfront, but his prick had transformed into a pragmatist calculating chances of escape refusing to acknowledge that he was a key player in the plan.

"It's no good. My John Henry is just limp and flaccid as if he has a mind of his own".

"I bet that he has a dirty mind still", countered Fumi. "Maybe he wants some dirty talk from me."

"Oh, please Miss Lartal. Think about our reputations", lamented Copperfield.

"Screw our reputations. We're dirty talking for our lives now".

"Yes dirty talk for my dirty willy." Jimmy's voice sounded remote and not quite in him.

"Yes he's a dirty boy", reproached Fumi Lartal. She knew how to follow a brief. She brought all her inquisitorial prowess to bear. " I expect he's been put into all sorts of dirty places. Like in your dirty fist. Like in dirty Mister Copperfield's mouth too!."

"Miss Lartal!"

Fumi has started to groan and is biting her lip ecstatically. "Now he wants to get into my dirty pussy, and if he does I'll give it a proper grinding in my cunt. I'll grind him down so hard he'll never get out. Perhaps big willy is not man enough to take on my comely cunt." Putting on a full islands lilt to her voice. "Big willy want to spill his load over me, but ain't no man enough to explore my ravenous cunty".

Jimmy started to moan. The primeval willy baiting was hitting a core in him. It was certainly working a trick on the capricious John Henry. It was pretty talk.

"Go on! Go On! Spill it over my luscious thigh, you big thick dick! You're obviously not man enough to bring me to orgasm. The only thing you can do is just get to your own gratification. Spill it! Spill it you little prick! Spill it, big dick."

Jimmy was sweating now and grunting in primordial ecstasy.

"Spunk it out loser! All over me! Come together right now over me."

Free abandon has been reached and Fumi's white left thigh is festooned with Jimmy's glue.

"By my top hat, for one who is a virgin you can certainly talk the language of the slut", observed Copperfield.

Fumi Lartal laughed. She looked surprised with herself yet coquettish.

"I have been a frequent observer of the criminal classes!", she riposted. She looked happy enough. "Now spread it around for artistic impression using that big thick member so that we can get as accurate a fabrication that we can."

"Yes, Marm", Jimmy dutifully complied.

"So what's next?", Fumi has in her induced orgasmic wriggling worked up a head of sweat adding to the artistic impression.

"Well my two good hearts will be waiting for news as to your dishonour. We have talked a lot, so I better get back to report to them. They'll be wanting to come in here and taunt you, and so in the meanwhile I'll have to figure a plan of escape. So hold your nerve and act it out appropriately. You too, Mister Copperfield".

And with that Jimmy hitched up his breeches and sauntered out of the barn into the evening.

"So what are Bellingham's precise instructions?", asked Kurt Tempels.

"To kill her spirit completely", replied Gloop.

"Being?", quizzed Tempels.

"I don't know what it is with our benefactor and Miss Lartal. There is also Lord Roy Gibbons lurking somewhere in the background on this. So you see, it is serious stuff. My instructions are that she is to suffer. Belsingham would like it that, via our slave traders, she be placed as a slave somewhere where she would have a very menial position. Somewhere where she would have only physical drudgery with no access to books or learning, a position which affords her no intellectual stimulation or societal contact with like minds. The lady they say is a very intellectual tour de force; quite possibly a genius. She has the skills set to become a leader in Great Society. There is a radical edge to her. She could be a bit of a reformer. Belsingham wants that intellect ground down and then expunged. He wants to punish that great intellect of hers. He wants a long suffering where she recognises day in and day out her intellectual starvation. Whilst recognising that she might be a threat to the state – she could be a future problem for Great Society – I would say that there is something very personal in all this. It seems that she managed to humiliate Belsingham in his public position. Made him look foolish in front of the Law Minister. Same with Gibbons and her. Some real personal sleight for Gibbons, but you would have to speak to Angus Oiler for more on that particular animus".

"Yes, there appears to be an element of revenge in all this", agreed Tempels, "but who are we to care when it allows us to do the work we love Mister Gloop!", and then he warmly clapped Gloop on the back.

At this point Jimmy returned from the exertions of his defilements.

"It's Jimmy Ram Mister Rod", gloated Tempels. "Did you ram her good?"

"I rammed and crammed into that tight sweet little clitty, and oh did she resist Mister Tempels. She fought like a wild cat. It was hot and exciting and the sense of defilement was added to by the constant limp admonishments of old man Copperfield! I'll jerk off thinking of that scene again. My, my, Lady Muck who wouldn't deign to cast an eye at worthless Jimmy ... well she had to get really close to me just now. I raped her entirely. From ranging my sweaty balls across her sensitive nostrils to my porker ram raiding her sweet treasure house. By Gad, that was uplifting. She was uplifted by me and then cast down in the morass you will find her broken and humiliated."

Jimmy surprised himself with the depictions of his villainy.

"A stirring account", offered Gloop. "Let's go and take a peek at the little bitch".

The three of them left the farmhouse together and crossed over to the barn arriving a minute later.

"How now my hearties?" shouted Tempels as he flung the barn door open.

He looked across at the dishevelled mess that was Fumi Lartal. "And how does the mistress like her new quarters? Shall I arrange for a hot bath to be drawn?"

Fumi managed to smile defiantly and hold her tongue against this baiting. Jan Gloop did not like that spirited demeanour.

"That's an excellent idea. We will have a scalding hot bath prepared to cook this particular lobster. For you, slut, are a mere crustacean in the eyes or our benefactors and employers. Our orders are to sell you into a lifetime of unremitting foul slavery and in the process to engage upon you all suffering that we can humanly imagine."

"Well that limp dick you sent in here previously precisely adds up to the fact that you have limited imagination! Is that all you can humanly imagine? Probably your little finger is even limper and that's why you can only imagine! Mind you, your limp dicks are horrible to imagine. I give you that", and spat in the general direction of Gloop.

'She's pushing it too far', thought Jimmy and fearing the worse. Gloop was already striding into her cell with a malign purpose.

"There you go", Fumi further taunted. "I'm sure that what's grabs your imagination to perform down here in another man's ejaculate! Do you want to clean me up first?", she demanded provocatively. Gloop could not but notice a large glop of semen resting on her thigh. It was evident with her arms restrained by the manacles to the wall that she could not have tidied it away.

"Be upstanding your Honour", urged Jimmy. "You will catch nothing from it. I am entirely clear of the pox and any form of perverse skin aberration".

Gloop observed Jimmy, strode forward and almost as an afterthought punched Fumi Lartal in the other eye. He then moved away from Fumi. He obviously did not want to go exploring after Jimmy, notwithstanding the personal guarantees.

'Two shiners will be a small price for deliverance', thought Jimmy.

"Have her cleaned up first thing in the morning and then have her wrapped up as merchandise for the slave market. We'll need to think about presentation, but I was thinking old style Oriental. I could have her stark naked and lead her into the market with a line attached to nipple clasps. What do you think, Tempels? I've always wanted to try the grand entrance once in my life. The old geezer can be sold too, but we can kill him if we are unable to raise a sou on his wrinkly flesh."

"It will be done with relish", rasped Tempels.

'I better have a pretty good plan pretty sharpish', considered Jimmy. 'This could be turning quite ugly'.

"See how he sleeps now", said the young Belsingham. "That's the effect of the chloroform. You will find him pliant and malleable now. Remember the discourse of our inestimable mentor, Professor Smart. Remember life is but a dream".

A rather unconfident and hesitant Alms-Master David Lincoln stepped forward towards the subject. The first subject that he had to perform high art social place conditioning on.

But Jimmy was sleeping now. Sleeping disturbed like a kicked dog and yet still chasing that elusive bunny rabbit. He was going down the hole after it; into the warren where all the dark snuffly rabbits lived. They might obliterate him with their silent unreleased outrage.

"Jimmy, you must listen to me now", murmured Lincoln.

"Say it like you believe it", whispered Belsingham.

"Jimmy, you must listen to me now", firmly spoke the Alms-Master David Lincoln. "Jimmy you are going to listen to what I say. Listen carefully. Then you are going to live the dream".

Andrew Brown : Walks for the Unemployed

Jimmy saw that he was just a big running slavering dog. A dog that had caught himself in a dark tight place. He was far away from sunlight. Far away from his master's voice. A voice that fed and sustained him. Yet he wanted to follow that urge to burrow further and reap carnage on all these dark bunny rabbits. He could feel them blending into the blackness emanating a pure and silent disdain. He could imagine their fine whiskers expressing their supreme displeasure and contempt for him. A rogue dog whose only business is to follow the sensation of his slavering tongue. A free slavering primeval spirit, but all those dark bunnies were united against him now. He could not see or identify it anymore, but he could really feel it. Their dark displeasure was on his slavering tongue. It was like biting into flesh that had been poisoned.

Jimmy saw that he was a big dog. He was strong. He could overcome these little dark bunnies. He could reap carnage on their furry flesh. He just had to bite and chew and do what's natural to achieve the rest. He was a strong dog, a young hound, but the pain, it was too strong and he felt his force leaving him.

Jimmy saw his owner kindly stroke him and his big slavering tongue rasped with pleasure.

"Been chasing too many bitches, has he?", said the man in white.

His owner smiled and nodded his head and Jimmy wagged his tail. We wag our tails even though none of us knows what befalls us next.

Laudanum.

"For the sterilisation".

The owner smiled and nodded his head.

"The surgical procedure done at the same time as the hypnotic conditioning reinforces the physical impairment", explained Belsingham. "He will waken with the firm conviction that his sterilisation is to prevent him bringing other rejects into the world. He will have reinforced that his blood line is unworthy of further procreation. It was important that we managed both the mental conditioning and the physical impairment in tandem. I am sorry you had to experience all the surgical parts, David, but you did an excellent job exercising the social place conditioning right through the surgical intervention."

Jimmy dreamt on.

Jimmy dreams on. Now he is a butcher lovingly grinding his sharp knives. He had to sharpen his sharp knives as he was among murderers and other ne'er-do-wells.

'Let Monday come', and so it did for Sir John J. Perriwinkle.

JaJa Point was out in the sugar mountains and normally about an hour's carriage drive from Sir John's estate at Chatham Cheap. However, it was October and the rainy season had started to set in. The road was turning to mud and the stage-horses were making tough going of it, especially as the road to the point was steep, and also due to the water vapour mist becoming thicker through the ascent the four horses were tentative in their progress.

Sir John was not concerned. They would wait on him and he was glad of the fresh dampness in the air ridding him of the noxious heat of the night. The mist enveloped the carriage and in the slow progress Sir John could not discern much out of the open portcullis, but he was able to discern much of the noise all around him. The noise of the yellow pappawaks, the noise of the Gringer Monkeys and Hoolan-Men clambering through the rain forested trees – the sheer wall of noise of the adjoining jungle. Then gradually he detected an amber glow in the mist and then slowly but surely they were out of the mist and into gilded sunlight where heat was burning away moisture.

"I see the Astronomy to port your Worship", called the rear outrider footman.

Sir John moved across the width of the closed carriage to strain to see from the left side the beautiful building known as the Astronomy. And there he did. A beautiful large onion dome in orange cream alabaster. An onion rising in the sky some two hundred feet and housing the finest astronomical telescope in the Occident.

Sir John's coach pulled into the neat entrance of the Astronomy where a delegation of liverymen was there to welcome him.

"The Baronet of Sandown!", called the most important looking one in Royal Society livery and that call was relayed from driveway to building interior. "Baronet of Sandown! ... Baronet Sandown!". This again was of no consequence to Sir John as it was quite the normal thing for a great patron such as himself to come and visit the patronised. There was no need for discretion for this site visit.

"Make way! Make way for the Baronet of Sandown!", with much scraping and scrambling and way was made for the Baronet to withdraw from his carriage appreciating the great etiquette paid to him whilst at the same dissembling from it with some disgust.

"My dear Sir John! I am so glad that you have made it safely through the storm and mist". It was Professor Riddell. "Well come Sir! Well come indeed".

"I thank thee, Sir", and Sir John ostentatiously waved a perfumed lace handkerchief as if to obliterate the rudeness of the open country air.

The Astrologer Royal led him into the yawning chasm of the great observatory building.

"Would you like a quick tour Sir John?"

"No. Let's get on with it."

" A glass of island tea or a Chablis perhaps?"

"No. Let's cut to the chase. Is your honest broker here yet?"

"He is indeed and ready to counsel you on the transaction".

"Show me to him, please. I presume he gets his cut from Catcaldis". Sir John has lowered his voice.

"He may well do, Sir John. I am not such of a business persuasion to opine truly, but you will find in the costings an agent arrangement fee that allows a government man to forget conveniently a windfall in war office provisions which does not in fact transpire. We might pay a handsome price for such selective memory".

"Ah well, let's see then", whispered the benefactor.

"Did you digest the detailed drawings and calculations on the BWT, Sir John?", also in conspiratorial tone.

"Alas, they are plain indigestible for me, and I can hardly call in my own experts such is the extreme secrecy of this project. I do trust in the integrity of Doctor Daedalus and yourself, Professor. Let's see the middle-man and the colour of his money".

Professor Riddell started to lead off.

"This business associate .."

"Mister Belsingham".

"Yes. What reason was he given for your involvement in the transaction bearing in mind that the fighting navy is the purported intended beneficiary?"

"Simple answer for that, Sir John. You contacted me to put enquiries out on the finance as no-one would connect the fighting navy with the Astrologer Royal and given your high regard for secrecy it would be impossible for anyone to trace the benefactor of the war frigates by connection through me back to you".

"You are a smart fellow Riddell".

"My mother always thought so. Whilst you, Sir John, can grant the greatest mortgage a bank can receive in these here islands".

Two sly smiles reflecting back at each other.

"Come Sir John", and Sir John is led through a huge chamber of light across gantries and mezzanine floors to a small bureau at the back end of the big telescope. On the door hung the sign:

Doctor Meritorious Egregious Daedalus
Astrologer Resident

Sir John was invited to enter in by a courteous Professor Riddell and entered accordingly. Seeing Dr Daedalus, looking even more like a scruffy boffin in his ramshackle office, remarked:

"My dear good Doctor Daedalus! Thank you for allowing us use of your premises to deliberate on a delicate matter. It is something that cannot be deliberated upon in fashionable settings. Hence the subterfuge here."

Daedalus smiled and gave a barely perceptible wink while looking Sir John full in the eye and shaking his visitor's velvet gloved hand most vigorously. Sir John was glad of his glove as the Doctor's skin looked even more diseased than on their first acquaintance and the Doctor looked as if he longed to scratch at it a bit.

"You are very welcome dear benefactor. I shall make myself scarce and look at the Morovain calculations which I fully intend to present at the forthcoming Royal Society dinner in your honour".

"Good, good. Keep up the good work learned doctor", Sir John artificially gushed.

The good doctor then left, in a whirl of dust and manuscripts, furiously scratching at the nape of his neck and Sir John was able to pay attention to the other person there shadowed in the bright light by the window. As he drew closer he could discern that the gentleman was tall (over six foot), clean shaven and of muscular build. He was unusually neither ugly nor handsome. Even though he was well preserved he dressed down conservatively and not in fashionable dandy-fop vein in which Sir John preferred (and even Professor James Riddell seemed inclined to do so too). He was very morning coat and sensible riding boots, but even so one could glean instantly that he was well attired.

Riddell: "Sir John. Let me introduce you to Horatio Beeswax Belsingham Esq., Provisions Clerk to the Treasury and often confidant to Catcaldis".

"Charmed, I am sure", said the clerk.

"Shall we have some luncheon?", ventured Professor Riddell.

"Business before drowsiness", opined Sir John.

"I agree", said Belsingham, "the weather could set in bad again making our return journeys regular tiresome. Let's get direct to the matter then."

"I'll ask the cook to hold the plush pork then, shall I?", queried Riddell.

"Regrettably, yes", yawned Sir John as Riddell was already in the process of embarking to the cooking and serving staff.

"So Sir John", said the man with an appearing natural confidence, "Catcaldis Venture Financiers are most impressed with your willingness to donate largesse to Great Society in these times of national and international crisis. Catcaldis is always very supportive to infrastructure and capital projects and commends your venture. Catcaldis prides itself in its support to Great Society, whether it be directly, or, in this present case, indirectly".

"Yes, you must understand my motives. I was born pure classless with a silver spoon on my lip. It is time to give something back to Great Society. It is not as if my estates could not bear it."

"True, true. The Fighting Temeraire is a beautiful and formidable warship, so modern that is bound to secure our seaways. Great Society will be indebted to you".

"Yes, indeed and the security of our territories leads naturally to the security of the Perriwinkle commercial estates so I am not totally disinterested by honour".

"Yes, yes", smiled the government clerk, "always everything is connected. One hand washes the other", the clerk smiled smarmily.

Sir John was starting to look irritated.

"Now where are we?", it was Riddell returning to the rickety office.

Belsingham was starting to look brisk.

"Catcaldis will take your mortgage on the estate of Chatham Cheap as security on a principal loan of two hundred thousand sovereigns of this realm".

"I want all the funds transferred into my accounts within the month", countered Sir John.

"That is highly unusual. Usually they would expect disbursement against construction progress payments for the ships. Likely some ten disbursements of twenty thousand each over the next five years. That lowers the risk on your side too."

"I know, but I have some inventive solutions with my ship contractors which call for payment up front. It is imperative that I have full disposal straight away".

"Are you looking to amortise the loan over a period? That would lessen considerably any insecurity over the loan."

"No. I am looking to pay off the loan with one shot payment after five years actually."

"That will cause the interest rate to look rather heavy", breathed Belsingham. "Also, it may take considerably more application of persuasion on my part to get their senior partners to be comfortable with the unusual risks involved. My arrangement fees correspondingly rise."

Sir John was unfazed. "Tell me."

"Well with no repayment on the principal sum within five years and with the risk of you repaying it all with a shot payment at the end of the period, then we would be looking at a yearly interest rate of eight in the hundred. Also my fee would rise by ten in the hundred due to the difficulty aspects".

"That means Sir John would have to service an interest payment of sixteen thousand sovereigns per year and eighty thousand in total over the five year period", clarified Riddell.

"Exactly", confirmed Belsingham.

Sir John intently studied Horatio Belsingham. The man was friendly and cordial enough, but Sir John felt that there was something deeply repulsive about him. He looked like the very type who would have a custodian position in Great Society; ambitious, venal, calculating. As a member of the old order Sir John found it easy to find himself despising these new militants. He could not quite put his finger on it, but he felt that there was something dangerous about Belsingham. Something treacherous that he rather not be too closely acquainted with. He suddenly felt that he needed to get the transaction done, and in getting it done not wanting to have much truck with Belsingham.

"I'll take it", he said abruptly and it seemed that silently within both Belsingham and Riddell that they were surprised, or maybe rather that they were actually relieved. 'Belsingham wants his money, but was expecting more of a fight for it', concluded Sir John.

"You are authorised to propose these terms, despite their highly unusual aspects?", enquired Sir John.

"A loan of two hundred thousand sovereigns at eight over the hundred cost of money for a five year term. Principal to be paid in full after the term of five years with a first ranking mortgage over the estate of Chatham Cheap securing the loan from Catcaldis."

"Precisely", said Sir John in mock resignation.

"It will take some persuasion to get the financiers on board. Nevertheless, I am confident that I can succeed given the aspects of national security that come with it. I am confident to go with it as your collateral is impeccable and once I have succeeded I'll have the papers drawn up and passed to Riddell for review", informed Belsingham.

"You know that Chatham is worth more than that, don't you?", asked Sir John.

"Do you offer other collateral then? Chatham Cheap is gilt-edged as far as my associates are concerned. Other forms of security can be accepted, but will take some time to review. Chatham is peerless security and with it the loan can be expedited quickly."

"The shipyards need to be commissioned soon, Sir John", urged Professor Riddell.

"Yes, we cannot have Jack Tar waiting", agreed Sir John. "Have the papers drawn up and sent to the good Professor for his review. Time is of the essence in this endeavour".

"It shall be done. Adieu!", snapped Belsingham and he was out of the room with one tap of his walking cane on the writing desk.

"Most excellent", remarked Riddell as soon as Belsingham was out of the room. "The most desired outcome, Sir John".

"What?", he snapped. "That you will get your hands on my money. The money that you need for your project!".

"Our project", clarified Riddell. "For we are partners, and consider this: Only three partners on the greatest and most valuable enterprise man has ever entered into. Consider what we plan to do and once have done it, the amount of time you will have to be able to accumulate multiple fortunes, the knowledge you will learn and the happiness you will garner by sidestepping death. And you will remain as you are John; a fine specimen of a man at the height of his powers! This is a gift greater than all of the gifts the world has even seen. It is the ultimate", he rasped.

"Be Gad, Sir! A fine specimen of a man. You sound as if you wish to bed me!", Sir John laughed.

"I'll call Daedalus back in", snickered Riddell.

"Wait a moment. Methinks I should have my advocate, Sir Stanley Slouce, look over the drafted finance documents once they are ready. He has a great eye for spotting risky areas and imprudent commitments."

"Agreed that Stanley is the best in the business for contract law, but by doing so we do again run the risk of exposing our most secret enterprise. Let me speak to Doctor Daedalus first. As the genius behind this, I feel he should be consulted."

"No. Fine. Leave it." Sir John rapped the desk top with his fingers. "You are right we are select partners. We should handle this as a matter of trust together. You and I, James, shall review the finance documents together. We'll leave the doctor to his tenderer contraption calculations".

"Good judgment, Sir John. I feel that our enterprise is making a splendid start and we are right on ticket to realise a Big Warp Tenderer – a most beautiful contraption - at the time we have forecasted. Let me get Daedalus in here so that he can give you the latest status."

"And tell them to bring that luncheon in here after all. I'm now hungry enough to eat a whole planetary constellation!".

The three partners talked through the afternoon developing and reengaging with the awesome plan of Doctor Egregious Daedalus. Sir John J. Perriwinkle had decided to embrace his destiny full heartedly trusting the true hearted nature of his cohorts.

It was dark and sweaty in the stables of the old run-down farm. The only livestock were the live humans being Arnold Copperfield and Fumi Lartal. Arnold Copperfield Esq. could not sleep. It was not for the discomfort, it was just his habit to be awake in the middle of the night and he listened to the shallow sleep breathing of Fumi Lartal. He imagined her breast rising and falling with her breath and he was strangely aroused. He knew that he had become old, but still found young women attractive and in a strange way there was a consciousness within him that though itself attractive and appealing. An old identity that refused logic and experience; a consciousness that dawdled in the light of the past reluctant to move on. An old identity that was and is him. He listened to Fumi's breathing and vainly hoped that she saw the old him; knew what he had been like.

"What ho, Mister Copperfield! Still bearing up?"

He had forgotten the strange power of women to reach you out of distant profanity.

"I thought you sleeping my dear .."

"I must have been catnapping. How it happens in these dire circumstances is beyond comprehension", she sighed.

"Well you will be sleeping forever if you don't look lively."

It is not Copperfield, but Suzuki. Somehow he has entered lightly.

"Do you have the keys?", anxiously enquired Copperfield.

"I do indeed", whispered Jimmy. "Thanks mainly to Tempels having with him a tub of rum and me volunteering to take first watch. They are in boozy sleep so we better make haste."

Jimmy unlocked both cells and then went to free off the manacles from Fumi Lartal. For Jimmy her arms were electric to the touch. He felt a bond to her and he looked upon her intently with the flickering candle that he held. She did not notice such earnestness in her relief to be released from her chains.

"Do we have a plan Mister Suzuki?", asked Copperfield solemnly as if he were tabling a motion at a shareholders meeting.

"Simply put, yes. To get out of here at high speed!"

"Do we have transport?", asked Fumi.

"Well, I'm not going to risk Big Bess. She's too clapped out to be a speed merchant. We will have to go directly by foot into the adjoining woods. I think then we can aim for the Coriander River which I would guess is not far from here. We could hopefully find a boat to speed our passage."

"What about alligators?", flustered Copperfield.

"I'm more worried about Tempels and Gloop actually. An alligator only wants to eat you. These two scoundrels will want us eaten by pain."

"Agreed", said Fumi. " We better hotfoot it out of here".

"Are you up to it, Marm?", solicitously asked Copperfield.

"Well the prospect certainly feels better than a horrendous period of devastating pain and humiliation followed by a lifetime of slavery. Yes, Sir, I am up to it. Especially if you did me the honour of lending me you top-coat; as you can see I have been rather reduced to the threadbare with my vestments!"

"But, of course", rejoined the noble Copperfield.

Jimmy smiled to himself in the darkness. At least the civilities had been done.

"Come", said the leader James Donald Suzuki.

And so it was that the fatefully brought together trio stumbled in a ramshackle way into the verdant woods on that balmy night with ironically the counter-professional leading the two esteemed professionals. Jimmy felt pioneering and proud as he pushed a way through the raskam bushes in the moonlit night. It occurred to him that he neglected to look for a weapon in the rush to facilitate the escape. He should have had a machete or a stangsword to cut a path through the ever pressing ever growing vegetation.

It was hard going during the night with Jimmy having to impress the vegetation with his full bulk as he ramrodded a path of clearance. Fumi Lartal was keeping up on his shoulder like his darling and he felt fuzzy and manly about her, though she did look a little weak probably due to lack of water. Jimmy felt like the old caveman, protector of yore. Copperfield though was struggling. He did not look fit for this tropical night jungle jaunt. His wheezing behind them and the strange hoots of the Hoolan-Men, Jimmy was starting to find it all rather unsettling.

"Can we rest for an hour, Mister Suzuki?", asked Copperfield wheezily.

"Yes, can we give him a rest, Mister Suzuki?", joined in Fumi.

"I would like to Miss. The trouble is we had no chance to cover our tracks to the woods. Come morning those two scally-wags will be able to see that we headed towards the woods and we have been clearing a fresh path for them to follow. I think it is vital that we keep pressing on until we hit that river. If they catch us before the river, then we are finished."

"He is right, Marm. I will fortify myself with new vigour so as to maintain our starting distance from our captors".

"We might have to speed up a tad then", implored Jimmy. "That Jan Gloop looks like he is a real countryman. An expeditious tracker and hunter, I would say."

"Then we better get our skates on!", injected Fumi.

They pressed on and interminably slow going it was too, but sometimes just pressing on and not thinking about it gets one an arrival somewhere. After painfully sluggish meandering through the remainder of the moonlit night the intrepid trio felt the first faint feeling of dawn. The noise of the Hoolan-Men started to abate as if their carousing were only to be done at dark, and the chirp of the birds began to hold fore as the first touches of deep red flickered the night sky, and as the sky hinted at an indistinct blue, Jimmy heard the flow of water.

"I can hear the river", he gasped. "Quick let's push down this bank and we'll be on the Coriander".

He started to slide down the bank with purpose. He could not bear to look on at his comrades. Fumi was rapidly weakening and Copperfield was starting to look just like a fleshy mass which his breeches could no longer contain. They just had to follow him this final spurt out of pure instinct.

They did.

Jimmy spotted a small wooden wharf on the placid river.

"There's a coracle boat there!", he exclaimed. "Maybe there is a village nearby and some fisherman moors it there".

"Should we try to find the village?", queried Copperfield not sounding very professional.

Jimmy felt like a steely pirate. "Too obvious, and too easy a place to get trapped by those cut-throats. Better that we get on the water. It will better afford our escape and also grant us the luxury to rest whilst we travel."

"Agreed", said the coxswain Fumi. Copperfield did not get a say. Nevertheless:

"Do you think the vessel will accommodate the three of us, Suzuki?"

"I'm hoping there will be a can to bail water, especially as I can't swim", added their leader.

"Well if we sink, I cannot imagine me rescuing you in these waters in the state I'm in".

"I can only worry about the next minute", was the stoic response.

"I need water", said Fumi.

"We better get to water", said Jimmy.

The craft appeared deserted but river-worthy. There was a bailing can therein and Jimmy used it to scoop water for Fumi. The men partook after her. The Coriander was a good freshwater river of the country and the water tasted not too bilious.

"We better get out there while we have the advantage. I expect it would take some time for those two to stumble upon some river craft. We just got lucky", mused Jimmy.

"Do you think they will be following us?", Fumi asked Jimmy. "They probably will have rude rums heads and all", she added.

"Don't doubt it. And they are fast. We only have this slim advantage".

"Set sail then Captain?", asked Copperfield with survival humour.

"Let's get to it", Jimmy commanded.

The three of them settled into the lightweight craft with cautious deportment. Jimmy pulled the line clear and started to paddle inexpertly, but to the other two he looked the epitome of competence in all aspects. Jimmy started to get a flow to his arm movements and get into rhythm with the feisty river. They were getting into the flow and were moving with accomplishment. A crane flew close and lazily over them with insouciant arrogance.

"We should have packed a picnic basket", joshed Copperfield.

Fumi Lartal smiled weakly.

"But there is some sort of bundle there", said Copperfield pointing to a bundle of cloths in one corner. "Maybe our fisherman has left some smoked fish or beef jerky", he mused hopefully. "Let's look see".

He put his hand on the bundle and it appeared to move in response.

"By Janna", Copperfield said and he was lifting up the covers to discover a small living animal. The small living animal looked back at them as if he had just been awoken rudely.

"Oh look, it's a beautiful little island sloth", exclaimed Fumi. "How cute!". She might have shrieked with glee if she had the energy.

Jimmy smiled fully as if he wanted to stroke the little monster.

Arnold Copperfield Esq. said nothing for a long short while and then screamed. He screamed with a passion. He screamed with an elemental dark fear. He screamed as if he were unworldly. By Janna, did he scream. It was astounding.

Jimmy's first reaction was why. What is the problem? His next instinct is that this primal noise is going to alert all river traffic this way. Within thirty seconds the Hoolan-Men were screeching in the hope of a continuance into another night of mad party.

"Take it away! Take it away!", screamed Copperfield.

It appeared to Jimmy that only he and Copperfield were on the coracle and he was paralysed in the vortex of Copperfield's primal scream. 'That mad fucker is going to give us away', he thought.

Fumi reintroduced herself to the reality. "But it is only a little sloth, Mister Copperfield".

Copperfield continued screaming with a new venom. How could such an old blagger produce such a noise.

"Take it away!"

And Jimmy did. He flicked the furry cutie out of the coracle and he could see its fuzzy bottom struggling with the currents to survive.

However, this did not quite do the trick as Copperfield persisted with the "Take it away" screaming as he was still living the experience of the sloth through his consciousness. Something snapped in Jimmy probably as he was still alert to his survival and wished a continuance with Fumi. It snapped in him and this meant that he suddenly and abruptly pushed Copperfield into the billowing waters of the river.

Fumi became suddenly very animated.

"Save him! Save him!", she cried.

"But I can't swim", replied Jimmy abstractly.

Fumi looked anxiously at him. "And to think that I might have loved you", she said, and that was enough to justify all the madness, all the other things that thereby transpired. With that Fumi got up and jumped after the sometime past Copperfield in the suddenly more ferocious waters of the Coriander.

Jimmy couldn't swim. Jimmy would find Fumi. Jimmy wouldn't drown. Jimmy would get the craft turned around to pick up Fumi. Jimmy would find Fumi.

Jimmy struggled to control the craft as the waters turned whiter by the second.

"Where do you think the other two got to?", asked Jan Gloop of Kurt Tempels.

They were standing on the edge of the river bank looking mistrustfully on as if there were gamekeepers contemptuous of poachers' traps.

"What's that?"

"Where do you think the other two got to?". This time shouting to be heard over the roar of the white water.

Kurt Tempels viewed the gasping form of Arnold Copperfield Esq. and said: "Drowned I should imagine".

"He must have had the foresight to jump from the boat just in time before they felt the full effects of the Trapago Rapids", conjectured Gloop.

"I guess they were blissfully unaware of those rapids. You are very lucky, Mister Copperfield Sah! You happy walrus you!", laughed Kurt Tempels and turning to Gloop said: "The governor will have to be content that she's brown bread now. You could tell him that all went to plan. He'd be none the wiser, would he?"

"I don't know", smiled Gloop sheepishly and the two sauntered off leaving Copperfield floundering on the shale river shore.

" A sloth, a sloth", murmured Copperfield deliriously. "My father said that I would live the life of the sloth. Nothing would come of me. Sloth, damn sloth".

The white water continued to roar as it always had for quite some long time.

Five: Resistance – "The Size of Jimmy"

Of course, being a counter-professional, Jimmy has a lot of time on his hands. He tries to keep going his artistic bents, especially as he has been labelled "Deviant Artist"; it was only fair to one and all to keep this perverted expression going. The problem is in the procuring of enough art materials on his paltry benefit, as well as the fact that he is not licensed at the Arts Wholesaler. He listens to the squawk-box a lot, and is especially fond of listening to the heroic exploits of *Yor Mama's So Fat FC*, particularly on their epic cup runs and last minute failures against the likes of *Weng Vengeance* or *Horrimort Rovers*. Not to mention those blue-shirted bastards who shall not be named. But besides that he actually spends a lot of time writing.

He is able to get hold of scrap paper by scrounging waste paper from the municipal rubbish bins. There are a number of professionals in the neighbourhood who have recourse to paper for professional notes, commentaries, essays, trainings and the like. Jimmy pillages what he needs; there is never a problem.

He is quite a slow writer. It is an onerous process with his stubby pencil and tattie knife with which he keeps it sharp. As a counter-professional it is difficult for him to get even a poor low grade pencil. People do not appreciate really the limitations of being a counter-professional. It is no bed of roses, despite what is said in the editorials of *The Thunderer*. Additionally, he has no writing table. He either has to lean on thick old broadsheets in bed, lean over the kitchen work surface, or, sit his papers carefully over the folds of his lap. It is a pencil manuscript. If it was good enough for the peerless Sir Jocelyn Perry and his tales of knights of lore, then it is good enough for Jimmy S.

Jimmy had resolved to write fiction, if only to blot out the humdrum of his fact; his life in fact. Jimmy does not possess a wide experience or the ability to do much research (he is only allowed entry to the Institute of the Scholars, *Poorhouse Bursary Section* for four hours on Wednesday afternoons and then he is often in competition with all the other ragged-trousered intellectuals and aspirants). Jimmy therefore has no recourse but to rely on his vivid imagination. His imagination is indeed rich, it sings and has no bounds, like the tatty starlings who fling themselves into the dusk skies. He may be slow, but he is working with continuing commitment and stamina on his complex opus *"The Bird Caged"*. He supposes that in the end inevitably it is a kind of autobiographical fictional account as it is about a social miscreant who is outrageously mistaken for a stage robber. The mistaken identity is blithely and cruelly corroborated by the fallacious evidence of a beautiful but small-minded duchess whose shameless sexual advances had been spurned by the heroic central character and for which she was exacting cruel revenge, resulting in the valiant protagonist, Cliff Citro, being convicted and consigned to the horrible bird island of Shamano where prisoners are forced to work unrelentingly all day to gather monster bird droppings, known as gagga-guano, which the dissolute rich citizens of Oriens use as a druggie ingredient in their scandalous psychedelic consume soups. Cliff Citro's situation is a fantastic fit-up and gross miscarriage of justice. Anyone rational, if they weighed up the evidence dispassionately, would see clearly that it is a diabolical fit-up. It would be an easy matter for just someone to say *"No! **This is all bloody wrong!**"* It would be so clear and moral to do so, but no-one does. When things are done wrong it is so difficult to right them back again. On the nefarious prison island Cliff, although continually worked to death, becomes more muscular and stronger, whilst everyone else is dropping like flies in the malaria infested wasteland. At the same time his continued indomitable principled defence of his most faithful prison lag friends generally leads to their hideous deaths at the hands of the cruel warders. With that Cliff, through his own very miraculous survival, has to suffer with great conscience by the fact that his honourable actions have resulted in those dearest to him inadvertently being led to their deaths or disfigurements. Cliff goes on to fall in love with the true and upright daughter of the chief warder, the beautiful Angela Devere. It has to be a clandestine relationship which is unluckily uncovered, but never in fact consummated. When the boss warder, Duncan Devere discovers the illicit relation, then he with his very own hands strangles his daughter Angela. Oh, horror. It is rather an epic tale and Jimmy is struggling to find a way in the plot to connect the pure anger of Cliff at the cruel unnatural death of his sweetheart to a means to escape Shamano bird droppings island. Maybe, in a fit of massive remorse upon slaughtering his daughter so cruelly, jailer Duncan Devere comes to Cliff to admit all his sins and the injustice of Cliffs frame-up and explains to him a secret passage out of the island. This he could tell Cliff before administering himself a fatal potion of poison. Jimmy knows that this should hopefully happen but is unable to conjure up the spark of ingenuity to make it seem feasible and for the reader to gasp in excitement and incredulity at the plot masterpiece. If he could then it really could become a potboiler of a story about Cliffs long drawn out revenge on all those who have viciously transgressed against him.

Jimmy has determined that before exacting his long drawn out revenge the protagonist Cliff is haunted by the idea that he can commune with the spirit of the delectable Angela. He becomes embroiled with a group of pantheists who convince Cliff that Angela still lives on in all moments of nature and Cliff becomes haunted by water as he will never find a way back to the guano islands and his few mere moments of magik with the everlasting beautiful Angela. Cliff becomes consumed by hopeless and debilitating morose indulgence dwelling upon a hidden fantastic past which bars him from moving out on the revenge required of him by the sacred laws of nature. Jimmy views Cliff's indecision as semi-autobiographical; the feelings of guilt and the persisting belief that he had been callously denied a delicious life with a wonderful partner that would have cured everything whole. The secret love that still had a life in his head. Alas, poor Cliff Citro sinking into a life of sloth. He knows what to do to improve things, but he simply cannot do them.

And so it was with James Donald Suzuki. Every now and then he would pull his old pencil to paper to write his book, but he is increasingly sunk in the morose morass of the dullest routine. It was comforting to suffer in it. Every now and then he would have a moment and these moments were usually driven by thoughts of Fumi. Fumi who was to be his. Fumi whom he had loved, but had never known truly. There had been none of that special type of intimacy and without it there were only longings that could not be requited. When one longed after longings a strange sort of indolence and drift into fantasy land would arise and which could only be countered by Jimmy through short bursts of activity portraying further and in more hungry detail the terrible pangs Cliff Citro had through his missing of Angela Devire who had been so cruelly plucked from her life and from their nascent but blooming relationship. Fumi, Fumi – all is lost. All is wrecked by the nincompoop Copperfield.

Jimmy thinks on about Fumi. He thinks also about finishing his novella; his epic and tragic romance. He cannot say how unfair life has been, but he must get Cliff

Citro to say it. Only Cliff now could form an escape from it. Only Cliff could dare to say and do what Jimmy dared not. The trouble is, is that Cliff is drifting into a terrible lethargy. Jimmy needs him to be decisive and a man of action who will right all wrongs. The problem is that Jimmy is getting stuck with how to write him. He cannot write a character who is not really like himself. All his characters have to be partly like himself. They are all facets of himself and now Jimmy is morose without Fumi Lartal and he cannot get Cliff Citro to spring to action and avenge all the various malefactions of his cast-out life . He cannot write up a good life for any of them. He has no experience of that.

Oh, Fumi.

Jimmy wracks his brain for a plot line, an ending where all that was put wrong can be righted again. Everyone wants a happy ending. Jimmy still continues to believe in the happy ending. He may be deluded, but he wants the happy ending.

'Perhaps Angela had a twin sister who shares her saintly character and attraction to Cliff, he muses. 'Cliff might think that he has been visited by a ghostly apparition but really it is the twin Charlotte, and although not quite like his first love Angela, is close enough for him to be requited at the end after he has carried out his ghastly admonitions', he considers.

But it is hard to write: There are many lines to script before he finishes. He cannot write faster than life. The pace of life brings in just too many experiences to be considered in the art of creation.

"I wish I had a nice moggy to cuddle and stroke again", he moans.

The wordsmithing is a lonely task.

Jimmy can be decisive and there again indecisive. It kind of depends on his mood and the support he gets from others. He can be cool and calculating and yet again fall back to the propensities of a full scale feebling. In that sense he is like the tragic hero from some of those novellas that the sensitive ladies from High Hammerfield like to read. One moment a man of action, the next a cowering procrastinator who tries to philosophise on the meaninglessness of everything.

It is at times like this that Jimmy likes to seek out solace in the support of others. He decides to seek out Sir John for courage and fortification. He makes an excuse to Sister Solice that he has left his towel in the steam house so that he can get a licence for a walkabout.

Sir John has been positioned in a bed in a busy thoroughfare corridor in the hospital. Another rouse of the Surgeon-Captain to humiliate him. Nevertheless Jimmy finds the baronet in good cheer.

"Your Honour, so this is where they have importuned you!"

"Fie, Sir! They shall soon have their comeuppance. Mark my words!"

It inspires Jimmy to see Sir John in fighting mood. He could do with some fire in the belly himself.

The corridor where Sir John is positioned is so noisy and chaotic that it affords great privacy. Jimmy can speak freely to his mentor amongst the melee.

"Sir John, you know that Matron Stoneywell is quite unmercifully persecuting poor Nurse Kendra. It is a scandal and I fear that there will be no legal way to kill this wicked innuendo."

"Have no doubt, sir. I have communicated to the Visitor and she will be here to settle things shortly. They shall be taken to account. Don't you worry."

"That may be so, however, I think that the Matron's devious actions are solidifying a position that even the Countess will be hard pushed to rectify. Stoneywell is laying down a case for the public prosecutors to pursue. She is fabricating this with innuendo and lies. She has put in place whispering allegations suggesting that Kendra administered poison to the late Arnold Copperfield."

"Absolute poppycock!"

"I know, but it is getting out of control now. We cannot wait for the niceties to be observed. I feel it is time now to nip this in the bud."

"Hmm, let's consider .."

Sir John shifts in his bedded sitting position and his sad weary eyes take on an impenetrable gaze beyond Jimmy as if searching into the past for some clue as to what constituted the fabric of the whole wrong.

"Let us see.."

"Yes?" Jimmy is hoping for answers to unfurl crystal clear.

"Well, what can I say? I was so unjustly wronged myself. I was taken to the cleaners by three scoundrels. I was sucked into a tale founded and fabricated by dark matter. I was hoodwinked and played with by forces of anti-mass and devoid constitution. Riddell, Daedalus and that creature called Belsingham plotted through base means to ruin me. They used what was base in me, after all it is the law of physik that there is something unwholesome in all of us. It is usually countered out by the universal law of balance, that there is always the same amount of pure and base, just that some of us have them in unequal parts, like in the cases of Riddell and Stoneywell. That aside they used what was base in me for leverage; that being my vanity. That I could possess the financial means to sponsor a machine that could buy practically eternal time was one vanity. The next that I deserved to live for ever. The vanity of having a consciousness. The impudent thought that a wealthy degenerate like myself should propagate my unworthy existence in tea houses, on card tables and in reputable ladies' drawing rooms. That a minutia such as myself could challenge cosmic existence!"

"These are unworthy thoughts, Sir John!"

"Are they really? Comfort yourself Sir that I one so mighty have fallen so low and I put myself here through my incorrigible vanity. You Jimmy had misfortune sliced up for you and force-fed by the cruel administrators of this Great Society to eat of it. I served mine up whole myself on a giant silver platter and went at devising my own misfortune without batting a heavy eyelid of doubt!"

"Please do not denigrate yourself good Sir".

"Yes, I freely gave those three scoundrels the two hundred thousand shiny sovereigns that they requested and gave the mortgage on Chatham Cheap, my prized baronial estate. Work on their magik machine was slow and results unforthcoming. To cut to the dash within eighteen months we were nowhere near the so-called divine-head machine and then abruptly and surprisingly income generation on my great estate started to fail. A mysterious fire in the grand plantain house, a blight of macca moths in the upper fields and payments to non-existent suppliers which thoroughly drained my liquid means. As a consequence I could not get credit from my bone fide suppliers and my business was starting to fail. I could not pay my own labourers. The income I needed to generate to service my debt to Catcaldis was no longer there. The financiers foreclosed on me two months later. I was made bereft and bankrupt. I was later to ascertain that my estate manager, one Jan Gloop, was colluding in this heinous scheme and he was doing all he could to destroy my plantation business in order to ruin me. I gave him free licence to ruin my business as I was so totally uninterested in taking care of my own business. I was too grand an aristocrat to look at accounts and speak to suppliers! I so wish Jimmy that I had not been leading a debauched life. In my arrogance I did not think to guard over my own business! I have been a sorry individual, I can tell you", and at this Sir John begins to volubly weep.

"Now, now, kind Sir. Pray do not cry. I shall help avenge you. By Jenna, did you say Gloop?"

"Gloop. His name was Gloop, yes. Avenge yes. To avenge is to carry through the course of natural justice. I think you should kill Stoneywell as I should have killed Belsingham and his cronies. The world would be a happier and pleasant place if you were to kill her. She shan't be missed. No, not at all. She will not be missed one bit."

"Dear Sir John, I shall take care of Kendra's business first, then we shall put steps in place to avenge you against your persecutors."

Sir John nods and closes his eyes to rest in the middle of the hurly-burly. Jimmy storms away down the corridor for the moment again the heroic man of action.

The Surgeon-Captain's office is large and imposing as it should be for a man of great importance. Great Society knew that he had worked hard enough for it. How many shattered shot out limbs had he had to saw off during the course of the Battle of Ferris Moor, for example? How many wards had he had to shut in the face of Great Society austerity measures, and all the resulting dirty business that was attendant upon it, which he had consummately and smoothly dealt with? How many scheming aldermen and chief chamberlains had he countered and fought in the scheming political abattoir of Great Society? Sir Fredrick Roper felt that he deserved the trappings of office. He was a somebody and he needed his underlings and his trimmings of office in Great Society. He had an original painting by Giugno for example, a large ravenous Tartary female nude reclining on a divan covered by a large circle of neck-laced beads which seemed to sink into every deep fold of her entirely nude body and as they sank into them they seemed to give her a sensuous pleasure. An eruption ...

'Oh my thoughts run away with me', he smirks to himself. 'The Giugno was given to me by the Minister of Good Constitution himself on the sly in thanks for dealing with the Minister's poor confused wife. Getting her off the hampa addiction on the quiet without the world at large having to know. It must be worth a good two hundred sovereigns even though it is decadent art'.

Roper considers the nude intently and further stretches down unconsciously his right hand in his breeches middle pocket. There is a knock at the door.

"Come!"

The door immediately opens.

"My dear Surgeon-Captain! I trust that I do not disturb you."

"Not at all, dear Matron Stoneywell. Your visit is most opportune. I was just thinking about that old reprobate who claims to be a baronet of the ancient realm. What a fantasist, but how to deal with him?"

"Yes, he is a problem isn't he? What's more, Solice and the other staff are reporting to me that he is becoming a centre of disaffection around the wards. He seems to be close to the iniquitous Nurse Kendra and the counter-professional Suzuki."

"Suzuki too indeed, the high grade counter-professional. We will have to take care to make sure that he is not disaffected. But what to do, what to do?"

"Well how about I sit on your lap for a while Frederick. If we get up close together we can harness the power of our joint thinking on the subject."

"Capital idea."

Matron Stoneywell plonks her considerable frame on the podgy legged lap of the surgeon and starts to writhe her bottom over the nether regions of the doctor. Stoneywell is not spritely, but nevertheless is able to cavort over the lap region of Sir Frederick exciting him to put clumsy hands on her ample bosom. The stout wooden frame of the desk chair is starting to gyrate with a convulsion. Suddenly there is the sound of uproar in the Surgeon-Captain's anteroom.

"Please Madam, you have not been announced!", an attendant cries.

"I will see the Surgeon-Captain this very instant! Move out of my way."

"By Janna, it's the Visitor. Hop to it!", snarls Roper.

The dumpy Stoneywell springs from his heated lap with the strength and grace of a prima ballerina. Roper spies first the entrance through the door of a prodding angry mauve parasol and then the Visitor herself in all her resplendent finery, Lady Elizabeth Swann, the Countess of Tischent. A different class to him altogether; old class.

"Good day, your reverence", wheezes Sir Frederick. "What a pleasant surprise".

"I understand that you have in your halls a person of considerable importance, the Baronet of Sandown himself. Is that correct?"

'Not even a salutation in return', thinks the hospital official. 'She must be angry'.

"We have someone claiming to be that august person. Quite preposterous. Such an amateur sham", giggles Sir Frederick. The Matron giggles with him in solidarity.

"Preposterous? I find it preposterous that you did not even care to check with me as to the credentials of such a person. You give me great embarrassment and you will certainly receive rebuke from the Republic's Palace".

Sir Frederick Roper is sweating profusely upon hearing this heavy threat. Matron Stoneywell stares at the Visitor with pure hatred.

"I want Sir John to be removed forthwith to your best private room. Understood? Good. Give the order now."

Sir Frederick shambles to his anteroom to make the arrangements. Lady Swann sits down on the warm desk chair of the Surgeon-Captain.

"And who might you be, pray?"

"Matron Stoneywell, your ladyship".

"You are dismissed".

"Pardon?"

"It simply means get out. At least for the time being." Her Ladyship gives Stoneywell an acid smile. "Leave us".

Stoneywell knows that discretion is the better part of valour and departs. Meanwhile Sir Fredrick shambles back in.

"Also Roper, I hear that you are not just persecuting poor Sir John, but also one Nurse Kendra too."

"She is absolutely not to be trusted. Matron Stoneywell has evidence to suggest that she stole strychnine from the hospital supply to poison some old fancy man of hers. It is diabolical."

"Drop it. The charges are totally false".

"But ..."

"Drop it I say! And have her reinstated with her old responsibilities. No arguments. Now get someone to show me to Sir John. We have a lot of apologising to do".

Lady Elizabeth Swann parades out of Roper's office prodding him in the chest once with her parasol for good measure.

"We have much to make amends on", she snarls as she leaves.

Six: Resistance – "More Than Just A Visit"

Jimmy is more than a little morose. He has been in White Cross Hospital a fair number of days now and since his mishap he has been in a deep morass of self-pity and self-hatred. Furthermore, he feels quite confounded by the latest missive that somehow has arisen again from the fair hand of Mistress Rosemary Dowd. He is of an indolence and feeling of "what is the point" that cloaks the forties - something person so that he vegetates in his hospital bed dropping off and dozing and drooling in the damp apathy of hospital world.

"Good morning! I am Lady Elizabeth Swann. The Hospital Visitor. Sir John J. Perriwinkle has made me known of your case and I am here to help you". A serene voice, a winning smile and an early mature lady of fine beauty and confidence. She makes an impact with minimum fuss.

Not sure whether in a dream or not, but nevertheless like the involuntary motions of a marionette Jimmy Suzuki finds himself lifting himself to a full sitting position in bed. The serene voice has an effect over him.

"And how are you today, patient Suzuki?"

"I'm fine thank you, your Ladyship". It seems so natural the urge to tell her everything is alright. Her whole demeanour expressed a desire for confirmation of order and propriety. Yet she is a full woman hinting of the ancient goddess under the fine lace of preferred society. She offers bounty within cordiality.

'From where surfaces such absurd thoughts?', muses Jimmy.

"And how is your treatment here? Have they been looking after you well?"

Jimmy is suddenly aware that there is a whole host of hospital officials standing there. What an illusion. Initially, during their opening gambit of conversation, he had only seen Lady Elizabeth Swann, the Hospital Visitor there. She stands afore him immaculate and full-bosomed in a lilac bustle dress, white gloves, ostrich plumed hat with matching parasol and all at the very height of full fashion and painstaking taste. She looks as if she is about to take afternoon tea at the palace. The Visitor is someone who clearly is concerned about her appearance and wears it to maximum disarming effect.

'I wonder if she is so spotless underneath it all', is his thought.

Jimmy feels very grubby against such straw blonde splendour. This concern quite takes any grumpiness out of him and the sharp juxtaposition is not exactly conducive to any whinging about his situation. He has been there over two weeks now with no further sign of his release, but should not grumble now. Sometimes the sharpness of another's appearance can be quite intimidating. Ugliness always submits to beauty.

Through his dense deliberations he notices in the entourage Surgeon-Captain Sir Frederick Roper, Matron Stoneywell, and Nurse Kendra amidst a bloom of medical orderlies, doctors and other restoration importers. Even more reason to make his answer moderate.

"The staff here are looking after me exceedingly well, your Ladyship".

"That is especially good to hear as the Poorhouse Authority have selected you as a representative of the Plebs Survey. I shall be interviewing you in due course in accordance with the requirements of the survey. Good day to you". And with that she and the entourage are off like a good dream dispelling in sunlight.

Jimmy catches the eye of Matron Stoneywell before she storms past.

"What is this survey she mentioned, Matron?".

"Nothing to worry about, Suzuki. From time to time patients are selected at random to give their opinion on our service. It is a normal part of the continuous improvement policy of Great Society. No doubt we shall be giving you even better treatment so that you can compli ment us to her ladyship!" And with that she moves off back to the main procession.

Jimmy can hear the Surgeon-Captain's booming voice in the distance: "You can see that we give our very best, Madam Visitor. Who would you like to see next, Marm?"

"Why our distinguished guest, Sir John J. Perriwinkle, of course. Who else?"

Jimmy notices that the Visitor also had the knack like Roper of throwing her voice so that all those for yards around could clearly hear. Yet she seemed to be talking quite moderately, whilst Roper was always roaring.

"Capital. Capital, Marm. Stoneywell direct us to Sir John's quarters!"

Eighteen set of feet in assorted shoes, clogs and boots clump down the long corridor to the area known as "Sunnydene" where Sir John J. Perriwinkle has been accommodated. Matron Stoneywell is leading the gaggle almost running as the Visitor likes to spirit about at a quick pace. They reach a room with the small door sign "Sunnydene 4" on the outside. Stoneywell opens the door for the exalted guest.

"Leave us", announces Lady Elizabeth as soon as the door starts to turn open. She enters the small chamber with a smile. "My dear Sir John!" and is a little taken aback by the picture she sees of this doyen of society.

"My dear Lady Elizabeth", answers the feeble voice of Sir John.

"What has become of you kind Sir?"

"Pray sit down Elizabeth and I will give you the gist of my sorry story. Use the little bell there and we can call for some tea."

"They will not have Earl Grey", she says.

"Your company will make up for far graver deficits", he graciously counters.

Three hours later Perriwinkle's account of his misfortune is finished.

"Do not worry Sir John I shall seek restitution on all this. These charlatans will not be humoured in Great Society. Rest assured I shall be asking the Earl of Tischent in his capacity as Master of the Rolls to ensure an exhaustive prosecutorial inquisition to get to the bottom of this. I will be back on the morrow after I have further set straight the unctuous Roper on how to treat one such as yourself who is from a most august bloodline".

"Viva Republica, Elizabeth! And please be sure to look in on James Donald Suzuki Esq. He has put himself at some risk to speak up for my case. He is a special one. A bit different from all those other malingerers."

"I already have today and will do so again tomorrow. Sleep well sweet prince!"

"You always make things sound so grand", smiled Sir John.

Lady Swann made her departure in sweetness and light.

"Brown Dwarf fiasco", mumbled Sir John in an abruptly returning bile of bitterness.

Lady Elizabeth Swann had entered his life. Jimmy, of course, had never had a bit of high class crumpet. He had never before been close to a lady of refinement. There had been one in the past that he had seen from afar at the Trenchtown Primary. She had been the Lady Governor to his school, and as a young adolescent, she had made an enormous impression on him, albeit only through mere glimpses from a distance as she was being accompanied and shepherded around by the anxious headmaster. He remembered feeling a frisson of sexual excitement at seeing this highborn lady of society. Part of the sexual allure was the Lady Governor's unattainability. She appeared as distant to him as a veritable goddess and he wanted to commune with her. The rare occasions that Jimmy would see her about the Primary would see Jimmy retreat into the sordid act of self-gratification. He was a growing lad and the sight of the remote and beautiful Lady Governor would pop his cork and he would do the act as soon as he could, but as a result ending in shameful feelings of failure and frustration that he could not ever be a man worthy of the affections of such a lovely creature.

So it was with this introduction to the Hospital Visitor, the delectable Lady Elizabeth Swann, the Countess of Tischent. Jimmy finds himself swooning silly over her titles and her fine marble exterior. He immediately has a rise under the heavily starched hospital sheets. He feels heavily starched himself. He lulls himself into a semi-masturbatory swell of frustrated happiness floating dreaming on about a slight lustful congress with her ladyship; perhaps too with Kendra, perhaps also moaning under the bountiful bosom of the rancid Matron Stoneywell. What did it matter once the arousal had been awoken? He would never be released from her ladyship's trance until the arousal had been requited. He had heard of a beautiful sorceress who had turned men into swine, and under the spell of the Visitor, Jimmy felt like a veritable pig who could never return to being a man. It was unrequited suffering.

Jimmy resolves to live off his intellect as thinking can alleviate suffering. However, three days later sees him uplifted into a different dimension of being. It starts like this.

"The Visitor is here and has just completed an interview on old Emily Parkinson", says Sister Solice. "She proposes to interview you now. If you are agreeable I shall bring along a bath chair".

"I am agreeable to the interview, but not to the bath chair", responds Jimmy. "Surely I am well enough to walk".

"If you insist. Why not?" smiles Solice. "Come let me take your arm, although I propose that we do not undertake the Skittish Walk!"

Jimmy slumps out of his bed. He brushes down his pyjamas and rushes to put on his regulation hospital dressing gown.

"Do I have time to shave, Sister?"

"I think not, Mister Suzuki, but do allow me to comb your hair and beard and we will have you looking quite dapper. You did have a bed wash yesterday?"

"Yes, I did", and Jimmy thinks on with displeasure at the poor ministrations of the ugly and ungraceful Nurse Girtles.

Jimmy allows himself to be fussed over a degree by Sister Solice and is charmed to be more charming for the Visitor.

When he arrives at the Visitor's anteroom he is in good form although still a little in awe at the beauty and civility he is about to congress with.

"Thank you Sister. You can leave me alone with the patient. He will wish to have the confidentiality of his views respected."

"Yes, Marm", and Jimmy is alone with the Visitor, except there is one other in the room quietly sitting in the corner.

"I hope you do not mind, Mister Suzuki, if my personal attendant, Elspeth, remains with us. She is of my service and not of the hospital, so you can rest easy that your views will be guarded in confidence."

Jimmy notices that the attendant is a squat plain looking woman in her fifties and is fashioned like a poor governess. Her clothes had seen better days, but that was something between servant and employer.

"Not at all, my lady", Jimmy courteously replies.

"Very well then, let us get down to business. Please take a seat on the cot."

Jimmy notices that there are only two chairs in the room and they are both taken. There is a medical examination bed and Jimmy takes it that that is where he should park his rump. He gleans that this probably is normally a doctor's examination room. For some reason the Visitor preferred to interview her charges in this environment rather than in one of the grander offices of the administration building. His is not to reason why, so he plonks his substantial frame on the solid examination bed.

"Are you comfortable, Mister Suzuki?"

"Quite so, thank thee".

"Have they been looking after you well, kind Sir?"

"Tolerably well, but I think …", Jimmy halts his breath abruptly.

"Is there anything the matter, Mister Suzuki?"

Jimmy is palpably nervous and focuses his attention to the heaving bosom of the noble lady. Her breathing seems to be shallow and quick, as if she too were excited about something.

"I wanted to mention a staff member, but how do I know that my remarks will be kept confidential; anonymous, so to speak."

"That absolutely I can assure you", replies the Countess. "This examination is to be the soul of discretion and in the course of this process I am hopeful that you will be examining me. Such examination too to be absolutely confidential, you understand?", she smiles sweetly and

Jimmy notices that she has applied a very liberal amount of
lip rouge so that her mouth appears very lascivious.

'She could swallow me up', he reflects.

"Yes, I understand", but he does not necessarily and
trips on to his next statement.

"Well, it's Sir Frederick actually. I find that sometimes
he can be a tad unpleasant, and even, aggressive at times."

"Oh, do not worry about him", she tartly states. " I have
my eye on him. What's the expression again? Ah yes, he is
a plywood tiger. Always bawling out the patients the
blustering bully – Sir John has mentioned it too – and
whilst all the time fornicating with the ghoulish Matron
Stoneywell!"

"Are they? Never!". Jimmy is instantly annoyed with
himself with his register of disappointment. He would have
liked to have withdrawn this outburst.

"What do you care, good Sir?. You are a man in your
prime who can do better. You can take a fine maiden, who
along with refinement has a lusty appetite!", she laughs
coquettishly.

"What do you mean?", blunders Jimmy.

" I mean …. Oh, let's cut out the pig shit, shall we?. We
are both mature adults of the world. What I mean is …
Elspeth, be a dear and start to unlace me, would you?"

Jimmy simply does not know what to say. He has never
been casually raped before, and, for that matter has not
been in for much lovemaking in the past. The lady was of
some standing, so it would not be good etiquette to resist
her view given the circumstances.

The lady-in-waiting rises without a sound at the same
time that her mistress stands. Without word or ceremony
Lady Swann stands confidently whilst Elspeth start
unlacing stays and bows. The lady's demeanour is as cool
as if she were standing there trimming flower stalks and
arranging a bouquet. Nevertheless, Jimmy sees the traces

of her bounteous breasts racing. There really was some passion there.

"Pray understand, Mister Suzuki, that today we can only afford for time a limited engagement. If we are both content then we can have longer more elaborate sessions in the future. So that means today I shall only be partially undressed, hence you can understand that I have to have my good helpmeet Elspeth here. It is quite essential for me to finish up again in full decorum. You Sir, in your loose pantaloons can fully disport yourself to me."

Jimmy starts quickly disporting, not wanting to disappoint. He notices that his good little rifleman is already standing fully to attention and ready to raise the colours up the flagpole.

"Well what a jolly fellow!", the lady exclaims. "The Master of the Rolls couldn't pip that could he, Elspeth? Thank Janna, I have you to play with his little mouse."

Elspeth is disengaging quickly from her mistress who is approaching fast at the naked Jimmy. She is attired in white linen petticoats and corset, but still looks at ease enough to take some musth.

"Why hello, boson. Looking for some juicy cunt are we?".

Jimmy starts to wither at hearing the language of the gutter. This is not the sensual refined love he imagined.

"We cannot be having that shipmate. Can we?", Lady Swann growls and proceeds to lick at the tip of his penis. Jimmy shivers but is securing leverage again so that she has something substantial to slot into her lascivious lipped mouth. She gulps at it and spits it out.

"Yikes. Birds and the bees. That is one salty monster! I love your seasoning."

Jimmy cannot believe how well he auditions.

"But now I simply must immediately have your love thrusts. Elspeth, help me to position."

The good lady still has on enough underskirts to put an umbrella cordon around her love jewel. Her assistant is required for the manoeuvres that get her a good landing on Jimmy's love probe. Without further ado Elspeth is positioning her head below the lady's rump as she lands down on Jimmy's shaft thus making sure that even without sight a good coupling is assured. Jimmy feels Elspeth's fingers joining connections and then the rubbing and grafting begins. Lady Elizabeth Swann is going off at a hell of a rate. She is riding Jimmy hard and even though he is not a fragile fellow he is starting to feel a mite suffocated by the exerting energy of the aristocratic lady. She is riding him full force and the lady's maid head is somewhere beneath too. Jimmy feels her tongue licking at his scrotum. It is a strange sensation and entirely unexpected, but he feels he has to be accommodating.

"Elspeth! Out with you", orders the countess. "This is not your fun time. Now, I need my retainer. I don't want to cry out in too an abandoned fashion, do I?"

Elspeth as if not at all unnatural to her retrieves a leather band which she puts between the teeth of her lady as if she were some epileptic sufferer.

"Onwards! Onwards!", moans the lady as the tether is applied and the recharge for full speed is now starting again.

Jimmy is being ridden hard. His big body is being shaken as if he is in his death convulsions. The little examination cot is being shaken around. Elspeth is trying to hold it from shaking too noisily whilst at the same time trying to keep the mouth restraint for her mistress in place.

Finally the lady is convulsing and moaning. His cannon makes the ceremonial shot and it is all over.

Jimmy is a bag of sweat. The lady perspires decorously. Elspeth's face is hoary red with effort.

"Please clean me of the discharge, Elspeth", orders Lady Elizabeth and she continues chatting as if she were at a garden party.

"Full marks, Mister Suzuki! I do hope we can get together for more extensive interviewing. You do understand that my good husband, the Earl of Tischent, is not one for surveying his wife's desires. His gratification is more on the gaming tables, or, the quick gratification of the hand-jerk. Is that not right, Elspeth?"

Elspeth nods her head as if in quiet resignation. Jimmy feels that this close intimacy with the acts of her mistress must be like a humiliation for the plain woman.

'But what was that whole licking thing about?', he wonders. 'That does not correlate exactly to being forced into the whole show'.

"Nevertheless, we must keep this totally discreet", the Countess continues, "and I shall make it extremely worthwhile for you to maintain that continued discretion. Is that acceptable?"

Elspeth is discreetly taking away linen handkerchiefs.

"Yes, fully acceptable. And I would like to explore your body a little more unhurriedly. I think you have a beautiful body. Elizabeth?"

Jimmy is surprised by his boldness.

"Yes, I would like that Jimmy. I think too that I have a beautiful body, so we will have to arrange for a further meet in the next few days. I take that you are not adverse to staying on in hospital a little longer, so that we can get to know each other a little better?"

"No, I am agreeable to that. I am starting to feel more comfortable here at White Cross."

"Good, perhaps I can arrange a private room for you. I will speak to Sister Solice. See you in the next days", and then pausing, "Jimmy."

Jimmy smiles back sheepishly and leaves the room clumsily.

The next few days sees Jimmy with some enhanced bath chair status in White Cross Hospital. He obtains an upgrade in accommodation. A single room in the "Sunnydene" area of the hospital materialises the very next day after his first visitation. The more select room is adorned with petunias and chrysanthemums. A spruce, dapper type of hospital attire is acquired for him. He has given to him good quality flannel pyjamas and navy blue worsted dressing-gown with White Cross Poorhouse monikers to boot . His bath chair is replaced for a newer model which has nice felt backstays. The bath chair pusher is upgraded too. No longer the poor gormless Nurse Girtles, but the far superior Auxiliary Nurse Leandra Legg. As far as nurses go, Leandra comes from the same model mould as Nurse Kendra, and Jimmy is very flattered with such a trophy pusher. Leandra is game too. She is frivolous and fun, and is wont to do the Skittish Walk with Jimmy as they perambulate along the long corridors of the institution. It is a bizarre progress, a strange performance, as the seated Jimmy and the walking Leandra coordinate their arms in the elaborate fashion of the Skittish. It means that he is often late for medical consultations, but nobody seems to care – their comic procession is simply applauded by orderlies as they flit through the channels of the hospital. All in all life is on the up for Jimmy.

Two days later Jimmy receives a summons again. Auxiliary Nurse Leandra Legg gives him a fine quality pastel envelope. A short note is therein which he reads in private.

I shall be coming to you this very day at three o'clock on the post meridiem. The interview will be conducted in your private room in the Sunnydene. It will give us the opportunity for extended questioning.
Elizabeth

"That is only an hour hence', thinks Jimmy. "Nurse Leandra", he calls, "Prepare me for ablutions. Bring in the bath chair".

Jimmy quickly bathes in the discrete ablutions hall reserved for the special Sunnydene paupers. He asks Leandra to procure for him eau de cologne and freshly laundered jim-jams. With a quarter of an hour to spare he is ready to entertain like a coffee morning doyen in the mansions of Ripside.

Exactly on the hour there is a faint knock on the door.

"Enter", calls out Jimmy lying like a notable dissolute luxuriating on his comfy bed.

Auxiliary Nurse Leandra announces the Visitor. The Visitor resplendent in purple headdress and this and that throws her voice down to an efficacious sotto voce so that it sneaks and carries down the adjacent corridor murmuring of *confidential questions* and *sensitive questionaries*. The good helpmeet Elspeth is also there, but she is shooed out by her ladyship and instructed to keep guard in the corridor.

And then after that. At last. The moment.

"Mister James Donald Suzuki, I do declare?"

"I believe it is the Lady Elizabeth Swann, the Visitor to White Cross Poorhouse Hospital, and Consort to the 11th. Earl of Tischent."

"My, you are informed, but methinks I am to be your consort for the next hour!"

"If the proper etiquettes are to be observed, then I should be accorded temporary status of the Order of the Red Garter."

"You can have the accolade of Most Noble Order of My Red Garter, but you have to gain it."

"I am on a Knight's Vigil! So where do I seek it?"

The great lady twirls her full skirt around like a little girl at a festive pageant.

"You will have to get down to some investigations", she growls in mock fashion.

Jimmy starts to move on the dark and secret place, but is stopped in his tracks.

"But first your clothes. Remove your clothes as a true supplicant. I would see you raise your colours again!"

Jimmy disrobes hesitantly.

"Do we need to lock the door", he nervously queries.

"My bull mastiff will let no-one pass", is the confident reply.

Jimmy continues undressing and he reviews his flabby form in the process.

'What the blazes', he thinks. 'If I can perform now I can trim up in future. I will make myself a new man.'

Jimmy is now a mighty nude. He is someone's taste in sex appeal.

"Now where do you think that garter is bestowed, Mister Suzuki".

Jimmy gives an evil grin.

"I shall have to go surveying in the folds of the good earth for it", he announces and without further ado he lifts up the skirts of her ladyship and goes exploring therein. It is hot, perfumed and soft. He sticks his nose into the area of her pudenda and sniffs her very femininity into him. He hears the muffled sound of her laughter and he starts to lash his tongue out in the area of her private parts.

"Stop! Stop!", he hears muffled above. "This is no quick form! For now please remove my garters with your hot sticky hands and then proceed to generally disrobe me. I will have you feel the charms of my flesh and the contours of my body. This time we shall have a more extended pleasure."

Jimmy rises out of the close quarters, his naked body feeling the cool of the room. Lady Elizabeth Swann points to the buttons of her waistcoat.

"You can start undressing me".

Jimmy is anxious to get started. His hands are trembling with excitement as he attacks the delicate buttons.

"Gently! Take your time. Undress me lovingly as if you were performing foreplay."

Jimmy slows his heart and his fingers. With less speed he is nimbler now. He starts to negotiate the buttons with finesse, he unlooses the stays as if he is handling fragile ornaments; he is undressing her as if it were a refined courtly dance.

Nevertheless he is still trying to cut corners in order to get to the main event. Taking off her blouse he allows it to drop to the floor, but the lady is not having it.

"You would have me leaving here looking like a fishwife. Pick it up and fold it. Put it on the chair."

Jimmy is so aroused by the aroma of her fine perfume that he is not back-chatting or mithering, he is just doing without thinking. His is a primal force enchanted by beauty. The undressing becomes a part of the lovemaking, but a controlled lovemaking where Elizabeth Swann is in control. Jimmy has been so used to being controlled throughout his life that he does not question it. Besides which he is in thrall to her loveliness. He has never come so close to such a woman. It was just fine to do it her way.

Elizabeth Swann is extremely well attired meaning that Jimmy has much work to do. He even unlaces her boots with a certain sensuality. All through this she never shows a stroke of passion and Jimmy just restrains it. Finally her naked form is all revealed. She is alabaster like a statue. Her skin is so fine. It is well toned. It is inviting to the touch and wafts of perfume. She is a form and fragrance that he has never beheld, or indeed held before.

"This time we do this so slow. So so slow", she whispers. "Today a slow tender lovemaking, so for that I should take the lead. I will train you in the sensual art."

"Yes", he gasps, but feeling like he would explode. The slowness was increasing the tension within him. He feels like a shooting star locked in great gravity wanting to burst into escape.

She has no strength in relation to his, but she turns him easily on the bed and quickly she is on top of him leading. Leading him to sweet insanity with kisses, nibbles, licks and slurps. He wants to pin her and push her back, but she is not having it. Just as he is about to manhandle her again she bombards him with sweet attacks of the erotic art; scratching, sliding, rubbing, nosing and ruffling. He is more than ready to point his thing to a direction without gravity.

"Now me", she says. "Make love to me. You have seen what I can do. Show me what you can do."

At this challenge Jimmy's flame is starting to abate through failure of nerve. Curiously it abates enough so that he can give attention to her as he is temporarily relieved from holding back his own eruption. Valiantly he tries to give as she has given; smooching, slurping, hugging, digging and sucking. His is a raw talent and she attempts to refine it. Showing how to apply less pressure, to do more caressing rather than arresting her special parts. She points his crude fingers and wet tongue to her clitoris. Jimmy is not immediately familiar with such advanced machinery and she has to coax and re-coax him to find the necessary finesse for such fine filigree.

The more attentive that he must become to his work the more aroused she becomes. Just as his driving force has been lost to attention her base driving force becomes alive and ready for dousing.

"Come inside me".

With his chubby fingers Jimmy can now almost not quite grasp his thing, so removed has it become in his work.

"Oh, where has my little soldier gone?", she asks. "It looks like he has got lost in his helmet!", she laughs.

Jimmy registers that she is mocking him, but in a sexy and coquettish manner. There was something so natural to it. It was the universal call to arms. Before he knows it the soldier is back standing to attention fully armed. Engagement is easy and she has inserted him before he can barely notice.

"Flip me. Put me on my back".

This is again done effortlessly. They are like a well-oiled machine together.

"Slowly, Jimmy. Take it really slow."

Jimmy concentrates on tortoises and snails. The slowness is driving him insane.

"And if you come before I orgasm I will fucking kill you", she adds.

Jimmy then drives on even more slowly and determinedly, trying to keep a cork on a bottle whilst thinking on old algebra problems from the schoolroom.

"Come on! Come on!", she hisses suddenly. "Faster! Faster! Come on really fuck me!"

Jimmy like a noble racehorse gallops the final furlong covering her to suffocate much of the sound of her orgasm before finally exploding himself. Like a driven hard and left wet racehorse Jimmy is ready to spin his head to life, love and the universe. Everything is there.

Out of this quietude he surprisingly hears a faint callous handclap. Clap slow. Clap slow.

"I say, well done. Well done. Well done, you two. Yes I express my admiration to the cheating harlot and the burly ape who services her."

Jimmy turns to look up. Mysteriously there is a finely dressed middle-aged gentleman standing there. Jimmy has no idea how he could have entered so silently. He has a confident bearing and looks a person of distinction. Jimmy

focus on his violet coiffured wig and his courtly dress. He
looks very old school.

"Thank you, Elspeth", he shouts. "I have now got my
evidence." Without further ado he leaves the room.

"Who in the hell was that?", gasps Jimmy.

"That was my very husband, the Earl of Tischent", is
the murmured reply. "So the evil old bastard has been
looking for evidence against me. It looks like I am hung
venison, Jimmy."

"If he divorces you, I would be more than happy to wed
you".

"That is very gallant of you, Jimmy, but I am really
here with you for your ram-rod, not your bank book!"

At this the hardly acquainted disconsolate lovers erupt
in laughter.

"So have you had time to read it?", Kendra asks of
him expectantly.

Poor Jimmy is deep in thought about one woman whilst
another is quizzing him so intimately. Jimmy could never
dare mention to Kendra his dalliance with Lady Swann.
Kendra and he had been at odds and now they were at
evens once again. Poor Jimmy marvels at the cavorting
over the emotions that people must accomplish. He is
responding to his doughty nurse whilst palpitating
inwardly about the lady Visitor.

"Yes, I have, but it is just as strange and enigmatic as
all the rest of them.", Jimmy splutters. "I have no idea what
Copperfield was hoping to achieve by all this, do you?"

"I do not understand the connection at all", admits
Kendra. "Woodford Valley, St. David's and all this pig shit.
By Janna! What is this *Unemployed*?"

"I am of the view that they are the counter-
professionals. Like me", adds Jimmy.

"I see", she says. "Let me read the section again".

Jimmy still propped up in his infernal hospital bed gives her the latest sheet from Copperfield.

"Why on earth am I still here?", he sighs.

"Hush", she says. "I need to read it."

Jimmy does not demur. He sees in Kendra the strong intelligence he had perceived in Fumi Lartal and is now similarly glad to be open with this woman.

"Perhaps it will tell me how you should atone for your past transgressions, maybe the mishaps you experienced with Copperfield, as well as your transgressions to me", she says quite seriously.

Jimmy does not argue. He needs the firm tender forgiveness of a woman. It forms a security that he is incapable of achieving on his own. Women had the capacity to forgive, but not necessarily forget. Kendra had been pragmatic choosing what she wanted and any hankering after the morality and suitability could be deferred to later. After their impasse in the bathhouse and Jimmy's sulky withdrawal had come their remission from pressure thanks to the intervention of the hospital visitor herself. The removal of that pressure and the raise of status in both of them, as well as that of Sir John, had been a natural growing olive branch of reconciliation which both grasped seemingly unthinkingly and without rancour on either part. Kendra had been given access to Jimmy again and things were naturally taken up again without any mention again of the elephant in the room: Fumi Lartal. Before they knew it nurse and patient had become closer than any normal professional proximity.

Jimmy ponders the efficacy of the healing of time while Kendra reads.

WALK 8: FROM WALTHAMSTOW CENTRAL STATION TO THE WILLIAM MORRIS GALLERY ON FOREST ROAD (0.7 Miles)

This is a walk I am doing for Stephen and it is practically straight down Hoe Street! It is a walk that my husband Stephen and I did together for this book for the purely practical sentiment that Stephen did his early "Ministry" work in the diocese of Walthamstow with the loving support of its parishioners and it was here in its Christian community that he truly found God. The other main reason is that the William Morris Gallery is our final destination and it is a place where Stephen took much comfort during his sojourn amongst the denizens of Walthamstow.

William Morris was one of our country's greatest writers. He was a socialist, although he did not take gladly to the label. Foremost he was a scholar and philosopher who looked to the simpler rudiments of life for inspiration and joy. He was a proponent of a simpler happiness and he was able to define our relevant contentment by what we do and what we set down for the community. He contemplated in his writings upon our basic moods of energy and idleness and how to balance the two to attain happiness. The attainment of happiness is at the heart of these contemplative walks. It seems an admirable objective to set our destination to an artistic centre that exemplifies this great man's passion for self-help and the pursuit of happiness.

But first the helter-skelter of the Victoria Line. It is a brisk cold late November Saturday and London is on the move to the shops. Walthamstow is a busy terminus and we have used the Victoria Line to come up after staying the night with friends in Islington. Most of the passengers have been going the other direction to the West End, as Christmas shopping is fore in many persons minds, so we have had plenty of space in our tube carriage. We ran into the occasional football supporter raucous and merry at the prospective of some great and valiant win over their opponent. Stephen even enjoyed an exchange of "Come on you Sours" with the hopeless optimists of his old club as the boisterous bunch departed the train at Seven Sisters station. Very much a normal winter's Saturday in north London.

"Damn, why are we served these elusive stories in only single sheets of manuscript!", exclaims an exasperated Kendra.

"I know. It makes my head giddy too", empathises Jimmy. "How do you interpret it? How do you interpret any of these barely started Mistress Dowd's reflections?"

"Do you think these words come from the ancient past? From a different time? A time that we do not recognise anymore."

" I really do not know. If it is from the past then how come we have never heard of this famous William Morris? Or Victoria Line? It's all mumbo jumbo. It is like it has come from somewhere else. It is too strange and distant for me."

"It might simply be elitist professional writing. We have to confess that the system has not accorded us the very best in education. I would not put it past Great Society suppressing information from our past when it suits their purposes. Didn't the philosopher Ho-Me once say that history is scribed by the assailant?"

"There is that. But how do we interpret it?"

"Why don't we interpret it as we would one of our dreams", suggests Kendra. " I have seen some medical writings on this procedure."

"Righto", says Jimmy looking vacant.

"The walks are like the direction of life. They signify progress. The fact that none of us is standing still." Kendra is getting animated and excited now as she sets her analysis on to an instrument of happiness. Her full islands accent becomes more entrancing and alluring in tune with the passion building inside of her. Jimmy finds it quite beguiling. He feels he should love Kendra no matter how unlikely their combination might be.

"So they convey a passage, a passage in our lives, do they not?", she continues.

Jimmy nods his head solemnly wanting more of that lazy lilting voice. Wanting more of her cheeks pouting, wanting more of the movement of those luscious lips. It is a spell to which he wants to be bound.

"Then they are to do with going from one place to another, and they are for you. In fact they could be for anyone. Anyway, Mistress Dowd specifically mentions here happiness. One should walk in the direction of happiness. That Morris geezer he represents a symbol of contentment. You can forget the museum and all that timpani. It is simple. Copperfield has designed all this so that once you have made atonement through me, that you then must go on and find your peace. You Jimmy are prompted by Rosemary Dowd or Arnold Copperfield – whoever - to move towards your happiness. To make your happiness your goal", she concludes.

"Ah, I see", murmurs Jimmy. 'I did not think she is such an intellectual maiden', thinks he feeling a little unsettled by the quality of her reasoning.

"Provided you know what your happiness is", interjects Kendra.

"I think I truly know it".

"Which is?", she coaxes arching her eyebrows in expectancy.

"I think to love you. I think that I love you. To love you and hopefully be loved back. That would now be my idea of true happiness."

"And what is the impediment to your happiness and our mutual happiness?", she prompts further.

"Matron Stoneywell. We should kill her." Sometimes Jimmy could be very decisive.

"Quite so."

Meanwhile Sir John J. Perriwinkle is on the up and is being restored to his old fortitude. He has decided to remain at White Cross although the Countess of Tischent was most eager to transfer him to the Sisters of Mazuma at her own expense. Sir John has admitted to himself that after the Brown Dwarf debacle he is ruined and financially destitute. He had been accorded special status in the Sunnydene suite at White Cross and he is content to stay there under the protection of Lady Elizabeth Swann. He should see how the other half have been living as he is now in future to be living with them.

There is a knock on the door.

"Come in!", cries Sir John.

"You asked for me, your Honour".

"Yes, dear Suzuki. Come in and sit yourself down next to me."

Jimmy is looking dapper in a new white dressing gown that the Visitor has acquired for him.

"You look in rude health!"

"You too look much better, Sir John."

"What we have both been through, eh?"

Jimmy sinks his manly frame on to the guest chair next to Sir John's bed. He looks at Sir John expectantly.

"I have been thinking about the war stories we have exchanged. Ludicrous really", sighs Sir John. "Fumi Lartal, Doctor Daedalus, dastardly bankers and Brown Dwarf systems. How have you and I been thrown together in this risible maelstrom called life, Jimmy?"

"I'm sure I have no idea, Worship. Pure coincidence?"

"It may well be, but there is one common denominator. This blackguard, Belsingham. He is the money man behind those scoundrels Riddell and Daedalus. He is the fiendish mastermind behind the kidnapping of the young State Prosecutor. Who is he? What is he? This fellow Belsingham."

"He is all that brings us down. Every negative influence in our lives", blurts out Jimmy. "Sorry your worship, I am just spouting nonsense."

"Nonsense, I daresay, but you may just have something there", soothes Sir John. "You may well be on my wave of thinking on this too. For he is a common bogeyman of misfortune after all. Yet he does exist. He is a very man. I have met him. So what is he up to?"

"He wants to remove rivals like Fumi Lartal and at the same time to embezzle away your great fortune."

"But why, Suzuki? Why does he need to do this, and wherefore does he get involved with ruffians like this Tempels you mentioned to me, whilst at the same time he can move in the set of the Astrologer-Royal? What does that tell you about him? He certainly played us both for fools."

"Well at least with you, Sah, it was foolishness of vanity. With me it was pig stupidity foolishness based upon revenging of all things a cat!"

"Yes", chuckles Sir John, "but you did it out of affection for the creature. You loved your cat. We all deserve to have some affection in our lives. Well, it has all been very bizarre, has it not?", continues Sir John. "But I have been thinking on. Maybe this Belsingham is a subversive? Maybe he is set out on a course to destroy Great Society?"

"You mean a revolutionist like Crikey Spoets?"

"I am not sure if I would classify him with Spoets. Spoets wanted to overthrow all and implement his new world order as he put it and make everyone a farmer. No, I think Spoets was an idealist in his deluded way, but Belsingham is about power. I think that he is hell-bent on overthrowing Great Society through subversion and replacing it with another Great Society with him at its head. What do you think?"

"I thought he just liked being an evil cunt. Simple as that."

"Oh, the rich language of the Gortal. How I love to hear a man speak so directly. That means your spirits are up. Unfortunately, things are never as simple as that. Cunt he may be, but cunt with an agenda I daresay. I think that he was so militant in the persecution of Fumi Lartal because she was so diligent in prosecuting the underworld of our great city. Belsingham receives the patronage of the underworld and the black economy. They are a power base for him which he has been cultivating assiduously. Should he get to power they would be an invisible army of his countenanced but kept quiet, yet instrumental to him taking power and fortifying his position. Lartal, although I am sure that he bore her personal animosity also, was just too much a loose cannon on the deck of his designs. Added to that, she dared to stand up to him and he could not forgive that. That is why she had to be dispensed with and you came in as an innocent pawn in his game."

"You really think so", queries Jimmy. Deep down in his mind he feels there is even more to this Belsingham dilemma. "But why then expose you to personal ruin? Did he really need to have your capital?"

"I have been thinking on about that and it hurts. It is so personally taken", states Sir John. "Like you I am dubious about his need for my personal fortune; after all he seems to have access to the vast undeclared mega fortunes of the underworld. I think that his action against me was an act of ritual strength."

"An act of ritual strength?", splutters Jimmy.

"Yes, a show of strength. For Belsingham it is never about the money. True he could have thrown a lot of my money at his shady cohorts once he had paid off Riddell and Daedalus, but it was more to show those partners of his what he was capable of doing. How he is a real player. How he is a real shaker and mover. To sway them to put him in power. To awe them as to what he is capable of doing once in power. To show his credentials as it were."

"You really think so?"

"Yes, I do. What better way to demonstrate your clout by destroying a mainstay of the ancient families. To sweep away generations of landed authority through the application of your intellect. They would sit up and take notice of that. Not even Great Society has managed to diminish the supremacy of the Sandown baronetcy in this land. He realises that in the future modern technology will be in the fore and he has just proved his credentials as shaker and mover to the cadre of new scientists. "

"You may well be right, Sir John."

"Thank you for all you have done for me, Jimmy. I appreciate greatly that you got the message regarding my plight to the Visitor. The time that I have had in these more private surroundings have given me the opportunity to succour my strength and get my thoughts back into order. You have really helped me, dear friend. Your friendship has rescued me from the abyss and I have found peace to reconcile myself to my very difficult situation."

"I did nothing, Sir John, but rest assured that once I am out of here I shall track down that spalpeen Belsingham and he shall pay I assure you!"

"Yes, I am sure he will", smiles Sir John. "What a world we live in".

Jimmy sighs not knowing what to say.

"One more thing, Jimmy. Lady Swann, the Visitor …"

"Yes?", Jimmy has said it too abruptly and Sir John gives him a wan smile.

"I have heard about the embarrassing scene with you and Elizabeth. It pains me that the Count has set out to humiliate her. He is a cruel man and has denied her. A grown woman has certain desires and appetites and I feel that she was probably forced to look for love. She is a great friend of mine. Her family, the Barretts, is of stock almost as ancient as mine. Tischent's family is of poor descent in comparison. Look, what I want to tell you is that she is my friend, but I have not partaken in any sort of sexual relationship with her. Yet, I understand that she has needs in that way. It is just that she abused her privileged position here to procure lovers."

"Lovers?"

"Yes paramours, you were not the only one. There have been others from the hospital, so I am afraid you were no special one in that regard. So there is a certain scandal, and I would advise for both your sakes to steer well clear of each other."

"I see".

"I will be saying the same thing to her. I suspect that Tischent is seeking to divorce her and ultimately, pretty soon, she will have to stand down as Visitor here. When things are done wrong it is so difficult to right them back again."

"So what should I do to help her?", entreats Jimmy.

"Leave her be ..."

Then there is a knock on the door. It is a nurse to perform some ablutions on Sir John and so ends the revealing talk between the two confidants.

Jimmy has with his chubby fingers calculated that all in all he has been some six weeks at White Cross Hospital. He has become comfortable and well situated. He has kept his accommodation in the Sunnydene wing and he is starting to live far better than he has back in Trenchtown. He has not seen Elizabeth Swann since the debacle. She had departed his room after a round of gallows humour and seemed in reasonably good malignant spirits. The Visitor on her departure did not look as cool as normal in her deportment. Perhaps as she did not have the disloyal Elspeth to put her back together to her normal fashion. Wisps of hair were out of place, her hat was not perched in her usual jaunty style. Elspeth no doubt having taken the Count's coin had disappeared. Nevertheless Jimmy still continued to enjoy his new privileges. It seemed that no-one was going to countermand the Visitor's instructions just yet. Lady Swann had so far not resigned her position as Visitor, and in the absence of change there, there was no change in Jimmy's circumstances.

However, a couple of sunny mornings later there is a loud knock on Jimmy's door and before Jimmy can pronounce "Enter", Surgeon-Captain Sir Fredrick Roper storms in.

"Good Day, patient Suzuki! I trust you are well?"

"I am indeed recovering, Sir", is the cautious reply.

"I would say that you have now recovered sufficiently. If you can dip your wick around the place that indicates to me a certain robustness of health, wouldn't you say?"

Jimmy is at a temporary loss of words.

"The ability to how's your father shows that you have recovered your strength and virility".

Jimmy continues to look abashed.

"You know she has announced her resignation?", says Roper more quietly now.

Jimmy now looks nonplussed.

"Lady Swann. She has announced to the Poorhouse Board that she will be stepping down as Visitor as of the end of March. The smart money is on the appointment of Baroness Hyko. A nice bleeding hearted liberal", gloats the doctor. "So with that I think we have an official discharge announcement to make. Let me call in the crew."

Sir Frederick momentarily disappears, but is soon back with Matron Stoneywell, Sister Solice, Nurse Girtles, Auxiliary Nurse Legg and some assorted others who had been caring for Jimmy. Nurse Kendra is noticeable by her absence.

"Well, on behalf of all of us with whom you have been in our charge, I think it is safe to say that it is really time to release your from our care and custody, Mister Suzuki", booms the Surgeon-Captain.

Matron Stoneywell sniggers and the rest stand and smile uncomfortably.

"I will have the papers raised for the morning and after signature you will be free to depart", finishes the Surgeon-Captain.

"I thank you all for your good ministrations", says Jimmy graciously rising to the occasion. "I am heartily sorry that my stay has ended in some difficult circumstances, that you all no doubt have heard about, but nevertheless I do truly feel mended and, once again, heartily thank you for that."

"Nicely said, stud", titters the Matron.

Sir Frederick and company do not respond to this and Jimmy simply beams back as if in a state of ecstasy. He beams and the company departs his presence.

'So that is that. Hospital time is just about over', he reflects and hopes that he shall never have to see another hospital again before his time of dying.

Jimmy is on course for departure and on his last night at the hospital he is gathering his things together in his room at the Sunnydene wing. Collecting his few paltry things when Nurse Girtles enters.

"Have you come to say goodbye?", smiles Jimmy.

"Yes, I have and to announce that Sir John would like to speak to you this evening prior to your departure."

"Right you are girl. Tell him I will be straight along", and he plonks a big wet kiss on her rosy cheek.

A quarter of an hour later Jimmy is bedside with the noble Sir John.

"I just wanted to bid you farewell Jimmy and to thank you for all that you have done to make my time here less discomforting. It is hard for someone so lofty to fall so hard and so far, but I have to say that one of the great positives I can take from it is my friendship with you. In my previous exalted position I would simply have not come across anyone from the underclass."

Jimmy looks uncomfortable with the depiction.

"I mean that sincerely, Jimmy. I use that word in that is what I was expected to believe about you honest folk. Pejoratives like white scum and cannon fodder have been commonly used, but I am truly grateful that my hubris has brought a quality into my life that had not existed before."

"Truly, Sir John, you do not have to praise me anymore!" Jimmy feels embarrassed.

"I will go on, Sir. My previous life had been a sum of superficial relationships without any depth or meaning. I lived the life of a dissolute cocooned in my enormous wealth. I have told you before how my overbearing arrogance was used against me to dispossess me of my fortune – and I really do not wish to say anymore on that at this time -, but that profound change in my circumstances has been the catalyst to taking a more complete view on life. I have no family, I think like you, and therefore I have now realised some great satisfaction in my friendship with you. You will leave tomorrow Jimmy and I hope that we can remain friends."

There are tears in the old fellow's eyes and for the first time Jimmy can see some weakness through the veneer of the brave old character. Jimmy presses Sir John's left hand with bear like affection.

"Of course, Sir John. I shall always be there for you. We have now been stitched together immutably."

"Thank you, Jimmy".

"I still do not understand why these cads did this to you. To plot your downfall. It is so unspeakable and puts me in a rage still."

"I have been trying to think on it dispassionately. After all I have nothing left to lose anymore. Even my ire has subsided. What if there were some truth in what Riddell and Daedalus were saying. I am beginning to think that there is ambiguity in this big warp tenderer thing. I think that there is no doubt that this Brown Dwarf thingy does exist. We have of late experienced an increase in seismic activity. People are complaining of an increased incidence of headaches and delusional bursts. There is definitely something afoot with the science. What I suppose I am saying Jimmy is that I happen to believe now that probably Doctor Daedalus was able to manipulate the temporal shifts caused by the Brown Dwarf. That the big warp tenderer in itself was not bogus. What was bogus was the very fact that they did not intend to use my capital to further this branch of science. Well they may have done so actually, but their true intent was to use this as the instrument to bring me down and bleed me dry."

"Do you really think so? "Jimmy is incredulous.

"Furthermore, I believe that there is a certain sentient quality in the Brown Dwarf that has been reaching out to manipulate our consciousness. Perhaps not consciously so. Perhaps simply because that is one of the gravitational effects. Riddell and Daedalus could have been manipulated by the Brown Dwarf. I am starting to believe that the Belsingham fellow is none other than a manifestation of the sentience of the Brown Dwarf. The Brown Dwarf in the form of what we can humanely conceive through Belsingham has been warping our reality perceptions starting with Daedalus and then on to Riddell and then on to all the other cast of characters that have come in to what one perhaps might falsely conceive as this blasted plot against me. This same perception reality shift could be operating on other levels. Inside this hospital for example, where I might substitute Belsingham for Stoneywell. Be on your guard Sir! When you leave this hospital adopt the

Skittish Walk! It is efficacious also against the likes of the odious Stoneywell and that nincompoop Roper."

" I shall surely do so."

"I must sleep now dear Jimmy. I am so tired. I believe that I had another opiate in my robush tea."

"Good night, dear Sir. I will come and visit you soon".

"Skittish Walk ...", but Sir John is already succumbing to sleep.

Jimmy leaves his friend disturbed by the implications of Sir John's assessment of the situation. Disturbed that this may all be madness.

Seven: Destruction – "The Shaping of Fumi"

Fumi Lartal was raised to be a professional. Although she came from relatively modest family circumstances, it was almost as if a subconscious feeling within the system recognised her virtue and waved her on through every step of life's process to fulfil the Great Society dream of becoming a model professional. One slight deviation to this unerring progress could have diverted her to the way of the counter-professional. She could have easily been side-tracked, for after all her mother was of poor immigrant Malaccan origin. Ma Lartal had not married Fumi's father, Mister Bruce who, though claiming impeccable island family stock, was of relatively impoverished means and lived on the fringes of recognised Great Society in the market underworld of Frasertoon subsisting as a bobotie purveyor. Thankfully her father did still have some connections and he used to the full the maximum leverage of the faded reputation of his old family name. There was something of the rags to riches about Fumi Lartal. She came from limited means rising to that of one of full standing in the GS meritocracy. In that regard, she was a bit of a poster girl for the inheritors of Porto Domingo's egalitarian regime.

What marks a person out for distinction? When you consider it, is it will or providence? A bit of both perhaps, but what is the right balance? How is it that some of us are thrown onto the scrapheap whilst others conquer all before them? A slight shift or unbalancing in the paradigms of fortune can unshackle a good person from the path of progress. A little thing, some coincidence or minor indecision can mar a life of good fortune. One break, one pull in another direction, an accident to another, one mishap, or a slight, can set a train in motion leading to a career of distinction or remembrances of wasted opportunities past. We should consider a life based off the back of small things; small things have driven our ineluctability.

What was it that set Fumi Lartal out for special things? She was special because she did not feel special. She saw herself as plain ordinary. Indeed even beneath that as she came from unsatisfactory plaintive stock, not of the full islands, nor of the full old blood. Dependent on the charity of an absent father and who looked even more impoverished daily on account of his charity to her. Living with a mother of poor immigrant status who confounded the security of Fumi by constantly questioning their luck. (" A hard rain is going to fall for those in the sun too long" and "Our family have lived off the scraps of blood, sweat and tears and then again simply miserable terrible misfortune"); such remarks made by Ma Lartal who was constantly chewing on the black quince making her teeth go rotten and her breath smell foul and malodorous. Fumi found it hard to ride the back of fortune accompanied by the daily rattle of a mother who breathed pest and misfortune. The juxtaposition was hard to bear. Days full of Dorothy's Girls school with evenings and non-school days with Ma Lartal who did not know how to set a table properly in their poor hut and could not really say what was the difference between history and geography.

Yet the young Fumi Lartal had a natural talent and she knew how to mimic the habits of her betters. She had the raw material in her to propel herself forward if someone were to give her the platform to do so. That platform provider was in the first instance her father Bobotie Bruce. His ambivalent instincts fashioned a track of progress for her. The first instinct was pride. Not pride in his daughter, but pride that the old Bruce family name could still count for things in the Delta. Bobotie had not made a success with his old nobility Bruce surname. However, he could make up some of the old family pride by utilising the power of the family name to the good of Fumi which he had not the confidence to do in promotion of himself. He was living what he should have done by transference onto Fumi. In doing so he was quite assiduous in getting the best education for his illegitimate daughter. He had not had the gumption to promote himself quite so vociferously when he himself had been young, and had not had the fortune of a Bruce family member doing so either.

The second instinct was guilt. Bobotie had been feeling bad about not doing the honourable thing and tying the knot with the mother of his child. Bobotie had freely associated and disassociated with Ma Lartal and Fumi and as the years progressed he felt worse and worse about not affording legitimacy to them both. Not that he would ever tie down his old blood to Malaccan stock, but he was earnestly prepared to make up this omission by canvassing for and funding the best education he could procure for his bastard daughter.

Then the system cut in and took over. If you can get the seed off the fruit the wind of change often will take it and sweep it up to new full pastures. Great Society was desirous to show a community of equal opportunity. Some from the minorities were to be uplifted and extolled into a token class. Token of the beneficence and progression of Great Society. There is nothing friendlier and nice than a Malaccan, or part-Malaccan, sounding like a member of your own political and economic class. Perfectly natural to promote a non-Malaccan speaking part-Malaccan when the vast majority of Malaccans spoke coarsely and without education.

Fumi Lartal had been put in a place where she could be selected. An embracing kindly arm had been put around her. Her natural talent was able to do the rest.

Lord Protector Phillian Williams had been on the look-out for fresh legal acumen in his great state office of Law Enforcement. His Grand office was responsible for all internal aspects of order and contentment within Great Society. Within his aegis he had control over the Chamberlains, the Rozzers, the Day and Night Watches, Poorhouse surveillance and Schools of the Suspect Norm among his dominion. However, most of all as a person who was schooled in the law, he had particular pleasure in having authority over the Prosecution. This was the elite group of his whole vast office as far as he was concerned, and he would only have the brightest and best in that exclusive fraternity. Williams had no qualms in showing that this group was where his heart and mind belonged, most of the time eschewing the formal robes of the Lord Protector for that of the black silk robes of a King's Counsel, and in that too , he had his peculiar affectations referring to anyone who he did not share opinion with as "my learned friend". Phillian Williams liked his people in the Prosecution to be the best, and to be the best you had to be sharp, cut-throat and quick-witted. If you could not be all these, then it helped to be good looking.

The Lord Protector liked his favourites, some might say his toadies, chief of which was one Tegan Snowchild. They were almost a couple, an unlikely couple in that Williams was sixty-five years of age and actually married, and one could never say he was a handsome piece of work. Snowchild was a pretty piece, dressing in appealing corset dresses which beautified her busty outlook and definitely made much of generous brunette looks for one in her prime at the age of thirty-six. There were rumours that the two were lovers, they may have only been soul mates, but she was his number two, albeit without position or portfolio at the Grand Office of Law Enforcement, and like the Lord Protector she too was an advocate. Tegan

Snowchild KC had a bias and a political outlook which she shared with the Lord Protector. The two of them had an animus against scroungers. That new class of people in Great Society. Neither professional or bone fide counter-professional, a group which was starting to swell and create a counter black economy which sapped at the revenues and ruling culture of Great Society. Williams and Snowchild were convinced that this group, the scroungers and ne'er-do-wells, were a slow dissolve on Great Society. Tegan Snowchild KC was instructed to root these elements out and those that would protect them.

Snowchild knew that there was corruption in the Grand Office of Law Enforcement and that there were officials who protected this underclass and their underworld entrepreneurs. Tegan was rapidly coming to some conclusions. One conclusion that she did not share with her superior was the dependability of one Horatio Beeswax Belsingham. She had grave suspicions as to his reliability. The Lord Protector, on the other hand, felt that "Beeswax" was one of the up and coming, counselling his acolyte that Belsingham was just too urbane for most tastes. The Lord Protector advised her that she would have to learn to work with his types in the future. An admission that Tegan Snowchild would never really get to the very top, rather the likes of Belsingham were of that political elite and breeding that would. Still, Tegan was keeping the book open on Belsingham and was actively recruiting new blood for the challenge on the scroungers in Great Society. So it was that Tegan Snowchild KC came across Fumi Lartal.

Fumi having passed her pupillage at Fustigans Chambers in Millbrook was already on the rise at the age of twenty-three and was just getting going to taking the lead on some defence cases. Fumi was already starting to garner a reputation as a ferocious defender of the rights of the citizens of Great Society. Many judges were being won over by her mixture of beautiful haughtiness allied with razor sharp intellect and in short time she came to the attention of Tegan Snowchild KC.

For Fumi coming to the notice of the great and the good was really something of a surprise. She had worked so hard to overcome her nerves within the bear pit of the courtroom. Every new case had been a big uphill challenge for her and maybe she had overcompensated with her acerbic haughtiness in court. What others saw as supreme self-confidence employing a destructive wit, Fumi internalised that she was below par and that she would have to pick up the pace in order to survive in the profession. What Fumi thought of herself and what others thought of her were nowhere the same. So it was a veritable surprise to Fumi, the daughter of an immigrant mother, to receive a recognition from the Grand Office of Law Enforcement.

It was a typical sultry day in December after assizes when she was invited to come and have afternoon coffee with the Lord Protector at yardarm six. This was only less than an hour away and she would have to rush, there not even being time to change out of her court robes. There was no shilly-shallying on an invitation from the LP. She caught a stage-cab and was there just about in time so that she had five minutes to recollect in the cool cavernous anteroom of the LP's bureau.

Fumi Lartal had arrived at the grand setting with her reputation. Her reputation was in the eyes of others. She could only see doubt.

"His Venerable Lordship will see you now", announced the thirty-second liveried official she had met since arriving at the building of the state offices. The thirty-third and thirty-fourth opening the huge double doors of the Lord Protector's Afternoon Bureau.

"Miss Lartal", boomed the thirty-fifth.

"Who are you?", intoned the Lord Protector.

"Fumi Lartal, your Honour. You invited me to afternoon coffee."

"Must be one of Tegan's", said a man dressed reasonably normally who was seated in an armchair near to the LP's giant walnut desk. "I'm sure she'll be here presently LP".

"Yes, yes", snapped the LP back to the rather gouty looking man. "Well you better take a seat then", indicating the plush armchairs to Fumi. "Have we had afternoon tiffin yet, Ebenezer?"

"Already twice methinks, my lord", replied the affable Ebenezer.

"Well, you better call for some more then! We can't have this pretty damsel supless can we?"

Fumi smiled sheepishly while Ebenezer got the many officials involved again for some more afternoon coffee to be delivered to the Lord Protector's bureau.

"So who are you again? I must say that I like a young woman attired in stern looking black advocate dress. Nothing like a woman in court uniform, I think. Did you dress like this to please me my girl? Now you are the niece to Countess Attol, I take it. The Serene Stella A'Droit? Did Countess Attol tell you to dress so prettily for me?"

"No Sir, the name is plain Fumi Lartal and I am actually a Junior Junior King's Counsel. I do practise at the bench really. I have come straight from court without a stop. That is why I am dressed as I am."

"Ah so, Tallulah did not send you?"

"No, my lord. I received an invitation from you to take afternoon coffee and here I am. I must say it is a privilege Lord Protector."

"Mm …. Must be tomorrow afternoon then".

Ebenezer was back and listening to their conversation.

"Losing our marbles then?"

"What?" The LC was known to be very direct.

"The under-aldermen have lost the order to the marble cake supplier. They've lost our marble cake. We'll have to make do with citron frips", clarified the knowledgeable Ebenezer.

"Miss Lartal?" A strikingly beautiful brunette materialised out of nowhere. She was dressed in the height of fashion. Her dress was quality, sky blue and accentuates her bounteous figure. She stands out amongst the drabness and fustiness of the signal colour of the great ministry. "I'm Tegan Snowchild. You may have heard of me?"

"Of course, good Mistress Snowchild. I am very aware of your great reputation", said Fumi rising from her armchair to shake the bejewelled hand.

"I'm afraid it was me that actually instigated the sudden invitation to you. No time like the moment, they do say. Perhaps we should take coffee with the Lord Protector and the Right Honourable Ebenezer Bolsover-Belsingham, and then you and I could have some private confidence directly after?", suggested her hostess.

"Naturally, I would be delighted Marm".

So this is how Fumi Lartal a young advocate got started in the gracious service of Great Society. This was the beginning of her fashioning as one of the most fiercesome state's prosecutors. A whimsical introduction to a dynamic vocation. The four characters sat at their afternoon tiffin drinking La Pur coffee and scoffing on citron frips with Fumi and Tegan Snowchild mainly listening to the two gentleman in rather frivolous conversation relating the scandalous accounts of Hussar-General Albert von Fritzheim and how Great Society would be much exercised as to how to get an efficient set of court proceedings on his many truly terrible transgressions.

"He said it was his favourite horse!", guffawed Ebenezer Bolsover-Belsingham. "What will Judge Rubicorn make of that?"

"Gentlemen, we ladies shall take our leave", announced Tegan. Fumi sensed that something more serious was about to occur and she was correct in her expectation.

Fumi was led by Tegan Snowchild some one hundred yards down an imperial looking corridor leading off the LP's bureau and was taken into a much smaller but still very sumptuous bureau.

"I think that we can dispense with further refreshments", suggested Snowchild.

"And dispense with a posse of liveried officials too". Fumi instantly regretted the spontaneity of the quip.

"Yes you are so right. We are drowning in uniformed underlings who fuss and bother around everywhere but don't really provide anything of use", smiled Snowchild. "There is much in this Grand Office of Great Society that is very ineffectual. We have enormous capacity problems trying to maintain and prosecute the law and good advocates and proponents we have but few. Nevertheless we have all these liveried hangers-on and I do not know what the point is of them all. I think there is one specialist who concentrates solely on removing cake crumbs from the LP's bureau! Well that's another matter for another day. I should get straight on to what might directly interest you."

Fumi shifted uneasily in her seat wondering if some great admonishment were to come where she would be decried as a disgrace to her profession for protecting and arguing for lowlifes and scum. Nothing escapes notice in Great Society. She knew that there were spies and informers everywhere.

"You have not escaped notice", tentatively began Tegan Snowchild. " Your performance in court of late has not missed our attention."

Fumi blanched. Her heart started to palpitate.

"And that's why I wish to confide in you. Great Society in my opinion is at a crossroads. That is the opinion of the

Lord Protector too. Before I go on I have to apologise discreetly for him. Phillian Williams has been one of the greatest legal minds that Great Society has been blessed with, and he still is most of the time. However, there are other times like this afternoon that that great mental faculty of his regresses into a foolish childlike senility. You see, I should confide to you, that the Lord Protector is suffering from Dagalov's Disorder. We are all aware that it will slowly and surely eat away his fertile mind. Nonetheless, he does not wish to lay down his rod of office quite yet. For he does not believe that we have identified an adequate successor, but I must say that is partly vanity on his part. There is me for a start!", Tegan Snowchild laughed artificially.

"I see", Fumi trying to appear sympathetic but not quite knowing to whom.

"But I trust you to hold all this in the strict confidence!"

"Naturally. Does an admiral have a poop deck?" Fumi regretting and recognising that she tended to say rather the wrong thing when feeling anxious or nervous.

Tegan Snowchild KC looked at her strangely and briefly, but nonetheless went on.

"Well apparently my acute and forensic legal mind is digressing. Back to the main issue, Miss Lartal!"

Fumi again shifted uneasily waiting for the coup de gráce.

"Yes, it is indeed very likely that Great Society is at a crossroads", continued Snowchild. "To use your analogy, we probably have to turn the ship or else we will hit the rocks. We cannot go directly on as always. We have to recognise the extraneous influences outside our pure ideal. Our country, our culture, our society is so very benign. I do not know where it could go better. The trouble is that our ethos is so wholly perfectly benign that there is no-one to challenge us about it. Our exterior façade is unimpeachable so we tend to rot from within. Our state officials represent an unflawed society so that their very own personal ethics and behaviour become flawed. Too many senior officers of Great Society have been made corrupt as the perfection of this society has perfectly accentuated their flaws. There's the irony of it.".

Fumi was not really sure that she was on Snowchild's intellectual level and was hoping soon that the apple would drop and open her realisation of what was being said here. She was not understanding much at all so far.

"So what am I saying here?", breathlessly enquired Snowchild.

For a long short moment Fumi was scrambling for a coherent reply but Snowchild allowed herself to be unanswered.

"We have done a good job with the professionals and counter-professionals. We are integrating well our immigrant folk – look at you as a model, for example Miss Lartal. Where we are vulnerable, where we have the unlatched back door, is in the incorrigible despicability of the scrounging class. We have a growing society of scroungers and ne'er-do-wells who do not pay any due to Great Society. These scroungers and freeloaders are creating a black economy and a bogus hierarchy existing within, but beyond the pale of Great Society. They would not exist, they would have been expunged if not for the forbearance of certain members of this very Great Office."

"Are you alluding to law enforcement officers on the take? Corruption?", ventured Fumi tentatively.

"Yes, indeed I am, and I can see that you are a quick brief", she stressed, "and that's why I want you in".

"In what, pray?"

"Have you heard of certain underworld characters, such as Dicky Dive, Lord Roy Gibbons and Fritz-Carla Delinqua?", probed Snowchild.

"Well, I have certainly heard of the iniquitous Fritz-Carla", rejoined Fumi.

"The other two are equally notorious, I assure you, and apart from their temerity in taking on Great Society, they should not be underestimated in terms of their organisation, planning and deployment. These underworld princes constitute a great menace to our state and their power has been enforced by those growing number of Great Society officials who they have put under their patronage. I would not be surprised if you came across at least one corrupt official even today in your present short stay in this building".

"Really?", gulped Fumi.

"This is not the time to voice my suspicions to you. Another time I hope, Miss Lartal. Instead now I want to put a proposal to you in principle. I want you to come and work here in the Prosecution. I make this proposition to you simply and boldly. We consider you - that's the LP and myself – to be one of the most principled and brightest advocates of this generation. We wish to recruit the very best to take on the scrounging class and secure successful prosecutions against these debased licentious members of Banana Delta. I believe you to be pure and honourable, as well as extremely capable and ingenious enough to give the scrounger scum a run for their money. For that you will receive the full support of the Lord Protector and myself. Meanwhile I shall be stepping up initiatives on wheedling out our enemy within. What do you, say Fumi Lartal?"

Her father, Bobotie Bruce, had always counselled her to seize an opportunity when offered. "I would have to say yes!", and simply could not believe it. "Pray give me the month to clear up my obligations to my present employer Fustigans"

"Miss Fumi Lartal, I am entirely delighted, and so shall Phillian Williams be, once his present temporary fugue has dissipated. A month's notice is entirely in order. You shall be working for me directly and intimately, you do understand?"

Fumi nodded expectantly.

"However, in the formal chain of command you will be reporting as an Associate to State's lawyer Horatio Beeswax Belsingham. He is a second cousin to the gentleman you met in the LP's bureau".

"Ebenezer?"

"Precisely. Please be aware that you may experience some resistance and difficulty from your new principal as he will probably be piqued by the fact that he was not consulted in your recruitment to his crew. We will develop circumstances to mollify that effect, however, continue to keep in mind that you shall be enjoying the full confidence of the Lord Protector and myself. You will have been recruited by the very top. I shall draw up the contract for your services. I am sure that you will find the remuneration sufficient."

And with that Fumi Lartal started out on her distinguished public service.

Cloppety-clop goes the progress of the slow horse in life, fully-burdened and struggling each day to extinguish a drop of its existence.

"Who is she, nuncle?"

"I do wish you wouldn't call me that!"

"Just a term of endearment for a cousin who is so much older than me!"

"Very clever, but I rather you cut it out altogether".

"Fair enough, but who in the fuck is she?", he barked, clearly used to getting his way with cousins, uncles and most others too.

"HBB, you know full well who she is. She is some smart up and coming career public official who will curry favour by doing exactly what their lordships want".

"Being what, Ebenezer?"

"To shake down our very painstakingly set of agreements with Dicky Dive et al".

"Fools! Don't they recognise that we need to keep in place these agreements to stop anarchy breaking out? Is the old fool such a fool?"

"He has his good days. Increasingly less so I'm afraid. Even when he is at his lucid best he is still prone to following the counsel of his slutty cohort."

"That bloody Snowchild!", rasped HBB.

"Yes, she has her winsome ways and his sexual appetite actually appears to be increasing with the Dagalov's. She wins him over with her sexual politik. I swear also that she is in cahoots with Countess Attol who is always sending along her very dubious nieces for audiences with the LP."

"What should I do, dear Coz?"

"You will have to let the Lartal woman prosecute her business to your very charter. However, keep her away from anything serious that could give grave complications. Protect those that protect the fabric of Great Society. Give her her head, and if she threatens to break yours, then arrange for something misfortunate. It is as about as simple as that. I wish I could offer something more clever."

"No cousin, that is sage advice and I would take it. Thank you for allowing me to vent my spleen. Nevertheless, we shall have to box clever to keep the balance of Great Society".

"I agree, HBB. There is nothing more dangerous than the self-righteous."

"Yes, you are right. Persecution is always public. Pragmatism is a force that wins over in private."

"She is starting within the month".

"I know how to play the game", smiled HBB.

Before he knew it Horatio Beeswax Belsingham, State's Prosecutor First Class, was welcoming a new junior to the group. He was effusive and charming to Miss Fumi Lartal. She was good looking. Her mixed Malaccan race inspired attraction and good looks from many of the male office juniors. HBB had to confess to himself that she also turned his head too just a little. However that would not stop him from destroying her when the time came. It was always a pleasure to expunge beauty. What more natural; after all, this was what time would actually do so naturally in the end.

HBB put her on little cases. He had her chasing down to Further Plokington, Upper Biddysworth, Jo Hopes and the provincial like. He kept her away from the main metropolitan cases, had her prosecuting obscure weights and measures cases, and had her scurrying around the lush countryside on the trahere trying to track down superfluous pieces of evidence. At first she did not mind. Fumi Lartal would learn the ropes. She knew that humility was essential for education. One had to be open to what was being taught to you. You had to learn it all and then later discard what was deemed unimportant or irrelevant to you. Her father, Bobotie Bruce, had taught her himself some rudiments of the science of pedagogy and she applied them with focus and thrift. Learning was trying in both senses of the meaning.

However, almost six months of being Miss Grey Mouse was starting to take its toll. She had minimal contact with Tegan Snowchild and the Lord Protector could have been in the pantheon of the old gods for he was so remote from her humble station. Principal Belsingham was no longer oozing such natural charm to her. He had begun to find fault with her and seemed to be more irascible towards her. When she was proud of something and reported achievements looking for approbation he was prone to dismiss her churlishly, often then praising to the rafters one of the other juniors, particularly Miss Anabella Goulish. She was tired of Belsingham's flirting with Anabella Goulish. Goulish was an intellectual lightweight compared to her. Not even a natural beauty like Fumi. Just a winsome blonde with a large gobbling smile who set herself out to accommodating to older gentlemen in the office.

'The slut would gobble her way to a comfortable living or a quick marriage', considered Fumi.

Fumi had one ally amongst the other juniors in the Prosecution. He was Strontius Maxmehr, a true Malaccan of the far islands who had similar to Fumi been raised relatively poor but supported by a true family. He had obtained the necessary schooling to raise himself up into the august realms of the world's second oldest decent profession. Maybe he had taken a shine to Fumi, but Fumi had noticed that he was prepared to speak out against Belsingham in support of Fumi. This was entirely merited Fumi considered, for in all objectivity, she was extremely good in the prosecution of her duties. Whether he fancied her or not, it was extremely fair of him to speak out forthrightly when things were being portrayed unfairly against her. Strontius was two years senior to her in the rank of the juniors and Fumi felt good to have his moral support.

One day: "Really Miss Lartal this is not the proper drafting of a Morteva injunction! What is this sloppy application? What is this unprofessional dedication? This will not do. Not at all, and by someone still serving her probation", hissed Belsingham.

"But Sir, you said that we should serve a Maressa interlocut", said Fumi quite reasonably.

"Do you dare to contradict me and speak untruths", countered Belsingham.

A quiet tear came to Fumi's eye.

"I am sorry Sir, but I really must intercede", it was Strontius Maxmehr. " I did also specifically hear you instruct Miss Lartal to draw up a Maressa. Of that, be assured, have no equivocation." Strontius flashed a pure sure smile. He had in his way quite a presence.

Belsingham was dissembling. "Then it must have been the hubbub in this room. So many advocates all talking at once in this large clerkship room. You must have misheard, or, pray do I take to mumbling?"

"You always speak cogently and clearly, my Principal" was his confident reply.

Fumi felt vindicated and more so supported so that she was able to compose herself and carry on having been provided with this temporary relief from the outrage of mobbing on her tarnished inner being.

Within the week Strontius Maxmehr had been reposted to the out-office in the Timber Highlands. Fumi never saw him again. She missed a true ally and gallant.

Y ou know how it is in your dreams. Your mind can expose yourself. It likes to prey upon your weaknesses.

They can all see through Fumi. The front is down and she has been exposed.

She is small and despicable. She is not worthy. What is she doing there?

Her mother is laughing at her. Ma Lartal is saying how have you grown so high and mighty when I know, and now they all know, that you are so useless. Bobotie Bruce is lying in the gutter, booze and other remnants retching from his mouth.

"I tried little girl. I tried, but all this family is really from the gutter. We must all go back to the gutter. That what we are about little lass. You may as well go back to the underclass where you belong."

"That you are someone is all fantasy. You are fantasy. You are nothing. After all you have made me up from your own perverted brain. I will exist not anymore! You have invented me up to be a real someone so that you can be someone by association". It is Tegan Snowchild talking now and a drunken sailor is taking her from behind. She speaks with irritation as she feels that she has to drop everything to scold Fumi and to be diverted from the real action at hand. The jolly jack tar who is shafting her suddenly assembles with the face of Horatio Beeswax Belsingham and from his stinky rum breath are heard the words:

"Malaccan dumbkopf! Miggera."

The language of her ancient oppressors even talks through the bloodlines. It is woven deep into dreamland consciousness.

Who do you think you are? Question. Question. Could you love me my sweet Belsingham?

Fumi Lartal had problems sleeping for quite some time not daring to be terrorised by the sweet deep anxieties of her over caring mind.

Then one day she said to herself that all hope must die.

All hope must die and she would ask Tegan Snowchild to kill it.

She dressed at her most prim. Yet another nightmarish night had been exacting. She applied her cosmetic stark but not over alluring. She practiced her look against her mirror. Her look of confidence. The body armour she needed for the day. She arched an emphatic eyebrow and taught her eyes to express again "come on – take me on". A full half-hour later Fumi Lartal was at Gaolers Knoll ready at the stage stop knowing that she must force her way into Tegan Snowchild's attention for an interview.

She would confront her demons of confidence by risking criticisms from the one who she most wanted approbation from on this very day.

When you resolve yourself to something then often it comes easier. Fumi arrived at the Grand Office just as the official coach of Tegan Snowchild KC was pulling into the main inner courtyard.

"Good day, Miss Lartal", smiled the KC as charming as ever.

" I doth need of urgent consultation with you Marm", Fumi went straight in like an arrow.

"Please speak to my appointments under-secretary. I have a very busy set of appointments the next days. He will fit you in with an appointment, or else your direct superior may be able to help". Tegan Snowchild looked as if she could not slow down due to cares of office.

"It cannot wait fitting in. I am at a predicament and will not enjoy a moment until it is resolved." Fumi could be bold when desperate.

"I see. Then you better come and take morning chocolate with me", said Snowchild. "Harris, the junior counsel is with me." Harris nodded courteously and opened the wide double doors of the Senior Annex of the building.

Fumi was again in the plush bureau of Tegan Snowchild. It had been a while. A footman was pouring morning chocolate and was then retiring discreetly leaving the two ladies at their leisure.

"What is the matter, Fumi?", Tegan chose to be intimate to make confidence more forthcoming.

"I am so sorry to bother you. I know that you have important matters to prosecute ..."

"Pray my dear, simply have out with it!"

"I am afraid I cannot go on with my position in the Prosecution. I do not have the confidence of my superior Horatio Beeswax Belsingham. He is making my life a misery such that I cannot sleep anymore. My position here is untenable. It is intolerable." And at this Fumi broke down into quiet sobs as Tegan Snowchild watched on solicitously allowing her to cry full sway decorously.

"Well spit it out. Tell me all."

A liveried official has knocked on the door and is entering: "The Solicitor of Ships has arrived for you Marm".

"Put him to wait in the Theodora Anteroom. Tell him to be patient as I have some urgent business to attend to."

The official has left and Fumi is feeling a little stupid to interrupt the august affairs of state.

"I'm afraid Marm that I am taking up your most valuable time", said she sheepishly.

"No not really. The Solicitor of Ships is a most tiresome and pompous individual. To wait upon me will put him in his place. I like the exercise of power from time to time", laughed Tegan, "particularly when that exercise is upon the very conceited. Your matters of concern are far more important to me than his. I think he wants to talk about his pet subject again − his uniform code for flogging on Great Society's fighting ships. I think he gets off on the whipping. The old pederast!"

Both women giggled mercilessly. The lewd nature of the quip allowed Fumi to feel more comfortable at unfolding her news. The relation of the peculiar desires of the SoS by Tegan inspired trust in Fumi. She opened up and told her mentor about the abuse that she had received at the hands of Belsingham. She related her loneliness, her feeling of being mobbed and her dismay about the treatment of her colleague Strontious Maxmehr. She found herself in a quarter of an hour expressing her full anxiety under the expert and sympathetic questioning of Tegan Snowchild.

"Well Fumi the time has now come to tell you this. Mister Belsingham has been under my observation for some time now. He is indeed one of those officials I first cautioned you about as being corrupt and in cahoots with the underworld hierarchy which is now threatening to dispossess Great Society. He is one of the major characters, in my opinion, who is sponsoring the growing influence of the scroungers. I have my eye on the gentleman, but unfortunately he is extremely well connected. The LP cannot believe that Belsingham would do any wrong. The old man has verily had the cloth pulled over his eyes. So it is my job to draw up the evidence on Belsingham and his like, but I have to do so very discretely as chum Belsingham is very well connected and my dear friend Phillian cannot be shaken in his faith in the man. This is where you come in, dear Fumi, so it is very providential that you are here today".

"Can I actually help?", Fumi croaked.

"You certainly can! First, by remaining in your position. Do not doubt whatsoever my full support for you. You shall be verily protected. Belsingham knows that he cannot touch you. He knows that you are my protégé and that I afford you my full protection. He may bluster, he may threaten, but he cannot remove you whilst my influence at the highest echelons remains here. So you have to put up with his bullying tactics, but realise that he is a toothless hound for you at the end of the day. Fortify yourself in that knowledge."

"I see."

"Second, I want you to make yourself a nuisance to him. Take on prosecutions in main town. Go looking for miscreants in Frasertoon, Hard Shoulder, Tinseltees and other less salubrious places in the main. You have served your probation and now have charter to take on investigations at your judgement. You do not always now have to be instructed by your superior. Start prodding at the hornets' nest. We need to start smoking him and his cronies out. We need to put pressure on Belsingham so that he starts to make mistakes. I want to force him to run to his underworld superiors. We need to catch him out and link him to his crooked cohorts. If he tries to block any of your prosecutions, then quote him letter and line of our ordinances. You will have the majesty of the law behind you, he cannot defy you. Be the demon good prosecutor of Great Society and I promise you that we will cut out this rotten core amongst us. The great and good will be indebted to you. I will be indebted to you. Your professional career in its future lofty position will look back and smile at the brave young Fumi Lartal. Think on it! Are you game, girl?"

Hesitantly, "Yes."

And then more assuredly: "Yes!"

"Good! I better go and sort out that old fart Sir Harry. Here is my address", handing Fumi her visiting card. "Come to my residence at seven this night and we will hammer out the details of a plan."

Thus was formed the prosecuting zeal and commitment of the Right Decent Fumi Lartal JJKC. Her reputation was about to burgeon.

"My dear Ebenezer. How nice to see you. What brings you from your lofty preserve to the front of my dingy desk?"

"Oh, your way with words cousin!"

"Well, what is happening", grimaced HBB.

"Now I am not sure that it concerns us, but I just wanted to let you know that I heard from Harris. He says that Fumi Lartal ambushed his mistress yesterday morning demanding an urgent meeting. The young filly seemed quite distraught, so said Harris."

"That's interesting".

"What is more interesting", continued Ebenezer Bolsover-Belsingham, "is that the audience was granted straight away and was intense enough that Harry Trueblood was kept waiting by Mistress Snowchild for over an hour! What do you make of that? She wouldn't wish to piss off old Trueblood too easily, would she? Ho hum. We will all commit 27,000 errors before we meet our graves."

"Something is amiss alright", conjectured HBB. "Miss Lartal had been starting to look distinctly rattled of late. Today she appears all sweetness and light. Quite calm and collected really. That surprised me as I thought I was getting her on the run."

"Do you think they are working a stratagem?"

"If they are, then that's not good for us?"

"What do we do then?"

"Devise our own stratagem", sighed HBB. "Let me talk to Roy and Slim. They are always very artful on ideas. Meanwhile keep pressing coin on Harris and tell him to keep a look-out. We cannot spring to conclusions, but the feeling in my water is that something is up."

"Very well, cousin", and Ebenezer was off.

Horatio Beeswax Belsingham was left alone in his bureau. He was left alone with his thoughts. His thoughts were like barbarians, but he knew how to deal with them. If you pursued their fanciful pagan virtues then always something artful and crafty would distil. He sensed that Fumi Lartal was here to stay and he further sensed that there was a strange elemental enmity on his part towards Miss Lartal building up. A strange elemental enmity that was making him feel quite libidinous. He would go with the feeling.

She must not be allowed to be built up to be a nemesis. However time would allow her to be built up to something high enough to be really hurt by the fall.

For now thoughts and time were on his side.

Eight: Destruction – "Lincoln and Common Humanity"

Like many a good family of snobs the head of the Lincoln family, Josemiah, had come from quite a humble background. So humble that it was approaching poverty; so much that the living of each and every day constituted a risk. Josemiah's family had been deep rooted island trash and their very antecedents had been traced back to the original Utone inhabitants of the islands. His extended Lincoln family had scrounged a living off the darker limits of Banana Delta. Fortunately, for them Great Society had never categorised them in whole as counter-professional as the gracious Porto Domingo deemed the original Utone aboriginals as "dex ruta" or Utone for "original root of the islands". In a peculiarly superstitious way Domingo believed that to deny the original inhabitants would be bad juju for the regime. The family was mixed race going back for several generations and for the most immediate of those several generations they had scrimped out a living under full GS licence. Josemiah's father, Harry, had officially been a tinker, but had made most of his krugerbands from illicit activity on the wrong side of the law. Josemiah's family lived in Straw Flats the most squalid area of Banana Delta that the City Council would claim as its own and Josemiah was one of seven children competing with his siblings for every scrap.

At the age of sixteen Josemiah had fallen down a sewer shaft in the Goldgluck neighbourhood of Banana Delta. As the name suggests the quarter was a centre for the goldsmith trade. Josemiah and some other enterprising cohorts scratched out a living by sieving off tiny fragments of gold which they collected from the slurry of the sewers. It was a dirty business, but where there is muck indeed there is brass. He had fallen down a sewer shaft of some twenty feet deep. Luckily for him his chums were able to pull him up with some rope and bring him up to the surface safely. However, Josemiah was badly injured and it was feared that he might have some serious fractures about his body. He was duly taken and admitted to the poorhouse hospital White Cross. After inspection and some, thankfully, minor broken bones being recast he was given a bed in the "Mercy" ward. There it transpired he was visited by the Hospital Visitor herself, Lady Clemency Swann. They struck up a conversation and there was something about the handsome Josemiah that Lady Swann took to. By the end of his stay Lady Swann had agreed to be Official Guardian to Josemiah. To that end court documents were drawn up and Lady Swann exuberantly poured money into Josemiah's education; it was rumoured that Josemiah in return poured affection into her. Lord Swann, grandfather to the present Earl of Tischent, was mostly at his club Milliwhigs. Josemiah Lincoln applied himself and before long had a double first in Commerce and Chemistry from Land University. Josemiah then took articles at the Dolphin Line shipping company. Within ten years he was running it and had increased revenues eight-fold.

Josemiah married Aliza Duncan. She was a society debutante and had been bred and groomed for a fine match. The Duncan family was big in commercial shipping. They ran the Continental line. Pa Duncan was mightily impressed by Josemiah's commercial acumen and seven years after the Lincoln–Duncan marital merger the respective two companies were merged to form Continental Dolphin under the stewardship of Josemiah Lincoln.

As if the young David Lincoln did not have enough to look up to in his formidable father there was also his older brother Adolphus. Adolphus was Aliza Duncan's favourite; her golden boy. Adolphus got the lion's share of his mother's affection, as well as his father's pride. Adolphus took a double-double first at Land University in chemistry / physik, as well as engineering / causal effect. Adolphus at the age of twenty-one was being groomed for the business and Josemiah had high hopes that Adolphus would cut a political career.

David Lincoln was a couple of years younger than his all-conquering older brother. Therefore he had just enough time to breathe a little behind all Adolphus's triumphs and achievements. He could catch his breath just long enough to realise that to compete in the area of his brother's exaltations would not be the best stratagem for him. Why play a particular game when it is not best suited for you? David had heard a maxim that people do not really change rather that they move to circumstances where it is better for them to prosper. Therefore, David liked to read and contemplate, not asseverate and postulate. He could do without the company of others. Why waste time listening to the commonplace or communing with wordy airbags? His route to power was not about posturing, it was about positioning.

Suffice to say that David was an ideas man and he was prepared to emblazon that leitmotif on his boating blazer and all other chic apparel he had begun to garner with a rapacious taste. He started to read Radisom, Emperry, Rottigall and many others too. The true classics of social empowerment. He also read Dantz, Hedelmeyer and Buttsie on political enfranchisement, and was gaining a rounder picture. But then he discovered *"The Acceptance of Truth"* by Franzi Joe (who had written this during his time in GS political office under the nom de plume of Agatha Berkely). Franzi Joe freely admitted in this masterpiece how he had leveraged his views off the earlier works of Gerontius Mander. Mander had not been published for many years due to his controversial views that all men might not be equal, or, even if they were, that it may be more efficient to the overall society interest that they were not all treated equally. David noted how all these ideas were rooted into the fabric of Great Society's state structure.

But this was more the conceptual stuff. If one could accept the concept, and David could, then the real exciting stuff was in the mechanics of implementation of social order, and for that you looked to the magisterial writings of Doctor Sally Dambey and her thesis on social place conditioning. The writings of Dambey convinced the young David Lincoln that true power was not getting into some ruling class position or getting perched on top of a pile of largesse, but rather to be in the "actual running truth" of the system of government. In other words the essence of power was to be the driving force of the implements of change, for change was always present and people accepted that you could not change it and it was preferable to go with the flow of it. What David recognised from the writings of Dambey, Franzi Joe, Heidelberger and others was that you attained power when you were the actual flow itself; for nobody could recognise where the flow came from but they went with it when it was there. True power was like the weather; people would recognise its elemental force and may not like its effects, but would never quibble about how it got there.

David Lincoln was constantly taking notes. He relished taking notes.

Social place conditioning.

Not social at all. Society driven and seeing overall society as one living organism that had to be in harmony to be able to thrive.

Place is mathematik. Universal physik has given that larger numbers are given life by smaller number. The smaller number of privilege will always dictate the larger numbers. Just as in the same way a single moment of time gave birth to eternity.

Conditioning is the hallmark of the human condition. We are conditioned permanently to stop us jumping and gnashing back into the way of the beast, but yet again the law of the jungle can never be quite quelled and because of that some of our human herd will have to be sacrificed. It is a constant process throughout life and we have to keep running for fear of being picked off.

David Lincoln dared to think differently as he could see that the ability to think into things marked the true difference between the successful and the truly powerful. He could now despise brother Adolphus as being merely successful, not inherently powerful. Porto Domingo had created a real hierarchy; a living microcosm for the government of the islands. David determined to attend the School of Modern Studies at Beltimore College. Most of the brightest officials were being identified and recruited from there. He wanted to learn from the radical Professor Jinty Smart. She was at the apex of this class of new thinker.

He told his father of his intentions.

"Beltimore College", snorted Josemiah Lincoln, "a reaping ground for pen-pushers and petty bureaucrats. Oh well, that's it. We will all commit 27,000 errors before we meet our graves. It's a good job then that we have raised Adolphus for a career of social responsibility."

"Yes indeed, Father", smiled David and he was on his way without anybody else's care in the world.

Thought processing: David Lincoln was about to coin the term and claim it as his own when he found the phrase in the *Kandy Literary Review* as he was leafing through the latest edition at the library at the Institute of Scholars. He read:

Professor Jinty Smart has taken a revisionist view to the writings of Heinrich Heidelberger and Sally Dambey and expands further on the principles of social place conditioning. In her seminal work entitled "How to Keep Society Free" (Social Press) Smart reflects on how Great Society can revitalise and maintain established principles on social place conditioning. This she maintains is best served by looking at the mechanics of the conditioning which is most elementally cemented by a process she coins as **thought processing** *......*

In advocating mechanical rudiments of **thought processing** *in relation to Dambey's central organising principle, Professor Smart goes further to advocate a new professional branch – the confessors of the professionals, as she calls it – to be known as* **thought processor,** *rather than the outmoded avuncular* **counter-professional therapist** *.....*

Professor Smart sharpens the thinking in this branch of science. **Thought processing** *is an entirely modern and intelligent approach to furthering the development of Great Society.*

David Lincoln was at once disappointed and vindicated. He had been on the verge of announcing his own views on what he had as a working title labelled thought processing (and not just the term itself, all the meaning behind the term was consistent to that espoused by Professor Smart), but had been beaten to the finish line by a renowned academician. David Lincoln was nothing but pragmatic. She had probably been developing this idea in academia for the past decade. She was of similar mind and likely more advanced in her thinking. The best solution would be to seek her out and try to learn further from her. She was on top of a movement that he wished to embrace.

Professor Jinty Smart with hair all ruffled, lip rouge smirched by moisture and clothes tousled looked cheekily at her young paramour.

"Dicky would suit you far better than that mouthful of name that you go by. Yes I could give Dicky a mouthful too."

"If you wish", he replied. "I come to you for experience".

"And what might that be?", she quizzed.

"Well it's not just for the clarity of your thought that I come so religiously to my late afternoon tutorials. Your experience in sexual adventure knows no parallel too. In the lecture theatre I hang on your every word and in your private tutor room I get the hang of working in other dimensions."

"Well said Dicky, even though I do not understand how one so young as you can compare my sexual arts to others?"

"I've been around", he ventured.

"Then maybe you're a Harry not a Dicky. Like Lucky Harry Haslam the legendary paramour".

"Oh, Professor Smart. I don't know why you have such a down on poor old Horatio, but in order to encourage you to give me the most glowing testimonial I would be happy to answer to you by any name .....Ignatius, Polonius, Rover!".

"Well Mister Belsingham ... or Rover! You'd better yap-yap your way down here and with your big Rover tongue give me a good slurpy licking!"

"Woof!"

"How I love young flesh!", she gleefully shrilled.

'How I love intellectual thigh flesh', thought Beeswax.

There was he. David Lincoln that was and his three debating companions, Manion Deadlock, Mamie Bissinger and Ruth Ratem, in the snug of *The Black Coffeepot*, a fine coffee shop and bedrock of radical ideas for the School of Modern Studies.

"Forbisher shows us that the tantamount conclusion is only operative upon the condition of deep-rooted long ingrained moral axioms being placed and then displaced in a continuous cycle of conflict in troubled individuals. Key to that is the non-acceptance by that individual of certain of those axioms which have been inserted through the application of extreme views rather than placed through subtle conditioning", asserted the pimply Ruth.

"Poppycock!"

"Pardon me?"

"Absolute tommy-rot! Forbisher was a dickhead who scripted such offal under delusions brought about by his rampant syphilis!"

"What!"

"I should know. I sucked his shrivelled dick!" The interrupter moved forward to the intellectuals stamm-table. "Let me introduce myself. I'm Horatio Beeswax Belsingham and I have come here to put you straight on radical discourse. Point one. It's all absolute kybosh. Charley, bring me wine!"

"And point two", enquired David of him.

"Yes, point two is to order some more wine to avoid additional waiting time", answered Belsingham, "but I see you're more comfortable with the straight-laced coffee pot and your coffee pot intellectuals."

David smiled and considered that he liked this discourse. He had not experienced such swagger since his last encounter with his brother Adolphus, but this brute Belsingham had obviously decided to forego all pomposity. That was refreshing. He had been tiring of over-academic discourse. It was so dry and pretentious and the intellectuals had forgotten all about the simplicity which was required to keep thought fresh and forceful.

"I know you", said Manion Deadlock. "You're the one in third year who's screwing Professor Smart".

"That's right, sah! But tush you do not use the proper language of the intellectual".

"We are not intellectuals Belsingham. We are 'thought processors'", countered David. Nonetheless David was surprised that Manion could speak so coarsely.

"Well I know about what thoughts you are processing", furthered Belsingham. "You are wondering what it is like to press your member into the generous flesh of Professor Smart's bosom. You are wondering what her chubby little fingers can do up the rims of your anus. You want to know what a prime condition forty-four year old woman can do with her tongue. Am I processing your thoughts correctly?"

"You're disgusting", snapped the beautiful but prim Mamie Bissinger and rose to leave the table. David's two other cohorts quickly followed her bustle. David held his position at the table though while Charley brought a bottle of fine Portman and two glasses.

"Then there is point three. Shall we?"

"Why not?", grinned David.

Belsingham poured.

"Portman. Where do you get the money for this?"

"I have means", revealed Belsingham.

"So what is she like, Professor Smart?"

"Really like? Well to get under those skirts and feel the flesh of those full thighs, it's like …"

"No", laughed David. "I meant her mind. Tell me the quality of her mind. That mind is one of the main reasons I signed up to Beltimore College".

"Such a dirty mind. I do not have the full vocabulary to quite describe it."

David laughed again.

"Well there is no such thing as coincidence David Lincoln. She is why I have come to find you. She is interested in you. The professor has heard reports about you. A particular glowing reference from your tutor Reader Tuttle, for example."

"Oh", smiled David.

'He is so earnest and charming. Boyish even, but we are in the process here of identifying a character and mind that can intellectualise good out of pure moribund misery', considered Belsingham.

"The professor would like you to call for tea".

"I would be delighted", stated David.

"Who is our Prime Minister and head of government", asked Belsingham.

"I'm not sure", mused Lincoln. "Maybe it is better not to know. Government of the people by the people, you know. A lot of people governing".

"Exactly we don't need personal accountability. The people are accountable to themselves! So many people governing".

Banter and discourse were in balance. The two new friends talked deep into the night.

That night was dense, and hot as so often was, and provided for fitful sleeping. The young David Lincoln was doing just that under the fine fabric of his mosquito sheets. The night so hot and lusty. He had tossed and turned imagining what he was going to say to the giant intellect that was Professor Jinty Smart.

There she was before him and her breasts were enormous and beautiful. Pearly white moonlight skin with nipples that could sustain any onslaught of lust. Naked lying on the bed she was a very majestic looking woman.

"I would play with everybody's minds for that is where true power lies", she said licking at her ruby red lips. "And I would play with your body first too so your mind might be more amenable to outside stimulus".

She was a magik woman.

Horatio Beeswax Belsingham was there next to her standing naked and erect. His erection like a tent-pole.

The magik woman pulled at the erection as if she were milking the intellect of a contemplation cow.

It was all so dreamy.

"Come", she said.

I was ready to explode. Discharge without responsibility.

"Come to us first David. Come to us first so that we can come together."

Belsingham's erection was expanding.

"Come and feel the strength and commitment of his membership", she seductively implored, "to our cause. Our membership you can see is plainly growing. Our members are rising. Join us!".

David Lincoln groaned wet and sticky on a too sultry night.

T he first words she uttered were: "Why do you think of yourself as a thought processor?".

David Lincoln had barely entered the commodious study and commodious mind of the Right Distinguished Professor Jinty Smart, Professor and Chair of Social

Placement Jurisprudence at the School of Modern Studies, Beltimore College. He had not expected to be hit straight in the consciousness with a question so direct and difficult. He knew from her lectures that she could be forthright and disarming, but had not really expected such an abrupt beginning to their meeting.

"That's a big question Professor."

And she smiled a beautiful lusty smile. "I like to think big, don't you?"

"I have read a lot. I have covered all the social scientists before you and I am firmly of the belief for a proper democratic society to be successful there has to be a fully functioning social place conditioning. That is the social philosophical belief. It is my belief. However, the belief is useless without the application. There must be a means for the people to believe in their social place conditioning and there have been many exponents on what it should be. Sally Dambey with her casuistry metrics, Smellie and his systematic aversion and Bloemthreetree and his postulations on place defining. These are very fine thinkers, but what you Madam have defined as *Running Flow Thought Processing* is in my opinion the most elegant and practical means for Great Society to adopt to continue and complete its great project."

"Oh well said, young Sir", said she with a lascivious mocking laugh.

"Dear Madam, I am not dressing you up. Believe me". David felt a little affronted as if he were not been taken seriously.

"Alright then, let's get serious, shall we?"

David smiled sheepishly. He had seemed to have parried the first attack.

"Social place conditioning, that genius idea of Doctor Sally Dambey is one that we all embrace and is crucial to the value norms of Great Society. However, the dogma cannot exude and take shape and hold without active evangelists to carry its anthem and whistle its tune so that it is catching and in our subconscious there and there again. There needs to be a system and an elite cadre of professionals to ensure that the organism of the professional is kept sacred and secure. Practitioners skilled in the business of making the selected ones feel and run counter — to make their conditioning to counter-professional complete, so to speak."

"You speak so smoothly, Mister Lincoln. So what's the hurdle to overcome?"

"We need to put in place quickly and smoothly a highly expert and skilled vocation …."

"Exactly", she interjected, as if she were convinced that they were of like mind, "so we need now the process and the method. We need new committed practitioners like yourself, David, to make this a science and an occupation. The occupation of Thought Processor. An elite position whose practitioners are able to spread out the thoughts of the deemed counter-professionals, to scramble them and unscramble them again, to weed out the base and impure; to get them to re-learn the noble and pure thoughts of sacrifice and denial. This is the new critical skill of the future; more important that the oratory acumen of a demagogue. Without efficient, meticulous and consistent thought processing Great Society could find itself under siege from the undesirables. I have coined the term "thought processing" and have set up the establishment of the profession of "Thought Processor", and we, all of us, are so vital for the continued success and prosperity of these islands. It is a noble nascent profession and I am deeply proud of what I have achieved following in the steps of the revered Sally Dambey. Equally I am touched that some of the brightest young things like yourself are embracing the creed."

"It is so patently clear to me Professor. I am surprised that there are so many among us that do not understand its clarion signal. Thought processing, therefore, may only be for the select. I hope that you do see in me that I am a radical thinker and can perform the skilled and adroit machinations of a truly qualified thought processor."

"Yes .."

"Indeed if you do, I would be honoured to learn from you, magistera."

"Hmn, I think you'll do", Jinty Smart smiled coquettishly. "Have you ever tried a ménage a trois?"

"No; I can't say that I have, but it sounds rather appealing".

"Settled", said the professor and rapped her chubby hand down on her portfolio desk. "Can you start as my pupil next week."

"Indeed I can!", laughed a triumphant David Lincoln.

"Well some pleasure before business", smiled the professor and called out to the ante-room. "Beeswax, get your hairy arse in here!"

The ambitious David Lincoln gulped.

"And then we will really drive this profession forward", she concluded.

David Lincoln felt like he was part of a living organism with Jinty Smart and Horatio Beeswax Belsingham. In the sex act they moved apart and then together like avant-garde ballet performers. Their love making and their radical politics was like a carefully orchestrated dance. They had to be in careful empathy and in abandoned coordination for their relationship, their partnership and their enterprise to thrive. Of course the Professor was the font. It was to her that he and Belsingham came to fill. She blew them thoughts, retuned their impulses, they kissed her for stimulation, they drew her orgasms and satiated into her well. Lincoln and

Belsingham probed around Jinty Smart careful not to be arousing the same area at once, flitting separately over the large gorgeous area to ensure that their queen was well fed. They were like honey bees – flying, dancing and copulating to build the hive of activities and fertile unstoppable ideas.

The three were intimate, but David felt closer to Belsingham. Jinty Smart wanted to be stimulated by not just ideas, so David took his lead from Horatio. Horatio put his head down and got to work diving for muff and David improvised on his lead looking for another orifice to flush out. They were isolated, the two men, but very synchronized, very kindred spirits. In the art of love making, in the art of stimulating ambition or desire, David would think of the arousal thought and even before he knew it Belsingham was showing how it could be best performed or implemented. David was thinking about possibilities and how his thoughts would be received and Belsingham would already be imploring "Engage, engage! Do it before you lose the thought." David could rationalise and think. Horatio could just improvise simply without too much over-contemplation.

The more David was in the company of Horatio the more easy he felt with his thoughts. It was as if his new friend had granted him absolution. That it was fine to be ruthless and extreme in your viewpoint to achieve the greater general good. That it was commendable to place yourself first before considering the overall welfare of others. That it was healthy and whole to place your appetites on to life's banquet table. That there would be no banquet if everyone could eat a little bit. Horatio taught David to recognise in himself deep debased appetite – one that might be called power. Horatio taught him to ignore morality; to despise grieving consciences that tangled up progress in a moral morass of self-pitying doubt. For the first time David Lincoln felt that it was quite proper and fine to be an absolutely selfish bastard. Belsingham liberated him. David felt liberated by not having a care for any other.

In exchange for fleshy devotion Jinty Smart gave the young aspiring David forceful patronage so that his ideas were received, debated and then generally celebrated. On the other side Belsingham put things into motion. He went to his sources at the Office of Ways and Means and secured a new civil list for the profession of Thought Processor. Belsingham then secured the appointment at the School of Suspect Norm for David; at Snoods Droop – the premier establishment, with David at the lead in this new position ensconced in as Senior Operative Thought Processor, Level II at an annual stipend of four sovereigns before tithe.

Belsingham paved a path for Lincoln. Lincoln could conceive of the destination to be achieved and Belsingham built a road to it. Lincoln thought and conceived, he weighed up things in the big balance. Belsingham went out and managed. Sometimes it occurred to Lincoln that his friend and kindred spirit had superhuman powers to manage time and activity. He seemed to be in all places at once and had a finger in every biscuit jar. He prosecuted the advancement of Lincoln's career whilst holding down his own demanding position in the Prosecution. Belsingham attended every intellectual soirée and was seen at every bigwig's party and was known to have danced with all the young unmarried female relatives of the Countess of Chame. Lincoln wondered if his friend Horatio could be human, but was then struck by his warm humanity. He was to Lincoln the nicest, kindest individual, although Lincoln frequently witnessed a side to him where he could employ a cruel tongue to people and where he could be unfeeling to persons whom Lincoln felt respect should be accorded. However, as his friend, Belsingham was to Lincoln fearless. Belsingham would take on the dogs of war and beat them to secure Lincoln's position. This Lincoln realised, and marvelled at the force of Horatio Beeswax Belsingham, and then again wondered why Belsingham should be his such loyal protector.

Lincoln hardly saw Horatio Beeswax Belsingham and yet again Horatio was always at his side proposing and cajoling good-naturedly. Every time the flux subsided (usually when the day was over) Lincoln would look up and his good friend would be there with some friendly comment, with some useful idea to progress things further.

One night Belsingham said to him: "What do you think of these sketches, David?"

"Huh! Hairy trolls and ring-eyed demons. I don't know. A bit ghoulish but in their way quite appealing. A little over melodramatic. Makes me think that a young person has done them".

"You are right, of course. It is the art of an adolescent, but I would say gifted. Would you not say that there is intelligence in this artist".

"Without a doubt", replied Lincoln. "The person must have some wherewithal to capture the sadness and the fury in these eyes".

"So this person could be countenanced as a professional for fabrication of art artefacts, would you say?"

"Yes, I would. Nonetheless the artist should be persuaded to craft something a bit more uplifting for the citizens of Great Society. I am not sure that the present specimens would accord with prescribed culture! Is the artist someone to be sent to the Society?"

"No, because I propose we break him", snarled Belsingham.

"What?"

"Think about it", purred Horatio. "We have been thought processing into counter-professionals mainly dullards and feeble minded folk. Riff-raff that would just be a problem for us if they were not cleansed into counter-professionalism. Easy meat. But what about the intellectuals whom we always have to cajole and persuade and are constantly accommodating them by giving them comfortable academic posts to neutralise their negative antipathy to Great Society?"

"Go on".

"Well we should be turning our theories to the application of sterner challenges. We should now be looking to prove our thought processing techniques as being thoroughly robust in treating all-comers. We should be turning some genuinely gifted and capable individuals. Great Society cannot accommodate too many fertile minds all at once, eh?"

"I see what you mean", intoned Lincoln.

"Are you game for a new challenge?", asked Belsingham.

"I might be".

"I know a chap by the name of Alderman Lennon who can arrange to bring this young aspiring chap to you here at Snoods Droop. He's just the type of challenge you need to perfect your process You could show Brother Jacob and his cohorts the improved efficacy of our new techniques."

Lincoln nodded. "You are right as always. Contact the Alderman. We could have an interesting case study here. Let's do it".

Nine: Resistance – "The Curse of Carnival"

Jimmy Suzuki has been brought up in a carnival kingdom but he has never enjoyed its monstrous cacophony. He remembers his father's passion for the silly season. It was a time when old Harold would really come alive and become animated. He would dress up in his silly troubadour costume and regale Jimmy and anyone else who was unlucky to be around about the tradition and remembrance behind the carnival tradition. How the islanders had sung out the Orientals and through their singing they had entranced and cursed the imperialists; that through dark juju songs they had crazed the spirits of their invaders. The carnival was the spirit of the islands that overcame the conqueror. Respect was to be given to the dark melodic songs with their deep malevolent juju within. Harold Suzuki would wear his crimson and orange troubadour outfit during the days of carnival and at night when things got altogether dark he would adorn the mahogany face fetish mask and play the wild conga drums with a wanton fury as if it were not Harold Suzuki at all. No carnival was not Jimmy's mug of rum at all; beneath all the promenading and giggling there was something murky and malign.

Carnival is a wild time. Jimmy never could get comfortable with it at all. There is something disturbing and distorting about the period. People become something other than themselves. Sober conservative characters transform into abandoned fools. Old maids suddenly have a glamour and young men lust after them in the ribald streets of Banana Delta. A very secular Great Society comes awash with tribal fetish and ancient juju rituals as if it were the most natural thing in the world. Rectitude is thrown out of the window as if a year of observance of it was not worth a second of lust. The good and the great of the community sponsor blood rituals and organised orgies whilst the Chamberlains turn a blind eye to it all.

Moreover there is a sense of cruelty to the air. It was like to Jimmy that a group of human beings revert to a pack of animals. The most base and crude aspect of humanity emerges in the pack and the pack picks off the weak and the infirm. The abominable behaviour is universally condoned in cups of good cheer. During the height of carnival people die, people are maimed and people are admitted into mental asylums because of what they see, or what they do, or what they have had done to them.

There is something of an ancient and barbaric time during the celebration of carnival. A time where humans walked the earth aimlessly in small groups and they walked in the style of Barber's Ape.

Jimmy would rather keep his head down during the time of Carnival. He would like to lock himself in his abode alone with a jar of Maltak rum.

This Carnival period has gotten Jimmy to thinking about his father. What ever happened to him? He had never received a notification from the authorities about Harold's demise. From time to time he would mull over the fate of his father and pig-out on his own guilt. Jimmy wanted to punish himself but receive no more punishment, so he funnelled his thoughts into maudlin emissions.

'Could he still be living?', he wonders.

Jimmy concludes that Harold may well be alive. Harold would be about seventy-seven or even seventy-eight by now if he were still living. It was conceivable. Jimmy is adverse to the Carnival, but still decidedly superstitious based on some childhood conditioning. Due to that he determines to seek guidance in the cards. He should not make the decision on further punishment for himself, but fate could prevail. The cards were a higher entity.

The Carnival period during its most intense period, called *the Finitude,* lasted four days normally, but this year it was an *Oliebol Karnival,* a special carnival that only occurred every twelve years. For such a special carnival the Finitude lasted a whopping twelve days. The entire carnival period usually started at the New Year and slowly ramped up to the beginning of March when the Finitude and its more intense carnivalista began. During the Finitude there was nothing other than Carnival. Nothing else simply existed apart from Carnival. For Jimmy the carnivalista was simply horror and mayhem usually occurring in the hottest dog-days of the year. If the carnival is intolerable in its annual period then the Oliebol Karnival is exponentially worse.

Nevertheless, it was a time when the gypsy ladies and their reading cards were abound. At least it was a good time for a consultation.

Therefore Jimmy moves his large frame with slow aplomb through the unthinking crowds. His bulky stealth parts the human waves like super moon gravity. His look of malevolence kills any human thought. Let him pass, let him pass is imprinted on the human cockroach of carnival crowd. Jimmy is heading for Banjara town. The Banjara town is a collection of tents, wagons and stringy looking horses parked around desultory looking fires that add to the sweat of the night. The night air is thick with smell of baked almonds and horse manure.

Jimmy comes to the outlandish tents of the fortune tellers. He walks past them peeping into those who are unoccupied and open for business. They seem in general to be occupied by rather hideous looking hags. That may be the effect of the oil lamps in the tents. Then at last quite a comely one. Under forty, ample bosom and appears to have all her teeth. His substantial frame shadows her tent doorway.

"Come inside enquiring stranger. I am Ceri Hatch, Mistress of Fortune."

"You can tell my fortune?". Jimmy wants confirmation.

"I am Ceri Hatch, Mistress of Fortune!", and then with a dramatic flourish of richly henna tattooed hands announced "I am of the Chara. Put silver here and I will address your fate." She indicated her eye-catching bosom with a flash of her green eyes.

Jimmy solemnly takes out of his purse a silver King Boris which he had won in a card game some long time ago and solicitously places it quite delicately on the very edge of her abundant cleavage. Without the same ceremony she quickly removes the ducat, bites on it and spits; all with a dramatic flourish.

"Good that you have come to someone with real knowledge of the cards, unlike all those unauthentic youngsters out there." Then she smiles and Jimmy senses the snarl of a cat or something more primeval.

"Sit stranger! I am Ceri Hatch and I will tell your fortune. You have come to me Ceri Hatch, and I may make your fortune".

"Wow, yes", stutters Jimmy.

"I have Savral Army cards".

"Savral Army", repeats Jimmy.

"Yes, the oldest yet that have not gone under the sea. They know ancient misfortune, present foolishness and are too good for literal truth. They are the best for divining".

"For divining…"

"For divining the future. But beware they do not tell the truth, only your fortune. Shuffle them." She hands the manky pack to Jimmy.

"Very few cards", he mentions.

"Yes, only six and very powerful. It is not the cards you choose but the order in which you choose for them to come out."

Jimmy shuffles very carefully the rather slim pack of cards and hands them pack to the fortune teller.

"The first is Gobblar", she explains. "He sneaks through the night, steals what you are scared to have stolen and he does not like it when it is bright. We feed our Banjara children with stories of his wanton craftiness and how he is like a phantom who steals away the souls of bad children. He can stand for something that you would like to suppress for fear of attacking you in the sharp of the night."

"What can it mean?", asked Jimmy.

"Who knows? Nothing at all probably. Possibly yes ...." Ceri Hatch closes her eyes and delivers a resounding fart. "Pungent! The smell tells me he is yet still alive. One Harold Suzuki is yet still alive and it would probably do you good to search him out as soon as you are able".

"I knew it", whispers Jimmy.

"Next card, next card. Think of my other clients. Ah there she is, Rhianna! I knew she would come next!"

"So what is she?"

"Why, of course, she's me. The fair fortune teller. All men will stake their fortune on her." Ceri Hatch again closes her eyes and belches abundantly. "Most aromatic. You must raise your flag to the mast of this Kendra. She is your fortune, but you choose in your heart to woo her. Do not worry that she is so much younger than you. Like you she is looking for a father figure too."

"Ooh ..."

"Next card, next card. Think of my awaiting clients."

Jimmy could not sense lines of further client outside the tent door, but dutifully removes the next card even so.

"Aha! Doktor Death. He always figures along with the beauty of life. He wants to put a dampener on your love."

Ceri Hatch closes her eyes and allows her stomach to rumble voluminously. "Most melodious. Get rid of Stoneywell before she takes down Kendra. If you want Kendra in your fortune, then kill Stoneywell. But you know that anyhow. That you have already decided upon!", she cackles mischievously.

Jimmy is shocked.

"This is rather interesting. Come on I cannot wait to know what is next. Fourth card, fourth card!" It turns. Mother Nature. She is the elemental force above all. She cannot be entreated for she is the balance. She moves everything in alignment to the coincidence. She is implacable as she just is." Ceri Hatch shuts her eyes again and suddenly retches on to the floor. "Most bile. You must cast natural poisons of nature's magik into the waters of that stony well we talked about. Go on. Go on!", and her eyes flash like cordite.

Jimmy is sweating profusely and Ceri Hatch is breathing angrily. He turns over the penultimate card.

"The Now!", she hisses. "Who would have thought it?" and she closes her eyes and hyperventilates most forcefully. "Damn you. I am the Now for you and I will procure for you the resources to put dark juju on this Mistress Stoneywell."

Jimmy had not expected all of this. On first pass it appears that he is primarily there for guidance on his father and now higher authority is directing him to skulduggery that already he had resolved upon, but had hoped might mysteriously vanish or be overtaken by events, or anyway disappear because of other reasons. There was no such thing as coincidence and Mistress Hatch was just rumbling up fire in the belly which was already there, albeit up to then perhaps only mere meek embers.

"So it is Carnival King", she says as Jimmy turns up the last card and at this point her eyes clang shut and she falls down dramatically and momentarily into a violent epileptic type fit with gyrations and foaming of the mouth and all. Ten seconds later she is on her feet again and perspiring heavily.

"I am Ceri Hatch. Most stimulating. I am the best at divining and I say that it is important that you seek out your father at the sign of the broken pony in the very immediate future prior to you again consulting me about deep dark juju which will kill Mistress Stoneywell at the very zenith of Oliebol Karnival at Midnight the Thirteenth! So hath the Carnival King spoken. So it is written. I have no choice in the matter. To resist will bring down a very earthquake on our houses!"

Jimmy rises from the table sheepishly.

"Begone! Begone! Think of my amassing clients."

Jimmy leaves awkwardly.

"Wait!", she commands. "It has come to me that he said that you are to take this manuscript too. I am not just the violence of Mother Nature, there is a paternal side to me too. Remember the sign of the broken pony. Find your father first, and then come back to me. I must, I must. Hurry, my clients are waiting. They are agitating for their consultations. There is no antidote to old Father Time!"

Jimmy goes stumbling out only to stumble in again. He is being played like a marionette.

"Wait!", she commands again. "My memory is not good. It is the effect of all these trances."

Jimmy looks at her nonplussed.

"What? What is it, you say", utters Ceri Hatch. It does not appear to Jimmy that she is addressing him. "Oh yes", she is plainly speaking to Jimmy now. "Find your father. You must, you must. But remember you may only find trace of him. You may not find directly. You may only hear good of him. Nothing is as it seems."

"What does this mean?", implores Jimmy.

"It means what it means and my clients are amassing. They will heave me to hell if I do not attend. Do you think I could not be less straightforward. I have given good for silver. Begone with you!"

Jimmy is too hassled to think straight and so scurries out past absolutely no-one and it is not for some five minutes that he thinks to look at the manuscript he has been handed, or indeed to consider the double caution she had administered to him, such was the force of him being scurried out. It dawns on him to examine the document and upon doing so in the dim fire lights he discerns the title:

Walk 6: From Salisbury Fayre to Lower Woodford

Without thinking or hesitation he backtracks to the tent of Fortune Mistress Hatch, no doubt to demand an explanation upon this strange set of circumstances, but he simply cannot find the tent again.

After an hour or so he gives up the search somehow accepting that he would find Mistress Hatch again when the time was ripe. Everything is a stage where he is being moved along and the props are there simply waiting. He has a stonking thirst well primed and appropriate for a carnivalista night. He finds a nearby tavern and parks his considerable frame in a quiet corner where dinginess and solitariness prevailed.

'How could a pony be broken', he considers.

To read on further with the mystery naturally was his mission.

WALK 6: FROM SALISBURY FAYRE TO LOWER WOODFORD (3.5 MILES)

Stephen has always counselled me away from the psychic esoteric. My husband and wise vicar is of the view that the Spirit of God is simple and pure, that his higher majesty is elementally in all forces of nature and plain for us to see, although we might not quite recognise or understand it. He says the mystery is complete without having to dig into it. I disagree. I think all the little components of God's mystery can be tickled out and examined. Being thrilled by one small component piece of the mystery does not mean that we lose sight of the majestic whole: God's purpose.

So do start a walk from Salisbury Fayre on a bustling Saturday. The Fayre, when we first took the vicarage in the Woodford valley, was in those days only run once every half year. However, interest in the activities in the Guildhall has exploded and means that the Fayre now runs every Saturday. It is not to be missed I assure you and will satisfy all those curious about the mysteries of life. "There are more things in heaven and earth, Horatio (Stephen), than dreamt of in your philosophy!". A whole range of fascinating activities, such as palmistry, reading Viking runes, and life coaching – to name but a few. It is a great place from which to start a walk out into some beautiful nature with your mind expanding out about how we, humankind, know so much about such ancient and secret things. No dark magic, I assure you Stephen!

Even if you cannot start out on a Saturday with the Fayre, the Guildhall at Salisbury is a splendid place to start out on this beautiful walk. Yes, even on non-esoteric days you can expect to see gypsy lady Beth Francis, from a long line of Irish Romany travellers. For a pound coin she is happy to give you a sprig of lucky heather and a pinch of Romany wisdom. Only last week she said to me:

"During the time of the great Civil War between Stephen and Matilda many of the citizens of Salisbury were dropping like flies from a frightful lurgy. People were dying, consumed with madness in their bowels, and yet this was no plague, for this was not catching on anywhere else in the country. It was poison in the well you see. They had dropped a dead cat made out like a demon and had cast it into the big stony well yonder to deprive
. . .

Jimmy is frustrated by reaching the end of the reading. Again he has received a single sheet of manuscript which runs out of volume just as its import was starting to swell, but this time yet the import was just so clear. A higher authority had spoken through Ceri Hatch and now once again through the esteemed Mrs Dowd. It was clear that the moving hand was instructing him to attack the stony well. The poison of deep juju and fetishes was to be administered, but first the order demanded that he speak to his long lost father first. There must be a clue in this somewhere as to the whereabouts of Harold Suzuki.

"Bar wench, bring me another beer!", he booms.

He ruminates and ruminates not yet seeing the answer.

"There you are good Master". It is the wench with a fresh noggin.

"What's that you got on your lapel?"

She is taken aback momentarily but answers true. "It is a sprig of lucky heather to keep me safe from the Carnival demons. They say it comes from the high volcano at Big Hawaa."

"Where can I get some? I have a particular fear of the carnival ghouls and demons and I would be afforded protection during these riotous times."

"There's another hostelry about two hundred yards down the road. It's called *The Broken Pony*. Ask for Elsie Manfield . She'll sell you a fair sprig."

"The Broken Pony, you say!", exclaims Jimmy.

"It's a well-known hostelry hereabouts, Sah", she replies somewhat surprised.

"Thank you indeed! Of course it is. What's your name, girl?"

"Mattie Rosebud from Ingeleter Island".

"Well Mattie Rosebud from Ingeleter Island. Here's six cents for your trouble".

"Why, Master. Generous indeed."

"And you can have the beer to resell again or to give to your sweetheart, for I must make quick!", and Jimmy bounds out to the next drinking hole.

Within six strides of a hungry mastiff he is in *The Broken Pony* and is being referred to Elsie Manfield.

"I don't have much left I'm afraid, just some old sorry sprigs. Here you are. Not exactly prime specimen, but it's yours free of charge."

"Pray Mistress Manfield, tell me, are you a supporter of Old Carnival?"

"Indeed I am Sah. Old carnival is in my blood. I'm a very Delta Dame of eight generations".

"I am only of seven generations a Delta Doyen, but Old Carnival also courses through my veins. Perchance do you remember a Harold Suzuki a Doyen of some renown?"

"Why, of course, I do. Harold was very close to the old Carnival King."

"He was my father. I'm his son Jimmy".

"Why I remember him talk of you. We used to talk a lot as his wife Doris – your mother - was not keen on the Carnival and she did not keep company with him here. She couldn't stand the silly season!"

"Indeed, indeed", concurs Jimmy.

"But why do you say was your Papa? Harold Suzuki is still very much alive. Some of us old Carnival Club members pay our respects to him whenever we can."

"Really?", exclaims Jimmy. "Dad got ill when I was still institutionalised on my counter-professional programme. I never knew what became of him. But I had a feeling deep in my gut that he had not passed from this earth. I have spent so much time wrestling with issues concerning being a counter-professional to ponder further on it."

"I expect that's been a real full-time job", she coos comfortingly.

"Where can I find him dear Mistress Manfield?"

Jimmy is speaking so calmly and rationally yet there appears to be a great wave of emotion that he is attempting to hold within. Another one of his givens was proving to be a fallacy.

"Why at White Cross Hospital. He has been at White Cross poorhouse wards all this last fifteen year or so."

"He has been right under my nose", murmurs Jimmy.

"Well Mister Suzuki …. Can I call you Jimmy?"

"Of course."

"I think them quacks have extended his stay there with all their potions, lotions and smoking concoctions. Harold was admitted for full scale dementia at the age of sixty-two. A little memory loss can happen a lot at that age, especially in these stressful modern times. For crikey sake I've been losing my marbles for some twenty years! He just needed a little rest and respite, but he suffered with all these doctors pushing their cures. For all I know he got caught up in some experimentations or something. By Janna, he's ended up in there for some fifteen, sixteen years now. There was no call for that. First I remember this Registrar Rickman; he was off his trolley. And by Janna he had a trolley, pushing it around with all his evil compacts. Then there's this Surgeon-Captain Roper; equally barking mad and always talking about having interesting subjects for his lecture tours. They are all self-serving and just interested in their physik research and not the interest of the patients at all."

"My dizzy sister. Roper you say!"

"Yes".

"Where do I find my dear old papa?"

"Down in the so-called *Demeans* in the basement of the hospital where there's no windows, only the gas light".

"Thank you Mistress Manfield ….. Elsie".

"You're very welcome Jimmy son. We carnivalistas should stick together. Good luck!"

Jimmy is all action. There is no time for thinking and he goes off bounding through the carnival crowd in the direction of White Cross Hospital. The stages are unreliable because of the festival, but eventually he is able to get one to Big Block terminus and from there it is only twenty minutes' walk to the hospital which he manages in eighteen. Festive-goers are relatively few in the area around the hospital and his progress is unimpeded.

Jimmy slows his pace just as he approaches the hospital. Suddenly he feels reticent and unsure.

'Wouldn't it be better to leave things undisturbed?", he muses and as he muses he is walking unintentionally to the great entrance of White Cross Hospital. He is lurching abstractedly through the great reception hall of the majestic old building looking as startled and confused as a man who has missed the boat to the fair islands.

Jimmy's abstract gaze becomes sharpened. There is a large entourage of persons looking at him. Through the oil lamp glaze he perceives that foremost among them is Lady Elizabeth Swann looking agitated and ill at ease.

'No doubt as a result of still feeling the stress of our relationship being exposed', he thinks.

"Has he called for you too?", she asks of Jimmy.

"No. Who?"

"Sir John. He has been admitted to the lunatic asylum below and I have been told that he has been shouting for me with alarming gusto. Seeing you here I assumed he had called for you too."

"What is about?"

"It appears that Sir John has attacked the Surgeon-Captain with a potato peeler. They say that the facial damage suffered by Sir Frederick is quite awful. He is being attended to by the surgeons at this very moment. They are trying to stitch back parts of his gums that had been hacked out by Sir John. Roper may have also lost his left eye too". Lady Swann is decorously weeping as she informs Jimmy.

"Oh, no. What was he doing with a potato peeler of all things?"

"I have not yet been informed, but I do know that they have forcibly admitted him in a strait-jacket to the asylum", she matter of fact informs. " More scandal on our great houses! What can we do, Jimmy?", she whispers with modulated anger.

"Get rid of the hangers-on first", he hisses back. "The Visitor wishes to be alone", he booms. "Pray all of you return to your duties. Leave us". Very officially stated from the person who least looked like an official in the whole ensemble. Even so the underlings look in askance. The Countess of Tischent peremptorily waves a hand at them and as if she had conjured a magical force they all start to retreat into the hospital fundaments.

"We have to go below, to the so-called Demeans", announces Lady Swann. "That's where we keep the funny farm here. I have been there once before and it is not savoury, I can assure you."

Jimmy makes the connection, but says nothing and the dread just builds up in him. They descend a staircase near the back of the main building. The staircase and connecting corridor to the mental asylum look unloved and forgotten adding to Jimmy's dread. Ahead of them stands a tall elderly man wearing autopsy like overalls and exaggerated arm length rubber gloves.

"Good evening. I am Professor Surgeon-At-Arms Lindsay Lucie, superintendent of the faculty."

"James Donald Suzuki, and this is the Visitor Lady Elizabeth Swann." Jimmy is observing male etiquette and putting a front foot on something.

"Ah, you are both here at the same time coincidentally? Yes, that is it. That's what has floored me", the man giggles squelching his great rubber gloves together in delight.

"Why would my arrival be a mere coincidence?", asks Elizabeth getting back to her imperious best. "Were you not expecting a visit from the Visitor?", arching her right eyebrow.

"No, I was expecting you, my Lady. It is just when I heard the distinctive name of Suzuki I presumed that it was a relative to pick the old man up."

"What do you mean?", asks Jimmy.

"We have had a long residing patient here who died not an hour ago. His name was Harold Suzuki. Remarkable a coincidence that another with the surname Suzuki happens to be in her ladyship's party."

"Truly", gasps Jimmy, "for I am in her ladyship's party and I am also the son of one Harold Suzuki."

"See to your father, Mister Suzuki. I shall attend to Sir John J. Perriwinkle", orders the Visitor.

"Charge Nurse Harris", calls Lucie. A burly male charge nurse comes running. "Take Mr Suzuki to see his father. Meanwhile Lady Swann and I shall attend to our eminent guest."

Jimmy is about to speed off with his minder.

"I will want you to see Sir John also before you leave. I will be expecting you in his chamber", says Elizabeth.

Jimmy nods curtly and follows his attendant. He is too shocked as of yet to register any further words. Charge Nurse Harris takes him to a very poor dormitory where there is the initial impression that the tawdry expanse is covered by the mentally ill, the physically ill and all in between. Jimmy sights persons who appear to be of rude health but who are not the authentic ducat and those in a miserably physical condition but who appeared to be sanely suffering.

Jimmy is being shuffled to a rather unkempt bed. Its occupant lies still.

The occupant of the bed to its left suddenly sits up and announces:" I've just had a mince pie, but he's forgotten his".

"Shut up Madrigal!" demands the Charge Nurse. "Mr Suzuki had been severely demented for many a year. He was almost part of the fixtures here in this institution, though I doubt that he had any idea where he was really. He might have thought that he was with the East Fleet for all we know".

"I see", says Jimmy.

"Anyway, three weeks ago he appeared to be suffering cramp pain in his stomach and where he had been relatively quiet and passive he became very vocal with the pain. Screamed a lot. Screamed a lot of stuff about "*down with the demons in art*" and *"bring our intellectuals home"*. All incomprehensible stuff. Anyway the proper quacks diagnosed pancreatic cancer and in the end his end came much faster than we could have conceived."

"Thank you, Charge Nurse. Was there anyone with him at the end? I imagine it is so lonely at the end. I did not even know until this very evening that he was still alive. I assumed that he had already been dead for many a year. In effect he had been dead for me."

"I was there for him at the end. Don't you worry I cared for him and loved him out of this life." A grizzled old crone appearing from the demented background had said all this.

"You are a fellow inmate who came to know my father?", interprets Jimmy.

"Do I look like an inmate?", she cackles.

'Yes, you certainly do', thinks Jimmy. She is wearing an old crone's cap as if she were going knitting to a public execution and looked like she slept close to the street.

"I'm your father's cousin, Jimmy. I was, rather. Aunty Hennie Suzuki. Don't you remember me?"

"Married to Long Tommy? Daughters Anthea and Petal?"

"That be me", she chortles. "I have been a constant visitor to your father. I've been loving and caring for him all these years and it was me that eased his passing on."

"Why didn't you inform me, Aunty Hennie? I have been back in Trenchtown these many years now."

"He did not want to be an imposition on you, Jimmy".

"An imposition. You mean something blocking my glowing career?"

"Harold didn't want you to suffer through seeing him suffer. He was a noble Dad".

"Surprising for one suffering from such dementia that he should be so specific with his wishes, wouldn't you say Charge Nurse?"

Both the Charge Nurse and Hennie Suzuki look at him sheepishly in silent response.

Jimmy realises that he still has not looked properly at his dear old dad. He turns away from the other two to examine the mortal remains of Harold Suzuki. It is a sorry sight. A wizened old body covered in dirty white sheets fringed with ochre. Harold's eyes had been closed but his mouth is still open looking as if at any moment it might attempt to suck life back into his emaciated form. Harold had a shock of white hair and the beginnings of a grisly white beard. He did not look as if he had been particularly well looked after. He must have died loveless save the affections of the dubious Aunt Hennie. Jimmy cries moderately. He realises that he cries not so much for the late Harold, but for himself. He cries at the frustration of a relationship he had lost, perhaps had never had and would no longer have. You had to be a big boy without parents. There is no imaginary comeback where all that frustration and anger garnered so young can be vented. The chance for little boy rage had been truly expunged. There is guilt too. Guilt at feeling that his own life had been fairly miserable, but that it could not have transcended the last fifteen years of his father living in this soulless and destructive place with no privacy with only mad-heads and warders for human company.

Mistress Suzuki and Charge Nurse Harris keep a respectable distance for Jimmy to boo like a baby.

"Did he leave any sort of testament?" Jimmy is back and glowering.

"Yes, he left you this." Hennie hands him a slip of crumpled parchment with the smell of urine upon it. Jimmy glances at the neatly printed words thereon.

the burghers of Salisbury of fresh clean water. This was a time when the city was being besieged by

There is a whole page of Rosemary Dowd's muse like wanderings. 'Is this all some tasteless joke?'

"What the fuck is this? I said testament, not this manic garbage!", roars Jimmy at his aunt.

"It's what he specifically said that I should pass to you, Jimmy", she croaks.

"Are you making this up?", replies he threateningly.

"Calm down, Mister Suzuki", intercedes Harris. "Manic garbage is exactly the type of stuff you are like to find in a lunatic asylum."

"He also said that I was to have his strong box. It has been stored down in the old cellars of the hospital. It is full of family mementos. Old journals from family members whom you would not know and so on. Probably nothing so interesting for a young feller like you".

"Let me see. You are the widow of my father's brother, yet you are very interested in keepsakes of the Suzuki family?"

"Yes."

"Well take it then."

"But I need the key."

"Where is it?"

"It's in the administration office. We require your signature as next of kin for the key to the box containing your father's belongings to be given over", informs Harris. "Do you have identification papers with you?"

"No, we'll have to do it later and I'll sort out the box before anyone takes away family mementos."

"But it is such hard work", pronounces Hennie. "Save yourself the time in your busy schedule, Jimmy".

"Marm, I am counter-professional. I have no schedule. Good day to you both."

Jimmy storms off quickly but only some fifteen yards down the vast subterranean ward. He stops abruptly realising he does not know the direction of Sir John's quarters.

"I know who you are Sir! You are the Unsullied Prince and you have come to claim your debt of shadows from us. We have made ready for you".

"Let him pass Silas". It is Charge Nurse Harris and he pushes the voluble inmate away. "No doubt you wish to be shown to where we have accommodated your eminent friend the most august Sir John J. Perriwinkle", he adds to Jimmy.

Harris leads the way. Despite his frustration with these adding pieces of parchment, Jimmy is tempted to read the rest of the Dowd missive, but does not think it proper to stop Harris in his ministrations.

"The weather is agreeably cool for carnival tide, is it not?" Harris says leading them down warren like corridors in the hospital's fundament. Jimmy does not reply. He has other issues to chew on. Some two minutes later they enter the private cell of Sir John.

Sir John is slumped on the floor like the noble dying admiral in the Bolingbroke masterpiece. Noble death contours are creased on to the frowning visage of the aristocratic Baronet of Sandown. Jimmy expected him to be surrounded by a gamut of naval commodores and lieutenants but there is only Elizabeth Swann, the Visitor of White Cross Hospital, swooning over him as if expecting the end of a gallant age to dissipate with his passing.

"It would not have happened if I were allowed to have gone to the Sisters of Mazuma! Damn you woman!"

"Sir John, I offered to do this some while ago at my own expense. It was your decision not to take my charity. I accepted that, but nevertheless afforded you with the best that this poorhouse hospital could provide. Please do not transfer you faults to me."

"I am sorry, Elizabeth", and in saying so the furrows on Sir John's face look as if they are to pain him into some unassailable death rattle. "I indeed am the architect of my own misfortune."

Jimmy is quiet and observing. They do not seem to notice his quiet entrance and they play their dialogue on as if they were actors upon the stage trained to concentrate on the relevance of their lines and not to be affected by extraneous considerations.

"What will this mean for me, Elizabeth?"

"By Janna John, where on earth did you procure a potato peeler? What were you thinking of? His family will claim a writ of lunacy against you!" Lady Elizabeth is upset about what she is saying and Jimmy can see that the plight of the discredited baronet hurts her deeply. "They say that you have maimed his face and neck beyond repair. Oh John, what have you done. I do not think that even I with my influence can extricate you from this", she sobs.

"Life is a veritable strumpet only worth living for the dying", philosophises Sir John. "That man Roper provoked me beyond human endurance. I am sorry for your embarrassment and humiliation, Milady, but I do not regret my action and the deserved punishment he received. I can only assume that Roper will not be able to work again and thereby will not be able to administer further cruelty on the helpless charges in this here poorhouse hospital. My only regret is that I did not get to take out that accomplice slut of his, Stoneywell."

Jimmy notes that what he first considered as sheets covering the abdomen of Sir John is actually a hospital issue strait jacket. 'This is really serious', he considers and is anxious to break the gloom of this scene.

"Well said great Sir John! You speak for justice and common humanity."

"Jimmy Suzuki. Thank you", and sobs the sobs of a broken man.

"Jimmy, how can you say that? Have you taken leave of your senses?" demands Elizabeth.

"I speak for natural justice. What Sir John did cannot be condemned. He has experienced the outrages that the common man here daily has to suffer, but he is of noble stock and therefore showed a reaction of noble spirit. A spirit that will not suffer such violations upon humanity that I and all of us have had to suffer in this gracious realm of Great Society. You will have to ask why you personally have propagated such a regime at this poorhouse hospital. How you have allowed the likes of Roper to become a tyrant without any restraints upon him. How you and the Earl of Tischent, who after all is Master of the Rolls, have sat on top of this Great Society and so blithely administered this exquisite cruelty. Beautiful and right you see it, and how so outraged you are that a common bully meets his comeuppance. Now it is just too difficult to help your old friend. You could do it, but you are afraid that any support of the baronet would risk your status and standing, as well as that of your impotent husband!"

The Visitor of White Cross Hospital wishes to hear no more. She rises sedately from her transpose over the weeping Sir John walks over to Jimmy and slaps him savagely on the cheek with the back of her jewelled hand. Jimmy can already feel faint blood seeping.

"You are no longer known to me anymore, Sir", and she leaves in seething emotion.

Sir John laughs nervously.

"I think that I may have really gone and done it this time, Sir John".

"I think that you may really have", replies Sir John, his tears turning to chortles.

"So what was it that finally broke this dromedary's back?", smiles Jimmy.

"Well it's back was broken by a million slow sutures, just to mix our metaphors", replies Sir John. "You know how he was with me", Sir John is suddenly turning deadly earnest again. "He ridiculed me right from the start. I have already told you about the accident where I fell down the Milliwhigs Clubs steps leading to my admission here. The fact that it occurred whilst I was under the influence did not help me and he used that to portray me at every chance as some sort of dissolute. At first a dissolute who was a sponger and a scourge upon Great Society, and then, after our gracious Visitor corroborated my credentials, as a dissolute dandy who milked the profits of the hardworking professionals of Great Society. He and his creature, Matron Stoneywell, were always looking for some opportunity to bring me down, humiliate me, or generally make things less comfortable for me here, and it became increasingly more difficult when Elizabeth's influence here was *"compromised"*. Enough said on that. Anyhow, he did not like the fact that I stood up to him initially and the loss of face to him when I was put under the Countess's protection. Well, you know my leg had to be operated upon after the fall that led to me being admitted here. I am sure that he deliberately botched that operation and there were complications leading to bleeding suppurations and the risk of gangrene. He was then always finding excuses for Stoneywell and her crew to carry out debasing bed treatments on me. Countless enemas, throat garbulations and anal explorations and the like in search of *"infection and hospital beriberi"*. It was a massive but slow progression of provocation culminating in Roper coming to see me this morning and earnestly apologising to me that as he feared the complications that he had been concerned about had come to pass meaning that he would have to amputate my foot on the morrow. Look at my leg. Look at my foot! Do you see any evidence for an extreme course of amputation? I was being ridiculed. I was being set up for a fool. Even that hussy Stoneywell could not suppress a smirk as Roper was relating me this hideous news. They wanted me for a cripple, by Janna!".

Jimmy solicitously examines the affected limb of Sir John. It looks rather wizened and gnarled. Not exactly the leg of a well-toned athlete, but nonetheless nothing to suggest the extreme course of amputation.

"I am no physician, but to me your leg and foot look sound enough for a man of your age. I could not believe that amputation of your foot is required. There is nothing to suggest gangrene or any other flesh devouring condition."

"Exactly!"

"So you lost control of your emotions? It was the fear. It was the injustice. It was the despair at the rank inhumanity of man towards its own kind".

"It was indeed, kind Jimmy. It was that what you describe. I went into a blue funk and picked up the potato peeler from under the pillow. I know that I had the authority and wit to reason and debate his proposed course of action, but the constant demeaning of my person caused me temporarily to lose my reason. I did not have the wherewithal to deal with it other than to lash out with the paws of a wounded animal. The paws of this particular wounded animal were the potato peeler and one could have not expected that such an ordinary implement could wreck such damage. However, it was the rage within me that translated into titanic force allied with irrepressible lightning speed. I have never been so athletic. I was like a bronze period hero wielding a scimitar! During seconds of bloodletting I was transformed into ecstasies of glory. It was the most consummate and satisfying moment, or slight moments, of my whole cursed life. That's why I could never regret this. Why I could not defend this action. It was just too pleasurable for me. His left eye hanging out of its socket, Jimmy, I positively whooped at the sight of it. The bitch Stoneywell was too quick. She got out of the room before I could get at her. I would have carved her up like a pig."

Sir John talks like a demon, but Jimmy sees a noble demon. If this were incarnate evil, he would then embrace pure iniquity.

"I will arrange for your defence. I will shame Swann to pay for the best of attorneys. As you know, I have dirt on her, don't you worry. But how did you have a potato peeler under your pillow? That could be a difficult aspect in putting together your defence."

"It was not an intentional thing to have that deadly potato peeler around my person. It was due to Nurse Kendra. I know how you love her dearly Jimmy, and she is very dear to me too. She was the only one of the staff here who treated us with any courtesy or gave any compassion to her charges. She too was treated scandalously by that malignant toad Stoneywell".

"I know too well".

"Well, because of the perceived connection to us, and the scandal over that Copperfield fellow, they maligned her most despicably and had her doing all sorts of skivvying instead of real nursing activities. Yesterday morning, prior to my visit from Roper and Stoneywell, she sneaked in to see me to say that, since Elizabeth's announcement that she was stepping down as Visitor, they were now treating her like a general scullery maid in the hospital kitchens and had her peeling tatties and neeps for a whole day's shift. She was distraught and came to me in tears and wanted to be consoled by deep hugs from a friend. She cried her pretty eyes out over my embrace on the hospital bed whilst still clutching the instrument of torture. She must have dropped the despicable tool in her emotion as after she left I discovered the thing lying in plain sight on the top sheet. I thought to hide it under the pillow so as to conceal her visit from the kitchens to me. For an hour or so it was out of sight and out of mind, but strangely naturally came into my recollection immediately in my blind fury. It just put itself into my avenging hand. I cannot ken the mental process that put the implement into my hand. It was fate, it was providence, it was at hand and in my hand. It was what goes around comes around. The immutable cycle of continual joy and despair."

"It makes sense now. We can argue no predetermined intent to use the potato peeler for an assault. I will organise your defence accordingly."

"No; Jimmy. I have had enough of this all. This Great Society. This crazy life which I have for so long wished to never give up. Yee Jenizens, I even strove for immortality! I want only immortal eternal peace now. Spare me no further agonies. Come back later and kill me, Jimmy".

"Are you serious? Do you mean this good Sir John? Think on what you are saying".

"Yes, yes, yes … I really do mean it, Jimmy. Please, please, please do this merciful thing for me. I entreat you!", croaks Sir John nobly. "I have no life anymore worth the living".

Jimmy nods and manages just to utter. "I will make sure that as soon as possible you will receive a big fluffy fine feather pillow for your noble head".

Jimmy does not see any point anymore to putting a gloss on things

"That's right, kind Sir. After all an old man such as me, his heart may give out struggling to release himself from an infernal straitjacket ... you understand? Leave me now Jimmy. Compose yourself and later do what your dear friend needs. Do not say a long adieu. I could not bear it. Just remember me fondly in your heart. Most of all it was my conceit and pride that led to this. Yet it has brought me humility which I have bought so exorbitantly, but in the end am so glad to acquire. Farewell for now, true friend."

Jimmy in his emotion can only nod his head in acknowledgement and then furthermore bowed in respect. He leaves the shabby cell silently.

He finds Charge Nurse Harris lurking outside.

"We still have to finalise on your father's affairs. You should come with me to the Administration Office to receive the death certificate and conclude on the transference".

"Very well", sighs Jimmy and like one who has to get past something unpleasant he follows Harris with reluctant stride.

Surgeon-At-Arms Lucie is awaiting in the shabby quarters which purports to be the Administration Office. There was something redolent to Jimmy in this conjoining of shabbiness and government office. All his life he has been treated by a shabby bureaucracy in run-down offices with shabby indifference by officials who wanted to close their eyes and meander through the working day showing perfunctory zeal for the rigours of Great Society and the noble counter-professionals they had to treat through their care. They were generally offices without much light in a land which was over gorgeous with sunlight. Darkened offices with dark memories and Jimmy felt strangely at un-home with this one too. It was kind of what he expected and he knew there that he would be comforted by them making him discomforted.

"A model patient, your father", consoles Lucie.

"How so?", Jimmy blandly asks.

"He knuckled down, observed the system and was never any trouble."

"Did he really have a mental illness?"

"Yes. A severe dementia known as *Dondinger's Fury*. It is a very serious debilitating condition. The only upside is that the sufferer retires into a world of extreme passivity. At least they don't give our orderlies any trouble as they are so entirely placid. They just have their little agitated murmurings, that's all. We are very surprised that he survived for so long after the fury was diagnosed. It is entirely usual for sufferers to die within four years of diagnosis. Well in all medicine there are exceptions."

"Such is life", murmurs Jimmy.

"You are free now to take your father's body for disposal subject to payment of the six sovereigns administration fee".

"Six sovereigns! Where do you think that I can get hold of that sort of money? Why so much?"

"Well, two sovs is the standard fee for body transfer plus your father ran up an account for political acclimatisation training which now totals at four sovs".

"How could a severely demented man take political acclimatisation training?"

"Yes indeed and it was one-to-one with Scout Trainer Reynolds".

"This seems preposterous to me. One-to-one training in political acclimatisation".

"Reynolds even came in to deliver the training at your father's bedside. He was devoted to your Dad and made sure that your father really understood the nature of Great Society", adds Charge Nurse Harris.

"But he was demented, wasn't he. He couldn't have been able to recognise a political party from a stage post!"

"He was not demented in all aspects", explains Lucie. "Your late father's condition is an extremely rare and complex one. On particular matters such as political philosophy, tax policy and alchemy, for example, the subject's acuity is enhanced by the condition".

"Oh, balderdash. I don't wish to take his body. The hospital can dispose of it as it wishes".

"But it is the law", further explains Lucie. "You must take responsibility for taking your father's body and pay the fee to boot!"

"Well I don't have the means to pay. What should I do?"

"We can take a charge on the payment whereby your release instalments to us through your future employments".

"But I am a counter-professional. I cannot work and I can only receive my Sacrificer allowance if I sign confirming that I am not working."

"I see, then we will take a lien on your note that you are not working by having you reside here in the interim until the debt plus interest is repaid. We have a spare bed now where you can pitch now that your father is deceased and we will vouch to the benefits authorities on your signature of compliance on non-employment."

"But that will take years. Besides which I am not mad."

"Maybe so", smiles Lucie, "but liquidity is not a pressing issue to this hospital and Great Society, but the debt is material. Regarding your mental condition; after a while I am sure you will acclimatise."

"Open the box!", she screeches. It is Aunt Hennie. She seems to have been there all along.

"Sorry, what do you mean open the box?"

"Your father's strongbox. They have it there underneath in the deep dark recesses of this here hospital."

"You think that I shall find a deep stash there to pay off this substantial debt? I find that inconceivable, Hennie.

Harold was a modest lock-keeper. Where would he come by the princely sum of six sovereigns?"

"Well", she cackles, "it is my experience that if you delve deep enough you can always find something of value in the belongings of loved ones. You just have to have perseverance and the wherewithal to search."

"Very well. Surgeon-At-Arms, with your permission I should like to take a peek into my father's strong box to see if there is anything of value to help mitigate against my father's debt."

"Capital idea, Sir. Harris prepare the paperwork for Suzuki's signature and then we can get him the key so that he can make the necessary explorations."

"Very good, Sah!" and Charge Nurse Harris makes haste.

"There were some family jewels that Harold had in his possession. Female frippery that a solid man like you would not care", begins Hennie hesitantly. "Heirlooms designed for the female line of the family. You are without issue Jimmy and I have daughters who can be bejewelled with the Suzuki family heirlooms. It was only natural that he would promise these to me his faithful sister-in-law. I can quickly go down to the vaults and return with these. Maybe one of the necklaces might be enough to pay off the debt. Shall I do that kind Sah so that you can free your head to consider the funerary aspects?"

"Promised, you say? Did you get that in writing from my late father?"

"No, but it was quite clear that was his intention. He mentioned that the jewellery would cover his funeral expenses expecting one of the pieces to pay for it and the remaining pieces to stay with the female members of the family in trust for future Suzuki generations. Of course, at the end he was not capable of writing all this down and having it witnessed."

"Remarkable again that someone lodged in the loony bin has the acuity to talk about material dispositions of will and trust. Is that again a paradox of the disease Surgeon-At-Arms?"

"Such acuity has been noted in the journals" replies the medical expert. " It has been recorded that such sufferers can discourse quantum fulfilment with a dog and then romp around barking mad thinking they are the dog. It is a verily strange ailment."

"Alright, I see. Let me sign for the key and lets discover what is down there. Are you ready good aunt?"

"Very ready!"

"And I am too!", and this insertion comes from a very musical voice. Jimmy involuntarily smiles for it is Kendra.

"I've just got off my shift in the kitchens and heard what had happened with Sir John. I was told that you were down here with the Visitor herself. How did you manage that?", smiles Kendra innocently to which Hennie winks coarsely. At this Kendra looks at Jimmy uncertainly.

"That is a story for another time, but now we have a more pressing concern."

"Being?"

"Being the matter of meeting my late father's debt so that I myself can escape confinement in this hallowed establishment!"

Kendra looks dumbfounded.

"I will explain whilst we walk. Hennie are you joining us as well?"

"I will ask Harris to accompany you as you will still be on the hospital premises when you go down to the vaults and we would want no harm to come to you", instructs Lucie.

"I would be grateful for a guide rather than a guard", smiles Jimmy.

The strange quickly assembled party, once a good oil lamp is found, then makes the short journey to the hospital vaults. Jimmy Suzuki expectant heir to great fortune, Hennie Suzuki treasure finder extraordinaire, Nurse Kendra Okvicha riding her emotions to who knows where, and Charge Nurse Harris who is solicitous towards everyone to mind the step and hopefully turn a bob or two and receive favour from his principal.

After eleven minutes of plodding along dark corridors and negotiating down uncared for steps the strange party reaches the area in the vaults where long term patients' possessions are stored.

"Let's see. Mister Suzuki was admitted in the mid-part of twenty-three so it should be somewhere along these shelves here", Harris usefully informs. "Should be a label with BL-2309 on. Ah, there it is! The old Burberry system never lets us down does it?"

"The old systems have proved the best", adds Hennie.

"Good. Well, bring it down", impatiently demands Jimmy which the burly Harris does do with ease.

"Shall I carry it upstairs, Sah?", asks Harris.

"I think we can have an intimate little peek here first", considers Jimmy. "What do you think, Kendra?"

"Open the box! Open the box!", cajoles Hennie.

"My interest is certainly piqued. Let's take a look", opines Kendra.

"Open it", orders Jimmy and Harris applies the key to the lock and opens the box to expose its contents to the low orange lamplight.

Jimmy puts his hand in to shuffle things around. He notes some old letters and family sketch portraits, but there is also a large purple velvet bag. He opens the bag and draws out in his hand a number of fine decorous pieces of jewellery. In the low light there is the impression of gold, sapphires, emeralds, diamonds and such fine filigree things. He delves his hand in again to find paper and he withdraws the note which he reads avariciously and earnestly.

James,
Here is all the fine jewellery, dear boy, you could have given to and adorned   upon Fumi. Find her and adorn her with these.
Your friend right from the start of this most glorious absurd adventure.
Yours aye,
AMC

There was also a single sheet missive of the prose that Jimmy Suzuki was becoming so well acquainted with and used to finding in surprising places. Another note page from Rosemary Dowd. He now had two new messages to decipher and ruminate upon.

Harris takes the party out of the dark vaults. They march like a procession cautiously and stealthily to get out of hell without waking anything in the deep. They march on silently and solemnly not exchanging words.

Jimmy's head marches in all directions.

'Why would the old fellow address me as James? Dear boy? What was this cant about being my friend right from the start of this glorious and absurd adventure? It is all rather cryptic. It does not make sense. A counter-professional is not qualified to decipher the many mysteries that have befallen me of late'.

It could be the tenth day of the madness of the twelve day Finitude, nobody really knows and somehow the Finitude clicks to the mechanism of its own clock. Already almost a week past its normal length and Banana Delta has gone to hell on the fuel of festivity. Every single soul on the street has gone barmy as if the debilitating exhaustion of this continuing celebration were tipping the balance toward permanent craziness. Jimmy with Kendra in hand moves effortlessly and purposefully through the bon-fired squares, the fire-lit avenues and the dark unhallowed crannies of the city. Demons are everywhere and the day seemingly has been turned into a perpetual duskiness hinting at night. Smoke abounds as if the fires of the camps of the revolutionary armies had set camp upon the eternal fiendish capital city of the Islands. Hues and cries rise through the air like the cacophony of hell hounds baying for a ritualistic pagan fury. The world is to be lost and spin abound and abandoned during the length of the Oliebol Finitude. For all who know the Carnival the only way back to quietude and replenishment of Mother Nature was to let the Goombeymen totally possess. And thus all became possessed, for before their possession they knew that Mother Nature would not move to redress the balance until she was feeling near mortally hurt so that she would have to dispel the Goombeymen. Reluctantly though, like a mother leaving a cosy bed to administer to a demanding wain, she would put up with a fair degree of wailing before she would finally act. The citizens and denizens of the Delta were becoming possessed. Pissing, vomiting and copulating in the streets was just standard fare in these later stages of the Oliebol Finitude. Jimmy kicks aside with his planter boots an old man in a demagogue mask who is trying to administer affections upon a hoary goat.

"Fuck off you old billy-bugger", he snarls, and turning to his Kendra, "I cannot stand this madness, but through it we must slice to find our oracle and fount of wisdom".

"I understand Jimmy. For me you cannot transgress against these abominable transgressors".

And so they plough on through the sea of demi-demons and small brats in animal masks and unerringly like a sea magnet to the metal pole are Jimmy and Kendra drawn to a small square with a single tent where insanity does not reign. As if it were written, the inimitable Ceri Hatch is within and waiting.

"Doubtless you have found your father. So where does she walk?", she asks cryptically.

But ineluctably Jimmy knows the score. "She traipse from Fortuners Cricket Ground to Old Sarum."

"Precisely!", Ceri Hatch responds with enthusiasm. "Old Father Time will always shed a tear for the lovers. He will spare his hoary frost for lovers to create more souls for his perennial perpetual harvest. It is just his wont, they say."

Kendra nods sagely at this divination and thinks to herself that she is rapidly losing the plot. She begins again to have a grasp on reality with the next utterance.

"You know the direction of the walk, but have you delved into its divinations?", pointedly asks the redoubtable Hatch.

"Verily, I have not as yet. I have just been too dazed and confused to concentrate upon contemplative walks."

"Read it out aloud to us. Read it do!"

Ceri Hatch's voice is clear and simple and does not brook any argument. Jimmy S is compelled by it so he takes the grubby sheet of paper out of his grubby pocket and reads aloud.

The title he mumbles over quickly and then enunciates a bit better on the real meat.

You would not normally find me at a cricket ground for I find the game confoundingly confusing and long-winded; I mean some of these matches can go over five days without a single meal opportunity being missed. Mr Dowd says it teaches one the virtue of patience. He says it is a slow game like life. The game can change slowly, or, there again, it can change swiftly like a hot knife through butter.

Well let's lay aside my prejudices. The prejudices of a field hockey maiden! There is a real game of harry and pace. Let us just establish that Fortuners Cricket Ground is today our starting place. Old man Fortuner established the club some 115 years ago. The story was that Arnold Fortuner was a very wealthy man and that he made the ground and pavilion (very fine it is) as an act of remorse for giving away his illegitimate son James to an impoverished family. He had heard that James had later been committed to the workhouse where he led a joyless life suffering on his intellect, but having one solitary joy; playing spin bowler in the workhouse cricket team. Fortuner had then gone on to meet his unwanted child when he was well into adulthood going under his adoptive name, James Ford, and had set up the cricket club as a form of apology to his disowned son. Little is known of James Ford thereafter.

Jimmy clears his voice. Like a fabled mechanical man he continues reading.

On leaving the ground walk straight along the little country road and look out for the signpost to **The Earls.**

"Stop, you fool! You have met your father and now the magik can begin."

Jimmy looks at Ceri Hatch taken aback. Kendra looks perplexed.

"Now that you truly know who your father is you can go on now to the next stage", reemphasises the sorceress. "What did you resolve for the magik? You resolved to do away with Matron Stoneywell. You resolved this to let your young love flourish".

"Yes, kill her!", bellows Jimmy as if he is too stunned to understand anything else.

"You abjure?" asks Ceri Hatch staring at Kendra.

"No, I am of the same opinion", asserts Kendra.

"Then I have a potion with a plan for the two of you."

The lovers wait expectant whilst Ceri Hatch continues.

"It is strange how the Carnival can take upon the modest and the moderate, the smug and the sufficient. Matron Augusta Stoneywell – yes, even she has a given private name – is carnivalisting with the blood-knife guzzlers. It is surprising what base and unspeakable practices are condoned and entered into – entertained - during this host whore lust known as the Oriebol Karnival. The matron connives with a filthy bunch of butchers who round up all the stray dogs in the Capital – well, as many as they can find at least – and they look to cut off the balls of these hounds in a ritualistic way using an acutely sharp knife to do the emasculation, after which they all in a frenzy lick the blood and all the assorted ooze from the sharp knife's edge. Being careful with their tongues and lips of course. When things are done wrong it is so difficult to right them back again. Ho hum."

"Why are you telling us about this disgusting practice?" Kendra is much put out.

"Because the potion is not much without the plan".

"And what precisely is this little revelation in relation to the plan?", politely enquires Jimmy.

"Fumigate me! I'm getting crossed with the curse of Carnival. Fumigate me of the curse of Carnival. Cross my palm with some of those dirty gems I know that you have found in the hiddens of the Carnival King and then the curse will leave me allowing me to talk clearly again. I am currently leaving this planet ..."

At this the redoubtable Ceri Hatch is in a golden glow of shadow light and is dancing possessed the dance of the mystic murmuring and masturbating while spittle of crimson spit forms at her lips.

"Cross her palm with the good stuff. Quickly before she loses it", hisses Kendra.

Jimmy attempts to secure in Hatch's hand a sizeable emerald.

"Fill my breast with it!", and her eyes are like fury compelling Jimmy without a second thought to cram the jewel into the very full and bounteous curvature.

"Fill me, fill me", she moans.

Jimmy has a raging hard-on. He is being possessed by the strange spirits of Carnival. Lust is compelling him to hear and perform the plan. But first he would grapple with Ceri Hatch, force her to the floor and fornicate his life-force into her. Hard so that the spirits would roar and adore. Jimmy proceeds to lick down her delectable throat and so with that Kendra has to boot him sternly in the arse to get him to desist.

"What was that?", he howls.

"Go now to Wheeler Street south not but a quarter of a mile", commands the redoubtable Mistress Hatch. "You will find Matron Stoneywell at this moment there", continues the fortune teller sitting quietly at her table. "Put on these cat face masks along with the underlays and take this very sharp knife. They are congregating there now around the poor trapped hounds. A big black furred mongrel will come bounding to you Mister Suzuki. Throw him to the ground and slice off his bollocks ruthlessly. In his testicles is deep juju. Make sure that you get that bloody juju on to the knife and then be certain to offer the venal juice to the assembled miscreants to lick your warlock knife. However, first you must appear to partake of the nefarious gore. That is why I have also procured inner mask mountings for you both. You can make the show of imbibing but it is absolutely imperative that the juju does not enter within you. These miscreants, this is what they are expecting – to have at the gore with their corrupted tongues. Stoneywell will be the one with the badger mask. She is in a frenzy at this very now for this weird primeval thing. I don't know what makes people tick, but I guarantee that she will lick the gore on your warlock knife with a fervour. Go do it now and she will be gone before Finitude Tide after much screaming heebie-jeebies. Dark is my art", she concludes.

"What will become of her?", enquires Kendra.

"How do you get juju into the dog's bollocks?", interjects Jimmy.

"Them, not just her", answering Kendra first. "They will be pursued to madness and slow death by the spirits of the poor debased animals. They will be possessed by psychosis and literally hounded to death. That what Carnival is about. That is the spirit of Carnival and these human animals deserve it". Ceri Hatch smiles cryptically. Then to Jimmy: "You only have to believe that dark is my art; no more. Think on nothing else for the time present. Go now for the moment is here".

They go from the tent and are immediately surrounded by demented celebrators as if the quietude had never ever existed there.

Straight they go to Wheeler Street.

Straight they go like compasses guided to the metal pole. There is no thinking required.

There was no thinking just the sheer joy madness of spontaneity for a fate kindly laid afore one. That is to say that a big fluffy black mongrel stray comes bounding straight at Jimmy and Kendra, up in Jimmy's arms as if he were the dog's long lost owner and their love had been dramatically reunited. It must have just escaped the strange worshippers and had been bounding to escape and turning a corner ran straight into Jimmy. Without pausing a breath, as if he had always been prepared for this, Jimmy hurls his massive frame on to the dog and floors him and before he can even begin to think about it debags the wretched cur. How does the mutt howl in helpless shocked indignation. Jimmy flicks away the rounds with the edge of his blade and melodramatically makes to lick the life-giving blood and gore. Thankfully his onlookers are still a tad away.

"Hullah!", shouts the first and foremost worshipper. A large man with a Leo the Lion get-up. "A man must fight to maintain his testicles. All the bitches in the world would take them away from him. Let me draw blood brother!" He is joined in the slathering by a man wearing the mask of a water buffalo. Jimmy the Cat proffers the sharp blade on which the Leo and buffalo gents ostentatiously sup and lick at the rough red glut.

"Let me! A bad bitch should be the one to have the goolies." It is a smaller personage decked out as a badger but with the unmistakable shrill syllables of Augusta Stoneywell.

'Death to the wicked', thinks Jimmy as he courteously shows her the blade for her intimate sharing also. He does not speak, but his smile speaks volumes beneath the fabricated feline face as Stoneywell begins to licks the blade's face like it were amber honey.

Kendra hears the unfathomable agony of another poor hound who has been reduced of his jewels without tender ceremony. Then more and more howling as the deletions gather force. People in an assortment of animal masks, apart from dogs, are dancing around like dervishes in their blood lust. Kendra is being offered a large hairy gory glut on sharp steel by a big bosomed mongoose.

"Come kitty kitty. This is better than Mama's milk."

Kendra is about to retch and give the game away when suddenly there is a shrill piercing cry: "Big Dog is coming. Big Dog comes."

Weirdly the crowd of dervishes opens up to reveal a large Carnival float being pulled by a group of naked young men and women in prime condition.

"The sons and daughters of the meat cleavers!", yells the plump mongoose as if she were some sort of declaimer.

"But look at Big Dog!", screams our badger lady. Matron Stoneywell's shrill tones are unmistakable. Kendra notices that she seems to be wearing an old doggy scrotum as a necklace. It is obviously part of this guild's ritual. Big Dog is a large Malaccan man muscled and noble in his birthday suit with a large hound dog mask disguising his identity.

"Big Dog", shouts Leo the Lion. "Our city is to be cleared of waifs and strays these every twelve years on the Oliebol. We give you the trophies signifying that the hell mutts will breed no more! We ask that you receive their life-force in exchange for keeping our great city free from vermin."

At this many of the assembled start to cast ruined disgusting scrotum sacks in the direction of Big Dog up on the podium of his carnival float.

In the course of this Kendra spots that Big Dog's member is suddenly and spectacularly on the rise and what an amazing whopper it is, she has to concede, and what a stentorian voice he has too. Kendra feels quite captivated by him.

"Let the fecund come and worship upon my fecundity!", proclaims the top dog around here.

At this is a spate of giggling from the female animals around the mask block. Kendra spies Matron Badger in that crowd immediately, and that she is suddenly clambering up the side of the float scampering to her dog god. She is up top first before any other of her kind, and is quickly and nimbly on her knees gobbling up dollops of the offerings cut up and skewered so far. She is oozing out and up Malaccan prime prick lubricating with her bloody red mastication. The Malaccan top alpha cannot be gobbled away so easily and merely wishes to perambulate further so at the instance of his finger click Leo the Lion is up Stoneywell's rear end to give more motion and rocking to the top hound's oral servicing. Lo, there are more supplicants. More female animals are clambering towards their prince whizz.

Jimmy is quite captivated by this macabre scene wondering in the back of his mind why he had felt a strange lust for Matron Stoneywell when he was a helpless charge in her ward. In a way he had also feared her and what a strumpet she looks now. 'Oh, how strange this world is.'

The women of this ritual group are obviously mesmerised by Big Dog and the posture he has struck. Jimmy notes that Kendra in his thrall too. 'Deep juju', he surmises. 'The whole world has gone mad and my Kendra too. This is the first Oliebol since the Brown Dwarf', he further muses. 'We are all going to hell in an arm-lock'.

There appear to be about five female mouths working, lucking and clucking on the Royal Hound's engorged status member while five male "animals" are shafting from the aft. Kendra is suspiciously looking like she is going to try her luck as number six. With the cat mask on Jimmy cannot read her face to see what she is thinking, but her body movement and motion suggest it strongly to Jimmy. And right enough a second later Jimmy is doing all that he can to ensure that Kendra's mouth does not envelope the majority of that gorge.

"Come with me young lady", he orders as if pulling away a tot from a sweet shop window.

"But Big Dog has the power! He wants to increase his power through me!", she cries.

She fights like a demon to grapple on to the good stuff, but Jimmy is strong, really quite strong, and he brings her to heel. He howls like a wolf in his exertions and she screeches like a night owl. It has become a contest of sexual frustration and Kendra keeps trying to rip away from his strong embrace. Jimmy is flagging with the manful exertion. He pulls out his own member. He feels excited and lustful by the primeval scene; by the healthy employ of his vigour on Kendra. He pulls out his own swollen member; a member that he had not seen so totem comely before and offers it to Kendra who gulps at it as if were some holy elixir.

Five minutes later in the midst of a street orgy of gargantuan proportion Jimmy and Kendra are sighing through spent toil.

"True love comes out top always", cackles Ceri Hatch. Jimmy sees her face clearly although she is kitted out in a glossy cat costume which covers her whole lithe body. "Look for Stoneywell on the morn. You will find her and some others of this motley crew in the Demeans of White Cross Hospital. Do you know where I mean?"

"We know it", replies Jimmy whilst buttoning up his fly.

"Well she won't spend long there. Her dementia will hound the existence out of her in a matter of a day; you'll see."

"You mean her life?", clarifies Kendra, but she is not articulating sufficiently.

"What?"

Kendra splutters back. "You mean her life?"

"What is life?", cryptically and rapidly returns the dark art oracle. "Don't stop the carnival!" she carouses, and with that she secretes herself into the passing crowds of inebriated merry-makers who run together like vast buffalo herds on their way to dust. Ceri Hatch momentarily appears to be like a wisp of gold dust and then vanishes from their view.

Kendra and Jimmy somehow return home to Kendra's abode in Gaolers Knoll. They part through the feverish crowds as if they were invisible gods ploughed on to their home in the stars with the vigour and force of amber nectar.

They wake the next morning in the simmering heat sweating and moaning wondering if it were all true or merely a classical false fiendish embellishment of Carnival. All is quiet for the moment. A lull in the carnival lunacy. It will build up its brawn again by middle afternoon.

"What just happened yesterday?", demands Jimmy to that invisible air knowledge. "What just went on? What did I see? What did I do? Was it all real or did I just dream it?"

"You didn't dream it", sighs Kendra. "It was raving madness. One thing though confounds me".

"What?"

"Am I now to believe that perhaps Arnold Copperfield was your natural father?"

"That's what I am maybe led to believe but cannot accept at this stage."

"We need to think on about this, but I think that the first matter is to attend to the business of the odious Stoneywell."

"Agreed, but what do you suggest?"

"Only one way to find out. I am on the early afternoon shift at the hospital", declares Kendra. "I will simply pop down to the Demeans and I'll have a snoop around. After all, I am a nurse in the hospital."

"I'll join you. I have an excuse in that I still have to tie up my father's affairs."

They both look at each other silently.

"My father's affairs ......", mutters Jimmy. "You know with Copperfield .... It might make sense, but I don't want to talk about it now".

"I understand, so let's return to the matter at hand."

Lunchtime sees the carnival lovers in the wretched Demeans. They cautiously move down the main administration corridor. Kendra in her starched white apron uniform, Jimmy in Karnival-rag flowered raincoat and silly stripy green and white Oliebol scarf. They were blending into the normality of the crazy season. Yet things in the hospital, in this corner of Great Society were just as they should be, so circumspection and civil convention were still the order of the day. They wish to be discreet in their search for their feared nemesis but they do not need to take their discretion too far as outside of Surgeon-At-Arms Lucie's office there is a stretcher with a bloodied sheet covering a body. Without so much as a "What do you think?", or any other hesitation, Kendra pulls back the sheet to reveal the white rigor mortised face of Matron Augusta Stoneywell.

"Stoneywell!", exclaims an exalted and animated Jimmy.

"Yes, unbelievable isn't it?" Someone has appeared. It is Charge Nurse Harris.

"She was admitted here early this morning complaining that dog packs were after her. She even accused the Old Man of being an evil big wolfhound slathering to rip its teeth into her bosom. She was really gone with insane imaginings. She looked a terrible sight. Her face was really bloodied. Janna knows what sort of thing she got up to in the unspeakable Oliebol."

"Really?", adds Kendra.

"Yes, and amazingly there were others that we admitted in a similar situation. A couple of geezers in animal masks verily claiming that they were being hotly pursued by rabid dogs."

"So what happened to the Matron to put her here exactly", asks Jimmy.

"Well she knew her way about the hospital I suppose, did the Matron. We were in the thick of dealing with a large number of processings. The number of psychosis cases always is high over the Finitude. Before we knew it, when we turned our backs ever so briefly, she was on her way as fast as frying eggs to the hospital kitchens down here on this same basement level. She got hold of a sharp butcher's knife in the blink of a moment and pronged it through her heart in a heartbeat. Apparently according to the eye witnesses – without a moment's compunction. It was like a demon had possessed her, one of the eye witnesses described. The kitchen porter said that it were as if something inside poor Matron Stoneywell were operating the knife as there was no hint of hesitation in this self-immolation."

"Golly", says Kendra.

"Even more efficacious than I thought", muses Ceri Hatch.

Jimmy turns to look but there is no-one there.

"So what can I do for you?", solicits the Charge Nurse.

"Just some further paperwork from the Finance Amt", reveals Jimmy.

"Good day, Mister Suzuki", rejoins the departing Kendra.

"Yes, good seeing you again Nurse", smiles an exultant Jimmy.

"Now that we are free of her we can be free to be together", she says. The lovers are lying in bed in her well-ordered abode and the noise of the ferocious Oliebol Finitude shows no sign of abating. That rampant noise without abandon has provided mood setting to a forceful and lusty bout of sex. Exhausted and satiated they both lie in bed thinking of the elemental force that had been conceived and driven by Ceri Hatch.

Jimmy is dripping in his own sweat. He had been really exerting in his exercise and now that he is sated he is grumpy and unsatisfied. He had captured his desires and now that they have been snared he just feels simply sullen. Matron Stoneywell had been despatched and Kendra is now secure to be his.

'Is this it?', he thinks.

He cogitates watching the sweat on his stomach furls slot into his fuzzy little catchment cracks around his navel. Contemplating his own sweaty navel he is aroused by feelings of self-disgust, but Kendra is not picking up on his surly silent rumination. She starts to caress his damp shoulder; a bit too familiar for his present temperament. He thinks on the past and through association is suddenly dwelling on memory of Miss Pussy's sturdy fleshly thigh, then quickly conceiving to the ugly piggy face of Matron Stoneywell and her firm swelling bosom in the expanse of her starched uniform. The protective love of the Matron's accommodating and protruding bosom. Now he feels exposed and weak next to her lithe form; a fair sex who would only offer risk and maintenance.

"Did we really need to kill her?", he murmurs.

"What?", asks a distracted Kendra.

"I said I am off out to get an ale in the Oliebol". Jimmy is getting dressed in a great flurry and he is not looking at Kendra as he makes his announcement.

"Can I join you", she hesitatingly asks.

"Better that I am left alone for a while. I have to reflect upon the enormity of what we have done".

"We have only done good; Jimmy", shrieks Kendra. "it was a battle for our survival. If we had not won she would have destroyed us!"

"So you say, but did we have to kill her? Did we have to kill her in the way we did?"

Kendra senses his raw anger and backs off.

'Better to let him be for the moment', she considers.

Jimmy looks at her defiantly and seeing no answer from her but her danger, he storms out of the room into the craziness of carnival.

Jimmy buys a heron mask from a street purveyor who was drunk enough to agree to a knock-down price. "Fair enough for a copper ducat, the Oliebol is almost done."

Although the streets are swelling with revellers Jimmy Suzuki makes a progress through the crowds. His great girth in his brown Tarajan frockcoat and heron face mask he looks an intimidating sight and even the most inebriated of revellers do not bother to hold him up with carnival trickery or raucous banter. Jimmy finds himself marching to his familiar haunt of Frasertoon. Almost natural to be dragged back to where this latest of personal calamities had its start.

Jimmy stopped at a couple of inns supping at a jar and then at a yard or two. Before long he has arrived at a familiar hostelry, "The Seven Bottoms" and where the atmosphere was particularly riotous. Jimmy could see that a Carnival King was holding court there. The King was set apart on a small stage attired in ermine supping from a golden vessel. The King looks resplendent in a glimmering emerald half face mask, and yet debased, for he has pulled from his robes his swollen member and is asking the ladies of the court to pay their bounty tithes to it. Jimmy watches mesmerised while the young ladies perform oral service to it. They take turns of a minute each until one of the women screams heartily "I have taken the fecundity of the Carnival King!" like the cat who has got the cream. After this eruption things start to calm down a bit and Jimmy thinks about moving on whilst the night is still young. He then notices that the Carnival King is motioning to him.

"His Majesty calls upon you to attend!", cries an ancient crone attendant who obviously attended to other ceremonial activities than her younger counterparts.

"Me?", motions Jimmy.

"Yes you", she shouts. "Come!"

Jimmy is curious and moves forward to attend his majesty.

"Sire?", Jimmy grunts.

"Humble minion?"

The voice seems familiar to Jimmy as is the leering smile and the poorly qualified brown teeth.

"Is it Mister Tempels?"

"Is it Suzuki?"

Jimmy grunts in surprise.

"Why it is you, Suzuki! I can recognise you by your great muscular girth even when masked! And you? You are surprised? Had you forgotten that I am a Carnival King? I wonder why providence has brought you here to my court, or, were you specifically looking for me?"

"I was not looking for you Mister Tempels. It must have been the spirit of Carnival that brought me here to you."

"Are you troubled Mister Suzuki?"

Jimmy does not know what to say. At the very least he is troubled by the acuity of the question.

"I am troubled Suzuki. I am troubled by her."

"Her?" Jimmy is troubled by Matron Stoneywell. 'How would Tempels know?'

"The Lartal woman. Our misadventure. Somehow we have to put this aside you and I. Don't you think?"

Jimmy nods glumly.

"I have a method. If you like a solace, or even …. a new beginning, a new awakening I would speak to you about. It would help you to be sure. It has been of great consolation to me. Have faith, Jimmy, I can guide you out of any troubles. I can cleanse your soul of Fumi Lartal and others too that you have transgressed."

Jimmy again nods neither agreeing or disagreeing.

"Meet me here at seven bells on Ash Mid-Week, then we can talk and I will reveal all."

Jimmy remembers the fateful encounter at the very same alehouse a number of years back, yet strangely he agrees to the meeting accepting that sometimes the movement of life is just what is good to flow with and that is simply for the best.

"Now must I return to the service of the party", finishes Tempels.

Jimmy smiles like a mechanical doll, turns and seeks out more madness out in the humid streets.

Kendra is confounded. She had expected a great surge of inexorable happiness. Instead she found only derision and doubt.

The next day finds Jimmy raging against a massive alcohol infection. He has a copy of the Daily Bugle open and is studiously reading trying to ignore Kendra. "**Star cluster hurtling towards earth**" blazes the headline.

"Well, aren't you going to tell me what you got up to last night?"

"I am trying to read. There are important matters in the world going on."

"And you think that all this blazing star shit is more important than our relationship?". Kendra seizes the newspaper from the table and screws it up in a ball which she flings to the floor. Clearly her night alone had built up a volume of rage.

"And you have the temerity to just ignore me now? Why on earth did you come back here then? Why didn't you go to your own place back in Trenchtown? The arrogance of you to come back to the comfort of my abode and then to deign to ignore me!"

"Why!", splutters Jimmy. "I forgot my abode keys here so could not go back to Trenchtown. Besides which I haven't been back since my accident. The place would not be so friendly."

Kendra stands in front of him furiously. Through her head rapid thoughts run as to what she is going to say translating into something she had not expected to say.

"Get out", she shrieks. "Just get out!"

"We should not have killed her, Kendra. Why did we have to kill her? You put me up to that. You made me commit that evil islands black magik."

"Get out", she repeats.

"Gladly", he answers and rummages for his abode key before leaving as he could not face the terrible image of Ceri Hatch no more.

Jimmy drudges his way back to Trenchtown. He is feeling too forlorn to attempt to take the stages. Besides which is it the Quiet Burial day, the very last, but sombre day of Carnival. The Carnival undertakers would be looking to make a reveller a corpse by the evening so that they had a fresh body to bury as the spirit of Carnival for another year. The spirit of Carnival would be buried in a coffin in the yard of Black Brothers tonight. Although it had always been the practice to make a cadaver of a reveller, it had been of late usual for the Carnival undertakers to kidnap and kill someone travelling on the stage after the bout of carnival revelries. It was a cruel unnatural practice but the people and Great Society ignored the crime going on with this tradition. Jimmy felt safer on foot where he could see those fiends coming, if they were to come indeed.

Eventually he arrives at the Massive Tivoli. The tenement building and the whole area looks horrendous compared to Kendra's setting in Gaolers Knoll. He is even more despondent upon reaching his own small abode. The place has not been aired in weeks and the smell of old food had made it rank. No-one had been in since his accident such a short long time ago. He misses the jazzy aroma of Kendra, her perfumes of jasmine and spice. There is no aura of the islands here; only dead Trenchtown. His spirit feels dead as if he is dying with Carnival.

He badly misses Kendra. He misses the late departed Nicole too. He misses all the lately late and departed souls who had the misfortune to come across him. Mum, Dad, Augusta Stoneywell and all. He misses Kendra though not dead. Although he misses her he still grieves his misfortune of being with her and what she has made him do to Matron Stoneywell. How the evil inside him has been drawn to bring her down. Fumi Lartal as well. He will have it out with Kendra. He ruminates a nasty clouded-out day on the ramshackle sofa with its persisting crumbs that jump inside the legs of his breeches and all is itching into a vivid distemper of mind and body. His thinking becomes clouded and morbid.

Before he knows it the afternoon is running on and he has an insatiable desire to eat and see the spirit of Carnival buried. He would get down to the Black Brothers for the holy ceremony. He would attend the ceremonial funeral in the yard there, although he had had no desire to ever attend before. He wants morbidity.

Jimmy storms out basically wearing what he had on the night before, less the heron face mask on which he has no explanation for its disappearance. He purchases a bag of fricadillos from a street vendor which he gobbles on the march to the nearest stage post. He feels a tinge of the wild abandon he experienced when on the search to Frasertoon for his beloved cat. He makes the post and without much delay a stage arrives and he is at the burial yard in just under an hour.

The yard is crowded. There is not a bench left free to share. The world and their dog appear to be there. Jimmy would rest his aching leg and find a place to sit to watch the ceremony. He spots a sad looking fellow perched in the middle of a bench. His fellow benchers look uncomfortable with his presence as if they did not want his incoherent intrusion – even too mindless for the death of Carnival.

"Too many old people eat warm luncheon!", the odd one is drooling.

"You are entirely correct, learned Sah", says Jimmy picking up the opportunity for comfortable accommodation. "They are waiting yonder in the back for you with warm luncheon for the sharing. Look they call for you".

"Where?", the queer fellow squints.

And Jimmy prods him along away from the bench in a false direction as the dreary blackguard is lurching away looking for warm luncheon.

Thus Jimmy sits awaiting the death ceremony of the momentous Oliebol Carnival. The funeral procession begins almost an hour later and Jimmy is able to observe reasonably well the goings-on from his vantage point. The deceased Oliebol is brought into the yard on an open carriage and the coffin is open too. Thus he is able to discern that the undertakers are interning a real human corpse. It is clearly evident to him that this is no waxen figure or mannequin being used. It is a handsome young man with blond curly hair. There does not seem to be a blemish on his face. A youth who would have been quite a catch to any Delta maiden. No more than twenty-one years old Jimmy surmises. Clearly a beautiful and tragic sacrifice for the Oliebol. The Oliebol that only came around once every twelve years. Nevertheless, even with the ghoulish confirmation, Jimmy is very moved by the ceremony. He is very mindful that this is the spirit of Carnival being buried away to revive itself with greater vigour in the coming year. Also that the relative youth of the victim who personified Carnival would withstand the ravages under earth of another twelve year cycle to come back as another glorious Oliebol Karnival after another eleven riotous Carnival seasons. A rebirth, a revitalisation was to take place, but first is the burial in the an all-enveloping darkness of things in the past.

Jimmy is sad and teary and he feels moved by the implications of all this; that he should bury away some past associations which he is not proud of. He wants to go darker and put things underground so that when he again sees the light it will be stronger and cleaner in its affirmation. He wants to see Tempels again for closure. To loosen off dark things from the past: Matron Stoneywell, Fumi, Kendra and many others perhaps that he dare not believe he has done any harm.

Such is the ritual. A collective wrong redeems the spirit of the individuals. Carnival has coursed with grim wild abandon through the psyche of the citizens. A reckoning and a peace should follow with thankfulness of having survived and symbolically resolving to go forward more pure.

Pure is his intention to open up to Kurt Tempels, Purveyor of Fine Natural Juyces. Jimmy is at the Seven Bottoms at the appointed time, but Tempels is there even earlier and is gesticulating to Jimmy to come over to his corner table affording discretion in the crowded tavern.

"Have a dram of sheep-schlog, Suzuki", says he whilst poring himself another libation too. "I know I shouldn't but I really ought to sponsor the business of these good licenced hosts. I have to support their honest business too", and he shakes a smile across the crowded inn to the fat ugly bartender who mystically returns the smile back as if they had communicated telepathically across the wave of noisy clientele.

Jimmy goes with it although it is not how he expected to open the dialogue between them.

"Why ever not? A wee dram is very efficacious to the health, is it not? Or is it now that Carnival is over you have heeded to a purge?"

"No, it is because my holy order frowns upon it. Actually it is forbidden to me", reveals Tempels.

"You mean alcohol in general?", clarifies Jimmy.

"Yes, alcohol in general, Suzuki, for I am of the Sand. We actually preach against it, so I do myself blasphemy."

"Really? You are of the Sand movement? I would not have credited it."

"Yes, I have been an upholder true for the past eighteen years. I am actually now of relatively high responsibility in our order. I am the lately proclaimed Mani of True Delta. Rasta Habs, the leader of our august order, proclaimed me himself. I am just getting acquainted to my new position and responsibilities. Therefore, I am giving myself a reasonable transition to crossover from my standard iniquities to more saintly behaviour!"

"What does it mean, this Mani thing?", enquires Jimmy.

"It means that I am the spiritual leader of the Sand congregation in Banana Delta. It is a big flock, an important position and that is why I wanted to converse with you, Jimmy."

"Look Tempels, I know that the Sand is not exactly establishment mainstream. You persons are agitators at the fringe of Great Society yet you still purport to hold the grand official office of Carnival King. How do you reconcile this to me and how comfortable should I be sitting next to a leader of a group who challenges the core of Great Society? I am counter-professional and my position could become a lot worse being seen colluding with a member of the agitating classes."

"You must have faith, Jimmy .."

"Fuck faith", he spits. "For me the only belief is certainty and for that I have my reasoning and experience where I take responsibility to know for what the truth is. You have already duped me once Tempels."

"I recognise that, and you are probably right to be suspicious of me and my creed, but believe me I was only acting a part to put my beliefs in a better position to challenge the fabric of this diseased and dissolute so called Great Society. I will reveal all on this in due course at a later time when we have longer to speak more freely . For today I would entreat you to tell me what troubles you, for

I know that you are troubled and I will listen and I will grant you full clemency on your anguishes."

'Who is this man?', thinks Jimmy. 'Every time I meet him he seems to be someone completely different. Pugnacious street seller, brigand, decadent carnival demon and then again man of piety. Is he playing me again?'

Against his better judgment Jimmy begins to talk. He tells Tempels of his unrequited feelings for Fumi Lartal, his dangerous relationship with Kendra and then finally the sad demise of Augusta Stoneywell and how he had involved Ceri Hatch in that. Tempels does not ask any questions, he just make short utterances to make the dialogue flow. Jimmy feels that he is opening up to an old friend and confidant.

"Well, well", says Tempels after who knows how long Jimmy has been confiding. " A sorry tale, but no worse than I have related to others in the past about my very self. Here have another libation. What has been endured on Fumi Lartal, where we were jointly complicit, I know that great Cosmos forgives you. Lartal was acting for this corrupt state. She was fair game for the purpose of our holy movement. Cosmos absolves you for that."

"Cosmos?"

"Cosmos is the great being. All knowing and the force who moves our hearts to pious purity. The Sand follows his divine cause."

" I see", says Jimmy knocking down another stiff one.

"Matron Stoneywell is another matter. She may have been hard on your fancy girl, but it sounds to me that she was just performing her duties. A reasonable suspicion on her part was no reason to bring in dark juju to slay her. You even remarked that she was quite kind to you in the hospital. For your part in her despicable demise you should make remission."

"How do I make remission?"

"You renounce the wicked Kendra and come into the true faith with me".

"Renounce Kendra!"

"Yes, she put a spell on you. I believe that she put the islands magik on you; that she was actually Ceri Hatch. She managed to make you believe otherwise. You have to cast her aside and come into the faith with me."

Jimmy is smiling wryly now.

"I don't think it was all Kendra. I was very much responsible too."

"May Sand have Salt! Come to us to lay off your transgressions."

"I will do as you instruct", without any hesitation from Jimmy.

"Good. I will arrange for you this very evening a safe house where Kendra, nor anyone else you do not wish to see, will ever find you."

"Thank you, dear Mister Tempels".

"Welcome to the Sand, Jimmy."

Jimmy a man of doubt sets out on the road to faith because the swimming in the current of life has become too rough.

However, there is one last path of the faithless that Jimmy has to meander down before he is on the road of the straight and narrow.

"How did they let you in?"

"I claimed habeas delicto".

"The right for the insolvent and insane to be succoured by their family and friends. By Sorno, you are a dark cock. Where did you get your education on our ancient rights?"

"You know on the street, in the public houses. Accordingly I have brought a large loaf of bazlama bread for you. It is warm from the oven and nice to the taste. I asked Lady Swann to make sure that you were made more comfortable in this cell and I see that her influence still extends enough when needed. I see that they have given you a presentable cot, blanket and pillow, even though you are still straightjacketed, kind Sir………. I can't , I can't", he bubbles.

Sir John is also weeping now. "You can. Please do it. No regrets. They told me that Roper died from his injuries, so they will either hang me or incarcerate me here for the rest of my miserable life. Sometimes it is necessary to have the courage to give it all up. Give me some of the bread to sup on for the last time."

Jimmy tenderly tears off some of the bread and delicately puts it in the mouth of his old friend who chews in its rich taste.

"No goodbyes", he chomps.

"Goodbye dear friend."

With speed and gentle force Jimmy takes the pillow and starts smothering. His friend offers no resistance apart from the involuntary death froes. Jimmy makes short work of it.

"Hark Sir John has had a seizure", bellows Jimmy. "I think he has choked on his bread and his heart has given out."

"Let me take a look at him". It is the medical orderly entering the cell. "By Domingo, I think he may have passed away. I'll call the physician."

Jimmy is not really listening. He is mourning the passage of his dear friend by throbbing out tears of emotion. In his grief he does not look like any murderer, more like simply a grieving good family friend.

"I will be back on the morrow to arrange for his funeral. I must get air."

Jimmy trundles off down the dark passages looking for exit from the terrible underworld. He reaches the air and relevant freshness of the upper normal part of the White

Cross giant structure. He seats himself on one of the large reception benches, joining the rank of the great unwashed. He wants to roll himself a fag, but he knows it is verboten to smoke inside the hospital and he cannot be arsed to drag his tired carcass outside. Instead he thinks to read against the latest mysterious missive from Mistress Dowd.

'This game cricket. It seems rum. Five days long with meals included', he muses. 'The old man who gave away his natural son. The recompense, the valedictory, the long lost ruined lives. Why did you forsake me father?', he screams in the soundproofed caverns of his distorted mind.

Jimmy is anguished and means to rip the latest Dowd paper into shreds.

"Wait! Don't do that fellow. I can use that paper to roll me some fags."

Jimmy gives the sheet of paper to the ruffian next to him and leaves the hospital silently.

So it begins and ends with a roll-up. Jimmy resolves to escape this life into the all redeeming comfort of faith.

Ten: Resistance – "Down in the Sand"

"Rasta Habs has laid down that the Brown Dwarf System is a redeeming demon sent by holy *Cosmos* to deliver the world back to us of the true faith – the believers. *Upholders true !* The Brown Dwarf will purge this earth of the unholy and the unfaithful. It will conjoin all infidel into oblivion. May Sand have Salt! It is the pledge of Cosmos. We have the pledge and my faith becomes stronger. We become stronger. And now to show our holy pledge to the infidel we must show that we have had holy aryah!"

So screams Kurt Tempels strong in voice and devoutness. He is on stage at the Adele Theatre in Googleheim; a place more accustomed to vaudeville acts and matinee stars – such now is the confidence of the secret people of the Sand religion. A movement that is starting to burn all over the islands. A faith that was a short while ago isolated and alien from a remote part of the continent in the far south – the desert region of Bogotain in the continent of Mamarazaarra, where all is desiccated and tumbleweed desolate, so that the sand has covered the tracks of the people's utter desolation. Let all disenfranchised minorities come forth with a pure hatred in their hearts and they shall be justly appeased.

"Yes, the time has come for the aryah!", he booms and his audience is ecstatic as Kurt Tempels again steps forward to centre stage.

They scream in unison a reprise: "Mumbah! Mumbah! Mumbah!". The holy terror has mystique in a foreign name of its own.

"Aryah purges our insecure thoughts. It cements our alliance. It singles us out from the infidel by the way we single him out. By declaring Mumbah we cast out the infidel to the far four span of the eternal mattress and Cosmos is fed and nourished by one more impure soul being banished from the world." He says without a gulp. "If the sore is minor you might prick it out. More large you could cut it out. A massive manifest sore of evil you would hack it away rather than it violate another. Hence upholders true, I pronounce aryah."

The theatre audience stands as one to its feet with arms uplifted and the sound of yodelling is infused through the air of the theatre's close confines. It is as if the many human beings in the auditorium have become an alien being unrecognisable to any of its individual souls.

"Aryah – Aryah – Aryah", in monstrous unison.

This is as music to Kurt Tempels, the lately proclaimed Mani of True Delta. The Mani of the poor and underclass of Frasertoon, Trenchtown, Hard Shoulder and the Wetlands. He wants to conduct the rising impulse some more and he is going to get all those instruments out there in the auditorium playing with a panache. He pauses dramatically for a moment, pressing the palms of his hands down in the air to push out silence and an eerie respectful silence arrives like the denouement of a high grade vaudeville conjuring act.

He hisses solicitously.

"I bring you upholders true, one Reginald Capling, tax collector of Deacon Docks, whom I recommend to you for righteous aryah!"

"Yeah unto us righteous aryah!", is the universal reply accomplished with no thought by all those with a passion to follow mass iniquity.

"So let it be so", states Mani Tempels and unsheathes a meat cleaver from an innocuous looking attaché bag. "Bring him forth".

A rather startled Reginald Capling is brought forth on to the stage. He wears the moth-eaten and dowdy livery of a minor tax collector of Great Society. Jimmy immediately recognises him as a second cousin on his mother's side. The Caplings, as mediocre as they were, always looked down their noses at their distaff Suzuki relations. Jimmy empathises with the figure of the rather pitiful tax collector, but does not feel inclined to intercede on account of merely an obscure family relationship. Blood is blood, but to some extent it becomes just blood, and Jimmy thinks things could be soon turning bloody enough as it was.

"So who is the first here to persecute this misfeasor?" Tempels cups his hand to his ear as if playing the pantomime villain in a Monday matinee. "Come forward, Marm. Jenny Howard, is it you?"

Jimmy notices an attractive young woman in the front row of the stalls standing up and approaching the stage with confidence.

"Yes, it is!", she cries. "This tax collector denied my tithe of Salt to Sand. He said that my first obligation was to pay my taxes to Great Society than to give freely my tithe to the moral authority of our creed. My bairns often went hungry as he forced collection of coppers from me as I was still wont to give freely my Sand tithe obligation. My bairns understood the priority of soul over stomach and preserved in the faith with me. Nonetheless my little Hans died last week of the piercing diphtheria on account of often going hungry and getting weak. All down to the actions of this here cur. A curse on him and all his kind."

"It's the people's religion. We come from the Sand and demand their Salt!". Jimmy is surprised that he has stood up and bellowed this statement out.

"Well said Sah! You speak for the people", says the aged crone sitting to the left of him. The crone then herself stands up and bellows out: "Chop off his balls!" Jimmy is amazed that something so small and wizened can deliver such volume and force through the packed noisy theatre.

"Right on, sister!", calls someone from the crowd. "Off with his goolies!"

"Yes, yes. You clearly have the moral authority", clicked Kurt Tempels as he offers the ugly looking meat cleaver to Mistress Howard. "Cleaver courtesy of Butcher Lamb", he diligently adds. "A round of applause for the good butcher!"

Butcher Lamb stand up momentarily in the front stalls to take recognition of the more restrained applause. The audience wants the main event to start.

The poor Capling fellow as small and slight as he is needs to be held fast in the firm vice like grip of two Frasertoon market heavies. Even though he is tightly held Jimmy can see the gyrating form of fear and hears the slow patter of urine on to the stage even from the distance of the upper fourth row. There is something mystical in the air and Jimmy feels possessed with extraordinary sensory powers. Mistress Howard is just getting hold of the cleaver and there is the look of long contemplated vengeance about her.

"What is there to be renounced, Mistress Howard?", enquires Tempels.

"That snooping of his. He was always snooping on me and my bairns. A bit unnatural I would call it. And besides which he had no right to look into aspects of my creed and demand that my faith be usurped by the mammon of Great Society. Yes, but most of all that wicked snooping into all my details. Wanting to know all my details like some dirty pervert. What I did with my money. What I did with my time. That snooping thing of his. For all his shameless snooping I say, off with his nose! Bloody nosy barker!"

At this she steps forward and without hesitation very hacks with the cleaver at his nose. Blood spurts up and out like a gusty fountain. Mistress Howard and the two minders are engulfed in it, but she continues to hack away at Capling's protuberance. Capling screams greatly but his frightful cry is washed out by the noise of the cheering and screeching. A minute or so goes by before Howard stands aside in a fit of hysterical laughing.

"Next persecutor?", calls Tempels.

Someone is already on stage. A large hairy looking middle-aged man.

"Angus Redskin, Mani", he announces. "Capling tried to falsify my tax payments. He gave me false record as I refused to provide him a cash bribe."

"Then?", volunteers Tempels.

"Off with his falsifying right hand." Redskin, a big bloke, starts remorselessly with the fingers. Jimmy is agog. He can barely look, but look he must. And then the hand from the stump is cleaved off.

Next on.

"Goodwife Treebee, your Mani".

"Well?"

"This gentleman would paw at my little Saralee. She being only ten you will know. He is a very predator, always at her with sexual advances".

"Off with his balls!", shouts Jimmy's crone.

"I'm minded to", replies the goodwife "Down with his pantaloons, good upholders!"

From this point Jimmy watches with a hand over his eye taking in a view of the carnage through the vented gaps of his stubby fingers lowlighting the absolute red butchery of the religious action. Capling's body rapidly becomes mincemeat with a final decapitation by someone called Chief Steward who claimed that Capling was a gambler and a dissolute. Something about Capling having no guts and then it is proved otherwise.

Jimmy keeps stumm while the show goes on. He slinks deeper into his seat and thinks on Yor Mamas So Fat latest football season campaign to try and make his mind avoid the horror.

'What players could improve the team? Could Honest Day Jackson be tempted? Would GS Strollers be prepared to trade?' The hacking of Capling's large intestine has reached a level of new ferocity and is taking quite some considerable time.

'Oh my goodness they're starting to burn it ….. but Jackson's a right-footer. We really need a south-foot."

Jimmy Suzuki wonders what he is doing with all this Sand stuff. He wants to believe, but he is just not getting it. He wants to suspend doubt, but it just refuses to be suspended. He is still sitting in the theatre stalls shocked at what he has seen, but yet unable to leave. He hears someone speak.

"You spoke up profoundly and true, good believer".

It is the Mistress Howard. She of the initial cleaving. She is as clean as a saint. All blood has gone.

Jimmy at one feels both disquieted and attracted by her. He feels great sexual attraction to her. Attracted by some dangerous quality that she has. Yet she is beautiful. Far more beautiful than would be perceived at first pass. He feels hot and nervous. Jimmy feels disturbed by her close company, but yet compelled to be a better man than he is. This is usually the effect extremely attractive women have on him, especially when they are an unknown quantity to him.

"Well I do indeed thank you, goodwife". He is so easily pumped up and manipulated by the fair sex. They could really play upon his strings.

"Tell me, Sah, why is it that I have not seen you at the temple before?"

"I am a new believer. The Mani has brought me into the fold".

"A new believer. Then you are truly blessed and we must adore you. I must wash your feet and anoint them with oil. I will be back in a minute. Stay!" Then she rustles off and Jimmy smells the whiff of fine jasmine.

Jimmy thinks about leaving but strangely stays put.

She is back after a myriad of emotions: "Come Sah, unsock and rest your weary peds in this here cleansing warm water."

Jimmy does so. It feels good. It feels even better when Mistress Jenny Howard start to administer to his feet with a bar of soap. Jimmy is mesmerised by the blondeness of her curls, her lily-white delicate skin and her piercing bright blue eyes. Looking into those was like peering into sunlit rock pools – comforting and mesmerising. Then Jimmy is touched by the tenderness of her touch on his peds. These hands, those hands, those lovely nimble hands – they may have been touching some other extremity in his body, such is their effect. Perfect touch from slim deft fingers anointing the oil into his toe crevasses and stimulating the cracks in his feet. He really feels like grabbing a curve of her body. There is a convulsion coming.

"How now you two! What are you up to?"

"I am making the ritual anointment for our new believer, Mani".

"Consider yourself lucky, Suzuki. I was ritually anointed by Grandma Jenkins!"

Despite the absurdity of the scene Jimmy has to chuckle. He looks at Jenny Howard's slim fingers – not a hint of blood can be discerned. Mani Tempels half an hour ago had been wading in blood, but now looks like a gleaming white angel in his ceremonial robes. The situation was bizarre. It was like sitting down to full afternoon tiffin after slaughtering babes. Comical and weird, so Jimmy thinks that he will try to generate some conversation to put himself at ease.

"You said something Mani in your sermon about the Brown Dwarf being a redeeming force sent by Holy Cosmos and that it is foretold in the good book. Can you give me further guidance on that, please your Holiness?"

"Yes, the scholarly research of Rasta Habs has thrown up evidence that the good book – the Sanda-Shi – predicts the very circumstances that we are going through now with respect to the Brown Dwarf system that the government has advised upon. We have certainly been feeling it effects lately. Tumultuous rain, flash floods, plagues of green fly and the like. Now what does Habs say?" Tempels fidgets to bring his thoughts into order.

Jenny Howard looks up from attending Jimmy's tootsies as if expecting a blessing.

"Yes", continues Tempels, "I have it. By the way, I must remark that the Temple would look upon you two as ideal sand-mates. Think on about it."

Jenny clucks bashfully and looks embarrassed. Jimmy great frame continues sitting in the stool looking a little abashed.

"What would an eminent gentleman like Mister Suzuki want with a poor widow like me?", murmurs Jenny.

"I could advocate some sort of case to him", states Tempels. "Nevertheless, the matter of the question posed – the Brown Dwarf System and its place in holy scripture. I have spoken at length with the most reverent Rasta Habs on this. He has delved deeply into the mysteries and the ambiguous prose of the Sanda-Shi and this is what he concludes."

Jimmy and Jenny are on tenterhooks waiting for the special revelation.

"You've missed a bit. You've missed a bit on his big toe", remarks the Mani. "I can see some dirt there still around the cuticle."

"Oh, right .."

"Yes. He says that the mass of the evidence defining the Brown Dwarf can be found in the Song of Sonia in the Testament of Abel. You remember the passages to do with Sonia's song and why she chose to sing it to the Khan and his ministers before the Clash Battle?"

Jimmy has no clue what mumbo-jumbo Tempels is going on about.

"Yes, they found her song very enigmatic and she refuses to interpret it even though she stresses that its import is vital to understanding the future battle, all future battles and Cosmos's direction for the world", replies Jenny.

"Precisely! And in her song are all the ingredients for the Brown Dwarf phenomenon that we have today".

"The Khan's scholars interpret her words of enigma that the brown earth will shift before the battle. That the Khan should move his warriors away from the Amagon lines which were known as natural fault lines. That he should move his forces to higher ground away from the massive floods that will hit Panacopia. That to do this the Khan will wrest control of Panacopia and wider Bogotain for the peoples of the Sand. That way Mother Nature in an entirely absurd and unexpected way helps the good Khan becomes representative of a bigger turmoil to come. That bigger future turmoil – a veritable tumult – will destroy and cleanse the world for the true believers who will wrest control of the earth. May Sand have Salt!", she barks at the end.

"Mistress Howard, you truly are a pious scholar. Tell me do you know the words of that beautiful song?"

"I can try", she says. "How does it go again?"

Across the stellar spaces
Through the furthest dark spun reaches

"Dark span reaches", corrects the knowledgeable Mani.

"Yes, yes", she continues.

Across the stellar spaces
Through the furthest dark span reaches
I send my harbinger to places
Where my light has never reached the faces
Of the poor and oppressed
Ugly and brown dirt like sand
I will lord over those who have you suppressed
Even though I come first with a small hand
I will rupture the world
And from its many creases
I will lay unfurled
A kingdom without the oppressors' diseases
A new world order
For the oppressed and the devout
And for those with the faith there will be no border
To the riches that will be received by those who are now without
But first must come a battle
And upholders true you must move to firm ground
Away from the earth's faults that rattle
Go to a high spot where you can survey all around
My brown dirt harbinger is coming
Like a small assassin in the night
It will creep whilst setting the spheres humming
A nature that will all unbelievers smite
Be ready now to fight
As my dark force is behind you
The obscure strength does not have much height
But that is to break up the brown dirt below you
And give up the world again to Cosmos.
Fight and do not Fright!

"So beautiful, so beautiful", splutters Mani Tempels. "And so beautifully said too", he adds.

'What appalling rhyme', thinks Jimmy. "Such moving language", he finds himself asseverating.

"That is why I and the holy Rasta Habs are insistent that we embrace the Brown Dwarf system", continues Tempels. "Great Society through the Astrologer Royal is describing the system as some sort of freak of nature arising from cosmic coincidence. Well we know that Cosmos does not move with abandon. There is always a divine plan. This interstellar contusion has been sent to our very world for a cosmic reason. It is clear from the Testament of Abel and Sonia's song that Cosmos was going to send a dark force of nature to assist the pious Khan win his battle against the Fillopians but that this signal portended far more, that it portended a later deluge of gravitational force that would break and smatter leaving a new world for the survivors. Those survivors being the good and the elect. The true descendants of the mighty Khan."

Jimmy thinks on about Tempels's input. The Mani had spoken. A different person he had known to the one he conspired with to bring dark malicious forces to Marmalade Fields and to wreck poor Fumi Lartal. When things are done wrong it is so difficult to right them back again. Still again he had received another viewpoint, another perspective on the Brown Dwarf. There was no such thing as coincidence and it appeared as if all extraordinary events of late referenced back into the Brown Dwarf system. This Brown Dwarf made him feel so very lonely. Its destructive force and its effect of disillusion made him feel so very alone. He wants a warm human comfort before the severe cleansing.

"Will you sprinkle Salt with me, good Mistress Howard?", involuntarily asks Jimmy.

"I would, good Mister Suzuki. I know a good hallah house in the near vicinity of here."

"Feed the stock of the believers", harrumphs the Mani and leaves.

"Shall I tell you about the history of the Sand?", she asks.

"The Mani has told me much about it", he responds.

"But he cannot tell the tale as a woman can, Jimmy. The secret of the Sand is that essentially it is a woman's creed."

"Why is it a woman's creed?"

"For it is about passion and the wholesome earth":

"Then dear Mistress Howard, I am prepared to hear a different viewpoint. Please do elucidate."

"So", she begins with an intake of breath as if before a long race. "There was the small town of Philomena in the heart of the desert of Bogotain. It is some one hundred and sixty years ago and Philomena is an oasis town that through excessive trade and outside influence has gone corrupt and has lost its spirituality. The people are awash with the artificial wealth of the oasis which is situated perfectly on the nexus of a new trading route. The town is the only hope of greenery and water in nigh two hundred leagues and Philomena was enriched by the trade brought by caravanners. Frankincense had been discovered in the High Isthus nearby. Philomena became the borne of robbers and the place for many corrupt acts, such as usury and slavery, for this was the immoral impact that the caravanserai brought to what had been once a pious and peaceful town. So many became wealthy through the new and increasing frankincense trade, many through immoral gains, but as in all things the majority of the people were the poor and when the rich got richer the poor simply got poorer! It is the story of the Sand."

"May Sand have Salt", exalts Jimmy.

"Society in Philomena had become pernicious and cynical. Someone had to do something about it and so someone came as great Cosmos willed it. There was a small family business of tanners in the Kolchecki district of the town. Righteous tanners Paul and Hera; their elder son was named Cyrus. One day Paul and Hera found that their nine year old middle-daughter Astra had disappeared. They searched and searched, but she could not be found. It soon became clear that slavers had kidnapped her. She would not be seen again and her parents knew that they had brought the child to life only to suffer a lifetime of abuse and torture. They could only hope that Astra's life would be a short one for they had heard how cruelly treated were slaves in the Farther Jonxta, they had heard about how cruel and inhuman the Jonxtans were; that they treated their slaves worse than their livestock. Such is the way of the Sand and the suffering of women."

Jenny Howard pauses for breath as there was still some to go. Her audience in Jimmy looks captive enough for her to continue with renewed passion.

"Well, when the twenty year old Cyrus heard of Astra's likely predicament, and saw the horror and dismay of his parents regarding their beloved daughter, he went berserk. His rage carried him out of their modest abode and down the main street he stomped. The first caravanner he saw in the main thoroughfare, he pulled from the man's own dromedary's back and took the man's own scimitar and slashed the throat of the poor dromedary. His rage knew no limits and Cyrus Trai was a strapping young man. May his memory be blessed! His anger continued unabated and he killed with the scimitar a passing town guard who tried to apprehend him after the assault to the dromedary. In his anger the commotion was escalating. Cyrus heard the commotion around him and a voice in his head told him to be calm as the town watch were coming in force to arrest him. The game would be up for Cyrus if this were to happen. He would have to flee Philomena and verily he did. Being a native of the town he knew well the back alleys and the secret places to circumvent the outer walls. Cyrus Trai, praise be his name, escaped into the desert by the skin of his little finger hiding by the city wall until under cover of darkness he was able to enter into the unforgiving vastness of the desert wilderness. There he wandered close to the edge of death surviving on thorn bush leaves and berries and moisture drunk from cacti at dawn. He was on the verge of dying and meeting his maker. He had been wandering on the brink of disaster for eleven days."

"Poor fellow", rummages Jimmy.

"Except his maker pre-empted this meeting by coming to our poor earth and meeting Cyrus himself. Holy Cosmos came to him in the far-flung reaches of the desert. He came in the form of Archangel Feanus dressed as a poor goat herder with a goat in tow!"

'How convenient', thinks Jimmy.

"The Archangel slaughtered the goat and immediately gave its blood to good Cyrus for immediate succour. The goat was then carved up by the good goatherd and roasted on a fire that had been created from a sudden electrical storm. Cyrus Trei ate the nutritious meat in a frenzy until he was sated with the old goat herder looking on. At the end of his devouring Cyrus let out an almighty belch so that the desert lions could he heard roaring back with the fright of it. "

" " You have just let out the fury of the world. That anger will be heard in the palaces and pleasure houses around the globe and the unjust will quake at the sound of that fury", said the old man. "Were it so", whispered back Cyrus Trei feebly. "I shall put fire in your belly from now on, for I am the Archangel Feanus", explained the glowing radiant young man who now sat opposite Cyrus and who shined with a clean force and vigour. "I am the emissary of Holy Cosmos. I am filled with his potency now. I am Holy Cosmos itself." Cyrus cowered next to a large boulder blinded by the majesty. "Come from the shadows into the light", said the kindly old goatherd, "for I shall tell you your divine purpose.""

Jimmy sits spellbound like a small child listening to a magik tale.

"Any questions", the narrator asks abruptly and unexpectedly.

"No, no. Please do go on."

"Well, the old goatherd told Cyrus of Cosmos's disgust at the thing he had built. A beautiful world being ruined by the iniquities of mankind. Mankind had been appointed custodian by being given a consciousness and a recognition of self, but had become a crooked custodian which would sell its own kin down the caravan routes given the chance for profit and would ruin the comfort of all other things in order to have an advantage. Cosmos would have a stop to it. It was time for righteous people to seize control from the powerful corrupt. The goatherd explained how Cosmos had been mightily moved by the suffering of the pure repressed folk and found the abduction of Cyrus's sister Astra to be just too much to suffer. It was the final outrage for Holy Cosmos. The straw that broke the dromedary's back so to speak. Holy Cosmos would take back the world for the righteous. The righteous people who would come out of the desert. The people who would come from the Sand to reclaim the world for the just and the true. Cyrus Trei would be their leader."

Jenny Howard pauses for dramatic effect.

"Well, the two of them talked deep into the night around the sturdy fire that would not go out. The Archangel instructed that Cyrus should go back and capture Philomena for the people. He was to use force also as he had the moral authority to do so. He should rid the town of the oppressor and corrupt and make Philomena into the first moral city."

"I should make pilgrimage to Philomena for my sins", whispers Jimmy.

"Yes, you should", she returns. "Then Cyrus was to use Philomena as his great moral base to expand the doctrine of the Sand to the poor and oppressed of this whole great planet. Cyrus was not to doubt or worry, Cosmos would always be there to direct him. Feanus described paradise. The running water, the choice virgins, the luscious figs and Cyrus fell asleep into the sleep of the righteous."

"So what happened then?"

"He woke to the sunlight and joy in his heart. The goatherd was nowhere to be seen, but a fully burdened and provisioned dromedary was there tethered to a rock. Cyrus knew that Cosmos has provided and he climbed on to the dromedary and without hesitation he rode within a day to the walls of Philomena never having to consult a chart or use a magnet. Praise to Cosmos! That same evening he explained to his family what had occurred to him in the past eleven days and he recounted to them his meeting with the holy Archangel Feanus. He told them of the hallowed design given to him, namely to capture the town for Cosmos and to have upholders true consecrated in the city. They could see in him the vision. They could see that he had been a party to a visitation from the divine", Jenny sighs in rapture.

"So they supported him in his plan to speak out against the oppressors and to take Philomena into the moral consecrated ground. They resolved to win over supporters from their existing congregation of the meek and the abused. Cyrus then went out to the market place and declaimed publicly the power and moral right of the Sand. The authorities soon were aware that his oratory spoke to the disaffected and they also connected Cyrus to the incident some two weeks earlier. Within three days of his return he was arrested and incarcerated in the small pasha's dungeon awaiting judgement on his perceived malfeasances. The small pasha of Philomena was a man called Ilonus Bas. He was not of true noble rank, rather having worked his way up through the administrative patronage. Essentially he was a politician rather than a leader. He summarily tried Cyrus Trei for insurrection, murder of the town guard and for theft of property due to the poor demised dromedary. Cyrus was sentenced to immurement the following morning; a cruel vindictive form of execution. Oh ye, Cosmos was right to condemn us for our cruelty. Ilonus Bas ruled that Cyrus would be immured in a brick shithouse that he was building for his guards. Cyrus could die with the knowledge that he was no better than the waste of his guards. The small building would be finished within the week according to the builders. Ilonus Bas ruled that he should be made an example of; insurrection would not be tolerated."

"Forgive my ignorance, but what is immurement?", asks Jimmy.

"It is a vile and cruel form of execution. The condemned is laid into the wall of the building and is completely surrounded in by the brick and masonry. They become part of the building after dying a slow inhuman death in the dark through dehydration and starvation. Of course, the cruel official made it aware to Cyrus that there would be some opportunity for sustenance from the waste pipes which would be connected through the wall in which he was to be immured."

"Oh, so vile!", protests Jimmy.

"Yes, but Cosmos had not forsaken him. Into the story comes the revered Rebecca."

"I have heard her name before in some of the Mani's preaching."

"Yes, but her full name then was Rebecca Bas. She is usually referred to as simply Rebecca as we upholders true do not wish her memory to be connected with her iniquitous father. Well Rebecca had heard Cyrus declaim and she saw the sense and reason in what he espoused. She had felt too closely the corruption of her father and the immorality of her mother who had many young bucks for lovers while her father ate and drank himself silly. Rebecca had heard Cyrus's call for a righteous world and she wanted to be a part of it. When she heard her father inviting her mother Olivia to the immurement the following noon day, she knew she had to take action so as to allow the Sand to engorge the unrighteous world. The dungeons were lightly attended with few guards. The administration was debauched in caution as well as outlook. It was a simple matter for her to steal her mother's sleeping potion and put it into the wine flagon of the dungeon guard. In the small hours of Cyrus's terror, who had been thinking a little that he had been forsaken, she came to him jangling the jailer's keys to his cell. The rapture of Cosmos took her. She demanded lovemaking with Cyrus before she released him as she wanted to mark before Cosmos and human alike that she was and would forever be the consort of Cyrus. Their lovemaking was sharp and erratic fuelled by lust and fear.

As he was being released by her Cyrus asked her why she was doing this. Why would someone from privilege come over to the Sand? "For I am woman", she snarled. "For whatever privilege we are eternally supressed. We have to bear the modesty of our sex and many miscarriages into the world. All women are of the Sand. The Sand is the creed to give womankind equality." "Blessed are the women in the Sand", enforced the pious Cyrus Trei."

"I see", says Jimmy.

"Well, I think Jimmy you know fairly well what happens next."

"Yes, I think my studies are taking my knowledge there. Philomena became a holy revered city. Cyrus and Rebecca wrested control of the town."

"Yes, but they had to be brutal", added Jenny. "Rebecca had to lead him to the small pasha's quarters where Cyrus butchered her parents with the pasha's very own scimitar. Cyrus held their severed heads as he called for the first time for upholders true to come to the cause. He was daring. He did this from the palace roof at the break of day. The people were exultant and the soldiers dismayed. In an instant they were his soldiers."

"Yes and within nine years the people of the Sand controlled the whole of Bogotain. Within eighteen years pretty much the continent of Mamarazaarra. The Sand is now blowing to all parts of the known earth. Now it has really become a world creed."

"It is the Creed!", she says sharply. "It is the women that makes it truly universal; makes it the Creed."

Jimmy senses an edge of menace in her.

"You will have to excuse me a while for I must pray".

'So she excuses herself', thinks Jimmy.

It is Sand this, Sand that. Jimmy is awash in a world of Sand and sex. Mistress Jenny Howard is awake and asleep imbued with the spirit of the Sand. It is a constant force in her life. It has become the constant force in their lives. Even Jenny's small children, Holger and Hannah, are expendable to the Sand. They are farmed out to Sand nurse maids whom Jenny has co-opted so that her Sand path politically and spiritually can soar upwards. Sand is in her spirit and the spirit of the Sand is within her and she is fast becoming a major force in the movement.

So it is all Sand this and Sand that, but then there is the overpowering sex. Jimmy has not known many women but would be astonished if there was another woman with Jenny Howard's libido. Talk of her faith just made her damn right horny and she would speak then of the spirit having to be sated. Jimmy became her riding horse and in the act of love it did seem that she became heavy and strong with the force of some unknown element, such so that she saps Jimmy's strength out of him through her libido. Jimmy is exhausted by the frequency and force of their lovemaking. He takes what opportunities for rest that he can find.

One such opportunity is the quiet contemplation offered by the silent study of the holy book, the Sanda-Shi. Mistress Howard carries a copy of it practically everywhere she goes. It is compact and precisely written. Fiats and commands can only stretch so far. It is ubiquitous to his spiritual guide and lover, although he has never seen her open it. Jenny Howard has gifted him a copy. A copy from the old Solomon edition. She has recommended that he read it daily and contemplate on its understated wisdom. Jimmy is glad to pore over the crazy ramblings as she will respect his personal devotions and will not take him out of them for furious fornication. His study of the holy book just about trumps her Oriens fly. When she is engorged, he can defuse her with spiritual reflections (most of the time that is).

"Just have to make my devotions with the good book, Mistress H", he calls while on the move to their sanctuary room.

"Good pilgrim", she responds. "I shall wait for you and with your good words we can have spiritual intercourse later."

Jimmy flinches and goes direct to the small sanctuary to expose himself to more mystic ramblings.

The sun shines, the sun shines, and do we ever doubt that it should not. Why has holy Cosmos placed this jewel in the heart of the universe? A jewel that looks so radiant and unflawed. Why has Cosmos perfected something so small in the vast speckled dark? Cosmos has created something so beautiful which covers a gross ugliness. Is it not? The world is full of beautiful people, but they do not know it for they are oppressed. They are the ugliness within which is the beauty and they are oppressed by the beauty of the jewel believing themselves just to be part of the vast speckled dark.

The beloved Rosemary says that so many of us do not know that the sun shines and will continue to shine; that we should walk, open our minds and then we will see the light. To walk on and to continue naturally puts the poor plaintiff on the road to spirituality. Our saint explains that you may be marching like Roth on Radandleur – his purpose was to take back the capital for the people -, or, you may be walking simply with the purpose to reclaim your value and find your soul once more, be that walk only be to Old Sarum or Saint David's ....

'May Sand have Salt', thinks Jimmy. 'This reminds me of something, but what?'

Jimmy scans forward through the text, his interest piqued.

A walk in the sand, a walk on this earth. Your feet just keep moving. You are my prophet. You carry forward my creed. You my special prophet take single steps. Sometimes when you start walking your feet appear heavy and the way unsure. With each simple set comes repetition like a heartbeat. A sense of feeling better, a feeling of satisfaction. You are in motion now acting. You are growing, procreating and dying all at the same time. This is mystery. This is my creed. This is what Cosmos wants to tell us. The only permanence is the love that is being carried as you all walk, all of you, have walked and will walk. The love for you and yours that is the thing that marks the only permanence in the Sand. Make sure that the yours is an expanding family. Always love those whom you can bring into the Walk. The Walk has no permanence. One day it will be finished and started again. It is as natural as hope and as painful as hope that will not go away. The beloved Rosemary has told us all the song of the Walk. The Walk on shifting Sand. May Sand have Salt!

'This reference to walks and the beloved Rosemary. Too much of a coincidence?', he ponders. 'Rosemary Dowd and her walks. The walks that have been revealed to me from umpteen sources, although principally Copperfield. It is like a complicated tapestry. Everything is entwined together. Is there something mystic? Are we all foretold and to be found in some ancient manuscript?', he muses further. 'Who or what could have brought all this together?'

His reflection is broken by the hurly-burly of life.

"Oh, Jimmy. Enough of the cosmic mysteries!", he hears the voice of Jenny Howard. "I am in need of your twizzle-stick and earthy fundament now. Come on, I will not be denied."

He leaves the good book somewhat puzzled, but more aroused by life than normal.

Jimmy becomes immobile with contradiction. His thinking points only to the pointless. As he continues to meander into non-conclusions and conflicting answers and spurious questions, things of the other life continue to run their course. For one Mistress Jenny Howard has become more strange over the continuing course of their mere four weeks together. Increasingly she is enrapt in the spirit, the mystery of the spirit. The spirit of Cosmos she has identified as being imbued in her. This ingress has altered an already very altered personality. Jimmy considers that the principal thing that is keeping her sane is her beauty. The beauty is a veneer over a raging instability underneath it. Jimmy concludes that commitment can endorse any irrational behaviour. That you cannot be mad if you are devout enough. If you delude yourself into believing what you say then that is alright. So it is with the divinely infested Jenny Howard. She has the physical manifestations of a goddess – she must be one.

He has moved in with the Howard family, almost without thought or consideration. He is shacked up with Mistress Jenny Howard, such a beauty and it has just crept by him. Before he knows it he is intimate without the time to have learnt and become intimate. He is part of the fixtures there and it has been such a short while he can hardly countenance how it transpired.

Jenny's relationship with Jimmy becomes a recurring wave of her revealing how holy Cosmos has spoken to her, how she is his chosen one, and how Cosmos has been guiding her through her special mission. When she confides to Jimmy these divine revelations, then after a few minutes, when her impassioned oratory becomes more frenzied, she would spontaneously become very randy with no effort or special attention on Jimmy's part. The first twenty or so times Jimmy would look at it dispassionately.

'Don't ask which side you bread is larded', he would think. 'Whoever would have thought that a fat lump like me would be shagging such a beautiful bint.'

But then it became rather exhausting and then rather intimidating. He needed rest for good performance. He needed to be relaxed to do it. He could not be relaxed under her scruples of high performance. He was starting to feel like a spent-out sex slave and she was becoming rather scary.

"Cosmos came to me again in the night".

It is just about dawn. Jimmy buries his head in the pillow hoping for her to subside, for it to go away and stop. He cannot be moved by the spirit no longer.

"Cosmos came to me again in the night", she repeats angrily and punches him in the stomach. For some unknown reason Jimmy is frozen from retaliating. If she dished it out he would not retaliate.

"Oh, I see. I did not register. I was still half asleep my darling. And what did the holy spirit impart?"

"Well, you remember I told you about how bold Cyrus became when he knew he was the chosen one of Holy Cosmos?"

"Of course, a beautiful story that you so well related to me."

"Well, Cosmos has called me to consider that this is another pusillanimous in Philomena moment."

"Pusillanimous in Philomena?"; Jimmy does not quite get it.

"Yes, Cyrus was rotting in the dungeon in Philomena. Quite gutless and in fear of his life. Rebecca frees him and emboldens his spirit to what needed to be done. To dispose of the small pasha and get the Sand movement to begin. Maybe I am timid in Trenchtown and I need you to embolden me to do what the divine spirit has marked out as my destiny."

"And that is to do what?"

"Why, to kill the Mani, of course. Cosmos wants me to take the Order forward and that cannot be done with old Mani Tempels standing in our way?"

Jimmy feels her twiddling with the foreskin of his penis.

"I see, and this is what the spirit of Cosmos has indicated to you that needs to be done."

"It is."

She is starting to pull at his testicles now and is descending a love bite down on him.

"And that there should be another Cyrus to carry on my divine mission. Give me a boy baby Suzuki!"

Jenny gets on top of him inserting on to his shaft. Jimmy does not wish to take another pummelling.

"If you get on top of me we will only make girls. I have to come on top of you."

"Do so, big boy. Do your missionary work."

"**H**ow do you think we should kill him?"

It is two days after Jimmy had first heard the sanctified murder ordinance.

"By the way I am showing as yet no sign of impregnation. We have been doing it some while now. Your cannon doesn't misfire, does it?"

"Well, I can't really say as …"

"I was thinking poison, but then again it's a bit hit and miss. You can never be entirely sure if you get efficacious stuff and then there is all the cloak and stiletto stuff to deliver it into his drinking vessel. Maybe we should simply strike him down with a knife whilst in disguise. What do you think?" She smiles as if discussing a choice of upholstery for the sitting room.

"Are you really serious? Wouldn't it be better if you simply told him about your visions and respectfully ask him to step aside for your divine backed candidacy?" Jimmy instantly regrets revealing his thoughts.

Jenny Howard looks at him with her beautiful face contorting, clear blue eyes smouldering their malice towards him.

"You dare to question the will of Cosmos? Do I protect you from this sacrilege? If upholders true knew about your suspect apostate thinking, they would stone you to death like a country crow. How could you challenge the immutable Spirit? Fear that you be struck down at any moment, unbeliever Suzuki!"

"No, of course not, dear lady, I do not doubt that you have been ingressed with the spirit of mighty Cosmos. I was just asking if there were a non-violent way. After all, Mani Tempels is a holy man, an upholder true."

"Is he?" She arches her eyebrows haughtily for effect.

"Well he is Mani. A senior cleric."

"Then why does Cosmos command me to kill him, you old silly?" She smiles mockingly. "It is a holy bloodletting that has been ordained on high."

Suddenly Jimmy has next to him canoodling a little thing of sweetness and light who is massaging at him deftly to get to the top of the bottom of his jim-jams.

"How about we take a look at the guard of honour for the new Mani of True Delta. Let's see him stand to attention at his post. Let's see him perform his present arms. After that we can talk about how to replace the old guard and all that", she giggles and falls into the mass of Jimmy's bulk.

Jimmy grunts not finding the talk of murder conducive to running the colours up the flagpole.

"Is big soldier weary? Can't he present arms? We'll have to do something about that!" She opens up her mouth for his member and gobbles him whole.

"It's a bit useless and soft", she murmurs. "Soft enough for me just to bite off actually."

Jimmy feels the muscle surprisingly becoming taut perplexed whether it has by the coquettishness or response to fear of actual castration.

"There, there tiger. I had to get that electric eel out of my mouth. Tip him to my clitty", she moans.

There then again Jimmy finds himself performing, enjoying and thinking what a beauty she is. This insane act of lust with the mad and quite beguiling Jenny Howard.

There then again they are lying in bed, Jimmy so exhausted that he could have turned his head around and done the next night of sleep.

"How do we do it Jimmy?"

"Sorry, what?"

"You know Mani Tempels."

"You simply strike him down in the street with a sharp knife. Three or four strong thrusts at his heart should do it. The knife should be extremely sharp. Take one of those from the temple. You know the ones they use for ritualistic killings. Dress like a beggar. Stop him with a supplication for alms. Do it quickly and with certainty and then flee like the mischievous wind running through the alleys. I will have your back and watch out for you."

"Oh, Jimmy why can't you do it? Or we could do it together?"

'She's like a spoilt little girl at times', thinks Jimmy. 'Absolutely terrifying most of the time, but then again so fragile.'

"I would advise not, Jenny. I think it is important to Cosmos that you take the blood of the old degenerate Mani. You are the fresh blood. Therefore it is the ritual that you let out the blood of the old."

"I see. You are right", she concludes unhesitatingly. "I like your reasoning. Let's carry out your plan on the morn."

And so it was. What was the thinking that was inside Jimmy at that time? Jimmy simply again evades a hard confrontation with the formidable Mistress Howard and dispassionately trades away that encounter in exchange for supporting in the carrying out of a heinous crime. Except that Jimmy does not see it as a matter of self-preservation, he simply cannot bear to let mad Jen down. He could not bear to see her disappointed and to accept the sad mad truth of her delusions.

There you have it. Very early on the next day Jimmy assists Jenny Howard in dressing up like a dishevelled beggar in rags furnished by a theatrical company. Jimmy applies a false crone nose and a wig of matted hair. He applies mud texture to her face as if it were evening rouge. Jenny is practically unrecognisable. She just needs the cushion for her back to make her look humpbacked to complete the disguise. Mistress Howard is pleased with the result and is excited like a girl going to carnival. The transformation reminds Jimmy too readily of the recent mess of the Oliebol. The good mistress is full of humour and gaiety while Jimmy is turning more morose and sombre.

"I have the knife. I went down to the temple last night and filched it."

"Yes, I like this knife. This one I do like. Didn't I use it on that odious little tax collector? Yes. I think this is the one."

"Be careful to keep it properly sheaved. It is terribly sharp. I whetted it last night."

"Yes, it is proper sharp", she gleams. "I'll have his guts for suspenders with this."

"Holy one!"

Jenny stops and looks with him with the purest pleasure for this.

"Masna! If I might call you this?.."

"You may."

"I have had dreams too of late. In them I spoke to a goatherd who talked about the Masna. She who would govern before the days of judgments. The goatherd was very wise and he talked about you. I have interpreted this to mean that you are the Masna that we the people of the Sand have been waiting for."

"Go on".

"The point is to put the point of the knife in his heart. You must take the blood of his life force. That is the chosha way. The essence of his life force you must take with your own hands. Do not touch his entrails. They are unclean and unritual. You should take his life by taking his purest blood. Aim for the heart. A few quick strikes, but be unhesitating about it."

"I have dreamt it so too", she exclaims.

"Then we should do it".

Jimmy is convinced that the more merciful death to Kurt Tempels is going to be achieved by eviscerating the heart of his mentor. He does not wish his old sparring partner to die in an inferno of ravaged bowels. Solaced by this good act intention he prepares with good mad Jen the despatch from life of the saintly cleric Mani Kurt Tempels.

"She has quite done me in Jimmy", says Kurt Tempels to me such a short time after the event. It is sometime when I am awake or asleep; sometime when I am alive or dead. It is sometime after.

Kurt Tempels, or I should say his ghost, the wraith or spirit of the late Tempels. I just knew that he was going to enlist me in the conduct of something underhand. I had witnessed directly his demise at the hands of Mistress Jenny Howard. My "mad Jen" as it was started to be whispered about in our Sand congregation by our fellow upholders.

In the silence of the witching hours of the night he lies in bed with me and I can smell his garlicky breath. I do not know where the Mistress Howard is; why she is not abed with me.

"An old beggar lady approached me for alms after lauds service yesterday", he explains. "Lauds is early and never too well attended, but we do it because we are pious. I am Mani, so I stop to offer her a copper groat. She was a hideous looking crone, but there was something very beautiful about her eyes. I was just about to reflect upon the familiarity I had with those blue eyes when I felt the blood being released from my right hand. Then she thrusts

with that savage blade swiftly into my dear old heart.
Once, twice, thrice, four times. There is the vague
recollection of someone shouting "Enough! Make your
escape." Then just as the lights went out, the last grasp of
consciousness. Jenny Howard."

"Jenny Howard?", you say.

" I want my revenge on her Jimmy. I want her blood.
She is taking my position. She took my very own life with
it."

"Kurt. Dear Kurt, I shall call you, although for years
you have seemed like my very bane. I cannot do it. I will
not do it. I have had enough blood for my lifetime."

"Then at least denounce her to our upholders true. Let
them know her evil ambition. That she wants to be Mani
of True Delta. She is dangerous and would be ruinous to
our faith, Jimmy. Renounce her and leave her and find
peace Jimmy. Do so and I shall provide you with facts that
lead to Fumi Lartal".

"Fumi? What are you talking about?"

"Yes, Fumi".

"Is she still alive?"

"Yes, she is. You must have known that she was, didn't
you?"

"And you know where she is?"

"Yes, I do, and I also know she is being held captive by
Belsingham."

"Belsingham indeed! Is she alright?"

"She is alright, but probably not for very long. He is of
mind again to sell her into slavery. You must have known
that he would come after us – actually you now – for the
double-cross those six years ago. He is more for revenge
against you now than to destroy Fumi. So you better move
out sharpish on a reprisal against the bitch Mistress
Howard. And if you do what I propose, then I will send
you to Fumi. You two could have a chance together." Even
as a ghostly spirit Kurt Tempels, Purveyor of Fine Natural

Juyces does not mince his words. I listen to a lot more words un-minced and nod in agreement that it constitutes a good plan.

So yet again I am to set out on a Kurt Tempels plan.

Yet again I set pace at someone else's march. I can again see clearly that I am being frogmarched into someone else's design.

Again and again still throughout the course of the continuing night a thing that looks like Kurt Tempels has come to Jimmy Suzuki again in a deeper dream. A dream now so deep and fashioned in its symbolism that all appears extremely vivid and real.

"I have come to tell you things that do not befit entering your day thoughts. I require your undivided unguarded attention. You still have two full chapters of the present past to walk through and reconcile. I am your ghoulish partner now and we have to walk together through those times you experienced at Snood's Droop, and your dalliance with the dark arts of Qin Chan, and from that the influence the spin meditationists have had on you. I am your unfettered deep conscience now, and although you would like to think that you are pure and have been transgressed against, we know that it is not quite that simple. You have to walk through the deserted passages of SSN. You have to amble on through the evil methodologies of Qin Chan and Le Bertet. You have to experience those again finally to purify. To be purified enough to reach Fumi."

"Speak on good ghost", Jimmy utters against the stormy night sky whilst he stands on the battlements. "Did I count the endless stars?"

"Walk on well through these old paths, but know this too of our old adversary Horatio Beeswax Belsingham, that he knows you only too well. He is the author of the good Alms-Master David Lincoln. He counselled Lincoln as to the nature and method of your social place conditioning. It was he who received your application to the Imperial Society of Gifted Arts. He looked at your primeval sketches and was afraid. He was afraid that you were an artist that would capture the spirit of the dissent of the time and hold the imagination of the people. He was afraid that you would go on to depict the rage inside our citizens. He thought that you had put a mirror within and the thought disturbed him. It was him who sent the brief to Alderman Lennon."

"The treacherous fiend", Jimmy responds while still continuing to dig up an old grave in a deserted moonlit cemetery. "Did I spin on through star light?"

"There is more", continues Tempels.

Jimmy is holding up a human skull as if it were an object of deep affection.

"Belsingham has been utterly ruthless in his ambition to control Great Society. He may even be Great Society by this very now. I do not in fact know, but keenly suspect it. Even your great consciousness cannot reveal to me the actual truth of where we stand on this matter, but we know we are pointing our joint consciousness in the right direction. Suffice to say the venerable HBB has been taking out individual enemies, as well as all his disliked cliques and sets which he sees could be in opposition to his vision of Great Society. Hence his associations with common hoodlums and villains such as Lord Roy Gibbons to bring down persons of privilege. Hence his targeted campaign using the Brown Dwarf system to bring down Sir John and his close associates. There is no doubt that the Brown Dwarf exists. He is beginning to reverberate through me now. Can you feel him?"

He continues.

"The business with Fumi Lartal happened to fall into the category of personal animosity. Belsingham cannot cope with opposing views. He can only close it down by fully opposing them who oppose him. She tried to close down the bully-boy barrow black market empire of Gibbons. She stood up to Belsingham's haranguing of her to leave off and let the under-class rule their own. Belsingham loves making the establishment in the mould of his own, but within making himself the law he has to have the frisson of living outside the law that he is creating; to have an ever darker side in lawlessness and revel in the reckless excitement of it all. Sometimes a high class criminal just wants to feel like a criminal and get excited by it all. Hence his association with the underworld. Therefore his penchant for white slavery. That and revenge on Fumi constitutes the greatest sexual excitement for him. That's where we are both tied in, dear Jimmy. That's where we became partners in crime and our fortunes coincided together."

"The very beast", says Jimmy as he and his portly frame remove themselves from his naked mother's bed. "What a blackguard! Did they consult me in the coffee houses and the drawing rooms?".

"Know this too", says the ghost. "I tried to play him. My reference and allegiance to the Sand was always to give us, the poor underclass a second chance. My plan was to expose Belsingham as I knew by exposing him we could bring down many of the other dark shadowy figures behind the anti-establishment known as Great Society. It was never my plan to sell Fumi Lartal to white slavers. I wanted to set up and engage in the plan in order to reveal with the greatest publicity that he was behind the kidnapping of an ordained official and officer-of-the-court. I engineered the plan so as to get Belsingham and bring him down. Alas, you did not know this at the time. You could not be made aware. I am sorry I played you too, but some things are necessary at the cost of individuals."

He pauses to listen twice to the hoot of a far off night owl.

"Dawn is soon breaking and you might ask what was my motivation. You would know that Jimmy? Well, it was just my antipathy toward my hard knock life. The Sand is all about liberating the people, getting them to rise up and take back the oases from the few privileged. That has always been my simple plan, and then one day a certain Angus Oiler entered into my life, led me to Belsingham and they told me of their plan for Fumi. At that point I recognised Belsingham as the new burgeoning power of this wicked establishment known as "Great Society". They told me of their plan to take out Fumi and I resolved to bring them down. You know the rest."

"Now things are starting to make sense", says Jimmy as he storms through the cloisters of a nunnery looking for Fumi. He is wearing full knight's armour. "Did they offer me the money?"

"You won't remember all of this on the morrow, but you will keep on having the feeling of the gist of it. You know what to do with Mistress Howard as I instructed you in our earlier dreaming thoughts. Do your duty. Complete your walks and you will find Fumi. Certainly she is not here in this convent in which you have set yourself. You know what to do, don't you?"

"Yes, please". Jimmy is in the chapel at prayer. Praying for guidance on the future of the kingdom.

"I'll go back in now", says Tempels.

Jimmy wakes up with a strange unsettling feeling. He believes that he has had a very weird dream. Nevertheless, he knows what he has to do. He has to take Mistress Jenny Howard out of the picture.

'It will be a peculiar thing to do', he concludes as he looks at the desirable naked frame of Jenny Howard still sleeping next to him. She looks so dangerous in her short shallow sleeping. 'The first thing I must do is to get out of this bedroom, out of her intimacy, out of the house and into the brutal Delta to start on putting my plan into operation".

He silently arises his ungainly naked frame from the bed. There are fresh scratch marks on the skin of his back.

'At least I won't have these to contend with in future'', he reflects.

He writes her a note out in the scullery.

Holy Masna / My dear Jenny,

I see it clearly now. Holy Cosmos has sent you to deliver us from the Sand. Cosmos has made me understand this in divine dreams and revelations – the latest and most compelling of which I had this very last night! It has been made abundantly clear to me that you should immediately be anointed as Mani of the True Delta – in place of that apostate Tempels - and you will shortly after that be elevated to Grand Demonizer. I have gone to tell the Elder upholders of my vision and how Cosmos has spoken. Please come to the Holy Crypt at midday where I will have all disposed for your anointment.

Your most devoted believer,
Jimmy

Jimmy gets dressed without much care. He starts to feel a little afraid now at what he must do. He must get out before she stirs. After all, Kurt Tempels had been a tough old biscuit. He was not the type you would like to have against you in a whorehouse fight in Frasertoon, but Mistress Howard had despatched old Kurt without a moment's compunction. She could be a formidable opponent so he would have to do this carefully.

He leaves the note under the chamber pot immediately outside the bed chamber door. It is six o'clock in the morning when he leaves the house. Six hours to get it right.

His first port of call is to Slim Tennyson. The Sand Believers had been tolerated by the Delta's ruling underworld hierarchy as they realised a certain amount of spiritual manna was required to keep everyone quiet. The fact that the religion was one that was opposed by Great Society lent a certain credibility to it as far as Lord Roy Gibbons was concerned. Tempels as the new Mani had been given the nod by Gibbons. Tempels was a known quantity to Gibbons. Gibbons had probably recognised that if there were a real conflict of interest then Tempels' first allegiance would be to the street rather than heaven. Jimmy felt that it might be politik to refer to the lay power before consulting with the astral movers. It is hard to get an audience with Gibbons himself, but Jimmy knows that Tennyson, as the eyes and ears of Gibbons, can grant an audience practically anytime.

Even though the hour is early Jimmy is received in Tennyson's bed chamber deep in the heart of Turnip Street. Slim Tennyson is propped up in bed sipping chocolate. Either side of him is a young catamite.

"Thank you for seeing me at such short notice, sah".

"Well; I was told that it was a request of extreme urgency from the devout of the Sand concerning the murder of our dear Mani."

"Yes on that I have extremely important news to relate Mister Tennyson".

"Don't mind them", comments Slim in reference to his bed mates, "they are both dumb mutes. Aren't you Sparky and Isaac?".

No answer from them.

"They won't be sucking up any rumours, but they are rather good at sucking other things!", laughs he.

"Well I am here to tell you that the Mani was murdered by Mistress Howard."

"He was murdered by Mistress Howard, you say? Mad Jen? Aren't you sleeping with her?"

"Yes, but I dare not".

"Dare not what? I don't follow."

"Dare not not sleep with her".

"I see. Then why are you here Mister Suzuki?"

Jimmy has some fast explaining to do.

A quarter of an hour later at eight o'clock he is finished explaining. Tennyson has sanctioned the doing from the secular side. Now he has to convince the pious elders. Jimmy resolves to go and see Stewart Braggs. Jimmy believes that Braggs is the most amenable, but yet the most influential of the Delta Council.

Braggs is an oil merchant. A grand name for someone who takes his cart and pony around the tenements of Frasertoon and Trenchtown delivering vegetable oil for those who are able to afford oil lamps. After some asking around Jimmy locates him on Tacktucker Avenue. Braggs is heaving onto his cart a large clay urn.

"May Sand have Salt!"

"May Sand have Salt!" The traditional greeting between upholders has been observed.

"What brings you to this part of town on a Monday morning, Mister Suzuki?"

"Actually you, Mister Braggs".

"It must be urgent". Braggs is a direct person.

"It is".

"Speak", says Braggs.

Jimmy moves him into a street corner out of the Monday hubbub.

"The Mani was murdered by Mistress Howard. It was no aimless arbitrary act of a beggar, it was her – Jenny

Howard. She has gone out of her mind. She believes that she is now the representation of Holy Cosmos on earth. Her all too consuming belief in her devotions has plainly driven her insane. We must take immediate action to take her evil malignancy away from our congregation. We must stop her in her tracks".

"I don't understand you. Why did she kill Mani Tempels?"

Jimmy explains to Braggs the grisly details behind the demise of Kurt Tempels. There is nothing else for Braggs but to believe it and on that belief Braggs has no doubt.

"I am not altogether surprised at her naked ambition, Mister Suzuki", he finally announces. "What do you propose we do?"

Jimmy outlines the plan for the noonday encounter at the Holy Crypt in Elsie Street and Braggs agrees to win the other elders around and get them together for the midday meet.

"I very much appreciate your forbearance, sah", adieus Jimmy, "and please note that I expect the venerable Lord Gibbons to be there for our meet also."

Jimmy hurries off. It is ten to ten.

Mistress Jenny Howard raises her pretty head at about quarter past nine that morning. She has slept full and well. She feels imbued with the spirit of Holy Cosmos. The passing at her hands of a Mani has refortified that inspiration of spirit within her. She has the Cosmos's blessing and she now has to consider how to ensure that, now being possessed with the spirit of the old Mani, she can convince the other upholders to confer upon her the position of Mani.

"Oh Jimmy", she cries. "Where art thou big boy? Your Mani needs her chamber pot soon. Soon!"

No answer.

"Jimmy!", she bellows and yet no answer. "I need to pee!"

She moves her naked form out of the bed towards the bedroom door.

"Need to take a piss", she snarls as she opens the door.

"Ah there it is", and she notices the note which she proceeds to read while squatting over the pot.

"Well he's finally seeing sense", she murmurs and smiles.

'Ah well, my believers are starting to register my holiness', she muses. 'Better pick out something suitably holy to wear for the day. I must look every inch the representative of Holy Cosmos'.

It is five minutes to noon and Jimmy is standing in the worship room of the Holy Crypt on Elsie Street. It lies underground street level and people are still amazed how a natural dome of rock has formed in this subterranean cavern deep in the heart of Trenchtown. Kurt Tempels had revealed it to the upholders true and pronounced it as the Cosmos miracle which established his prelacy in the Delta. The natural dome looks like the dome of a temple pushed up by the hand of Divine Cosmos from the deep dark earth of the Delta. Since Tempels has revealed it, the Holy Crypt had gone on to become one of the holiest of holy sites of the Sand religion. Water and rock salt crystals ooze from the dank walls and this was now the site for the most intimate of mystic observations for the select few in the hierarchy of the upholders true.

Jimmy stands with the elders in the mystic semi-circle. In lieu of the missing Kurt Tempels, the other elders have invited him to form up as one of the Accession of Nine. Six men and three women all garbed in ceremonial cowls and yellow berets. The Accession of Nine represents the half-formed nature of the universe with a circle of humanity that has been broken. It is talismanic to the Sand and is the procedural element necessary for all important decisions and confirmations.

The Accession of Nine waits in silence. Jimmy stands between Stewart Braggs and Agatha Minky in the oil lamp glow patiently waiting for the supplicant.

And lo she comes. Jimmy hears the ceremonial knocking on the Sardis door. The Venerable Rod which symbolically guards the Sardis Door is used for this purpose and any supplicant to the Accession of Nine of the Holy Crypt would be expected to adopt this procedure. Jimmy thinks it cute that Mistress Howard modestly represents herself as a supplicant to the Nine. Even though she is madly insane with the overriding conviction that she is some sort of mystic chosen one, she still evidences the political savvy that she is working everyone into her camp. 'Insane undoubting belief, but yet on the other hand some element of doubt concerning her holy credentials', muses Jimmy. 'Do these holy persons deep down recognise their selfish naked ambitions?'

The knocking goes into a second round of bashing as it is required under the convention to do. Bash, bash, bash.

"Who comes here?", shrieks the Elder Stewart Braggs, as he is required to.

"A poor penitent and sinner. A supplicant who would ask your inspired guidance on a matter. Pray may I enter for your audience?" It is Jenny Howard's voice as clear as a bell.

"You may enter", shouts Braggs, and the large teak door is opened by silent attendants.

Mistress Jemmy Howard enters and Jimmy thinks she looks gobsmack gorgeous. She is wearing her full blonde hair laid out and adorned with glittering braids. She is wearing a tight deep purple frockcoat, accentuating the ample fullness of her bosom, with matching full length taffeta skirts. Bejewelled ('Where did she get those gems from?'), but much more than that was the application of her make-up and body art. She looks like one of those mythical old Delta queens of legend.

'My, she has been industrious in just a few short hours to be bedecked so splendidly. You have to admire her elemental force. Where does she get her energy from? How can you get so insanely organised? If it were not for Tempels I might have lived further with this threatening life-force and perhaps ultimately sacrificed myself to her', Jimmy contemplates. He marvels at the application of Delta Douge eye-shadow and the complex henna tattoos on her ringed hands. 'What a goddess! Can she really be taken down? Maybe she is the Cosmos's reflection.'

"My dear fellow upholders true. Thank you for welcoming me." Mistress Jenny Howard smiles luxuriantly as if on the crest of a great self-fulfilment. She enters the commodious audience chamber like a queen who know she has bought a large largesse very cheaply.

'Too regal. Too strong', thinks Jimmy.

"I have had wonderful visions. Apparitions from Holy Cosmos who have inspired me and fortified me in my mission to be strong and to do what is required by Holy Cosmos. The Holy Cosmos informed me of Mani Tempels's apostasy and faithlessness. Later the Archangel Prime himself instructed me to remove his poisonous cancer from this devout Assembly. That I had to do without question, although it pained me to do down one who had been seemingly so devout and had fallen so far from the way."

"Really?", queries Braggs.

His tone is doubting and questioning. 'Surely this will unsettle her and put her on her guard', fears Jimmy.

"Yes, there can be no denying the divine truth", answers Jenny Howard confidently.

"Might I attest to that truth too for Mistress Howard has been imbued with the spirit of that truth?", adds Jimmy tentatively.

"Go on", prompts Agatha Minky.

"Well", says Jimmy responding, "we all know Mistress Howard as an upholder true for some time now. She has been one of the earliest members of our faith here in our diocese of the Delta and has been absolute true in her following of the true doctrine of the Sand. She has suffered to uphold the testament of this "the only Belief" ......"

"Mumbahs", resound through the chamber.

"Indeed, so had been her absolute faith and conviction", continues Jimmy, "that she lost her son Hans in the struggle to uphold and maintain our beliefs. So no-one can question Mistress Howard's faith and belief".

"Hear, hear!", sings a strange little man in the corner by the vestibules.

Mistress Jenny Howard smiles lavishly accentuating desire in Jimmy through those ruby red lips. She still arouses him even though he knows he has to do her down.

'It is strange how much we desire that which would do you harm. Are we rational people?', he wonders.

Jimmy pauses and continues.

"There is much more to consider, my comrades of the wind. Mistress Howard says she has had the visions of grace. The visions of grace that mark her out as remarkably special and the true communicator of the spirit that enwraps and guides us. I too have had similar visions. Visions which affirm the divine mission of Mistress Howard. For a number of nights the Archangel Prime has come to me now to attest to the holy mission to be accorded to the Mistress Howard. The Archangel has related to me in clear dream visions that Mistress Howard is indeed the next Chosen Prophet. The Archangel told me to remind all doubters that it was in just such a way the purity of the first Great Prophet Cyrus was revealed first to him and then to all upholders true."

"May Sand have Salt!", quietly says Agatha Minky. "Tell me Sir, you have been living now for some little time with the Mistress. How can we know that you are absolutely objective?"

"Exactly", confirms Braggs. "Is there anyone else that can attest to the special character of the Mistress Howard? Is there anyone else that can bear witness?"

"I can!", bellows a voice from the back audience. It is the strange little man again back in the corner near the vestibules.

The man looks like he has been sleeping rough for some time amongst the tenement alleys of Decayed Barrier. His hair is unkempt and his face is smeared with dirt. He is basically dressed in an assortment of rags and he is foul to behold. The Sand had many of these outlandish types and such beggars were usually considered as particularly devout and holy due to their humility and closeness to the earth. It was no surprise that someone of this ilk would be in the congregation. An endorsement from one of the poorest of poor, if presented with the appropriate spiritual passion, could go a long way to endorsing Jenny Howard's candidacy.

Mistress Jenny Howard looks on superciliously at the foul one expecting only resounding endorsement.

"I have had most strong and unequivocal visions as to the holiness of Mistress Jenny Howard. The Archangel himself has spoken to me amongst the poorest brutes of the sewers. There stood Archangel Prime himself amongst the street rats and told me: "She is the Chosen One!"", boomed the little man with a majesty which one could not think possible from the possessor of such a slight frame.

Mistress Jenny Howard is licking her lips at such approbation, and Jimmy is thinking that she is thinking that it is in the bag for her. She will get her confirmation as Mani. She moves forward to the centre of the semi-circle with confidence.

"And indeed, Archangel Prime has instructed me to take hold of the position of Mani of True Delta. Holy Cosmos has much work ordained for our flock. The spirit has instructed us to be at the vanguard of the next wave of a holy mega aryah. We are to purge Great Society of all its ungodliness and corruption, and the blood of the unrighteous shall flow through the drains of our streets. We are to make Banana Delta the holiest of holy cities throughout this wide earth and whoever tries to stop us or stand in our way shall be annulled."

'She would incite holy war', thinks Jimmy.

"Oh Divinity, you are so right!", again the little wizened man who is now hogging centre show. "You should be Mani and rid us of all our enemies with fire and steel. I can see the divine nature in you now. You are positively glowing with the splendour of Holy Cosmos within you. He hath truly touched you! Through you I feel his might. Might I kiss the majesty of your person to imbue a too small part of your sacred spirit?" And with that he shifts on to his knees in a position of extreme pious reverence.

"You may", she haughtily deigns like a malevolent goddess from some old style religion .

With that the scrawny one is crawling over to her and kissing at the hem of her robe and slavering at her boot heels.

"O Divinity, O Divinity. You are a goddess are you not, indeed?", he obsequiously asks.

"I may just well be", chuckles Mistress Jenny Howard and she is not embarrassed.

There is a sense of great tension in the hall to which Mistress Howard appears immune.

"Oh, I think not. I think not. What would the great Sand think at some other usurping the godhead. This is not right. This is sacrilege. This will not do!" And with that the wizened beggar with a powerful stroke rips the entire length of her skirts apart with a majestic stroke of a small stiletto blade which he had concealed up his dishevelled sleeve. In this one stroke he entirely removes from Jenny Howard all allusion of sanctity and holiness.

"Mani of True Delta. Methinks not. All I see is the scarlet fleshy hue of a great whore, and trust me Roy Gibbons knows a whore when he sees one and you, you fucking street bitch, are one of the biggest whores I've cast my eye on. We the pressed upon, the supporters of the street religion know what to do with common strumpets, don't we? We fuck them royally, that's what we do."

Howard is completely shocked and taken aback and is in the vice like grip of Lord Roy Gibbons.

"Tennyson, come and help me hold the bitch. She struggles like one truly deranged."

Slim Tennyson, immaculately garbed as ever, comes out of a dim corner of the room with two street brutes to restrain an extremely desperate looking Jenny Howard. Once they have her firm and secure, although still gyrating, Lord Roy Gibbons continues with his condemnation.

"You, you stupid tart, did a monumentally pernicious and idiotic thing in killing Mani Kurt Tempels. I and my street clans have always supported the new faith. Some, like myself, are devout upholders true. I did not have to come to holy congregation to attest my faith. Mani Tempels converted me and counselled me in the teachings of the Sand. He told me of his plan, which had been worked out with agreement from the eminent Rasta Habs, to win many new converts from the poor and oppressed; to build our congregation from the many non-value providers of this perverted Great Society and then to start to oppose and attack Great Society once our numbers were strong. I thought the stratagem of Tempels to be a good one, but of course you had to come along, with your deluded behaviour, and destroy all that. Verily, you have obliterated all that, as well as a good and extremely pious person. It would be easy to kill you, but I shall not grant you the easy path".

Jenny is struggling in the grip of her assailants. She starts to scream from a fear and a knowing.

"Accession of Nine, I call upon you to get him to release me. I have been chosen by Cosmos. Do not allow anything to occur against me which will mean that this city incurs the wrath of Holy Cosmos", she entreats. "There will be holy hell to pay if my majesty is touched".

Slim Tennyson kicks her hard in the crutch to get her to stop, but Jenny Howard just starts to scream louder. "Stop them! Stop them!"

She screams and screams as if a temper tantrum will strike down her assailants and restore her to glory.

"This will not do, Mister Tennyson", and Lord Roy steps forward and brutally and callously cuts out Mistress Howard's tongue with the sharp blade of his stiletto knife which tongue he proceeds to cast towards Jimmy with a peremptory "Catch!", which Jimmy automatically does, holding it tentatively with much disgust, but not daring to do more than show that contempt.

"You can keep that as a memento of all the tongue lashings you got", laughs Gibbons. "Now that aside", continues Gibbons, "a whore should concentrate on sucking and not be engaged in talking. A whore don't need to talk so much. We have had quite enough of you postulating your anti-dogma. Now let's talk about your penance little Miss Jenny Howard! All this blood. Good job, I'm in my beggar's attire and not in my usual finery."

Her mouth is with blood asunder. Slim Tennyson calls on someone to bring a barber with a solder. "Before we are all drowning in blood, as she prophesised!", laughs Tennyson.

As the barber is looked for Lord Roy Gibbons take the opportunity to expound on the nature of her penance.

"Death after your foul betrayal would be too easy for you. Your tongue was going to go anyway as it has been the means to pass your malignity to others. I had always intended to dispose of your evil tongue. I had planned on an expert extractor to do this, but you couldn't shut up and I had to do it perhaps more messily than you might have wished. Your teeth will be extracted expertly as I want your remission to be as a worm in the sand where you can only suck for your existence. Where you are going you'll only be fed a sickly gruel I understand. I'll leave your eyes and ears as I want you to see and hear the brute ugliness of your future oppressors".

Jenny Howard in all her bloodiness is sobbing inconsolably now. She has lost all hauteur.

"Oh, yes. Eyes are good for tears too, and you'll want your eyes as there will be plenty of tears in your long short life to come. What else?"

"Branding?", ventures Slim Tennyson.

"But branding for sure", replies Lord Roy. "After all we have to notify everyone on the holy continent of your anti-Sand beliefs. We shall brand you *Great Whore and Apostate*. It won't be any easy task to brand on you all these letters, but I know someone who is very expert and patient and probably get it done in the course of a fortnight. Of course, we will do the branding down near your nether regions so that you will get no comfort from all the forced sexual attentions you will receive in your long short life to come."

'I wish I had simply agreed with the after-life of Tempels just to kill her', ruminated Jimmy. This devastation to Jenny Howard prompted mercy within him.

Lord Roy Gibbons pauses for dramatic effect. Everyone is looking truly shocked by his pronouncement.

"Rough treatment you might consider, Mistress Howard, but know that I had a vision this very morning from Archangel Prime too. He told me of your treachery and directed that Holy Cosmos had directed this penance. Prime said that you would not be truly redeemed without you truly knowing the suffering of his original people in the Sand. That means once you are fully beautified like the harlot you are, you will be transported by despicable white slavers of my choice to far-off Bogotain in the holy desert continent of Mamarazaarra. There you will work in the salt mines of Tanatarus as so many of our oppressed Sand predecessors were forced to do. You will be worked hard and long until your last day which I vouch will not be long, but which you might think is more than long enough. This way you may have the chance to achieve a state of grace to atone for your crimes. Ah, good timing. Here comes our honest barber. Cauterise the tongue! Expunge this mess!"

Lord Roy Gibbons sweeps out of the hall to the tune of horrible screams from what is left of Mistress Howard. Jimmy stands frozen in a negative despondency which Tennyson rescues him from.

"Come my dear chap. Let's get away from this awful cacophony!" Jimmy allows himself to be secreted away from the rack and ruination being witnessed by the most devout of the believers. The Sand had been all blood to him and he was glad to be freed from it even only for a short while.

They are walking into the daylight of the street and Tennyson continues: "Lord Roy Gibbons is very grateful to you for alerting us to this problem. He would have me say that he is very pleased with you and will take your petition in future. If you need a favour in the future then my door shall always be open to you. Please feel free to ask for my assistance."

"Thank you, sah", returns Jimmy. "But who be will be Mani now?"

"Well that is for the Nine to decide – even now at eight –", Slim Tennyson smiles, "but my principal opines that it will very likely be Agatha Minky".

"Agatha?"

"Yes. We believe her to be the most devout of our congregation."

"I see." Jimmy remains earnest.

"I think Cosmos was sending us a message. We are a liberated cause. Time to have a woman."

Slim Tennyson takes his arm away from Jimmy's shoulder and very slowly assumes the slow walk of the Skittish Walk.

"Good day, sah", and Slim Tennyson very slowly and bizarrely moves off down the street followed very slowly by two big street roughs as if they were participants in some very esoteric reel dance performed at the court of San Iago.

Jimmy pauses to look upon the scene and to wonder upon the next stage of his always new life.

He feels something mushy and slimy in his hand. With horror he recoils from the fragment of tongue once in the vitriolic mouth of Jenny Howard.

"Oh, so horrible", he shouts and drops the slavered tongue on to the ground. He goes to look for water to clean up the too much blood on his hands.

A quarter of an hour later Jimmy is in the public ablutions at Sandown Square. Surprisingly, but yet there is nothing surprising, he is alone in the common men's ablutions washing blood from him like the demented protagonist in an old style melodrama. He is looking into the mirror at his own grimy face. Kurt Tempels, Purveyor of Fine Natural Juyces, is staring back at him. The image of Tempels speaks:

"Thank you for that Jimmy. There had to be some natural justice."

"Are you requited now?"

"It is all finishing, Jimmy. It is all winding down."

"It will never be finished with Fumi. I must go to her".

"You will find her where this all begins".

"In the temple? In the tenements? Where does this all begin? Where?", snarls Jimmy into his soul.

"Where the injustice erupted and still now continues to fester", the mask responds.

"You mean the SSN?"

"Go to her at Snoods Droop, but first unload your conscience to me about the whole rotten experience there."

"Yes", says Jimmy.

"Oh, there is another thing I should tell you Jimmy".

Jimmy looks hard and intently at the image of Kurt Tempels in the mirror. He looks quizzically until he can only find his own image staring gravely back at him.

"If you win back something from your past, you will lose something you have today", they both say at the same time.

'Kendra? But why would I wish to lose her?'

"Well, could you keep both her and Fumi?"

"But how could I be so disloyal to her? It would not be honourable of me to dump her."

"Does it feel right for you with her, Jimmy?"

"No something is amiss between me and her".

"That would be the poison...."

"Poison?"

"Could be that she poisoned your father?"

"Old Harold? What in the hell do I believe now?"

"Think about it", says the ghost and disappears.

It all makes sense somehow.

That evening sees Jimmy waiting outside the door of Kendra's abode in Gaolers Knoll. He knows that she is due to return from her shift at White Cross Hospital. He does not have to wait long before she arrives. He has judged her arrival with accuracy. She does not appear to be surprised to see him.

"Oh, it's you".

"Kendra, I need to talk to you. Can I come in?"

"Yes."

They both enter her well-appointed commode in entirely civilised fashion. Kendra turns to close the door quietly and abruptly spits in his face.

"Well I never. Finally after all these weeks I hear from you. The business with Matron Stoneywell is still all my fault, is it?". She laughs harshly.

"I expect you are here to grovel for me to take you back", proposes she saucily. She arches her sensual eyebrows at him as if she were a judge awaiting supplication.

'Her voice….. it does not have music anymore', thinks Jimmy. 'I am not so easily entreated by her now. She misestimates her influence upon me. A spell has been broken'.

Jimmy rather circumspectly wipes the spit globule from his nose with the sleeve of his shirt.

"Rather the opposite, Mistress Okvicha". He does not know why he has resorted to formality.

'Perhaps it keeps a distance from emotion. I need to operate against her negative passion'.

"How so?", she more tentatively asks and looking a little taken aback.

"I wanted to be clean with you. I want you to know that we are finished. I have nothing more with you. I am going to be with Fumi. I am giving you up because I love Fumi".

"Fumi? Fumi? Does she even exist? Did she even exist?", hisses Kendra. "Fumi, what is she? Let's see now. F is for Figment, U is for Useless , M is for Miserable and I is for Imagination. Figment of your useless miserable imagination. That spells Fumi, your nowhere nothing girl, Jimmy Suzuki. Your fantasy lady whom you have kept in your heart even whilst you these last weeks have been shacked up with that mad malicious cow Jenny Howard. Don't think that I don't know about her. You didn't think that I thought you had been at a mountain spiritual retreat all this time. I wasn't born this morning. The whole of Trenchtown knows that you are with that evil bitch"

"Well if she was fantasy, then why did Copperfield ask you to speak to me about my involvement with her? Riddle me that if you can."

Kendra glares back at him with anger.

"So why on earth did you put pressure on me to learn about my involvement with Copperfield if she were just some figment of my imagination", continues he with his pressing.

"Words, words, words….. but what is the reality of it, Suzuki. That old Copperfield fellow was as mad as a ranter. He was one pork pie short of a picnic. I can tell you. All these strange oblique references to you being family. I think that he was just as deluded as you about this Fumi. I think that he colluded with you about this pretend princess because he wanted you to be some prodigal son. Even if she had ever existed in the way you have described her, why would a witty and charming young woman be interested in a fat fuck like you. A counter-professional for pity's sake."

"Think what you like, Kendra. I have simply come here today because you deserve closure. I am ashamed of my affair with Jenny Howard. I am sure you will hear more about her from the usual gutter sources .."

"Why what happened to her?", she interjects.

"I am simply here today to tell you of my love for Fumi. I will talk on no other aspect with you."

"And you still blame me for Stoneywell no doubt".

Jimmy does not speak.

"What if she had been right, after all", Kendra offers. "Does that increase your guilt?"

Jimmy is amazed by what he is hearing.

"What do you mean if she had been right? What are you suggesting? Wasn't it her who was doing the poisoning, figuratively so to speak? I have always believed your innocence. You have always maintained your innocence to that ridiculous charge", he stumbles on. "I have always believed that woman to be absolutely putrid. Are you now insinuating something else?"

"Yes."

"Are you saying that you did poison the old fellow?"

"What if I had?"

"Then I would hear you out and would probably have even greater reason to separate entirely from you."

"I thought you had separated from me, Jimmy", she laughs mockingly.

"Perhaps never truly in my mind Kendra until this point".

"Then I will put you at ease. A bit of confession may take a weight off me too. I did wish to poison Arnold Copperfield with strychnine. I was after his fortune. He had already alluded to me the existence of a bank strongbox and money that he had secreted away to give to deserving claimants like you and I. I think that Stoneywell had some evidence about missing strychnine mysteriously gone from the hospital's medicinal cabinet. It was me that stole the strychnine with the intention to use it on the old lecher ..."

"Lecher!"

"Yes, he was always pawing at me and grabbing my bottom and feeling my breasts under the guise of all that easy charm."

"Kendra, that is hardly grounds to kill a man. I would have been murdered tenfold by now."

"Well, I did not get the chance to commit the act. The old bugger did his heart in during the act of fornication with the tavern whore. There was no poison in his blood found in an autopsy. That was just a rouse of Stoneywell's. She just knew that some poison was missing and put a couple and a pair together. I suspect that's why there was no follow up with the Chamberlains. There was no actual evidence for it."

"How sad and sordid."

"More just sad. I did have the intention, but did not get the chance to commit the actual offence. Auspicious providence is what I call it."

"You can dress it up how you like", rasps Jimmy. "You have committed a wrongdoing, then coerced me to commit another delict. We are done now. Goodbye."

"Jimmy …"

But Jimmy is already out of the door like an express trahere fathoming through the night and his heart is closed to entreaty. He was not quite sure what this Arnold Copperfield meant to him, but he now felt extremely disquieted at his passing.

"Do you feel better now having that off your shoulders".

Jimmy hardly acknowledges him, but then curtly says. "Take a letter down Tempels. I want to set the record forward with the authorities".

So Suzuki dictates and Tempels scribes.

To the Attorney of the Day Watch and Zentralpolizei:

Your Affable Honour,
I am committed by spirited public duty to Great Society to inform.

I inform against Nurse Kendra Okvicha, a professional of White Cross Hospital and burgher of Gaolers Knoll district in Banana Delta.

I inform of her murder of Matron Augusta Stoneywell, once of White Cross Hospital. I inform that it is my knowledge that she callously poisoned the said good Matron.

I am sure that you will be rewarded by investigation.
Yours faithfully,
A Concerned Citizen and Professional

"Thank you, Tempels. Writing is not my strongpoint".

"I write and you are just. The words of the just are a power that cannot be restrained", says the face in the dirty shaving mirror.

Eleven: Destruction – "Snoods Droop"

I got out of the carriage. I had been travelling in it for some four hours and for the whole journey it had been raining heavily, so the road had very much mud on it. As I put my feet down on the road I could hear and feel the squidge of the mud. I felt totally disconsolate. At the tender age of nineteen I had been wrapped up like a package and delivered to the School of the Suspect Norm in Snoods Droop. Snoods Droop, a place that I had not even been able to find on any map. My whole environment looked miserable, the place was well inland and far away from the freshness of the sea. I felt miserable and unfresh too.

["Well, it was just as bad for me laddie", snarled Tempels. "I was pressganged into the fighting Navy at eighteen."]

I looked ahead at this imposing edifice, the School of the Suspect Norm, commonly known as the "SSN"; some of the Alderman's men referred to it as 'the penitentiary for pricks'. It was large walled and forbidding. It stood comfortable in its repose as if it had been there for some time and sometime still. The Alderman's men walked me to the large wooden door. I still remember fat young Bailiff Buckie, barely older than myself, taking hold of the big cast iron door-knocker and pounding it to make a large rappity-rap on the oak door. The door was immediately opened by a large bearded man wearing seemingly only a brown cassock with attached scapular and cowl with brown open-toed sandals. He had a shiny bald pate as if it were regularly shaved and glistened. His demeanour was curt and perfunctory.

"Good day, kind officers", he murmured.

"Penitent petitioning. Sponsor is Alderman Godfrey Lennon, and I am Bailiff Andrew Buckie presenting for you one James Donald Suzuki for penitence and re-education".

"I am Brother Tikhon and I will receive the penitent into the School."

"Then I will sign him over to your charge Brother", and then Buckie produced a shiny roster portfolio for a humdrum of signatures for the Brother Tikhon to scribble. I can tell you that I was very sad to see Buckie and his crew depart for the carriage as I was taken in to the tender care of Tikhon and whoever else; for Buckie and his band represented the outside world, the banal but accustomed misery of my life. I knew nought what was therein on the other hand and that unknown element made it scary. In the midst of all that fear and foreboding my nose was already taking in the mouldy smell of farm animals. It seemed they worked animals as well as penitents there.

"Come this way", said Brother Tikhon as he showed me into an inner courtyard of fountains and climbing plants. He led me up a stone staircase leading to a handsome house within the walls of the SSN. The rain was abating and the sun was coming out and as we ascended the stairs we were joined by two other brothers in brown cassocks. They were younger than Tikhon and did not speak. No-one spoke, we just moved as if we were a choreographed movement in a quiet ballet.

We entered a room with the sign "Sanatorium" outside it. No-one spoke, no-one smiled and no-one evidenced any flicker of human emotion; myself included.

"Take your clothes off", said Brother Tikhon. Standard procedure for a medical I thought and prepared myself for the entry of a quack, but no doctor was forthcoming. Instead the two younger brothers started to whet rather sharp looking surgical razors.

Perhaps Brother Tikhon sensed my fear, so maybe he said for some sort of reassurance: "We will shave you whole of hair. That only. For every penitent here has to come to us like a babe into the world once more. We would have you shiny and pure. That only".

I had been resigned for a death of any sort, so I held perfectly still as the two younger men applied the shaving soap, expecting arbitrary mutilation at a moment's stroke. I held still as they made me fresh pure flesh. It was strange to feel the approaching of baldness and I held still even as they performed diligently in the vicinity of my nether regions. I was resigned to the worse and I held still as the hopeless do.

["All to make you feel like a non-person, laddie", rasped Tempels.]

In a surreal progress, as soon as when the shaving process was done, Brother Tikhon proceeded to whip my arse with a bunch of stingy nettles.

"We bring you back as a babe to the world and then that babe into the world must then acknowledge and experience the pain of suffering. It is the process of reconciliation", he clarified as he applied the nettles to my sensitive rump.

He apologised after every stroke of this thrashing, explaining that it was partly symbolic, but that every entering penitent must partake in it.

After some ten or more strokes, strangely I cannot recall the number, my infected rump was applied with a soothing restorative balm by the two juniors. I wondered who these two strange acolytes were. I was then given some light undergarments to wear and led to a simple cell with a solitary bed and latrine and ordered to wait. The sound of a lock turning accompanied their leaving, but that did not faze me. I was applied resolutely to my resignation of life.

I waited throughout the day with only my disturbed thoughts. I was in discomfort from the nettle weals. Much discomfort and much disturbance allied with grim resignation, and then sometime finally at last I slept into the sunlight of the next day.

Almost after waking I heard a knock on my cell door, then the sound of keys in the lock.

"Good morning, my dear James. I've brought you a nice hearty breakfast!"

A smile. A trace of humanity. The first human warmth since I left the big outside world. Maybe I was to be redeemed after all.

"Yes, indeed. A lovely warm breakfast". The hearty person was carrying a full tray of food and drink. "My name is David Lincoln. If you like you can call me Dave."

["There's a turn-up for the books!", another response from the knowledgeable Tempels.]

"Hello, Mister Lincoln", was about what I could immediately muster.

Well, I tore into the pieces of streaky bacon with gusto and whilst chomping down toast, Mister Lincoln poured me out a hot cup of strong brew. I imagine to the observer the two of us would have looked rather incongruous. Me in light undergarments and bald to the world as if I were something stage managed to look villainous and repugnant. Lincoln looking slick in Espirito dandy-down casual attire looking every inch the doyen of desired attraction.

["You come across as a very educated raconteur, Sah!" – "It is the very faith that moves me, Mister Tempels".]

"Officially though, James, I should introduce myself as Alms-Master David Lincoln and I am responsible for the Ward you have been assigned to. It is called the Burgess Ward after the well-known benefactor Sir Hubert Burgess", the kindness dispenser explained.

"Jimmy. Call me Jimmy. No-one calls me James anymore."

"I see ..... Jimmy. Well Jimmy, I wanted to say that I'm going to be responsible for your welfare here and to ensure that you get the very best treatment that science knows."

"I wouldn't call being shaved down and all over, and then being thrashed with stinging nettles as good scientific treatment."

["You actually had a way with words even then! – "I may have had something, but they wheedled it out of me, Mister Tempels." – "Touché!"]

"Jimmy, I confess I am no proponent of such a process. The Principal of SSN is a bit of a traditionalist and is firmly fixed on the Franzi Joe principles of our patients entering here as so-called "penitents" to be cleansed. This is not an entirely modern view and even those continuing proponents of it see it as symbolic; that being that the participants in this process come here as newly born so that they can enter anew into the world. The first thing they connect to upon that re-entry is suffering. Suffering conditions humility and contrition. Two attributes that build to a social new self-realisation. I am sure the good brother tried to tell you that in his way. Tikhon is not an enthusiast of the cat. Good job you did not have Brother Jacob having at you instead. You would not have been able to eat this breakfast. "

Utter claptrap I thought.

"Do you understand what I am saying, Jimmy?"

I nodded sagely.

"My, you are intelligent, young man. That's why you are so important to me. My mission with you will be a complex and inspiring one."

"So what do I ask penitence for?"

Lincoln raised his right eyebrow quizzically. I was a fast learner and I read the signs.

"So what am I being treated for?"

"Your delusions".

At that he sprang up from his sitting position on my modest cot, collected up the breakfast tray with its dystopian remains and proceeded to leave my small room.

"Rest up for the rest of the day. The Brothers will be back with more food and drink later. Rest up. Your programme will begin tomorrow". And off he was.

For the rest of that day I was very alone with my thoughts.

"So tell me about art", he said.

David Lincoln was staring intently at me. He was always looking intensely at me as if he really cared for me. As if he really cared about what I was saying. That look of concern of his, that appearance of solicitousness – all as false as a free Friday. He was about to have one of his "at the root of it all" discussions.

This discussion was taking place some five days after I had first met the Alms-Master. In that time we had already had four good discussions together after that initial breakfast meeting. These discussions had involved conversation of a general nature; my background, my favourite types of entertainment, sport and the like. For example, I found out that Lincoln was also a follower of the mighty *Yor Mama*. There had been no such acute questioning such as this so far. I sensed a change in direction, even though there was no change in the solicitous portrait of his face.

"So tell me about art", he said.

"Art is the boldness of the imagination", I boldly replied. "It is the mind's depiction of reality. It is the fusion of past, present and purpose. It represents life's vicissitudes, and seeing into what is usually unseen to the consciousness we affect to sustain ourselves through every day. By that I mean, it stands apart as to what we have to set apart otherwise we would despair".

"I find this rather disturbing". Again the all concerned voice. "Your thoughts about art are dark and unsettling. Surely art is uplifting. The artist brings colour and beauty to the beholder. Art inspires, it describes and it fulfils the very best elements of human endeavour and spirit. Great art is a flag for our people. It is the standard for our society that motivates and invigorates our very souls."

"It could be that", I countered. "It just depends what sort of artist you are. Just like what sort of baker you are. I would bake rich course bread and no frippery pastry or the like. Perhaps I could be a baker? Or even a chef?"

"You know that you cannot be that. Your calling is more noble. You are being purged of insincere thoughts for the most lofty of purposes. You are to be unhinged of callow emotion to have a true calling in life. That true purpose as deemed by Great Society is for you to assume true counter-profession. Yours is the noblest calling; to serve through disservice. You really are to be a special one. However, first we must address the rudiments of suspect thought. What is art, really Jimmy?"

"It is fucking fame! Or it should be for being recognised for producing something challenging and different. It is that fucking bloody standard to put on a hill taken from the enemy with emblems blazoning that the human condition is all doubt and nothing, for once there is nothing where there is no doubt about it. You see?"

"Jimmy you are deeply confused. I think we are going to have to send you to the Danver Class for more base suspecting. Until then, we cannot talk of finer ideals."

Lincoln rose from his chair.

"Take him to the Deep Militants!", he snapped and two dragoon guards came to life and shuffled me like wind-up toys down the stairs deep into the dark orifices of SSN.

["I expect that was no picnic", offered Tempels. - "It wasn't at all".]

Everything about the SSN is some delusional euphemism. I could say the same about Great Society. GS, that could actually stand for Ghastly Shit, is constantly changing ghastly shit into something more perfumed all the time. Just so with Deep Militants. Just another set of safe words for the dungeons; so politically correct. There are no dungeons in the meritocracy of Great Society. The SSN dragoons dragooned me down to those Militants darker and darker down into those holes, and the darker it got the stronger became the sounds of shouting and wailing. I was not fazed as of yet as the dank corridor was lighted by torches every five yards or so. The dragoons were steady in their footing as they careered me down into the caverns until we came to a pitiful dank office sitting there like the administrative archive of the underworld.

Dragoon One knocked upon the dirty door.

"Come!"

"Another one for you, Mister Danker", announced Dragoon One.

"Splendid! Splendid!" said Mister Danker as he approached me and kissed me fully on the lips and the foul odour of his neglected gnashers penetrated right into me. "Welcome to my passion".

I was much taken back by this strange welcome and Danker was sure on its effect and laughed.

"Don't worry boy. I'm not after your back passage. It's just old wives tales that we jailers are all shirtlifters. I just wanted to give you a hearty welcome to these here "Deep Militants". Just for you to know that we care. Isn't that so Mister Pellegrini?"

If Danker was a large hairy fellow standing at some six feet three with a large collection of warts and facial sores, Mister Pellegrini was small gnome like, bald with sallow skin. He had a glowing white quality about it as if he were able to glow in the dark. Perhaps he had been too long down in the Militants away from daylight.

"These Militants are his deep passion. That is verily true", he wheezed. His voice had the timbre of a constant hanja smoker.

"These Militants are called so because we deal here with the downright bolshy. Isn't that so Mister Pellegrini?"

"Just so, Mister Danker".

"You are put down here", continued Danker, "to think on and contemplate why you are here in this institution. You will have dark and straw, no other, to give focus to your concentrations. If that don't work then Mister Pellegrini has ways of wonder with the needle to make you think and contemplate further about your place in this system of order. He can needle in tattoos deep in to your skin that will fill in the vacuum of your soul. Tattoos so far into the skin that will make you positively itch with despair. Yes, positively itch before you buckle down in despair. Ain't that so Mister Pellegrini?"

"That be it", said Pellegrini and he rose from his stool in the corner and I could see the little man was positively covered in tattoos, including his face. What had seemed just sallow skin had been a trick of the poor oil light down in the dark chambers of the house. I noticed that in his hand he had a hanja reefer which he proceeded to light.

"Medicinal. For the pain", Pellegrini added. "To give truly effective pain one must have received pain; must know pain. Look at my skin, boy. Wish not for what I can give. Buckle under, learn, conform".

"So endeth the lesson, Mister Pellegrini. Take him under", ordered Danker.

If it has seemed a long descent with the dragoons to the dark office then the descent was equal again following Pellegrini holding a lighted torch whilst hopping down mouldy steps as if he were some demented gnome.

But I felt under his thrall and followed in true submission. I was in fear of him.

Eventually we arrived at a door and all was silence. There were no groans or shrieks. On the door hung a jaunty sign saying "Happy Thoughts".

Pellegrini showed me inside. There was a draught of air and straw upon the floor. No else.

"You'll be in there for some time. No point telling you what time as time has no relevance in this darkness. There will be nothing to count off. You can only retire to your thoughts. If you need to drink you'll find portions of the floor damp enough for you to lick at. It don't taste so good they tell me, but it will sustain you. Anyway I best be off as I have a nice piece of tongue awaiting me. It has been some time since I've taken my tattoo needles to a woman's tongue, but what can I say? That particular miscreant, she'll never learn. It will be the pudenda next. Quite the project. Let's hope Jimmy boy that it doesn't come to that for you. Nice Mister Lincoln will be so disappointed"

And with that the little man in an elegant jujitsu movement tripped me up and launched me on to the floor straw and was off and the door to "Happy Thoughts" was locked and bolted before I knew it.

There was darkness. I knew darkness.

Such darkness. Such an awful torture for me. I am terrified of black darkness, Mister Tempels.

So what is art?

My stay in the institute at Snoods Droop had come about due to some darkness in me. I had sketched hairy demons and hobgoblins from within the darkness in me and I felt in such compelling darkness that I was one of these creatures forever to be cast away from the sun.

What can I tell you of my perception of this all enveloping blackness?

It was the darkness of the coffin. It was like the finality of nothingness. It was soundless too. It was the end of life.

For me that first impact of total blackness was a moment of utter terror. I strained my eyes to see some chink of light, but none was forthcoming. I thought that my heart would seize and stop, but it went on plain pumping and the noise of its beat added to the terror for me.

I called out and I called out, but there was no answer from the overwhelming silence. I ran into the wall in the darkness and hurt my leg. There was a throbbing pain in my knee which added to the beat of my heart and to the beat of the darkness.

I wish I had the power in my words to depict my total fear of the darkness. It felt like an existence on the edge of death. Like being comatose, like being paralysed within the mind. Then the darkness became my internal thoughts and those thoughts were sad haunted imaginings. Alderman Lennon beating me with his staff of office. My disdain of my parents. Me taunting and demeaning poor Doris. I was presenting an exhibit of my paintings and the audience were laughing at me. They became an audience of art critics in the form of hairy demons. Then Pellegrini heating needles over hot coals ready to tattoo eyelids with the emblem "Loser". Monstrous thoughts of copulation with fat amputated women. My member having at it amidst the conjunction of bloody stumps. Some truly disgusting thoughts in the tenure of the murk of this hell.

["They were really breaking you". For once a true voice of sympathy.]

I was being broken down through my own insecurities. They and the darkness knew what I truly was. The discomfort of the stony damp floor was like the discomfort I found in my inner being. I was made afraid by my fear. I was laid bare by it. Their torture was simple. They just had to out me there alone with myself. So simple. So effective.

Andrew Brown : Walks for the Unemployed

The longer I was alone with my true blackness, the more fear I felt about Pellegrini's monstrous needles. The more profound became my shame of myself.

I had no sense of time, just wave after wave of crazy thought, bleak thought, then foolish fantasy, then moments of quietude, fits of sleep and then more boundless moments of fear and then utter disgust about myself.

I did not know how long I was down there. I did not know how long and hard I shouted, but somehow what was the allotted time passed where the passage of clocks still counted. Someone was counting even though I did not count myself.

Somewhere on the edge of time and place the door to my cell must have been opened. I was not really aware of it. I then became aware though of blaring torchlight.

"So what is art?", asked Danker. I was blinded by the light. The very substance I yearned for was doing me in, but I was ready to beg for more of it.

"It is light. Happy light heroic things. It is feeling good and showing that through noble depictions of beauty!", I splurged out.

"Sounds promising", said Danker.

"How long have I been in here?", I asked.

"We have a little procedure of chance", clarified Danker. "Mister Pellegrini throws a simple die for fortune to decide how long is needed. He threw a three for you. Three days. You got away relatively lightly."

"Only three days", I gasped. "I must have been away for much much longer".

"Have no regrets, Jimmy. I won't be scheduling a further meeting with Mister Pellegrini. One Dee Danver is keen to see you now. I always think it has a happy ring about it to say from Danker to Danver. For me that is like ending things on a cheery note."

And with that I was transferred to the Danver class for Base Suspecting. The dragoons took me off once more and I did not see Danker again and thankfully I never experienced Pellegrini's fine arts.

I sat there with Monsy, Pete and Sam. We were the new entrants to the Danver class for Base Suspecting. I suppose we were just left alone together for a while to learn our new society. We were sitting on stools in as semi-circle and I eyed them all up.

Monsy was a mousy looking young woman about my age. They were all of my age roughly. We were a new intake. She was overweight and no picture. Hair was lank and her complexion was bad like she had eaten too much fatted sheep.

Pete looked hard core stupid and indeed was. He had very short hair, red marine cut and had very tattooed arms (not Pellegrini's work; I hasten to add). He had a lazy lip which made him look as if he was continually sneering at you.

Sam was one obese skin. He looked like he had emerged born from a deep bobotie fryer in Frasertoon. He kind of looked like he was just sprawling in a cushion of his own fat. His speech was monosyllabic.

I thought to myself what a fantastic foursome we were. There was a quiet comforting security to be in that group. I felt no competition here.

"So what you doing in here, big yin?". It was Pete and he had his right hand rammed into his crutch. I presumed he was talking to Sam, but he was sneering at me.

It did not matter that I had not replied because he went on with the sound of his own voice.

" I did try to get into the services. The Red Marines actually, but I had some difficulty with all that training, you see? Sergeant was always bollicking me. Me mates always larking and larfing at me. That drill sergeant always cussing and putting me under pressure. Got me so fucked up with loading and unloading me weapon. I only shot the sorry fucker in the foot with me musket. Complete accident mind you. Anyways they then says maybes I'm counter p. Now's I'm here to see like".

"I just canny stop eating, man". Sam wanted to hold sway. "Canny find the time to do nought as I gotta eat. Canny hold a job. Too busy shovelling the shit to do anything. Fuck I'm so hungree noo".

I felt like a very professor of letters amongst this crowd.

Then Monsy got started.

"Derek's got a good job in the market as a lard loader". A promising start. Quite articulate. "He's saving up for us to buy a mansion in Devon Tor. He's already saved ten gold sovereigns. He gave up that Janice. She wasn't good for him. Mam says Devon Tor is an amazing place to live. I'm descended from Franzi Joe you know. Derek says you can see that plain once you know. Those handsome locks, he says."

"Theory of art", I said.

"Mary's your tart?", Pete confirmed.

"Yeah, she gave me the clap and I've been a bit anti-p ever since, like."

I had decided to keep things at their level. It might be best just to bond.

"It's the old mercury applications for you!", rejoined Pete.

"What time's lunch around here?", from Sam.

"We have just had breakfast, have we not?", said a newcomer entering the room. "Good morning. My name is Dee Danver and we will be doing group therapy together into base suspect thoughts. Just at basic level you understand."

"I don't know any Dee, but one of me best girls is called Heidi", said Monsy.

And so began my group work in the Danver class of Base Suspecting. A seminal seven months stint for me.

Thankfully this first session with Danver involving our quixotic quartet was the first and last in this quorum. After that first morning meeting we were involved into the wider Danver class. It was actually a big group and by the time we were introduced into it we numbered some eighteen souls. Within the wider group there were *regulars* and *irregulars*. Our new intake, our quartet, were irregulars. We were not expected to stay forever. Our participation was expected to be a relatively short affair. However, in the group there were four regulars who had been attending the treatment for some number of years. These four regulars were not progressing - perhaps really they were not expected to progress; the illusion giving GS the chance to keep them there indefinitely. They could not be released back into Great Society as bone fide non-professionals. It was kind of accepted that they would never complete the programme. They attended the treatment in the Danver class and from time to time they were sent back down under to the Deep Militants for more radical therapy.

In that bunch there was Roger Abel and out of all of them he had the most tattoos. He wore them with a perverse pride like military decorations. He was positively breaking out in a rash of them. On his neck was a depicted a ferocious snake biting into its own tail. Roger was constantly rubbing at his neck as if there was real snake venom coursing through his veins there. His arms were pretty much covered with tattoo designs looking like little demons. I never got that close to him to recognise fully what they were. He was not the type of guy one would get close to. At about forty years of age, he was mean and muscular and too mad for our own fighting navy by all accounts. It was rumoured that he had blown up some of his own shipmates whilst under the influence of pog-rum and playing with matches in the explosives section of the hold. No-one was able to explain how Roger had survived the incendiary explosion though. Nobody could really understand Roger. He was a person of few words.

Then there was Vicky Spimm. I admired her spirit and intelligence. She sailed close enough to the wind so as to be a constant thorn in the side of the establishment there, but never so close as to capsize the ship. Although she did once reveal to me that she had a little ornamental love bite on her left breast. The tiny fangs she called them. She claimed that Pellegrini had tattooed them as a little love offering. Pellegrini had claimed that her libido would increase because of it. She assured me that Pellegrini never had the chance to test the veracity of his own claim. Vicky was twenty-two and had been at SSN for five years. Apparently at the Ninian Girls School she had tried to form an official school society called *Shadow Reform* calling for opposition parties to form with the aim to perfect a viable democracy. Hot talk for GS. To rehabilitate someone like her would be a real challenge for the SSN as Vicky could articulate very precisely shortcomings in the Great Society democracy model. She was able to attack the deficiencies of the system in a cool logical manner and she held conviction in her voice. This sort of intellectualism should have no place in the true professional world. It could never be tolerated as credible persuasive opposing views would provide too much doubt and uncertainty in what for Great Society was always a struggle for the independence and prosperity of its peoples.

Vicky was attractive to me. Brown haired and busty and full of pure spunk and vitality. I felt close to her as she was the only one who came anywhere close to empathising with my condition. As with me, I could not understand why Vicky had been put into this group of clodhoppers. I think Lincoln did it to take the "special" away from us. He really wanted to class us two under so to speak.

Then there was Dolores Agnew. She was older than Vicky, about thirty. I am not sure why she had become a permanent member of the Danver class. She certainly was no intellectual tour de force or festering arsonist. I think it was simply and absolutely purely because she had an immense downer on everything and everybody, and although no-one would describe her as educated, she was particularly articulate in delivering a withering put-down. Dolores Agnew was a profoundly malignant force which was elemental rather than in any way reasoned. She exuded a sense of negativity which was positively all consuming and overpowering. She looked of extreme negativity, she spoke with such extreme negativity and she emanated such an aura of extreme negativity that it made one feel absolutely depressed and eventually very violent. She was only five foot two and of slight frame, pimply and morose, but she had the attitude of a cannon ball coming right at you. Her lank hair and acne ridden face and her dull eyes all reeked of and oozed spiteful despondency. Frankly she scared me to death as I could not resist her evil brooding through my own natural traits of optimism and usual behaviour. More so, Dolores could put the whole group into a mass downward spiral. Master Practitioner Dee Danver called for her contributions most sparingly for fear of making everyone suicidal and destructive and putting the whole group to vitriol. We were all affected by her, except Roger Abel who was too crazy to be affected by anyone or anything, and who was anyway constantly sniffing and rubbing at his angry flesh to be diverted into the path of Dolores Agnew's downward spiral.

Then there was Dodung Waters, the fourth regular participant of our group. He must have been in his mid-fifties by the looks of him. He was like Vicky Spimm, what I would call an interesting character. He spoke with such a quiet voice. It was so difficult to hear him that one had to hang on his every word. After I got to know him better he claimed to me that this was because he had so many little tattoos put on his tongue, tonsils and nostrils by Pellegrini to moderate all the evil words he was capable of spouting. Little tattoos but concentrated in ink he told me. Every word he was able to utter came at the cost of pain. Like Spimm, Waters had theories about what Great Society should be delivering to its populace and he was critical in a reasoned analytical way which put an almighty fear into the hearts of the custodians of Great Society.

Waters kept on asserting that "he was not going to go with the flow". This was his stock expression during our group deliberations. He asserted that in his belief as a social scientist, if man were to do that, then man would eventually revert back to the state of the more base animal from whence he came. He held that with each new invention we became less spiritual and less free so that in the end we were running in a wolf pack, or, more likely for the majority of us now, a deer herd. With every new regulation and with every new level of organisation we became more base and selfish. Increased laws led to increased avarice. He was critical of Great Society arguing that the regime was turning us all into slaves.

["You see you can remember and state these things now. The Sand has liberated your thoughts!"]

Dodung Waters was obviously a deep thinker. He was a little man who had to use eye glasses, and was diffident and unassuming. It must have been a supreme humiliation for him to express his well-reasoned convictions in a group consisting of the likes of Monsy, Pete and Sam. Waters explained to us his theory of social conditioning which he called "the actual running truth". How he did it amongst the titters and belches of many of the more apish group members there, I do not know, but now looking back I wonder if I have held the truth of "the actual running truth" in me over these many number of years since my release from the institution. Maybe out of all the things I had to experience in that place the views of Dodung Waters got through to me more than anything else there.

In essence the actual running truth explained by Waters was the manipulation of truth by Control over the Controlled. If the Control told the Controlled lies enough times then lies become the perception of reality. The lies are then reinforced by conditioning through exercising and altering behaviour to make the operation and belief of the lie more compelling and self-fulfilling. Dee Danver had from time to time to accept Waters' call to contribute in the group exchange. After, for example, Sam wailing about how hungry he was, or Roger bellowing on about the serpent in his blood, then we would go from the ridiculous to the sublime. At this synthesis Waters was then able to reach out and compel me with his arguments, especially as he did it with great patience and courage against a backdrop of hilarity and asinine behaviour from my class counterparts which did much also to convince me that Waters' reasoning was correct. I got the impression that Waters had originally worked on the "inside" of the system; as if he was some kind of guard turned prisoner. This impression even more reinforced me in the man's convictions. I think especially he must have felt it his penance as a man perhaps who had created something evil to keep repeating his message in remission of his sins. The only ones really listening were, and really capable of understanding were, Vicky Spimm, myself, and, of course, Dee Danvers.

That brings me to Master Practitioner Dee Danvers himself. What can I say about him? He was not like Alms-Master David Lincoln. Lincoln was every inch a political animal, a product of the system and a political animal that propagated the system. Lincoln was ingrained into the system.

⌜"But why am I talking about Lincoln? I wanted to talk about Danvers". – "Why are you talking to me at all?"⌝

Danvers was something else, however. He was older for a start, around fifty years old and he always wore the most unassuming livery. He always wore a drab beige livery with tan beret. You could only recognise his official functionary position through the three pip stars on his upper left sleeve. Let's say he was rather unassuming. Unassuming yet he had presence. I think he had a certain moral courage and fortitude. His counselling style was open and expansive. He positively allowed us to express our prejudices and his questioning style would cause that we had to build up our prejudices more extreme in defence to his line of reasoning and that allowed him later to caricaturise them and then they were easy to knock down. He would then argue back the Great Society method and view on things, but I do now consider that on that methodology, every time there was a little deviation, a little different spin and always a little yawning left open for a tiny seed of doubt. I did not dislike his reconciliation sessions. I only disliked the explosive combination of characters, ideas and gobbledegook that he was handling.

It is difficult to remember now, after so long away from there, the nature of the discourses within the Danver class. They all seem to merge together over the course of those seven months or so. We had three three-hour sessions per week on Mondays, Wednesdays and Fridays. So all in all I attended some eighty to ninety sessions. Remarkable when you think about it and Dee Danver was always there, never ill or absent for any other reason. It was roughly the same set of characters who attended with me, the four regulars, as well as Monsy, Pete and Sam and some others who came and went during the course of my penitence confessions. This was the high end of my education there – I'll get to the baser components of it in due course – and in some ways I received some enjoyment out of it compared to the other methods of my instruction. Incidentally, Monsy and I were released from the Danver class at the same time.

I have never determined in my mind what Dee Danver was about. On the one hand he was a fearful inquisitor, turning back our arguments back on us. He could be crass and pompous, entirely intolerant of our views. On the other hand, he did allow some line of discussion which must have been plain anathema to Great Society. He allowed it to be voiced in that room and for me that was quite thrilling and liberating. I do not understand at all, however, this fusion of putting together some malignant intellects with quite frankly the views of mental incompetents. I suppose it was to demean any among of us who could actually think for ourselves. For example, I remember one session which ran something like this.

Dee Danver: On Monday Vicky was telling us that Great Society could never be totally deemed "great" without a fundamental opposition. What she might describe as an opposing voice to state policies. I might say in counter that why would we wish to oppose all that is tested and true. Where is the reason in that? It would only insert doubt and destruction in our peoples and in our institutions. Roger Abel, what say you on this?

Roger: Mimas, Enceladus, Tethys, Dione, Rhea, Hyperion, Iapetus, Phoebe and …. Fuck me I always cannot remember all me fighting ships! This snake is eating the insides of my brain. I cannot remember what is important anymore.

Danver: Titan. Flagship of our ships of the line. Admiral Jason Bellows currently presiding.

Dolores Agnew: Admiral pig shite. He has a bunch of banana boats with hyped up names to make them sound better than the festered wood leech that they actually are. We got a snowballs chance in a hot harbour of scaring off any of those Orientals with that decrepit shower.

Roger: A knob of waterfowl, a pity of prisoners, a gaggle of geese, a clowder of cats, a herd of pigs, a malapertness of beggars.

Dolores: A malapertness of pedlars you imbecile.

Roger: Drat! A mistake. We will all commit 27,000 errors before we meet our graves.

Dolores: Oh, fuck that! So what manner of truth are you peddling today, Danvers? What's today's official truth then truth pedlar? And don't you start again dung boy with your actual raving running mad actual but unnatural truth!

Danver: Do you want to explain that to me, Dolores?

Vicky Spimm: Master Practitioner! Aren't we going off the original contention that you raised as to the precepts of a true functioning democracy? How can you contend that to discuss differing views is a destructive element that would be introduced into our society? Why does Great Society have the only claim and title to what is tested and true? Who is Great Society?

Danver: I first offered this thought to Roger Abel. So what do you truly say Roger?

[“By gad. Dissemination! He is avoiding the point!”]

Roger: A rookery of penguins, a string of racehorses, a chattering of choughs ….. Fuck I 've forgotten again the one for merchants.

Vicky: A faith of merchants and a faithless of truth merchants.

Dolores: She's got a point, maestro. What GS merchandise are you merchandising today? Great Society, a chattering of charlatans and what Sam had for supper? Draw the comparison class!

Sam: I'm hungry. Is it lunchtime now?

Pete: Shut the fuck up you fat cunt!

Dodung Waters: I have to appeal to you. What is the point of these fruitless discussions. If the gentleman is hungry and that bothers you, then simply ignore it and get back to the real point of the discussion.

Pete: Speak up you whispering wanker! Can't hear you ... can't hear you. Have you got Mister Danver's dick in your mouth cocksucker?

Waters: I think Vicky made a fair point, which is who is to say that the Great Society view of things is the absolutely correct one?

Danver: Alright then. That is the contention. What do you say then, Suzuki?

James Donald Suzuki: I agree with the next speaker.

Danver: I haven't called the next speaker yet. How do you know what they are going to say?

Jimmy: I am sure they will say the right thing. In the end we will all say the right thing.

Vicky: Or we might die trying to express it.

Roger: A bevy of quail.

Dolores: A shortcoming of competence.

Vicky: The death of collective. The birth of individual.

Danver: Ego gives us no hope. The individual rides roughshod over the greater good.

You can see that the fusion of two sets of incompatibles in a strange way provoked a powerful and emotional set of discussions. I do not know where I was placed. Was I categorised with Vicky? An outcast due to her articulation of alternative views. Or was I with Roger Abel? A bit crazy, a bit useless even.

To this day I am unclear as to why I was put in the Danver class for Base Suspecting. Why me? I can assure you that there were plenty of others who were not afforded this type of questioning. Why in the Danver class the questions were big. We were allowed free range over a number of big issues that are permanently under the surface in all the walks of Great Society. It was like the University of SSN Snoods Droop. The other times were like being a borstal boy in comparison. Some 250 hours or so out of a total period of six years. I attended other group counselling sessions, but these were for real low lives; all sorts of addicts and incompetents. I was put in with these poor sods for the misery and drudgery of it all. I think the purpose behind it was to tickle out my real views and then design a real programme to deal with them. The likes of Vicky Spimm and Dodung Walters were simply too smart to pin to a programme, although I am sure they had from time to time to endure the "Deep Militants", and they added the likes of Roger Abel, Dolores Agnew, Pete, Sam and Monsy just as an extreme irritant.

Suffice to say that they did conclude on a programme for me. I had started with the confessions with the Alms-Master and then had endured the charms of Danker and Pellegrini and then took the counselling sessions in the Danver class. Then they had me with Monsy.

I do not know how many days I attended sessions with Alms-Master David Lincoln, but I do remember certainly that I did not start off these long drawn out sessions alone. I started with Monsy.

"Am I in your head; Monsy? Are we getting through to you? Why are you here again? Think about it!", Lincoln bellowed.

Monsy picked at her acne ridden face and ran a sallow finger through her lank hair. She could withstand a lot of bollicking. It did not seem to get to her.

"Derek encouraged me to take a spa trip. He says it is good for my complexion."

"Derek is fucking fried bread, isn't he? You knocked him out with a shovel and then drowned him in a vat of oil!"!

Some reaction. Monsy had started to sob quietly and with a bit more dignity than she would normally conduct herself.

"There, there. Jimmy take the poor mite in your arms. Comfort her. She's missing her man. She needs a man now in her hour of need", continued Lincoln.

"Well go on!", he snapped. "Do I need to attach the encouragers?"

"No, no Mister Lincoln."

I cuddled the poor ferret of a lard trap with her perfume of callow tears.

"I think you make a handsome couple. I think you two should get closer and be a bit more intimate. It might ease you with your thought processing. But you will need the Life Enhancing Vasectomy Plus package, won't you Jimmy", he winked. "Have you applied for it yet?"

"The application is in process Alms-Master".

"Well give her a good cuddle. She wants consoling. Now that's nice. The lovely Monsy in your strong arms Jimmy".

I could see Brother Jacob and one of his sadistic cronies smirking as they stood in the background.

"So she can listen to you in your strong arms about the reason why you are here. Maybe she will learn something that will help toward her own thought processing."

"I am here because of art. Deviant art to be precise. I sought to paint what was without value to Great Society. I wanted to indulge myself in the meaningless and absurd. I wanted to capture in some depictions what was not the norm. I was at risk of corrupting myself in meaningless valueless manifestations which would simply unsettle and disquiet all good value providers. I was risking corrupting others too through my depictions leading to meaningless questions. I was at the point of creating meaningless deviant art. To pose the meaningless to the good population of Great Society would have been to insert a canker into the heart of our benevolent state. I recognise that I was pretentious merely but in that pretension I was at risk in confronting the good public with the real meaningless. That indeed would have been too much for us all to swallow and many of us would have been subsumed by deviant doubt. Truly did my thoughts need to be processed as they are being processed now and I feel much better."

"Only some of us have an outcome. Amen", said Brother Jacob from the back.

"So what is art, Jimmy?". The Alms-Master is all smiles now like peace after a hard fought day.

"Art is the representation of serenity that is felt in all the good souls benefiting from the care of Great Society. Great art captures the culture and values of the citizens of Great Society. Truly brilliant art shows the being and happiness of contributing to the noble virtues of Great Society. It is the joy of bringing up your own family."

"Well said, Jimmy."

"Are we going to have a baby?", asked Monsy.

"We'll see", rejoined the consummate professional. "Methinks you two will wish to share a cell to continue your thought processing on a more informal basis. Can we fix something up Brother?"

"I am sure we can", leered Brother Jacob. "And best we find the quarters quick as the mood for thought processing seems to be rather strong".

So there I was consigned to share a cell with the pitiful Monsy, a maiden who was not attractive at all and I am ashamed to say that I did copulate with her a number of times over the next weeks although she appeared to have the mental strength of an infant. There were many times in the heart of the deep and steamy nights I could hear voices talking as if I could hear observers commenting on some sort of trial experimentation.

"You see Lincoln they can be trained into doing things contrary to their very elemental natures. You can make them believe anything; to do what you believe them to do."

"I have to say, you are so right. So right, dear Belsingham."

[_"Yes, but the experience! Didn't you break your pigeon? — "Yes, she was my first I am ashamed to say. From there on I have shared my love with shame."_]

Then one day several weeks later I returned from the male ablutions and went into the small syndicate room to start a session with the Alms-Master and Monsy, but there was no sign of Monsy.

"Monsy won't be continuing with us now", informed Lincoln.

"Why?". As before I had at least some sort of companion.

"You put her up the duff, Jimmy. That will not do and that is why I have had to speed up your LEV Plus application".

"LEV?"

"Your vasectomy."

"Oh, I had forgotten that I had put that in."

"Some here are saying that it ought to be another form of procedure so that we can protect our maidens from the likes of you. We might have to think about, you know?"

"I am sorry Sir, but I would say that all we did was freely encouraged and accepted on her side too. I did not force myself on her."

"Well maybe not brute physical force, but the force of your intelligence. What can we do with that intelligence of yours. We all know that poor Monsy is one trotter short of a hog feast. She is very easy for you to take advantage of, is she not?"

"Well …."

"Well the question is whether it is your brute passions or your devious intelligence that we should be concerned about? If the former then I can just instruct the sawbones to use a less intricate instrument. They are prepping up for your vasectomy surgery – it would only mean getting out the other implements. Or is it your mind that we need to correct? That mind of yours that seeks to exploit and disrupt good patterns in Great Society?"

My mouth had gone dry and I blurted out: "Yes, I think that there are aspects of my attitude that can still be worked upon and sorted out. I did not mean to prey upon the disadvantaged, but maybe I simply do not recognise these bad traits in my character. I agree to the vasectomy to purge the line of the valueless, but given some more coaching on mental perception I am sure that I can find service in sacrifice and conform to the ordains of Great Society."

David Lincoln rubbed at his perfectly groomed facial hair as if weighing up some great gamble.

"What do you think, Brother Jacob".

Jacob – I had not even noticed his gloomy malignant presence.

"I say off with the bastard's balls, but you're the one who processes thoughts."

"Have them scrub up, good Jacob".

"And?", he snarled. I was gulping on the reply.

"Have them ready as before for the intended procedure", he smiled.

What artful malignant malice mastery.

⌈"That's why the Sand came to save us!"⌉

So it came to pass that my line had passed and that I can never pass any loving without the feeling of shame.

And there was more. Much more.

I was effortlessly moved in to single questioning with the Alms-Master. I missed Monsy and her wet cabbage kisses. I missed the warmth of human company and solidarity. I was then kept mainly in isolation. Not the isolation of the "Deep Militants". It was an isolation of sparse accommodation and daylight. Comfortable enough but uncomfortable in that I was alone with my thoughts. These thoughts inevitably harked to my past; my hubris and my disdain for my poor uncultured ignorant parents. I was left for hours alone most days. I began to look forward to my sessions with Alms-Master David Lincoln. I began to look forward to pleasing him. I started to dream up phrases to show him my deep commitment, better ways to describe my redemption, my renewal into his faith.

Then there was Brother Jacob. One could sense some fundamental decency about Brother Tikhon and many others of the general staff there. None of that could be sensed about Brother Jacob. Someone in Great Society had recognised what a misery scourge he was and how he could provide the opposite of Great Society's promised paradise to anyone who held a deviant view to the norm. Everyone complained about how ruthless and bad he was. I was surprised to hear that as it felt as if he were around me every spare waking moment, so I wondered where he found the time to share his unabated malice with everyone else. At least I could take comfort that I was not the only one apparently. Maybe the others invented stories of his cruelty to dilute my dejection.

Jacob had the propensity to come into my thoughts just as I was assembling them into some sort of sense. When I was about to get a view into my emotions and my feelings and was starting to see their length and fabric he would violate me. He would storm into my single cell as those times where I was close to realisation and scream profanities at me. Kick me in the shins too just for effect. If Lincoln was the thought processor, Brother Jacob was the thought dissembler. It was if they had decided that it was only Lincoln who could put my thoughts together. If I ever tried then they would be scrambled by the gruesome

Brother Jacob. I have looked into the art of the spin meditationists and their contemplations to gain great insight; that great quest to know the quality of nothing. For that deep thought and peace are required. The irony was that I had that time and that relative quiet, for I was often in isolation with nothing to read or write upon, but Jacob was like a firebug in the brain. Just as I was achieving some sort of realisation he would come in like a mechanical cannon shot and break it all up leaving a disturbing and all-encompassing sense of doubt. He would humiliate me and demean me so that all my thoughts were absorbed by self-deprecation and questioning my fundamental worth for anything.

For example, one day I was lying comfortably enough on my hard cot, thoughts flicking across the width of the ceiling in a reverie of pale late afternoon light. The sweat of the sticky cell adding to my transcendence. I was safely in a sense of nowhere and protected by its nothingness.

"Playing with yourself are you? You're a dirty sheep-shagging Monsy boy, aren't you? Good job vermin like you are cut so that you cannot breed on your malignancy!", he leered at me through the slide grail of the cell door.

I looked back at him with fear and loathing and before I knew it he was in the room like oiled locomotion and flinging the mattress along with me on to the hard floor. He was big burly man in his mid-forties; bald with a warty face. Muscle for muscle I was no match for him.

I bumped on to the floor but my dignity felt more outrage than my body felt pain.

"I was not masturbating, good brother".

"Yes, you were. I have been around base men for too long not to know when they are self-gratifying. You know that it is explicitly against our ordinance that the semen of miscreants be spent around our pristine institution where we are trying to bring lost souls back to decent society.

You know that such indecency is unconducive to the general health here and absolutely forbidden".

With that he pranged one of his marine style boots into my sensitive parts making me scream.

"There that should stop all that indecent rubbing for a while. Next, let's get you concentrating on remedial punishment as through just punishment we all can be saved. Clean out your slop bucket. Silver standard!"

That meant I had to clean out my slop bucket into which I had to perform all my bodily movements. Not just to clean out the bucket but to clean and shine it to a ridiculously meticulous level. The odious Brother Jacob pulled me out of the cell by my ear and pulled me to the ablutions point. There I had to wash away my composites before then laboriously cleaning and shining the old rust bucket. It literally was an old warped tin bucket with many dents and folds in it making it a devil to clean to the meticulous degree that the sadist required. Jacob then delegated the overseeing of this activity to Acolyte Archer, a young up and coming sadist who was being groomed personally by Brother Jacob. Archer, of course, was able to find fault at all stages of the cleaning. The humiliation became a ritual. The most effective conditioning was ritualistic. Both myself and Archer did not quite understand its effectiveness, but we both quite accepted that it had to be applied. Only that Archer always was in the position to apply it better than myself.

Brother Jacob was no doubt away terrifying some other recidivist, but like an orbiting planet he was back as timed to end the sunny splendour of my day's degradation.

"Well done Acolyte Archer. Sterling silver service and supervision. However, the real test Mister Suzuki, your Honour, is that you are able to eat your own dinner off your slop bucket. Let's test it, shall we? Let's have you lick every corner of that here bucket. Archer, bring him his porridge meal and spread it into the bucket."

And there I was on all fours licking and slavering at my own excrement receptacle.

"Come on! Give it a good licking, sunny boy!", screamed Jacob with Archer sniggering at his side. "Imagine that it is fat Monsy's fanny that your are giving a good licking to, but don't let it turn you too much randy", laughed Brother Jacob.

They had me doing this for some quarter of an hour like a demented animal.

"Do you keep your own slop bucket spick and span, Archer?"

"Why I do, Sir. Like Mister Suzuki scrupulously clean. Clean enough to eat one's dinner from."

"Good as Mister Suzuki looks clearly half famished and I would want to give him some of what remains of the Brothers' breakfast and alas all the dining plates are currently being washed. Let's serve him up a treat in your fine shiny bucket, shall we?"

"Of course, Sah. It would be an honour to oblige."

Archer brought his own slop bucket. I did not evidence much cleaning on this particular implement and into it Brother Jacob poured some sad fried potatoes and motley peas.

"There you go, dear Jimmy. Dig in. Extra rations for once", he laughed.

I looked askance only to receive two hard kicks in to my midriff. I started to eat but I could smell shit and I was disgusted. I had to retch.

"You'll have to eat that vomit too. You're not wasting anything, you sad fucker", commanded the heartless Jacob.

This time two quick hard blows to my face. Somehow I downed this slop to a background of ridicule and amusement. Somehow even Pete was there in a growing disquieting audience to my humiliation.

"What a sad plonker", he exclaimed. "Not just licking the warders' arses but their shit cans too".

["By Sand, how cruel and inhuman"].

The next day the cultivated Alms-Master is saying to me: "They tell me that yesterday you tried to commit suicide by gorging excrement into yourself. This is most unusual. Not that you have suicidal tendencies, but also that you wanted to away with yourself in the most debasing manner. How long have you held these suicidal tendencies, Jimmy?"

The bloody fucking reasonable questions of Alms-Master David Lincoln. Lincoln at the vanguard of the new professional thought processor.

"What do you think happens to you Jimmy when you die?"

"I think then I become a malignant avenging force who wipes out Brother Jacob, Archer and all his other cronies. I think I will become an invincible spirit that wrecks Great Society and brings all you blackguards down."

"Me, too?"

"You too".

"Your counsellor".

"My chief tormentor".

"What do you think happens to you Jimmy when you die?"

"Nothing of course. If I had a mum she would cry for me, but nevertheless I shall simply turn to dust and then nothing at all."

"If that is so, then why don't you make something of your life? Make your mark."

"Because you cunts won't let me. You've made me a fucking counter-professional."

"So you see no service in sacrifice? We have all had to make sacrifices for Great Society. Are you so morally bereft as to not want to make sacrifices like the rest of us? Our sense of life is one of shared community is it not?"

"Fuck you Lincoln! I would take your noble sacrifice any day of the fortnight against what I have suffered. You've sacrificed me big time in relation to your small discomforts. Don't talk to me about sacrifices. I want to enjoy myself now. Live my life. Be an artist."

"Then why did you try to evade your responsibilities by attempting suicide. Not just attempting it but trying it in such an awful shocking way?"

I laughed. "You know that was no attempt at suicide. I was simply a victim of wanton cruelty. I can't win, can I?"

"You better clean yourself up thoroughly. Have a complete clean of your body before we return to cleaning your mind."

Then the next time, and then the next time, another round of endless reasonable questions from Alms-Master David Lincoln.

The questions were always so moderate and tempered. Like questions one would pose to a small child. They were questions that shocked me to my core. Lincoln might have been administering convulsion therapy. They had the same effect in shaking me to my basis. That is how all these questions felt to me.

"What is art, Jimmy?"

What is art, Jimmy? And this is having survived Danker and Pelligrini and being now in fear of my life from Brother Jacob and Acolyte Archer. Again what is fucking art, Jimmy!

⌜"This old spirit is at the point of weeping. That is why you had to embrace the Sand. The Sand will protect now all you poor and oppressed."⌝

So I replied. "Art is a magnificent elephant alone. It has no partners. The herd has thrown it out as it has grown too big and vainglorious. It's presence is hurtful and destructive. We see it alone in its beauty, but we do not care to live along with it. That is art."

"I think I understand your parable, Jimmy. It is insightful. We might be able to proceed with that."

"Why don't you just walk out of here, Jimmy?" David Lincoln has so many questions hiding there in his finely groomed beard.

This time Brother Tikhon was present with the Alms-Master.

"Because out there I have no sweetheart, no musical instrument to play and no empty canvas. I have no family and no community. Here is everything I need. A purpose, a society and a future. You are my family. Great Society is my mother."

"To serve and to disserve preserves our balance", chanted the good brother.

"Only some of us have an outcome", whispered the Alms-Master.

"We are family", bubbled I.

"You have been here a number of years with us now, James Donald Suzuki. Perhaps it is time for you to leave us now and go out into Great Society as a fully committed and staunch counter-professional."

"Yes", I sighed sadly.

"But we shall always be your family. We shall always be with you on your way", and David Lincoln smiled warmly at me.

Those were not hollow words. They have always been with me every step of the way since.

I have spoken of great injustices done to me. I have recounted unspeakable sins committed against my person. I have told of their wicked experiments to alienate the spirit and individuality from one's consciousness. I have related all this from the viewpoint of a tough young adult who had spirit and guile and stood against it where he could. I have dealt with the bizarre humour which was backdrop to it. In all that craziness there was something risible and preposterous to it all. If it were not for the sheer fright you were constantly experiencing you could belly-ache with the sheer buffoonery of it all. Evil can be so absurd.

The one thing, however, I have not spoken about was the lack of love. The absence of any love for me. A base elemental love that takes me without question and showers me with affection. A love that is circuited across the years and then is bound and cemented. I missed love. Stupid simple love. I had never been away from home before. At home I could live simple patterns and I could ridicule them from a place of safety. I was loved, so I could despise and then drop my despising to be simply loved again. I had disdained my simple folks, Doris and Harold, and their small-minded relatives and friends. I could be very critical of them and caustic in my behaviour towards them, but I was never lonely. I was never alone as their love – no matter how corny- persisted. Their love survived all my admonishments and I missed it dearly then.

In Snoods Droop, throughout all the horrible facets of fighting for my survival, one thing I could not overcome was the simple ache of feeling all alone; deserted and without company to come back and cry on. I was small and there was no person adult to protect me. I just simply wanted to point out that every conceivable chance I had where my mind was not combating against fear, then I had a simple stark despondent blackness of loneliness. No-one

I could really tell it all to and lay bare to them the charge of all my ragged emotions.

There, I have said it. It was a great hurt. They did their profession credit. That loneliness has persisted to this day.

I t was a cloudy day with the threat of rain when they set me out of that prison. A prison of the soul and the body. I had been suddenly told that I was able to leave by someone I had never seen before in all my years there. I just had to leave summarily my cell and head to the big cavernous front door to the institution. There was no-one there to see me depart or say adieu. Strangely it was the same Bailiff Buckie who was to escort me back to the Delta. He looked considerably much fatter and older. I wondered how I had changed externally. I knew my inside effects.

My time at Snoods Droop ended so plainly in comparison to what I had undergone there.

"And now you know why you are a supplicant to the Sand", concluded Kurt Tempels.

Twelve: Destruction – "Spin Meditation"

The spin meditationists said that everything was about dark matter. That it all came to dark matter in the end. Dark matter was not something to be feared they said, rather it was something to be desired and attained. The spin meditationists prayed to dark matter and preyed upon those with the nervous sensibilities to fear its ghastly force. Doctor Egregious Daedalus, due to his research on the far beyond the fringe, was naturally drawn to the spin meditation movement and he had contemplated deep and long on the unfathomable being of extreme dark matter. He had seen into the deep darkness and beyond therein the incredible numbing mathematik of all eternity.

Doctor Daedalus was a scientist. He understood the natural forces of the universe. He understood the simplicity and consistency of its universal principles. It was like music to him, and like the greatest music with its clear simplicity, that grandeur of simplicity, could be unravelled into connotations of absurd complexity. Doctor Daedalus had started as a scientist with redeemable faith. Faith that the beginning of the universe, its creation had been undertaken for a supreme purpose. Nonetheless the good doctor was prone to be drawn to research into dark matter. He simply could not withstand the unassailable charm of its algebra. Dark matter taught him to be less certain about intentional principles in science. Black mass and anti-gravity put in him a growing sense of doubt of a creation. A period of intense study into the mathematik of Brown Dwarf parabola systems had denuded that faith altogether. Then one sunny morning in May, upon staring at the abstract cornucopia of his collection of middle period

Deissenböck paintings in his possession, there came to him the stark and sudden realisation of the absolute randomness of all the coloured drops and spots and splurges on the canvases. The more he gazed into the deep myriad of all those dots the more the beautiful colours came together to merge and in their deep penetration form nothing so that he was lost in it all, and then he knew nothing but an overwhelming doubt.

He knew doubt and that knowledge was terrifying. A series of numbers that he knew could not stop and would never have an end to them. A loss of sentience whilst those numbers continued to collide against each other was pure fright for him. Then a feeling of desolation and loneliness. Daedalus had a self. He saw himself as an individual. A someone with an ego and an id. He felt that he was something of importance, a somebody who should have an imprint on his life and the lives of others. Then again there were the numbers of the meaningless which shattered this whole notion. Myriads of atoms that he was made of. Trillions of synapses that governed his every thought. Billions of years before his most distant ancestors had their first primal walks. Billions of years before he had awoke and trillions of years to sleep without his consciousness ever knowing. How could he be assembled and so exquisitely crafted so and then disassembled again and left for so long? What was it for? And this after millions of sperm having competed to be him and died in the mad dash. The very fact that he was such an improbability made an absurdity of his life. The numbers, their sheer colossal mind boggling scale took away the foundation of his existence and ate away at his sense of self. He was just lost in the huge insignificance of his solitary number.

He was in despair. He needed another view-point, another frame of reference. The man of science, Doctor Meritorious Egregious Daedalus, would consult Mistress Qin Chan. Mistress Qin Chan, the mentor to the notorious

Jan Le Bertet's movement *"Purposeless"* and eminence grise of Spin Meditation.

Spin meditation – meditating without faith.

Doctor Meritorius Egregious Daedalus was not very well known, but he was extremely well known to that select body of Great Society that was in the know. To the public he was a nobody, but to the great and the good he was a somebody. If you were extremely well connected then it is very likely that you might have heard of him. Mistress Qin Chan was immensely well connected; so well connected that she did not need to know of him, but would have someone well connected to enquire as to who he was and have the answer forthcoming shortly. Doctor Daedalus was well connected enough to have heard of Qin Chan, otherwise he would not have heard of her. Professor James Riddell knew of her, but did not fully approve. He was not quite powerful enough to entirely approve of her and her principles. It was anathema to Great Society to learn that the universe was unprincipled and that basically there was no point to anything. Mistress Qin Chan therefore had to stand on the periphery with her eminence radiating in. The most powerful persons of all could contemplate her points of view and wrestle with them. Professor Riddell could not; he just did not have that type of authority. Daeadalus probably should not, but he was getting so dammed melancholic he was willing to risk it and screw the consequences. His dejection on the nature of everything being nothing was starting to overcome him. When you doubt all, doubt yourself and doubt your existence, then you simply cease to operate. He was not functioning and needed some words to stop him from falling apart. He would persist with analysing all schools of thinking, established and non-established, in pursuit of true enlightenment – or darkness – whichever was correct. He put his visiting card into the Institute of Spin Meditation.

"Who is this man?", croaked Mistress Qin Chan. She was old, toothless and blind. She held the visiting card as if she could read it.

"He has presented his visiting card for you, your reverence", said the retainer. "Doctor Egregious Daeadalus. A leading light at the Royal Society of Science, I understand. He is expert in big mathematik and the cosmos."

"A Sand?", she hissed.

"No not that type. The one with all the stars, you know".

"I see. Tell him to go away."

"Yes, Reverence."

The good doctor was in such a nadir to bother a care, so the very next day he tried again as if the previous incident had never occurred. He doubted it mattered.

"Ah yes, the good Doctor Egregious Daedalus. Let him in", she hissed.

Doctor Daedalus found himself standing in a darkened room full of plump cushions set up amongst very non-occidental looking rugs and carpets. The smell emanating from the many incense sticks in the close enclosed room was initially quite overcoming, but like the dark light the good doctor was getting used to it. He had been instructed to go right into the room and this was it; standing in gloom. 'This must be the first message', he cogitated, 'to make some sense out of the haze of darkness. Living your life against the haze of darkness on the ever present horizon. Every night the light goes away. We are addicted to it. We must have it again. Good lesson', he mused and was beginning to lose himself in the stinky smell of the joss sticks.

For a brief moment he wondered, 'Could I be spinning?'

"Why you stand there without talking? Are you spinning? Maybe you have understanding that speaks from only within."

The doctor was startled. He had not realised that there was in fact someone else in the room. He peered into the murk to locate the source of the voice.

"Doctor Daedalus come close to me", and the voice was in the imperative so that it guided him towards it. There he saw her a tiny individual cross-legged on a cushion in the far corner of the close cornered room. "Why you not say hello to me?" She talked as if speaking to a child.

"Hello, good Madam. I am Doctor Meritorious Egregious Daedalus, fellow of the Royal Society of Science and Astrologer Resident at the Astronomy at JaJa Point".

"That's a hell of a mouthful", said the little one. " I am Qin Chan".

And indeed Qin Chan she was, cross-legged on a cushion and smoking a large long ivory pipe which the doctor had not detected amongst all the incense smell.

"Welcome good fellow", she further said. "What can I do for you? But first you better get closer to me so that you can see me at least."

Daedalus moved closer in and snatched a plump cushion from the floor for his delicate bottom. He could see her a bit better now. Nevertheless, she still appeared murky as if she were an apparition.

"You can light a candle if you wish. They should be at the wall close to you. I'm sorry, but I have no need for them. I have to concentrate on a different type of seeing now."

"You are blind Madam?" Scientists have a tendency to state things straight out.

"Yes and you are a scientist. I like scientists. They have little fear because their curiosity is greater than their fear. Scientists delight in life because of their curiosity. Consequently they don't give you any shit because they don't like to hide things."

"That is scientific axiom. Are you a scientist too Marm?"

"No, not really. I just a peasant girl. Just a peasant girl who found an old book one day. A wastrel who was reading a book whilst the rest were out a reaping".

Daedalus was scrambling around the wall edge in search of candles.

"Ah, got one".

"There are matches too somewhere", she said.

"You are right. I've found those too."

Qin Chan heard the flash of the lighted match. She heard all things now so precisely.

"Self-igniting matches. You are very modern", he chuckled.

"You see. There is your enthusiasm in life. You are like smart child. Smart child always has hope and enthusiasm".

"Enthusiasm I can science, hope I cannot. What does hope mean?", he asked.

"Only the hopeless ask that question of me".

Daedalus was left breathless by this exchange and began to consider. That was his training.

Daedalus decided to drop the dialogue momentarily and observe more his discussion partner. He noticed that Qin Chan appeared old and venerable. He observed her sightless eyes. Her hair was lank and unkempt, greasy from absence from water he guessed. She wore a peasant smock which appeared not to have been laundered for a while. Most noticeable was her skin. Parts of her skin tissue had been removed exposing muscle flesh and in some cases he thought he could see actual bone. She looked like she was thoroughly diseased and it made him a little uncomfortable.

'Perhaps it is a trick of the dim light here. I must not spring to firm conclusions as yet', he reckoned.

"You second fellow here today", she continued. "He here an hour or so ago. He also had a big question. Not what does hope mean, but something equally profound and smelly. Smelly question, yet he smelt of fancy cologne, so must have been gentleman of leisure. Let's see next will come E. You are D for Daedalus. E for Egregious comes next as you will speak to me and the rest of our group under your personal name and not under the weight of your so many titles and propagandas. Yes, your conversation with us will be long and valuable. E. Big fellow yesterday was B for .... I forget, but I know that your universe is full of these unnatural coincidences. Must be big plan after all. .... I forget what I wanted to say, must be all this smoking. It gives big clarity, but you miss little detail."

"I see", helpfully added Daedalus.

"Yes, the other fellow today with big question was C for Copperfield. You D for Daedalus. E for what is later to be revealed as you. B for big fellow, I don't know. A...B...C. Mathematik must be just putting a frame on randomness. D...E. Anyway this C for Copperfield, you know, he wanted to know about D for death."

"C for Copperfield and Comfort, D for Daedalus and Death", the doctor's mind was making symmetries to put a frame on randomness. "E for Egregious and Eternity", he further mused. "Big, big issues, and the stars burn on for unfathomable time and we are worrying about our little deaths."

"Yes. You smoking this stuff too? You is spinning. He wanted us to think out death together so that he would not have fear of whatever it is. Death that is. Big smelly word. He wanted to rationalise away from faith so that he would not join the living dead of the faithful. Quite a struggle for him wanting comfort but by taking that comfort he would be as blind as me."

"So what did you tell him about D for death?", asked Daedalus. He spoke softly in the groove of fascination by her diseased state. "He seems to be in that classic conundrum place of distaste of life and terror of death.

Wanting a faith but really knowing that the all is faithless".

" I told him that it was the wrong point of view. He has to look at things differently if he were to succeed in releasing him from his big paralysis. I told him that actually I do not know much about life even though I am old and venerable and having been smoking at the laca for the most of the adult part of my forty-seven years in this life. How could he ask me about death when I am so casual with life?" The sightless eyes were smiling macabrely.

"What do you mean so casual?"

"I am of the extreme spin meditation. I am so old and wise at this young age of forty-seven. I have been smoking at the laca for every conceivable waking moment of the last nine years. The opiate gives me profound clarities which I disdain my bodily functions for. I am of the extreme spin meditation. I am of the laca. I am of the true philosophy of decay. He should not ask me clever questions about life. It is like asking a child if the moon is made of white chocolate. The child don't know, she just wants to eat all the chocolate."

Daedalus again felt uneasy. She appeared so unworldly like some demon dwarf of legends lore. He would have to phrase his statements carefully to avoid her displeasure and querulousness.

"I am not here to implore from you the meaning of life or even to ask for the absence of death from the heart. I am here to discourse with you the all", Daedalus framed with the greatest of exact precision.

"The all?"

"I am of late of the disposition to live on a different dimension from that of science and faith. The trouble is that I do not know how to hook up to a different state?"

"Explain yourself."

"I have tried to comprehend the natural laws of the universe. I have tried to dispel notions of faith. I have tried to remove purpose from my life. I have tried to lay aside principles of coincidence and chaos. I have tried to rid myself of inconsequential feelings of happiness and good."

"You are doing well. What's the problem?", she giggled.

"It's just that I cannot conceive of it all anymore. I only doubt. I cannot conceive of such abstraction no longer. It is the vastness. It is the sheer scale of the numbers. There is no scale or relevance. The numbers are simply off the scale. The numbers are so dense how can I be found anymore? How can I matter anymore? I calculated numbers. I have so calculated numbers. I have calculated numbers beyond the bounds of possibility so that I cannot fathom anything. I cannot go on when the numbers are crashing down on me and inside eating away at me. I can only doubt in everything. I do not matter. I am anti-matter."

"The numbers are so immense", Qin Chan said, "that they have to obliterate into oblivion. There is no other way and no other nonsense. That is why I am of the extreme spin meditation. That is why I smoke the laca. The numbers are reducing through my clarity and soon one day they will come down to one in nothing. In oblivion where they began".

"Yes", sighed Daedalus. She had given him a number. She had provided him with a benchmark to understand. The holiest of numbers. The enigmatic none.

"Come closer Doctor Number. Observe what I have become. What I am becoming."

Daedalus shifted closer to her and found himself kneeling in front of her as if some holy acolyte.

"Hold the candle up to see me properly. Do not worry about expressing in your face your horror. I am now fully blind and will not see it."

Daedalus did as he was told and held the candle close to her and gasped. Mistress Qin Chan was in a terrible looking state and although she was wearing a simple peasant's smock he could see a lot of horrible aberrations about her body. Clearly she was profoundly blind. What's more her face was pockmarked with dark ugly patches as if her facial skin was being eating away. Her right ear appeared to be hanging off itself and her thinning hair was awash with yellow and purple pustules. Boils seemed to be erupting above her emaciated breasts. Worse still were her limbs. On both her arms and legs her skin was ablaze with anger, and in many areas of the limbs Daedalus could see actual exposure of the bone. She was actually falling apart. Her skin was actually being eaten away down to the bone. It was as if her skeleton wanted to discard her coat of flesh and was breaking out from within.

"The pox? The infectious pox", he groaned in dismayed realisation.

"If it were, why would you fear it?", she rasped. "With your devastation of numbers, why would you care?", Qin Chan continued. "Is it just a numbers game for you or do you indeed really seek cessation?"

Daedalus was naturally recoiling. His scientific conditioning calling that he withdraw from the plague.

'I might now have been here too long', he considered. 'What irony that this may be the release from all those numbers that I had been crying out for'.

"Still yourself Doctor. This is no pox. I take the laca. I take the laca now all my mortal moments and I find my resolution. I am of the extreme spin meditation. It is the laca drug that I smoke so constantly and committedly that eats all this joy into me. I do not sleep, I only smoke the laca. My attendant from time forces some water and gruel into me. Have no fear, this reduces the number. I am serene. I would be serene amongst the pox also."

"Should I smoke too?" asked Daedalus timidly.

"You might well do and receive many revelations which you might not count as blessings", she grinned.

Daedalus looked perplexed.

"Excuse the count and the numbers", she added momentarily later.

Doctor Daedalus was at a loss for words as if he were now communicating with her telepathically.

"That's right", Qin replied, "extreme spinning is a hard road, especially without any initial knowledge. I smoke the laca. The laca opiate gives me great clarity and insight. It allows me the ability to spin deeply and gain great understanding of this realm of suffering. The laca releases my mind into great spin meditation whilst it eats apart my flesh, and I keep smoking and gaining the big picture knowing that the big insight will come once the laca has eaten me apart."

Daedalus the scientist had difficulty being comfortable with this philosophy.

"You know when I was peasant child I thought that I was going to remain child forever, then I was not, then I was. Go to my secular protégé.", she instructed him. "Go to our leader. Seek out Jan Le Bertet. You can find him at the Purposeless Institute on Beaver Street. I will grant you access direct to him and his. Say to Him and his the phrase: Bat droppings shall be my food. They will know then that I confer my blessing upon you."

"Bat droppings shall be my food", repeated Daedalus uncertainly.

"Yes, that will certainly get their attention. Now depart me now."

Daedalus got to his feet and nodded his head in devoted farewell. Upon leaving the room he heard ever so faintly small moans of agony.

Later that day Doctor Meritorious Egregious Daedalus arrived at the Beaver Street institute. He mumbled the insane words to the doorkeeper whilst looking abashed.

"You are most exalted, Sah!", said the doorkeeper upon hearing the words of power. "He is about to speak now. He is about to address the dignitaries. He is about to give vision."

"Who is?"

"But Le Bertet, of course", answered the doorkeeper. "Be quick and collect your ceremonial robes. Go to the garde de robe. He will be speaking in two minutes precisely. Now if I can deal with the next visitor before the proceedings begin."

Daedalus notices hovering in the doorway a chubby shabby type who looks anxious to break in to the party if he can.

"Who might you be?", said the doorkeeper examining a sad scrap of paper. " A counter-professional? And why not? After all we are here to agitate! My boy is called James as well. I named him after James Jungles, the champion bridge player."

With that the supplicant Daedalus hurried off to the cloakroom in advance of the riff-raff. It seemed that the society opened its doors to some of the great unwashed. At the cloakroom Daedalus was given a very white cowl vestment to put on and then was immediately ushered to a large reception hall. He took a plump cushion and sat down on it at the back at the edge of the sea of very white dignitaries who were largely men, some women — but all appearing to be specimens of middle age and poor physical condition who laboured to sit comfortably and straight on the rattan floor on their plump plush-red cushions. A tall bespectacled man, balding and of the age of the fifties stood on the podium garbed in a white toga wearing artisan sandals. He was the very virtue of simplicity.

"Friends, I am Jan Le Bertet", he announced in a quiet voice; a quiet voice that filtered and carried throughout the auditorium. "Great Society doyens, I am a guru of spin. Islanders, I am grounded although my thoughts kiss the sky."

With this opening Daedalus noticed that the doyens did not seem so restless on their discipline cushions. They appeared to be spellbound by the speaker. He spotted someone who was familiar.

'Is that Baroness Letchworth? So hard to tell in these clothes', he wondered. 'If so, he might really actually be addressing the good and the great; so great that they could play with the subversive and get away with it.'

"So what do I stand for? Why do I stand before you today? What is our movement? Why have we named it *Purposeless?* So many questions, I daresay, but recognise that each day our own brains present ourselves with a volume more questions than answers every day. We are questioning minds. I think you will agree; so does that mean we do not value certainty and security? I think so. We think so. We like to think that security and purpose is paramount to our being. However, essentially, our animal mind holds sway. It is written into our deep code to question and upturn. This questioning is vital in that it is the process, that has to continue so long as we have energy left, because it is that which holds off decay. We inherently know this, as do we know that decay is the only permanence. A permanence which we are secure in the knowledge that we wish to avoid."

Daedalus notices that the audience shifts in their sitting positions, not through agitation but rather through straining to hear. Le Bertet's voice can be heard by all, but it is faint enough to question one's senses as to what had just been heard. Daedalus was puzzled too. For a man versed in dealing with numbers, this was abstraction without governing principles. It was difficult to conceive as to where this discourse was going.

"What I have to tell you is this", continued Le Bertet. "You will not be surprised by it as you intrinsically know it", Le Bertet stressed the its. "As animals, who simply sacrificed self for communal well-being, it is deeply ingrained in our psyche. We all know that this existence, that we accidentally go through, has no actual intrinsic meaning or value. Look to the universe. Our astrologers will tell you, that none of us, no single human being, or even the entire human species, can be of significance when you regard it for what it is. Frankly, we are without purpose and unlikely to change anything in the totality of existence, in the totality of the universe, in all the meaningless myriad of atoms. That why we acknowledge our movement as *Purposeless*. Each one of us is an isolated being born into the universe. We seek to know why we have been born and what we are. We die to determine what everything is and we cannot ever know why, because there is no why. Therefore, we all make our whys. We join groups of whys. We today are a group of whys. We make them with godhead, fear, intolerance and we also fabricate them from our calumny of a knowing universe where we conceive there is the most complicated inconceivable plan. As complicated as our collective thinking, you might all say. Recognise that life is without purpose. It is existence without meaning. Although ironically I have had to put much intention in explaining to you this truth today", Le Bertet lightly smiled. "Life is the sum of our aberrant prejudices and subjective confused thinking. It is existence without meaning, yet existence is the only meaning. There can be no other."

"So what do I ask from you today after this little homily? Just meditate upon existence. Mediate to that oblivion. Spin, spin, spin."

"What is this spin, Master?", asked a fat bald headed supplicant with a wealth of a haunch. "Is this the spin meditation I have heard so much upon?"

"I am not the foremost expert on this. Mistress Qin Chan is, but what I have learnt from her is that to spin is to turn and move with the velocity of the unforgiving spheres. Our consciousness has no place in this existence. It is an aberrant anomaly that makes us suffer. Spin your consciousness away. Blind it out with the velocity of the moving spheres. Spin at great speed. Wipe out the future and the past to be omnipresent and along with the atoms heading into nothingness. As Qin Chan would say: *We are a tray of goat's cheese on a dragonfly's back.* That gives us some perspective, wouldn't you say?"

Daedalus felt great affinity with the speaker. He spoke the truth that there is no consciousness in the immutable laws of Physik. Consciousness had no place in the raging universe. He was mightily impressed that Le Bertet was coming to the same conclusions as he, but from a different tack.

"Is there anything else that we should conceive, Master?" This time asked by a young woman acolyte on the podium with the mystic.

"Yes", is the certain reply. "Question hard all those who propose to know the answers. Question them harder. Doubt me for I have already started formulating answers. Doubt yourselves. See yourselves for foolishness and pomposity. Abhor great art. Tear away at the institutions. Govern your conditioning to be free. Govern your emotions to be irresponsible. To be free as the aimless atoms. To be as licentious as the cawky crows. Down with them! Down with them all! Down with you all! Down with Great Society!"

The acolyte started clapping her hands in applause at her leader's exhortation. The audience was quiet and dumbfounded. Jan Le Bertet left back stage at a hurry and then disappeared sleekly and swiftly. The podium cleared of acolytes almost as quickly and the assembly was left to their own devices without any more ceremony.

Everyone assembled had a look of bafflement about them. Silence prevailed. Then astonishment. The mood was turning a little ugly.

"Should we call the Chamberlains?", someone asked. Daedalus could see that it was Baroness Letchworth. He figured that it might be best to scarper before there was even a sniff of a rozzer being there. He started to edge toward the auditorium exit as discreetly as he could.

"This way, Sah". It was the doorkeeper that he had met earlier. "I have your day coat with me. You need not return the cowl. I will arrange that after. The eminence is awaiting you. Bat droppings shall be my food, after all", he smiled mischievously and winked.

'As crazy is as crazy nought', thought the good doctor and followed his charge up the stairs of what was becoming an increasingly grander building. The doorkeeper took him upstairs and opened the door to an unassuming back office. There seated on the floor on a physikrattan mat was Jan Le Bertet eating a peri-apple.

"Ah, my dear Egregious! I have been expecting you. You are going to tell me about the numbers; the numbers that no doubt support my reasoning."

"The numbers will certainly prove you right", replied the doctor smartly. "The only trouble is that if you are conscious enough to understand the Brown Dwarf system, then you could synthetically lock in consciousness into physik."

"Now that would be a surprise", returned Jan Le Bertet. "Tell me about science and the art of doubt."

"Well what about the Chamberlains?" Daedalus was a little agitated. Too agitated for grave explanation.

"Well don't think on them and they won't think on us. We just lose consciousness and we are in another place."

"Alright then. How can I even begin to explain?"

"Just try me".

Daedalus started with his explanation even before the noise of the growing hubbub downstairs started to abate.

Doctor Meritorious Egregious Daedalus after that first discourse had many further discussions and insight revelations with Jan Le Bertet and his principal acolytes. During the course of his numerous discourses with Le Bertet he had felt less and less feeling of disquiet. He could not call it peace of mind, but at least most of the raging doubt had dispelled. His worry had been backtracked and more acceptance of it had sunk into his behaviour. It was increasingly more and more seldom that he woke up with feelings of panic.

Daedalus found Le Bertet extremely clever. He definitely had a scientific bent. Daedalus mused that Le Bertet could have easily become a master astrologer like himself. He had the intelligence, aptitude and love for the subject. Le Bertet was able easily to correlate the nothing holistic philosophy of *Purposelessness* to the astounding knowledge Daedalus had on random and pitiless numbers. Le Bertet was able to spin out a nothing philosophy from Daedalus' complex mathematik. Daedalus' complex mathematik and Le Bertet's simple nothing philosophy merged together and became one and the same. It was so perfect as to be perfectly accidental.

'There was no such thing as coincidence', thought Daedalus and then balked at the thought of it with a sharp ice like shiver.

Daedalus went from certainty to doubt to faith to fury to nothing to abject serenity. It was a process as accidental as it was unintended. Daedalus had feelings towards Le Bertet; the feeling that Le Bertet was a friend. He became fond of the other man and relished his company. Le Bertet, of course, did nothing to generate warmth, but the atoms in the universe did unthinkingly, and, for the first time in his life Daedalus experienced what it was being with one. He had exchanged his many numbers for affection in a single person.

One stormy evening in November with the palm trees looking like they would take flight to the heavens, Jan Le Bertet said to Daedalus: "You should go to her again now".

"Do you really think so?"

"Yes, I think that you are really ready for further insight".

"So be it", said Daedalus slightly uncertainly. He looked into the blazing heart of the flicker in a stout candle. The candle blazed on impervious to all the bigger presences surrounding it. No storm would unsettle the contented burning to its end.

"Yes", comforted Le Bertet. "She is particularly prone to open up after a storm such as this. The clearing of the weather clears her clarity."

"But what are you to her, Jan? How do you and your movement connect into the ethos of extreme meditation? I do not understand how you two work together."

"Simple, I suppose", answered Jan. "The spin meditationists are spinning away existence. The trouble is that there are so few sentient things that know of existence. Therefore my role is to disrupt consciousness in those that have it so that they can no longer focus on their existence. Focus that is lost on existence, their lives, makes the job of the spin meditationists a lighter burden to bear. They can only spin away the universe when the Ching and the Chong are diverted away. That is why we have to challenge structures to get unstructured. To reach beauty. That is why we are relentless in our opposition to the pompous structures and machinations of Great Society."

"But that involves only these here Islands. What about Oriens and all other places on the map?"

"Well, first of all we just concentrate on wiping ourselves off the map."

Daedalus was puzzled but used to being answered in riddles. Nevertheless he pressed for clarity.

"Well, why is it that with all your agitation that no-one from Great Society comes and closes you down? Why don't the Chamberlains come and arrest you all? For after all you are subversive!"

"Because we do not exist."

Before Daedalus could pose another question Le Bertet disappeared from the room. It was the last time Daedalus had sight of his friend. It was as if he had been taken into the ferociousness of the storm. Daedalus was left to his own reflections for a moment trying to work through the implications of that which Jan Le Bertet had portrayed to him. It was perplexing. There was a knock at the door and Daedalus saw the perennial doorkeeper standing at the doorway.

'I still do not know his name', considered Daedalus.

"Good doctor, the master has asked me to give you this with his compliments".

Daedalus saw that he was holding vivid flashes of colour consisting of an infinite number of splurges and dots on a large canvas.

"By Janna. It is an original Deissenböck. True middle period I declare."

"I would not know about this Deissenböck. This is one of the master's own works. He was a painter before forming the movement, but Great Society became more and more critical about his work which they considered deviant art. He said that his paintings were simply an abandon of essays and mistakes. He felt that we are compelled to an endless cycle of trying and failing until we expire of the process of making mistakes. Then it ends. What did he say? Yes, that's it. We will all commit 27,000 errors before we meet our graves. Good night, Sah!"

Daedalus had been told that Georg Deissenböck was a recluse who had cared for no man's society. Apparently he had not been seen for years. 'I will have to revise all my notions about randomness, coincidence and mathematik of uncertainty', surmised the genius.

The next morning as the cock crowed Daedalus was outside on the street surveying the storm's devastation. Less than he imagined based on last night's lambast of noise. He thought about the random disorder of his Deissenböck paintings – like a storm on a canvas, yet contained; threatening you with the onslaught of a mass of numbers if they could ever break out of the painting's frame. He thought about the enigmatic discussion with Le Bertet the night previous, but he was unaltered. Really though, he felt fit and well as he went out to seek the ministrations of Qin Chan. He glowed with a hue of healthy and transient pleasure. Before he knew it and without thinking he was in her presence again. Without thinking was far more comforting than a pleasant dream and without thinking he had been moving on far further.

"You not been thinking. You've been spinning", Qin Chan immediately noted. "Spinning along on the cobweb of the universe."

Daedalus smiled back the smile of disingenuous ignorance.

"It don't matter what you catch. It doesn't matter anything at all. All that matters is that you spun and you did not think about it. You live your life like a bird that looks for worm in the morning, like a dog who dreams of food in its dreams; like a bigot that does not doubt his displeasure. For you shall be sure and stride out only with the unthinking purpose of reaching the horizon."

"I must confess, I do not understand enlightened one."

"Who gives a fuck? Isn't that the whole point? The storm last night could have wiped you off the web of the universe and that would have simply been that. Nevertheless you would turn up somewhere again on it, probably as something else. Hopefully without the arrogance of thinking, without the egotism of self-awareness and self- analysis. I despise it to the point where I could break my bones down to be rid of it. Time for you to bite the skunk!"

"Sorry?"

"Time for you to smoke the laca. Do you want to smoke some with me?"

"Yes."

"Yes. Yes. Yes. Yes. Yes. Then we lose all the pig shit. We can spin together", the old and abused body of Qin Chan cackled. Her body seemed to be used and abused even more than the time he saw her a few weeks before. He noticed briefly some hideous suppurations on her weeping elbows with small skeleton bones exposed. Yet, Doctor Daedalus saw much to admire in the blue eyed blond haired young beauty sitting cross-legged in front of him. He would congress with her.

Qin Chan filled an old ebony pipe for her acolyte and they smoked slowly and intensely together.

"When I was a little girl in the cold north", she said after about an hour, "I was very frightened by my shaman. He was a hideous bully and he was very horrible to me as I asked questions about what was he was saying. I used to ask how could Santos eat Old Hoary. Old Hoary was an immense titan. How could little Santos swallow this huge giant and spit out his bones over a period of eleven months? It seemed ridiculous to me even as a child, but the shaman did not share this view. He was so certain that this had happened. He believed it and could not understand why anyone else would not believe it. The shaman was certain that his belief was the only certain one. He could not suffer any doubt. He persecuted anyone who doubted such was his fear of doubt. He persecuted me as I was doubting. My childhood hence became miserable and my parents were horrified by my special persecution by the holy shaman such that they gave me their special persecution themselves. Only my elder brother, Han-Wan, was able to give me solace and some protection. He was training as a warrior and a very good one he was in the making. He had killed five bears by the age of seventeen. When he protected me he was not greatly challenged as they needed his future strength for the tribe. They needed his strength contained in the frame of the tribe solidarity. Also, Han-Wan found me a book. It was "Polar Zone" by Esturges. It was a sort of mystic book, but Esturges taught me to think. He took my thoughts out of the frame. "Polar Zone" is about polarity. The connection of opposites to hold together a balance, a kind of Zong and Zeng attitude, and it released me with full abandon into doubt."

"I see, I see", murmured Doctor Daedalus. He was having very sensible thoughts about bears dressed in shaman headdresses reading philosophy. They were spouting wisdoms to him, but there was a background of hammering blurring the holy bears' words. They were hammering nails into their own furry flesh whilst complaining ruefully about the cold of the polar zone. They were white bears whose furry flesh was weeping. "It's the laca", they said.

"I was able to understand then that doubt is the only healthy viewpoint. To have doubt is to fully conquer fear", she continued. "Those who want to control cannot stand doubt as it places doubt into their belief systems. The doubt eats away at these systems like the laca. It is a virulence on their belief systems. Their belief systems are there to fortify their selfishness and greed. There will always be pain in the world but their beliefs are to propagate our pains and release theirs. We have all been marching to the tune of their beliefs. Their religions, their values, their standards, their morals, their piety, their music, their principles, their maxims, their creeds, their ethos, their objectives, their duty, their future ...."

Qin Chan had trailed off and was snoring.

"Their beef stew", said one of the angry white bears. "Sorry to interrupt, enlightened one", the bear excused himself.

"Accordingly all their belief systems are to be challenged. All these systems should be razed to the ground so that we can start again. I bring you the beauty of the thought of anarchy. Not having to care for their shibboleths hence more. We are to be released from the pride of survival on their terms. We are to be released simply into our simple suffering beings with no regard for anything else apart from our simple solitary suffering. We are travelling unthinking to the horizon of polarity. We shall get there and not know it. That shall be sublime."

"Who are they?", gasped Daedalus as a spurt of smoke expunges itself from his nose.

"They are us. We have to correct our own behaviour. We have to halt ourselves from buying into their vision so that it becomes our vision and thereby self-propagated. We have to stop our own manifest capability for evil. We have to stop the institution of wide scale evil. That is why we have set us this institution for spin meditation to combat that".

"I am on your wave", said the Doctor even though he was experiencing his own wave of sexual ecstasy. His state of arousal was high and he would congress with the sleuth of white bears congregated throughout the room. He stroked his throbbing penis and saw a number of other crossed-leg individuals smoking assiduously away on their pipes. Did they all look like Qin Chan?

"We must create a wave", Qin Chan continued. " A wave of elemental and natural force that destroys their beliefs and the institutions that have been designed to propagate them. It is time to rid ourselves of their order and to reconstitute natural disorder."

"Of course, entropy – what could be more natural".

"Natural disorder", she repeated.

"But who are they?", the Doctor was himself repeating himself.

It was no matter to Qin Chan. She revelled in questions and took it in her stride of smoke.

"They are us. They are the shamans, the sky helmsmen, Great Society, the Imperial Society of Gifted Arts, the professionals, the Sand religion and their like. All those who have the arrogance to declare they are right without the shadow of hallowed doubt!", Qin Chan positively shrieked.

All the other sitters in the room have begun to hum in some sort of divine fervour bringing mystical force to Qin Chan's declamations. Then suddenly the humming abruptly stopped as if Qin Chan were in command of some human musical box which she had metaphysically snapped closed.

"Your Big Warp Tenderer can be used as the instrument of their destruction.", she whispered loudly.

This statement was as loud as a giant temple bell ringing next to his ear for the learned astrologer.

"You know what a Big Warp Tenderer is? You can conceive what it can do?" Daedalus was decidedly lucid now.

"Yes." Qin Chan's sightless eyes stare back at him. "Yes indeed. My countless thoughts have ranged wide through the fabric of this disordered universe and like you I have become aware of the existence of the nearby Brown Dwarf system. It is imperturbable and disinterested. It is a force that knows nothing of its force. It spins like I do. It does not care if it is a captive or a slayer. I am aware of its destructive cleansing vitality. I know its boundless energy can be harnessed. To leverage its energy then extreme spin logic leads to the necessity of a machine that can manipulate the energy perturbations. The Brown Dwarf's space is dense in dark space matter which is highly warped and can be tendered to enhance particular physical mathematical possibilities. There can be no doubt that you have conceived of this machinery".

"Yes, true", spluttered Daedalus, "but how could you even calculate such mathematik without any instruments or observatory?"

"It is the laca", she rasped. "It is most self-edifying. There is a science in the smoking of this ganga".

"But how can you even be aware of the Brown Dwarf system's appearance in our near space? It is at the very outer range of my deepest space telescope. I could only verify it through applying the veracity of advanced Kötzen-calculus?"

"Why, my dear Doctor. The Brown Dwarf sings to me. It sings as it spins and I hear its verses of unimaginable travel across the universe to near distant horizons."

"Incredible", whispered Doctor Meritorious Egregious Daedalus. "Tell me more".

Mistress Qin Chan continued as the group of toke-smokers sustained their humming in crescendo around her. She explained her understanding of the Brown Dwarf system which Daedalus had believed could have only been known to him in Great Society. She explained how a BWT could be assembled. She explained how the temporal warps of the Brown Dwarf system could be accentuated by the manipulations of a functioning BWT. She explained her plan to leverage off the Brown Dwarf to cause natural disasters which would shake the fabric of Great Society and its institutions to its core. She explained her view that the Brown Dwarf was there to cleanse out belief systems and bring us all to the unassailable clarity of doubt.

Doctor Daedalus smoked a lot and assimilated a lot. He became clear as to what to do. As of now he had no doubt.

Doctor Egregious Daedalus worked hard and toked endlessly. He was working on his plan. Part of the overall plan he understood. He had been touched by the wisdom of Qin Chan, educated into action by Jan Le Bertet and then again taken into the confidence of Qin Chan. He was working on the plan to make the world run amok and bring all back to entropy. It was naturally satisfying, the numbers did not startle him anymore and he felt an ease in the passing of time. It was not happiness, it was not so uncontained, but it was something that put him quite right and he was working on a plan; maybe indeed he was implementing on the plan. It did not matter, it just felt right.

Qin Chan had shared her views on the Brown Dwarf system and the utility of a BWT. Now he would set out the fine detail to her inconceivable notion. She had told him that the anti-matter had a spirit. This sort of thing could not be gleaned by particle physik. One could only determine it by listening to its music, by listening to the clangs in its cacophony of spheres, and to do that you had to undergo deep spinning. For deep spinning one needed to always spliff the skunk. Doctor Daedalus was doing that and he was understanding even though he was heartily itching. He had to ignore the great itching and he did this by deeply concentrating.

Qin Chan told him that deep effects of the dark matter in the approaching brown system would make it as if the universe had a character; a personality. Albeit a character as perverse and cruel as Nature would create so that such disharmony be received in smiles of sunlight. She said to watch out for something or somebody with a *B*, like B for brown, or, Brown Dwarf or the like. If something or somebody with a **B** were to come along then, then if it felt right then to seize it like it were an opportunity and a means to developing mass contusions and disharmony. The Brown Dwarf system would form itself like a plan as there were no coincidences in the universe, there just is what there is, and there is no thinking more on it. She told the doctor that there were many elemental unseen aspects to the fabric of the cosmos and that all matter is destroyed eventually by 27,000 chemical reactions upon it and would then simply form into something else. So what was destruction really when after it all something else just pops up in its place. The universe liked to give new chances.

Egregious knew that he just had to work on the parameters and finesse the measurements and he was well down the road of creating a miniscule warp tenderer when Professor James Riddell came visiting him to talk over a notion. This miniscule warp tenderer would be as Daedalus conceived be capable of producing heavy atom fission. The type of atomic fission that could produce magma shifts. Magma shifts that could go from altering the geography of the earth, to clouding the clarity of mind, to make earthworms hiccup and for all to doubt all they had held and perceived to be indubitable. Magma shifts would make the earth spin on its head. Daedalus shared the mission of Qin Chan and Le Bertet and was working assiduously to make it happen.

And like there was no such thing as coincidence the Astrologer Royal sauntered into his ramshackle laboratory one fine March evening.

"My dear Daedalus".

"AR".

"I have a handsome business proposition for you to consider. If you had money, serious money, what would you do with it?"

"I would take a holiday first. I would holiday into the Off-Jox islands to look for and collect specimens of Tiger Moth. It has been my dearest wish to add these fine specimens to my collection."

"And then what?", prompted Riddell.

"If I had anything left over?"

"Oh indeed you would have a princely sum left over."

"I would plough it into hefty scientific research."

"Such as?"

"The Big Warp Tenderer. The divine-head machine."

"Can it exist?"

"You know that I can make it exist given infinite capital."

"Is two hundred thousand sovereigns infinite capital enough?"

"More than enough. You know that I would have to be conservative with the figures. It could probably be done at one hundred and fifty thousand at a pinch."

"And what could we do with it?", further enquired the AR.

"Pretty much everything. Change the weather, find gold, make the ill feel well, cause earthquakes and distort the balance of time and temporal reality. All in all we could challenge the natural laws of physik. Giving enough time in the research we could cause the parameters of the universe to shift."

"Hmn, interesting. To do that would you work with a mystery benefactor who might without compunction leverage the idle rich to achieve such a scientific landmark?"

"They say good ends justify foul means. I can live with a bit of casuistry. Who is the mystery benefactor?"

"More the mystery organiser. The benefactor might not be so plain on their investment."

Daedalus arched his eyebrow for more.

"Our chap is named Belsingham and I think he is keen to tell you more. He somehow has heard of the concept of the divine-head machine and would like it to move our civilisation ahead", revealed the Astrologer Royal. "But he would incentivise us as he is confident that through his planning that we should be able to raise the two hundred thousand. If we can bring it in cheaper, then we can keep the difference for our other scientific pursuits."

"Where did you meet this Belsingham? How could he have possibly conceived of the Big Warp Tenderer?"

"Actually, I met him in Milliwhigs. I had not come across him before, but his credentials are impeccable", further revealed the AR. "As to his understanding of atomic fission and the divine-head, I really cannot say. Perhaps I was too surprised to question him about that."

"Does that mean we have lost our edge on the research? Could he be in league with the Orientals?"

"Who knows, but if he were, I would like to know what we are dealing with."

"Yes, you are right AR. Sign me up", said Daedalus. "I would welcome the chance to meet the gentleman."

'Qin Chan certainly knows a thing or two', he thought.

Mistress Qin Chan meditated on year after year. She positively spinned as she fell apart. She floated on air, the thinning hair on her head brushing the ramshackle ceiling. The smoke from her pipe lacerating the high assembled cobwebs within the astral room. Everything was getting ready to come together. The world, the universe, the everything was fashioned upon a series of indeterminate and indifferent occurrences so widely variable that if anything ever happened from them there could be conceived a plan; a destiny. Qin Chan knew this to be stuff and nonsense. All that had to be done to disprove this shallow fallacy was to draw things together, connect them and put all invariables variably commensurate with themselves. This was the connection to destruction. If things were unable to connect this system would keep moving and thereby provide its own stability. Connecting the parts together would dissolve away necessity and provide instability for destruction. The requirement of what had to become of things to be able to start again. There had to be a coming together of collisions and incidents to fashion a furnace for all cleansing newness. A fissure, a fire − something to burn out all consciousness. The old consciousness that always hung about causing all to be seen in the future with the memory of the past.

The people would be mad with fear of the Brown Dwarf System. They would be aghast by the threat of earthquakes and tsunamis that the colliding system would be bringing. Their fears would be accentuated by the negative effects on consciousness and reality perception brought about by the perturbations of the anti-gravity. The black matter ingress would form delusions and people would look to divine shibboleths and creationists to give them comfort in their deluded state. The Sand religion would form as the world in its anarchy takes on the principles of the biased and uneducated.

The spinning was making them. She was there sitting and spinning and making them. A team of dream makers are spinning along the skirting boards and the bookcases of the room feeding on her emissions and weaving the tale accordingly. They are bouncing off the dust like atomic particles and destroying floorboards in their febrile state. She spinned a cosmic weave and what we meditate, we believe.

'The time has come to destroy the world', conceived Qin Chan as mandrakes moaned in their sleep. 'How do I do it? How do I make it again that we do not matter, that we never mattered at all?' She spinned even more intensively.

Beneath her all her acolytes who were there in the room with her rose up from their spinning, and stood out of the meditation pose to strike up attitudes like actors on the stage.

"Let me introduce the Cosmic Play", said one. "The principal actor shall come on stage".

Another came to the fore of the room as if it were centre stage. Qin Chan looked down on him interested.

"I am James Donald Suzuki, actor dramatic", said he. "This drama sets out the many injustices and gross inequities done unto me. Mine is the tragedy of a life ruined although I truly had not possessed any hubris with which to fall".

"Except his art!", hissed the chorus.

"I know you. Why you are Doctor Daedalus", said the oracle. "Who is this Suzuki?"

Doctor Daedalus moved forward, his skin looking much diseased and his creaky bones protruding out of his awkwardly fitting clothes. The good doctor as if staged fell to the floor gripping his stomach in agony. Whilst he is writhing and groaning something is born from the death in his insides.

A big brown bat flew from the doctor's insides and there suddenly was stood a brown skinned pygmy. The little pygmy shook as if in the death throes of swamp dengue fever. He shook so violently that he fractured a maw in the floor and the earth stopped spinning to swallow him up and as he was spat out laughing he imitated the voices of deathly dark singing spheres.

"I am Doctor Meritorious Egregious Daedalus".

"I am David Lincoln".

"I am Nurse Kendra".

"I am Sir John J. Perriwinkle".

"I am Mistress Jenny Howard".

"I am Kurt Tempels".

"I am Lady Elizabeth Swann".

"I am Arnold Copperfield".

"I am Rosemary Dowd".

"I am the one and only Horatio Beeswax Belsingham".

"And I am he .... I am Jimmy Suzuki".

"And am I the one you are looking for?", enquired Qin Chan.

"Sadly, no", answered Jimmy Suzuki.

"So it is woven", said Qin Chan. "The world can be destroyed now. The sand has met the sun. I have seen how it can be done".

Thirteen: Fusion – "Come Together"

I have never thought of myself as a writer. I was raised into a deeply religious family where women were always expected to be the little supporters. We were not designed to have a leading role in things. Women were always encouraging from the background and lavishing care on the children. Women were not recognised as having real intellects. We were set as the teachers, not the thinkers. We were not seen as having original thoughts. We were not developers; merely sustainers once things had been developed by the will of men. The church held us strict in this dogma. It was as if we were born into sacrifice. I have posed that one to God; how is it that everyone who is anyone has had a whole team of sacrificers pulling them into the light?

Actually, you might wish to know, that my maiden name was Anfield. I was born in Rochdale in old Lancashire. My father was vicar of St. Anne's. I was unlucky to have five siblings, all of them brothers. I was the second oldest, so I rapidly assumed the role of Mum's understudy. I spent a lot of my later childhood and adolescence as mother's little helper, so that my younger brothers saw me as an extension of mother. I was married by the time I was fourteen, except that I wasn't if you see what I mean. Experienced in care, but lacking in being cared for. Somehow I muddled along with my studies. I had no time for boys, the Gulf Town Rollickers or netball. A lot of my set at school were into riding, but with five hungry brothers we could not afford lessons for me. Mother was so obsessed with coffee mornings and tea parties that she had no time for me, unless it was to issue a set of day instructions. No time to take soundings on my unhappiness.

Amazingly through this all I was still able to attain fairly good A level results so that I was able to qualify for a BA course in Theology and Religion at Oxford University. Quite a boon in my family, but tarnished by the fact that my elder brother, Arnold, had not done so well at school and had gone into teacher training college in Coventry with the aim to teach physical education and woodwork. At the tender age of nineteen in the autumn of '14 I entered my course of studies at Wyfranke Hall, Oxford. I had a reasonable time at Oxford sharing some digs with my chums Marjorie and Peach. I suppose the three of us were considered to be cannon fodder for the Church. We studied hard and attended all the right associations (Young Christians for Change, Christian Militant and so on). However, it had been inculcated into me somehow that I was never going into the ministry, so I worked my way to a reasonable 2.1 and had designs to apply for employment in Christian publishing. With that modest aim I was again successful in securing a position with Rainfall Publishing in Truro.

But then I met Stephen and it all changed! Well, in fact, I met him over the course of two years. He was in the year below me at Oxford, although he is actually five years older than me. I had been attracted to him during the course of that time, but had never dared to speak to him. I was too painfully shy and he seemed to be very dashing and worldly for a theology student. Two years of anguished admiration for him and after all that I was about to let my big opportunity slip by. Summer holidays in Rochdale and then the new job in Truro would call. I would not be having much course to come to Oxford again.

Of course, as a good Anglican girl I had been taught never to touch the demon drink, but one of the handful of times I did, I struck amazingly lucky. My flat-mate Peach in her way was a bit of rebel rouser. She was the adventurous one of us three and persuaded Marjorie and I to go out wassailing at a new club in Gloucester Green called "Apple Crumble" – a frightfully stupid name that I can still remember. This was the occasion of our very penultimate night at Oxford together. We had made it through all the summer balls in an appropriate demure fashion. Well, in any event on this exceptional night we all got extremely loaded on a cocktail called "Killer Zombie" – a good name for it too and I had at least a couple, but I can still taste the after-effect of that vile rum to this day. I am ashamed at the brazen way we behaved that night and surprised that I did not end up in the bed of some randy lad; maybe I was simply too drunk even for the most randy lad! To cut a painful story painless, I ended up totally brainless in the street, lying on my back drunk as a skunk like one of those white heel stiletto lasses from the Tyne. I was told later that I had been lying half-on and half-off the pavement of Arbuckle Street with my skirt rather up and my inebriated friends trying haphazardly to haul me away from the road before any traffic came. It was just my luck that Stephen lived at 27 Arbuckle Street and upon hearing the hullabaloo was good-natured Samaritan enough to come out of his house and engage actively in my rescue. Doubtless with his superior manly strength I was despatched to safety and can live to tell the tale.

I woke up the next morning terribly hung over and in Stephen's bed. So I had ended up in some boys bed, but I had no idea how I had got there. I felt somewhat humiliated at the thought of what must have transpired the night before, but glad finally of the chance to speak to my handsome stranger who I had for some time admired from afar – and more than that in my most base thoughts, I must confess.

"Subconsciously I must have known", I said. My voice seemed distant from me as if something else was in control now.

"Subconsciously known what?", replied he.

"That to get into your bed would be the only way I get to talk to you", I blurted out. Who was this me?

"What do you mean?"

"I've been dying to talk to you for some two years!"

"Me too", he solemnly asserted.

"I've been too shy", I added.

"I thought you too good for me", he countered.

"What makes you think that?"

"Maybe it is not thinking, but it just is".

"I see."

Pensive looks.

"Your friends. Marge and Peach? They said they were alright to get home, and they were sure that I would look after you alright".

"It's all shit. I'm leaving tomorrow Stephen. Going back home to Rochdale." And I cried.

"I'll join you next week", he stated smiling. "I have always wanted to try fish and chips with mushy peas."

And so he did, but my parents did not take to him. They could not empathise with persons outside of their own experience, even with my father being a man of the cloth. Incredibly they remained amazingly prejudiced and unlike Jesus very slow to forgive what they perceived as transgressions. You see, the reason that Stephen being five years my senior and a year behind me academically was that he was in fact a recovering drug addict. Stephen had demonised his teens with cocaine abuse. That abuse had led to terrible behaviour involving stealing and mugging the elderly to gather money for his coke habit. Somehow he had managed just about to stay out of prison, but all at an enormous emotional cost to his parents. He had admitted that his own parents were still extremely mistrustful of him and were still dubious about having active contact with him. They still had no confidence that he had changed his spots.

Stephen had really communed with God, however, and had committed to the light. Stephen recognised in the depths of his shame and depression that he had no hope. To have hope he had to let God back into his life and he began to pray; for he knew how to pray, his own family being devout Anglicans. Stephen had a hangout in a downtrodden hovel in Walthamstow, and it was there in a Christian Anglican community in modest Walthamstow that he found the support to put him on his feet again. Through the patience of these kindly folk he found the support to get help to kick the habit and put him in parley with God once again. Stephen was so grateful to them and to God too. He had found his vocation in life. He knew he had to carry the mission himself. He applied to Oxford to read theology having received a bursary from the Bishop Longbroke trust. The Walthamstow parishioners had taken Stephen's story nationwide and raised enough sponsorship funds to get him through the Oxford entrance examination and inveigled him to the Longbroke trust officials.

Within two weeks of our joint summer sojourn in Rochdale Stephen had proposed to me. I accepted unhesitatingly and with delight. The news was not so joyful to my mother.

"I'm just worried that once a crackhead always a crackhead", she actually opined and more in a similar vein. Mum whined on in the kitchen in this way much to my shock. She saw no long-term redemption for Stephen; even with the support of her loving and resourceful daughter.

Father was the same without the emotion intensity. His was a commentary lacking positive endorsement, analysing his prospects as poor in good parishes because of his track record, and stating that our likely parish would be one plagued with drug addicts and like ne'er-do-wells.

"Don't do this. It's not the life for you", father counselled.

I remember that night I had cried myself to sleep. This occurrence had happened on a number of occasions in my life. Too many occasions and the sobbing myself to sleep felt like a perverse comfort blanket. Nevertheless, I reached sleep and tended to dream and the dream was a familiar genre of dream.

She would come to me as I lay in bed. I was a child. I was now. I was ninety-nine. I was a kind of a spirit of the age.

"Child".

"Yes, Nan".

"You are to say nothing of what just occurred. God would never forgive you to speak of it."

"Yes, Nan".

"Pa is a good man. A devout man. He is consumed with God's spirit and works selflessly for the poor of this parish. He is extremely sorry for what has happened. It's just that working with so many sinners he is sometimes touched by their demons. You do understand, child?"

"Yes, Nan".

"The demons consume him. It is part of Satan's plan, but he always recovers to fight on. And of course ......"

A silence.

"I cannot let Satan get close to me. I just cannot. I cannot. You understand me, child?"

"Yes, Nan".

"Your parents will be back in a couple of days. You are to say nothing. It is part of God's plan to defeat Satan. You will know God's wrath if you are to say anything about this .... your poor Pa."

I cry. I always cry at this denouement.

"God will grant you no happiness should you say anything".

And at this point she storms out of the darkened room leaving me with the sense of despair, disgust and soreness. Then I cry frantically until the strength of the tears wake me up and I loathe myself but in emotional exhaustion fall back into a clearer round of sleep.

He got joo joo eyeballs

He one holy rollers

I dream of an Indian family on a tropical island. The daddy is a bit of a tyrant, but he lets his little daughter dance, which is nice. They sing together a funny song with quaint lyrics.

I did not mean to break my discourse. I was explaining a fundamental rebellion of mine against my parents – and a thing always lurking in the backdrop - and the battleground was Stephen Dowd.

What more is there to say? I did assert my rights. I did marry Stephen against the approval of my parents. Against the approval of my paternal grandparents if they could have given it. Pa was long gone. Nana in senile dementia in a home discoursing with demons. I fled back to Oxford to be with my man and we were quickly and discreetly married at his parish of Walthamstow. Stephen finished his degree at Wyfranke and I took work at Mongoloid record store in Oxford. Upon Stephens elevation to the ministry in the church we took an impoverished parish in Tredegar. The Church of England in Wales. Then on to a parish in Milford Haven where Stephen became close to the diocese head Bishop Joy.

We were happy working in these underprivileged parishes far from the posh areas of the country. We felt our mission and felt that we were helping people. We were getting things done. We were happy, particularly in Milford Haven. It was nice to be close to the sea. The sea air made me feel quite peppy and gave me an edge of horniness that I had not felt below before. I was married to Stephen and we enjoyed our sex in a robust and rumbustious fashion! I would have bouts of amazing sexual excitement, then it would subside altogether and I was left with feelings of self-disgust and alienation. These cycles must have been most disquieting for Stephen. Going from being all over him to recoiling from his touch.

Alas, I could not conceive. In my cycles of libido I was loved hard and pummelled through lustily, but the seed of life was not sparking and occasionally I would get disconsolate about this. Stephen was very phlegmatic and reverted to God's plan. It is probably the only issue on which we have not had consensus ad idem. A big issue for me, but apparently relatively minor for him. He wanted to count God's blessings. As far as he was concerned there was nothing missing if you were filled with the Spirit. That was enough. He avoided discussions on medical intervention. I held my bitterness in check, pined for a child and determined to get a medical opinion.

A long time passed before I mustered the courage to get that professional opinion (and I explained to the doctor the problem of getting my husband's acquiescence), but the outcome came flying out like a bullet.

"There is no need to persuade your husband to come in. You cannot conceive", and then a battery of technical reasons mollified by Latin terms. I did not wish to know the reasons. I just wished to see the ways forward. In the end like a crazy kaleidoscope the way forward was the most obvious and the most mundane coloured; that was to embrace the Spirit and to continue with God's work along with my dear husband and spiritual helper.

There was an orphan boy at Milford Haven called Jimmy. Jimmy Scott to be precise. Eleven years old and freckly with a beautiful Welsh accent. He looked like an angel and did not speak much. He could really play football too and was a terror on the left wing. I liked the look of this boy and wanted to mother him to death. Despite his attractions he had had problems getting an adoption or holding on to a foster family. His father had been lost to the sea and the pollack catch. His mother had another type of catch by lying on her back to buy her crack. She had choked on her own vomit and Jimmy had discovered her body at the tender age of six. For a period social services had introduced Jimmy and some others to some of the parish events and activities and I mulled relentlessly over the thought of him. I even took Jimmy down to the Watergardens on The Rath from time to time for an afternoon's jaunt. Eventually I worked up the courage to approach Stephen about adopting young Jimmy, or, even fostering him. I could never argue against Stephen's earnestness and he convinced me upon Gods greater purpose being that we were to look after a flock rather than a single child. We all had to make sacrifices to that greater object and purer love, and that was that. I sneakily got hold of a photo of Jimmy Scott in his school uniform and from time to time I still secretly take it out to gaze and wonder what if.

Bishop Joy used her influence to gain us a good parish in the rather well-heeled Woodford Valley. That meant it was the end of my ambition towards Jimmy Scott and any other sprite for that matter. Stephen still does phenomenal work for his parish. He and I do not have that fundamental passion that we used to sadly. We have a dog. A black Labrador bitch called Sally. Then I have my walks. My spiritual reflections which reach out to the unemployed and others feeling not quite right with the might and mystery of God's plan. I walk, I write, I empathise with those confounded by the mystery of God's plan and I empathise with myself.

I put a brave face on it really.

Jimmy Suzuki, apart from his faithful moggie Nicole, did not hold much truck with animals. He was not particularly keen on house pets like parrots and farango hamsters. He was positively adverse to creepy-crawlies such as bugs and daddy-long-legs and such. He had heard that everyone had an aversion to a particular type of animal. It was clear now that in the case of Arnold Copperfield Esq., it had been the Island three-toed Small Sloth. That much was clear. How such an innocuous lazy looking thing could have inspired so much terror in Copperfield was beyond comprehension. For Jimmy though it was bats, and, as much as Jimmy loved the green sites of Banana Delta, he would never visit Mulberry Park because of the many fruit bats there.

His mother, Doris, took him to the park one fine day in May. He must have been about four at the time he supposed. There had been a festive feel to the day he recalled. Mum had wanted to see the Grand Pancini or one of the other well-known band masters of the time orchestrating fine brass music from tuba and flute at the celebrated lakeside bandstand. Mum adored that sort of thing. No doubt Dad was away with the racing greyhounds losing his hard earned wages. Mum had often taken Jimmy out on her own; even so Jimmy still holds deep affection for his somewhat lacking father.

Before seeing the Grand Pancini, Maestro Moore or whoever it was, Mum had bought them cool malted macks – a simple pleasure on a hot day. They had gone under the shade of a mulberry tree to enjoy the macks. The infant Jimmy had heard a shrill screeching and had looked up to see a cloud of fruit bats hanging upside down from the mulberry tree. At the moment he looked up one of them must have peed and a wave of bat piss hit the face of young Jimmy. My did he cry; my was he outraged! Doris had seen the funny side of it and could not constrain a laugh. Even so in her best motherly way she had cleaned up her young son as best as she could. Even so young Jimmy was mortified and feared and loathed bats to this day. They absolutely disgusted him.

The bats had always stayed within him, in his head. On the rare occasions in his life when he felt peace, quiet and happiness, it would not be long before the black bats would swarm. They were a terror that could arise at any time. They could spring out at you at any moment, particularly if he had temporarily put them out of mind. So in a way it was the bats that had to be dispelled for Jimmy to find freedom; for him at last, finally to put an end to all the bad things and find freedom.

And so it was that Jimmy found himself hitched on to a slow horse and farmer's cart which he had negotiated the passage of for a double-farthing after alighting the trahere at Basil Down. He is morose and down after finishing his business with Nurse Kendra the previous day. He alights from the wagon and says adieu to Farmer Morgan. He stands there alone on the familiar patch of road at sunset outside a very deserted looking SSN at Snoods Droop. Jimmy notices that there is a cloud of bats flying towards him. Did he summon them for confrontation, or, were they choosing their moment as usual? Coming at him as if they were the dark guardians of the School of Suspect Norm. He had come back to Snoods Droop to confront all that pain of a wasted life. He is back at Snoods Droop where it all started to go wrong and he is prepared to destroy if he does not get satisfaction. He has no plan. He is simply aware that being here on this cool September night will just have to lead to something.

Yet the collection of bats is coming at him. Such a blackness emanating out the deep red of the dusk. Such a black cloud represents his life and why he has to be here. He is terrified, but he knows he has to confront these creatures that have morbidly frightened him since early childhood. He thinks of going to ground; to let the blackness pass, but knows that he will never close anything if he flees the crowd once more. He stands his ground. They will have to pass through him. He will destroy them or they will destroy him. It is simple and that is why he has come to make his stand at the School of the Suspect Norm, Snood's Droop. He does not know if he is really here to make a stand, or, to make an attack. He is simply here to have an outcome here. Here standing on the stony road outside the institution that has permeated and infringed upon his every adult living moment. And the bats keep coming closer and closer, flying nearer and nearer on a beeline; an overwhelming force which will permanently cripple or stupendously enforce him.

'Let the bats come', he grimly determines.

The first wave of bats fly into him with overwhelming force and he is toppled to the ground without ceremony. He hits the ground hard and immediately feels the earth begin to shift under him. Something fundamental and enormous is happening which could explain the extreme movement of the bats which are still crescendoing past him in the direction of the far-off coast. He feels himself being sucked under the soil while the bats are still driving at him. The bats are suffocating him and the earth is swallowing him. There in the trance of loss of senses he hears the voices.

"Look let me be first. There is never time for moral compunctions in these things. One has to act for the greater interest. I'll be short. I'll be brief. To serve and disserve preserves our balance. You could have been born a bat or a goat. Just your bad luck that you have consciousness. It's a curse, a blight that never goes away. Yet we fight to preserve it every day and are terrified by the thought of that final day when it goes away. There are mystics who teach that we should aim for nothingness. To not be able to think at all. Is that what you wanted, Jimmy?"

"I suppose".

"Those blasted scientists were right. I never listened. I am a social scientist. I never listened to all this brown dwarf stuff and maelstroms and earthquakes and the like, but I see they are right. All their theories are coming together and killing us right now. Before it does, I just wanted to say ..."

"What? That you were just doing your job?"

"No, it was more than that Jimmy. It was my credo. I really believed that society has to provide the looked for missing aspect. That crucial aspect being quality of life. A happiness and comfort in life. However, there is only a limited amount of it to go around. Everything of nature relates to balance. If there is something then equally there has to be something else. However, much you push toward the good balance there has to be some of the something else, otherwise the good stuff learns towards the precipice and falls out over the edge. The mystics and religion spouters have always known this. That's why they have always reverted to creating the allusion of purpose in punishment. The common man took his punishment stoically in this life in the knowledge that in the after-life there is a boundless supply of joy and delight to go around. In these modern times of physik we cannot support that hocus-pocus so easily and that's why we have had to inculcate into the punishment detail this social conditioning of sacrifice and disservice. I was doing my job - true, but I also really believe in this for the greater good. There is no denying that life is completely unfair. We just have to make sure that we reduce to the minimum the amount of those who have to suffer through it and where suffering is to be done on those unlucky few then we dole it out with a consistency and a rationale. You know, I really wish I was something fluffy and gormless like a rabbit and did not have to think about it. Just munch my grass and avoid the hawk. Even in privilege we can be miserable. You know what they say. Life's just a dream. I'm sure you'll thank me for it."

"Thank you David. Why do I say it. It's your bloody conditioning isn't it?"

"Yes. Yes. But it is all turning to dust now."

The earth is really shaking up. Jimmy sees the nearby building and institution of SSN, Snood's Droop gyrating and shaking, and starting to disintegrate. The bats have passed now, but maybe starker dangers are starting to reveal themselves. Brown Dwarf doth truly hath force.

"I'm next", she says. "Oh, Jimmy what have you done? What have you done to me? It is important that I get in and say this quick to you before I care again for your sensibilities. I had started to think that I had become important to you, Jimmy. What happened? What went wrong?"

"I don't know what you mean".

"Men! You are all so fickle. You follow your own wagging tails and hunt your own preoccupations. My life has been ruined on the impulses of men."

"This is too cryptic for the world falling apart", splutters Jimmy in the maelstrom of dust. "Just accept the simplicity of destruction. It is not a moral argument."

"I'll ask a question direct then. Was I just a stepping stone to your beloved Fumi? Riddle me that back!"

"How can you say that? I loved you from the moment I woke up in that hospital bed seeing you as a lovely apparition in front of me. You are a lovely apparition even now, Kendra, as my feet sink into this morass of I know not what. You are a lovely apparition even now, dear heart."

Lovely apparitions have a terrible countenance when angry and their beauty enhances the purity of the rage. "Then what was it all for? The risks that we took with Arnold Copperfield, the relationship with Mistress Howard and then to let me down in the end as you did?", Kendra positively spits.

"I suppose that it was just me trying to be normal. I had not wanted always to be abnormal. I had not always wanted to be counter-professional. I wanted the selfish id as you all main players had. I wanted to plant my seed for someone more legendary. I wanted to have my oats and really let everybody down. I wanted just to want without rationalisation anymore."

"I don't understand you. You are far too cryptic!", Kendra screeches.

It cannot be Kendra. Kendra's voice has always sung. It never had to screech.

"I don't know myself. There are just too many layers of explanation. I cannot sort them out into the right order anymore. I am simply inarticulate to express it."

"Adieu. Adieu." Kendra's terrible beauty fades.

The dust from the crumbling ruins is starting to merge with the dark tint of the enveloping sunset. Jimmy spots a sign in a last ray of recalcitrant sunlight with words approaching him hot like a stellar flare.

"*School of Suspect Norm – Closed until further notice*".

Jimmy realises now how Belsingham is able to hold his beloved Fumi there. The school had been abandoned and is derelict. Belsingham could hold Fumi there without anyone noticing. Furthermore to hold her there, where Jimmy's demons had first been created, was the perfect setting for revenge upon Jimmy and Fumi. It all made sense now. Kurt Tempels, or his wraith, had been right all along. This place of denouement was peopled by more ghosts than just jolly old Kurt. There were many old ghosts there for Jimmy to meet. Dee Danver, Vicky Spimm, Roger Abel, Pellegrini, Monsy and all. He has just started the experience.

"Well, of course, my dear friend, my dear James Donald, at least you had the luxury of not having anything to lose. My tale was of a classical hubris. I stood high and mighty to take a great fall. You were placed so low you had nowhere to go. You were able to avoid the unrighteous tempests and the hurricanes of malice as you were lying so low those winds could not reach you. You were lying low licking your wounds and I am very grateful to come to know you, dear friend."

Jimmy sobs and cries at the fear of friendship but is touched by the sentiment of Sir John J. Perriwinkle nevertheless.

Sir John picks up a lute and starts to strum on it.

"I never knew you could play it", says Jimmy.

"Always could, just never chose to reveal it."

Sir John sings. His voice is luscious and brute like a louche baritone. He sings of old land and legendary glory. He croons fair ladies and immortal everlasting love. He warbles black night and pestilence. He free refrains Jimmy and those who might have loved him. He curlywurgs an ever giving friendship to James Donald Suzuki. Jimmy is tremendously affected by the emotion of the song. He looks at the beneficent Sir John J. Perriwinkle sitting on the rocks surrounded by bounteous blond river maidens. Sir John is young now and virile. He looks of the great good humour of worldly youth.

"I was so mighty. I should never have met you, but through my own vanity I did indeed meet you. I moved into your anti-social circle and through that I believe I met the truest friend in my life."

"But I haven't even read Manticore's *Old Nobility*", entreats Jimmy.

"I learnt through you that there is more to life than Manticore, fussiness and petulance. Dear Jimmy, you have signified something good to me in life and a realisation that we should look for real value in persons that we put close to us. Your saga has all been about you not being a value provider, but indeed to me you have given a great value to me. You have given me friendship and the belief in the true kindness of straightforward folk. I hope that I have reciprocated in some way".

"Indeed you have, great worship", bombasts Jimmy. "Simplicity and honesty".

"Simplicity and honesty. Please engrave it on my tombstone".

Jimmy is again quietly crying in front of the forlorn gravestone of Sir John J. Perriwinkle 15th. Baronet of Sandown and Protector of the Wold.

The grave of Jimmy's great friend and confidante was strewn by awful dead flowers as if Sir John had died an age ago and no-one had come to visit in quite a while. The light of this last sunset is weak and confusing. Jimmy's eyes are deceiving. The earthquake is continuing its rumblings and is continuing to cast the core of the world away. The earthquake continues its unsavoury clear-out. Jimmy is dreadfully affected by it, but appears to be in an air envelope of magik so that he is protected from the horrible extraneous tumult in order that he can be intimately stricken inside it.

Dead ugly flowers on the final resting place of true Sir John. Flowers that can move. Plants that can move. Manacles not plants. Limbs not manacles. Plants, tendrils, gesticulations, the Skittish Walk, a form of a man motioning Jimmy toward him. A living moving thing sitting abstractly where Sir John's grave should lie. A representation of a man whose skin is hanging off him. Jimmy had heard of zombies – animated corpses who come to get you. Was this some gruesome jape of the dangerous

Ceri Hatch? A post-world penance for what he had done to Matron Stoneywell? Was this the golem of final retributions for one who wanted his comeuppance from the past?

"I don't think we ever met although we have always been related". The dripping flesh thing finds a voice too with the other strange visitations. The eyes stare at Jimmy weirdly and piercingly.

"Related? Are you from my mother Doris's side?" At times of high tension we sputter such nonsense.

"No, I mean related in terms of our fates being connected to each other. I am Doctor Meritorious Egregious Daedalus and I am largely responsible as to what befell your close friend whose tombstone you now pay respect to. You might have heard of me."

"Yes, I have, and I want to know why you were so evilly pernicious to this late great benefactor. Why did you and the ignoble Riddell set out your stalls to destroy him."

"It was not him, dear Sir, but what he represented. I had my faith, my anti-faith so to speak. I took on the belief to be faithless. I had my dogma, my marching orders. I was under the influence of the spin meditationists. I did not wish to harm anyone by thought or by deed, knowingly or unknowingly. I was mystified by the creed. The great spiritualist Qin Chan convinced me that the Brown Dwarf system had no purpose and held a purpose at the same time and if I wished to draw out a purpose from the purposelessness of this universe I could purposefully harness its power to bring even more purposelessness and disharmony to our lives. That then would be living for a purpose. Jan Le Bertet further convinced me to agitate against order, to destroy establishment, and Sir John was a target emblematic of achieving this disorder. They both hated the certainty of Great Society and its system within. They both believed in war against belief cultures and the destruction of dogma and money were prime targets".

"But why? Why did you sign up to such malice? You are an eminent scientist. You should be working for the common good", bombasts an indignant Jimmy.

"Because I found something in them. Le Bertet and his movement. Not hope, no not hope at all. Just something that made a little sense."

"You are too cryptic for me Daedalus."

"I was panicked by the numbers".

"The numbers?"

"Yes, the vastness of the numbers. The sheer overwhelming helplessness of all those astronomical numbers. I had calculated that my consciousness had been sleeping for seventeen and a sixth billion years. I did not know how it could sleep before time at all. I reckoned that it would soon again be sleeping for another twenty-seven trillion trillion years until a point I did not know how it would be possible to sleep at all. I surmised that my id, that is so important to me, could be represented by half a grain of sand of all the known sand in the expanding universe. I was assailed by mortal loneliness by understanding the colossal scale of numbers around me. I was drawn into the infinite points of loneliness in the middle period Deissenböck paintings and understood and saw only lonely pointless desolation. I went to Qin Chan for guidance."

"May Sand have Salt! And she guided you to destruction?"

"She finally got me to realise the fundamental disorder of the winds of Nahib. Her counselling in a way was spiritual. Le Bertet taught me to tear down pomposity. I do not know why, but I found that to be an axiomatic truth. Doing down Sir John was just my slight contribution to spreading out disorder".

"I see."

"Do not forgive me. Do not reproach. Just know that I am on the permanent path of destruction that comes from

smoking the laca. I am on the path to destruction. Always
have been. We all always have been. My dripping flesh
only is a visceral depiction. Only remember this problem
that no-one yet has solved."

"Being what?"

"That the ability to think is outside all the parameters
of the universal law of physik. That is the large anomaly
that dooms us all."

"What is consciousness?", Jimmy forms.

However the image of the good doctor disappears like a
cosmic flash.

"That is why you must uphold the Creator. That's why
we have loved and revered Holy Cosmos. Without the
spirit and grace of Cosmos all crumbles into disorder. All
is lost. I let her spirit enter me, but you betrayed me; you
betrayed her divine purpose and turned the world back
into purposelessness! For that you will suffer again and
again without water in the sands of Nahib. Their atoms,
their granules will absorb your consciousness whole so
that you will know only the pain of the wind. You will be
dispersed and never feel whole again."

Mistress Jenny Howard's terrible beauty still held him
transfixed and he would not interrupt her.

"There is evil in your heart Suzuki. It can never be
expunged. For you there can never be a redemption."

Jimmy can only see her face hovering above the mist in
the twilight. Her beautiful face covers the vast auburn
horizon. Blonde hair curly as the distant clouds, piercing
blue eyes holding the expectation of another bright azure
morning and arched eyebrows raising up like roofs of
comfort in-laid with a frisson of danger. A complex
beautiful visage holding within it the terror of perfection.
Jimmy could sink into the pools of exquisiteness and held
in amber there all eternity surviving out a punishment of
voicelessness. Just one more moment of her gaze would

drive himself back into himself so far and beyond that he could not articulate an escape.

"For what you did is so fundamentally condemned that there can be no redemption. You were disloyal. You breached my trust. There is no more elemental and atrocious a sin."

"How about vanity? How about self-righteousness? How about intolerance?" Jimmy is surprised by the spark of life that has come back into him.

"You dare, Sah!"

"I do."

He picks up a sturdy rock and throws it hard at the perfect visage of dusk skyline. The horizon smashes like glass and large shards of the glass fall to the ground and in all of them Jimmy sees reflections of himself.

"We put a mirror into your soul", he scoffs. "Is there anyone else here who wishes to give me aggravation? I have done my best. Is there anyone else who wishes to disapprove of me?", he bawls angrily into the darkening sky.

"Only me. You knew I would have to be where I sent you."

"You have sent me to many places Kurt. To Marmalade Fields, to the Sand, to the arms of Mistress Howard, and back here to Snoods Droop where I never wanted to return. You have led me into some real scrapes and escapades. Against my better judgment you have always managed to get me to engage in things which would not have been my own volition."

"Consider me like a parent then. Your Dad who would be guiding you to take responsibility."

"And how responsible has it all been, Mister Tempels?"

"I won't answer that. I did not come to a pretty end. But didn't I make you come alive, Jimmy? Will you not grant me that?"

"Yes, I will grant you that. You have told me some home truths and given me a valour that I thought I had not possessed. You made me a running man and put power and fortitude into my limbs which I would not have summoned by myself. You put a plan into my passion, a race into my rage, and I hated you for it as you would not allow me to fester in my indolence. You have given my life a certain colour, an escape from the drabness of the counter-professional."

"I loved you as my own, Jimmy. I put you through these trials Jimmy as I knew they would be good for you. What does not kill you is put down to experience."

"If you say so dear Kurt", says Jimmy sobbingly. "But what about the monstrous Jenny Howard? I had to summon up all my sap to dispel all her fury just now. Was that an experience that made me strong? I think not, she did you in after all."

"That be true, but you know I loved my belief. I loved the Sand. I loved the fact that the great one loves us poor and oppressed. That Cosmos gives us belief that we can manage and take back the salt from greedy hands. Our Fumi Lartal escapade was founded on that credo. I knew that you had the core in you to be an upholder true and I roped you into Fumi's kidnap as it was important to launch an attack against Great Society. I hope you accept this and that is why I wanted you to come back today to reclaim your Fumi whom you learnt to love during the desperation time at Marmalade Fields. You and I are now immutably connected through the Sand. The Sand has saved you from the clutches of those pernicious spin meditationists. If they had got you, you would have been skin and bone by now, and not the fine figure of a man I see standing afore me today. I look at the bigger scheme and recognise sadly that we both suffered at the hands of Mistress Howard, but the life line was one worth pulling to set a sail. It could have been much worse …. for you anyway."

"Nautical to the end, Kurt."

"It is the end for me dear Jimmy. Time for me to meet Cosmos. Go and rescue her and be redeemed. Now my spirit fades into Cosmos."

"Goodbye purveyor of fine natural juyces", Jimmy bids farewell with strange and enduring affection.

"So what did you learn from me?", she asks.

"That no matter how refined we become it is still only a veneer to the animal that is within us all. You taught me that all refinement is simply our consciousness putting a lid on our animal realisation".

"Which is what?", she poses.

"That really we know that we are nothing but beasts, but the beast does not make the assumption that it is important; that its life has any relevance. All the social niceties, all the importance we put into our lives is just to inflate up some relevance to this crooked story."

"You have become quite the philosopher, Jimmy."

"I'd like to think so Elizabeth. At least you showed me something of the fine life and that the fine life has its problems too; that we are all relatively miserable in our course through this crooked tale."

"It gives a new dimension to sex, wouldn't you say?", she smiles weakly through the darkening clouds with bats stuck and dying in her whitening teeth.

"It certainly does, Lady Swann."

"But I have to hush away as a gentleman comes."

"You had a better father", announces the gentleman. "You have to have had a better father", frets the old gentleman.

"What was it with the sloth? Why did it repel you so? Such a cute humorous looking animal. Not at all loathsome like all these bats."

"My father was always comparing me to the thing, constantly admonishing me for being slothful. He was always saying that I would waste my life away, and I did in my constant fretting upon death".

"But you were honourable, kind Sir".

"I did my best to make amends. I did not wish to see you waste your life away. I tried to put you on the right track. I endeavoured to get you to contemplate and see the spiritual in a mean life."

"But you planted a seed of doubt in my life. Why did you leave it unexplained?"

"Because I could not explain it to myself", replies Copperfield. "Nevertheless she wants to clarify."

"You have read my musings, Jimmy", states Rosemary Dowd.

"Yes, but they only confirm that I shall go to my death knowing absolutely nothing."

"Yes, you are probably right", she responds. "As the time increases for me I more and more wonder what it is all for. One moment of intoxication, a couple of transitory thrills and a derring-do moment and we live with a commitment for the rest of our recorded time. And …"

"We wonder at all if we ever at all did the right thing at any time right through all of it", finishes Jimmy.

"I do not wish to write any further", she sighs.

"But thank you anyway you both", cordially interjects Jimmy although he does not know why.

The two of them nod their heads in deep deference and fade into the deep dark night.

Then there is Belsingham. It had to be. He knew instinctively who it was. Belsingham! The Belsingham that he had never met. Belsingham whose rumour he had been meeting all over the place. There as Tempels had predicted stands Belsingham about to roar out his challenge over Fumi. The showdown that inevitably had to be the catharsis to this chronic unrequited love.

Belsingham stands on the grand stone staircase persisting alone in the grand humbled ruins of the School for the Suspect Norm. It gives him a more imposing authority and makes him appear a grim figure. The wind is howling with a greater fury now. Belsingham presents himself majestically against the elements in shiny brown riding boots, grave frockcoat and jaunty cravat. He is a lion of a man who will go down roaring. He looks as if the storm will not assail him. Jimmy sees that in his powerful arms he is holding a damsel who looks to be in distress. In the darkening howl Jimmy cannot make out her features, but it must be Fumi he discerns. Jimmy cannot see whether she is dead or had merely fainted, but she stirs not. So stands Belsingham holding aloft the abject figure of Fumi Lartal, just as he himself had once done when disembarking the steam trahere at Lamb's Slaughter.

"What have you done to her?", Jimmy furiously cries.

"What have I done to her?", roars back the veritable demon. "It was you who did this. You have left this abject form here at Snoods Droop for me to collect and to try and resuscitate".

"Stuff and nonsense!", cries back an increasingly irate Jimmy.

"Lose the outraged demeanour. Do not depict that you only had a bit part in your own downfall. Let's face it, you never had the guts to become like me", says Belsingham. His words are cool and they cut like ice projectiles through the wall of storm projecting from Jimmy's persona. "You have never had the courage to go out and take it. Grab it with both hands. We set out to break you, Lincoln and I, and it was easy game for us. You were meant to be a challenge with your intellect and your degenerate art, but you didn't even rise to that challenge did you? Even though you had the natural attributes to equip you to do so. Now when anything bad befalls you, you just want to blame me or someone like me for your woes. You are miserable Suzuki."

"I am not ..." Jimmy says these words although a wall of sound is about to explode him.

"Fumi was just your fantasy", laughs the thing. "Your representation of a true and meaningful love. Why else would you have all your failed dalliances with all the other damsels in your tale?"

"It's not true!", screams Jimmy. The retort seems to have incredible strength because it had to outrun the vortex to be heard.

"Here is the thing that you have come to challenge me for Suzuki. Is it your beloved Fumi Lartal, or, do I hold in my bold forthright arms simply the spineless life you have lived?"

Jimmy is not sure now as to the form of the thing that his nemesis is holding. The storm is shaking at reality. Perception is getting down to the core.

"In either case they are both as dead and limp as your wretched existence", continues the bad-arse and hurls the lifeless form high into the angry air. The form is not lifeless though. It has been merely sleeping and awakes. Jimmy finds himself careering through the air in the direction of the late departed bats. A short while ago he had been grounded and now suddenly he is an air spirit – just as fury.

In the air he becomes one with the storm. In the night he is one of the fears. In the wind he is only irrationality without awareness. He becomes absorbed in the numbers of the universe and as part of their infinite energy he blows Belsingham over. As the violence of the storm he drives the crumbling ruins of Snoods Droop into more perfect shambles and decay.

"List, list, o, list!", says the spectre of Belsingham before Jimmy sweeps up in the air once more to make Fumi

Lartal alive again from the swirling atoms of the electrical storm.

He has made her new again from a bolt of lightning and a thunderclap so black.

Jimmy and Fumi lie in the ruins of the building. It has been a great escape. Jimmy feels untarnished. A bit shocked maybe, but just in need of a good dusting down. Dust from the debris mats his hair, but Fumi looks a lot worse. Her head is clearly visible to him. It juts out from fallen rubble covering her whole body. Theirs had been an embrace in the catastrophe thwarted by this bedrock of reality the earthquake has shook up. Fumi's features are clear, eyes alert, but her expression pained as if she was feeling the heavy weight upon her body. Blood is streaming from her mouth. Lips blood red and to kiss.

"My darling…" Was he to lose her again so quickly after so long to win her back?

"It was you who wanted me kidnapped all along", Fumi says. "There was no Belsingham. Only you all this time."

Jimmy Suzuki nods his head quietly.

As he nods, she vanishes.

"Yes, it was me all along. Just me, only me. I am all too well aware of it all".